The
Martini
Effect

Also by B.J. Morison
from North Country Press

CHAMPAGNE AND A GARDENER
PORT AND A STAR BOARDER
BEER AND SKITTLES
REALITY & DREAM
THE VOYAGE OF THE CHIANTI

The Martini Effect

• A Little Maine Murder •

B.J. Morison

NORTH COUNTRY PRESS • UNITY, MAINE

Cover design by Susan Gross, Bar Harbor, Maine,
after a suggestion by the author.
Composition by Typeworks, Belfast, Maine
Manufactured in the USA

Grateful acknowledgment is made for permission
to reproduce part of Dorothy Parker's "Resumé,"
published by Penguin USA.

Discussion in "Mrs. Farnum's" class culled from
Introduction to Biblical Literature, © 1984 by
Boynton/Cook Publishers, Inc. Used by permission
of the author, O.B. Davis.

Library of Congress Cataloging-in-Publication Data

Morison, B. J. (Betty Jane), 1924-
    The martini effect : a little Maine murder / B.J. Morison.
       p.   cm.
    ISBN 0-945980-38-8
    I. Title.
PS3563.087167M37   1992
813'.54 — dc20   92-31610
                                                          CIP

This story is dedicated to Kent School, Kent, Connecticut, for many reasons, but chiefly because it truly is as Porter Sargent's The Handbook of Private Schools *describes it: "One of the nation's great schools, simplicity, self-reliance and directness of purpose have characterized Kent since its founding."*

Acknowledgments

For advice on matters in which they are expert, the author expresses grateful thanks to the following:

Theodosia Gray, former Chief of Police Dan Herrick, and Mark Kandutsch, M.D. (all of Bar Harbor, Maine), Jamie Scott of Antarctica, and Marel Rogers of Sharon, Connecticut.

But the most gratitude is due Alaraby Jane Johnson of Bar Harbor, Maine, and, at present, Brown University, for not only did she live some of the incidents in this story, she also made many invaluable suggestions.

Foreword

TO A GENTLEMAN AND A SCHOLAR

My very dear Tim:

Since the kind authorities at a school we both know — you much better than I — and both admire once permitted me to attend classes there for some days, eat in the girls' and boys' dining halls, use the libraries, talk informally to the teachers and students and generally roam around absorbing the atmosphere of a private preparatory school, it might be reasonable to deduce that in these pages I am portraying that school. *Not so*, or, as the kids at the school would say: NO WAY!

No person I met there is pictured in this fantasy, nor is any of the interesting gossip, or the titillating stories I heard — what institution of any kind does not have these, usually completely untrue? — herein related. I repeat: no one and nothing in my fictional "St. Augustine's School" in the slightest way refers to or reflects on the real school I was permitted to inspect. Of course, since I was there to discover what such a school is like, some — but by no means all — of its speech, customs and rules have crept in. The rest are invented, for even though I had not the (very real) advantage of an education in prep school, I have absorbed many facts and tales in my life and it is these, as well as the imagination any writer of fiction must possess, on which I have drawn.

Nor, of course, as you know, is there any preparatory school at all, let alone one that might be "St. Augustine's," on Mount Desert

Island. If there were, it could not possibly be located where my school is. I have changed the geography of MDI to suit my purposes.

I close by thanking you, most sincerely, for the gracious hospitality you showed me on my several visits to the place where my daughter was being superbly educated, and I wish you, and the admirable school where you teach, many more years of success.

— B.J.M.

Bar Harbor, Maine
1992

The Characters in the
Order in Which They Appear

ELIZABETH LAMB WORTHINGTON — *a young girl of inquisitive nature*

MRS. OTIS (*Elizabeth*) WORTHINGTON — *her grandmother; a Bostonian grande dame*

VITTORIO (*Vito, Nonno*) VINCENTIA — *a man of the world, soon to marry Mrs. Worthington*

*The following are all of St. Augustine's School,
Mount Desert Island, Maine:*

MR. LYMAN SALTON — *Admissions Officer*

JOLENE TREBLE — *Senior Prefect of Girls*

MR. HARRY PRESTWICK — *Algebra instructor, coach of Boys' Crew, and a former Olympic sculling medalist*

MRS. OLIVIA LESTRANGE — *Dean of Girls*

DORA DORR — *an assistant cook (general factotum, in the summers, at Mrs. Worthington's MDI cottage, The Bungalow)*

LARA JANE OLIVER — *the Sixth Form's Girls' Representative to the Student Council, and stroke on Girls' Crew*

JOSAS (*Josie*) OUTERBRIDGE — *a Third Former, roommate of Faith O'Malley and Elizabeth Lamb*

FAITH O'MALLEY — *a Sixth Former*

MOLLY PEALE — *a Sixth Former, prefect of Falls Dormitory, member of Girls' Crew*

LIZ FYORDBERG — *a Sixth Former, member of Girls' Crew, and Molly's best friend*

LEIGH URSON — *a Sixth Former, roommate of Lara Jane, Molly and Liz*

MISS THEODOSIA MCMURTRIE — *Biology instructor, coach of Girls' Crew and swimming*

FATHER WILLIAM FARNUM — *Headmaster of St. Augustine's School*

MISS SALLY GREENWELL — *Latin instructor, and housemistress of Falls Dormitory*

MR. THEODORE ALSOP — *Greek instructor, and boys' swimming coach*

MISS MELINDA CURTAIN — *Creative Writing and Drama instructor, a former film star, and an outgoing lady*

WILL (*B.B.*) DICKINSON — *a Third Former*

MR. J.P. SULLIVAN — *head of the English Department, assistant to the Headmaster, and editor of the school newspaper,* The Hippo

MRS. WM. (*Electra*) FARNUM — *the Headmaster's wife, and Biblical Literature instructor*

DAN GARDE — *a Sixth Former, Faith's special friend, and stroke on Boys' Crew*

PORTER CORNWALL — *Dan's friend, Senior Prefect of Boys*

MR. TIMOTHY CRANSTON — *French Literature and English instructor, author of an immortal book*

LIEUTENANT ALFRED (*Buzzie*) HIGGINS — *a state detective, an old acquaintance of Elizabeth Lamb's*

Also servants, relatives, other staff and students, incidental innocents, and the shade of Jay Colket.

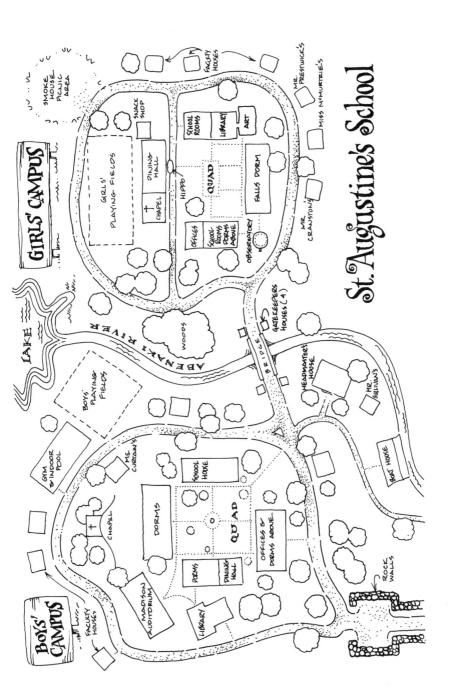

St. Augustine's School

• CONTENTS •

• CHAPTER 1 •

Foot of the Charles

T HE YOUNG WOMAN driving the large station wagon stopped abruptly at the corner of Mount Vernon and Charles Streets, switching on flashing red lights above the front and back window signs that read SCHOOL BUS. The heavy traffic on Charles reluctantly paused and a few stern-faced Boston pedestrians, as they crossed, allowed her smiles that were both grateful and distant.

"Move it, you Elizabeth Lamb Worthington," she said curtly, turning a fat, petulant face towards the tall, slim child who was struggling to open a door while with her other mittened hand trying to get a firmer grasp on the books and notebook that had been dislodged by the sudden stop. "You've been getting off here for five years now; you ought to be ready. I've got more kids than you to get home, you know."

"Well," the child replied calmly, "I thought I *was* ready but I just don't seem able to get used to your driving, Miss Milton. Even after five years. I know my getting-off's improved after five years, but your driving—" She smiled politely and shut the door on the

15

appreciative laughter of the five or six others still at Miss Milton's mercy.

She ran across Charles and started down Mount Vernon, towards the river, her low, rubber-soled boots slipping in the slush on the brick sidewalk. A cold March wind blew back her long, silver-blonde hair and misted her large green eyes, beautifully set off by dark lashes and brows. She shivered under her heavy jacket.

"They can't have freezing winds like the ones we get off the foot of the Charles up in New Hampshire," she murmured aloud, the breath from her open mouth steaming in the cold air. She had formed the habit of talking to herself when she was very young and often alone while her mother worked to support them both during a long absence of her father. Even when he had returned, with the proverbial pot of gold, or, rather, diamonds, and at the same time she and her mother had finally been presented to and warmly welcomed by his wealthy family, she had retained the habit.

She smiled up at the sunflower on the colorful front of a walled house on Mount Vernon. It was one of her favorite houses in her grandmother's neighborhood. "Though why Grandmother insists we live 'at the foot of the Charles' is beyond me," she said now. "I've told her the real foot of the Charles River has got to be in Charlestown, where it goes into the ocean, or maybe at the Charles River Dam."

Her grandmother, being so instructed, had replied that her mother-in-law, whose father-in-law had built the Worthington house on Brimmer Street in the early nineteenth century, had always maintained that they lived "just at the foot of the Charles." Elizabeth Worthington had smiled at her favorite grandchild and gone on: "You must allow old people some latitude, Elizabeth Lamb. I find living 'at the foot of the Charles' most poetic. And, too, this street and the rest of the area was the Charles once, or at least marshland attached to it, before it was filled in less than two hundred years ago."

"Old! Grandmother, you're not old," Elizabeth Lamb had answered, ignoring the geography of the Back Bay. "If you were, Mr. Vincentia wouldn't have asked you to marry him. With his charm *and* money, he could have anybody! But he wants you, because you look and act as young as he does. And because you're kind and beautiful, too," she had added diplomatically.

Her grandmother, who knew when she was being buttered up, had merely smiled and made a request that Elizabeth Lamb stop addressing and referring to her step-grandfather-to-be so formally: "If you're too young to call him Vito—which you are—and don't want to try Grandfather, then I suggest *Nonno*, the Italian for Grandfather."

Thinking of this, she escaped the biting wind that was, or was not, from the foot of the Charles as she ran around the corner into Brimmer Street and climbed the three granite steps to the heavy, windowed double door, pulling off a mitten with her teeth and fumbling through several pockets for a key. She saw with relief that the solid walnut inner door, up another two steps and also double, was ajar, for that key was in another, deeper pocket. "I suppose I'd better find my key ring," she muttered, as she entered very cautiously and quickly made for the stairs across the entry hall, directing a glance at the mahogany hall table, bare except for a lamp whose light was beautifully reflected in the octagonal, blue-and-gold-framed Empire mirror hanging on the staircase wall above the table.

At once, the whining of a vacuum cleaner in the drawing room to her left stopped, the doors were thrown open and the tail of her jacket was seized by a large, rough hand. "No ye don't," the owner of the hand said loudly. "Set yerself on that chair and git off them filthy clodhoppers."

"Well, Alice," lied Elizabeth Lamb, "I was just going to, of course. I know Grandmother has guests coming tonight and I know you don't want to clean the stairs again, with all the work you have to do." She smiled prettily and bent to her footgear. Alice glared at her, her small round face and little, cold grey eyes below frizzy, thin red hair appearing inadequate to top her huge body.

Then her expression softened and she knelt with a loud thump to struggle with the stiff, wet leather laces. Elizabeth Lamb was astounded. "Niver seen sich ugly things," said Alice, "at least, not

17

since I left the bogs of County Kerry. Why a pretty colleen like you wants to deform yer feet like this, I do not know, nor kin I understand why yer grandmother lets ye wear 'em."

Elizabeth Lamb was even more astounded at being called pretty by the belligerent cook, always her sworn enemy during the times her parents were off on one of their mining ventures in remote parts of the world and she made her home with her grandmother. "They're practical, Alice," she said mildly. "Grandmother bought them in Maine last fall on our way down from The Bungalow.

"I saw some girls as well as boys wearing them when Aunt Isabella took me for my interview at St. Paul's. I bet in a few years L.L.Bean boots will be just about everywhere, not just on hunters and fishermen and the few kids whose parents get the catalogue."

"Niver!" Alice proclaimed. "People got more taste. What's wrong with a nice pair of red rubber boots with yer name on 'em, I should like to know? Ye always had fine ones from Best and Comp'ny."

"They're for little children and, anyway, Best's been gone for four years now. You know that."

"Humph!" Then, glancing up at the dark-haired, fresh-faced young woman who had followed her from the drawing room, dustcloth in hand: "Katie, git a towel from the kitchen and dry 'er hair. And rub them ears. They look frostbit."

"My ears are fine," Elizabeth Lamb protested. "Alice, do you feel all right? It's not like you to be so — worrisome." Then, looking again at the hall table, "I see Grandmother has the mail upstairs. Did you notice a letter that said 'St. Paul's School'? It should have come today."

" 'Sif I even look at madam's mail!" Alice exclaimed virtuously. "I got more to do than snoop, worked off me feet as I am." Elizabeth Lamb and Katie, who both knew Alice shook every package, held every letter up to the light of the hall lamp, and then listened at doors to hear if any interesting-looking missive might be being discussed, smiled at each other over her head as she got creakingly to her feet and handed the shoes to Katie. "Wash 'em off," she ordered, "and brush 'er jacket before ye hang it in the cloakroom."

"I can hang up my own jacket," Elizabeth Lamb sighed. "I

always do, and you and Katie have your own work. Lots of it. You just said so, and I'm not an infant."

"No," Alice decreed, "all *you* do is go up and git on some house shoes and then there's tea in the liberry. It's early today, 'cause of the dinner party t'night. You're to eat beforehand in the kitchen with me and Katie, but not to worry: they're havin' a nice roast of beef but I got three fine feelays miggnons fer us.

"There's raisin scones for tea, like ye always have a fancy fer. Ye jist make a good tea, like the fine gerrel ye are; ye're young, y'know, with a long life ahead. Ye don't need to worry about little things that don't mean nuthin' in the long run. I perdict ye'll go far, I do."

Elizabeth Lamb started slowly up the stairs, looking back unbelievingly at Alice, who was regarding her with a strange expression, almost of sympathy. She stopped dead. "Mummy and Daddy are all right, aren't they? Alice, did something happen to them? They're in Pakistan now and anything could, I guess. Alice!"

"'Course not," she was assured. "I'd of seen the letter or heard yer Grandma talkin'." She blushed slightly and then, hastily: "Himself is up there, havin' tea agin. Don't know why they don't git married and have done with it. He's here more'n he is in his own house next door; though, with that door they had cut through on the landin', it might's well be one and the same house."

"They're waiting till he gets all his business concerns settled; you know that. It'll be next spring, I guess."

"Humph!" said Alice again. "Guess it does take a long time to git out of the Black Hand. Not that he ain't a perfick gintleman," she added hastily. "Open-handed as they make 'em, too. And I guess nobody knows fer sure how he made his money; plenty of it, all right."

"Alice," Katie put in timidly, "you shouldn't talk so. Whatever Mr. Vincentia's businesses were, he's retiring now and bygones are bygones, you always say. All he does now is run his publishing company. He gave me some of their books and I enjoyed them."

Elizabeth Lamb, who alone of everyone in the house, except the person under discussion, knew perfectly well what his concerns had been, smiled at her and ran lightly up to her room on the third floor. On the second floor landing, she called, "*Buono sera, Maria*" to the maid who was visible through the open door pushing a carpet sweeper along Mr. Vincentia's hall rug. In her room, she quickly brushed her hair and washed her hands, then ran, humming happily under her breath, down a flight to the library. Before she walked towards it, she went quietly into her grandmother's room, at the opposite end of the hall. A man's handsome dressing gown of heavy brocaded silk was lying on the *chaise longue*.

"As usual," she said under her breath. "Alice is right: why don't they just get married? Oh, well, none of my business and, whether they do in the fall or not, I sure won't be here! I'll be away, away, away at school!" She walked sedately towards the library.

• Chapter 2 •

*Despised and rejected of men…
acquainted with grief…*

— Isaiah 53:3

T HE DOUBLE DOORS of the library were shut but voices murmured behind them. She opened them, still wondering a little about Alice's transformation, and smiled happily at the two people sitting by the tea table, placed before a modest fire. She thought, not for the first time, what a handsome pair they made.

Elizabeth Worthington was slender, her oval, aristocratic face pale and almost unlined. Her sleek black hair, showing only a few threads of grey, was pulled back into a knot low on the base of her long, graceful neck. Her pallor was heightened by a touch of pale pink lipstick on her pretty mouth. She was dressed in her usual winter daytime costume: a twin sweater set topping a tweed skirt. Her graceful legs were crossed at the ankles and, below her brown tights, she wore beautifully polished brown brogues.

The voices had stopped when the doors were opened. Her grandmother had looked up briefly, nodded pleasantly, and then, sipping tea, turned again to the newspaper she was holding. Mr. Vincentia had risen as Elizabeth Lamb entered and crossed to her, kissing her cheek, and saying softly, "How cold you are, *cara*. Come by the fire and I will pour for you."

He was tall, slim-hipped but broad-shouldered, with an agreeable, olive-skinned, weathered face. His black hair and thin mustache were as dark as Mrs. Worthington's hair. He wore a turtle-necked cashmere sweater in his favorite shade of red. He filled a cup for Elizabeth Lamb and continued to stand, thrusting his hands deep into the pockets of his grey flannel trousers and, now frowning a little, rocked back and forth on the heels of his Gucci loafers.

Her grandmother glanced at him and busily began to read from the *Boston Globe*. "Anne Klein is dead, Vito; can you imagine that? So talented and so young and such a ridiculous, unwarranted thing to die of in this day and age! I liked her clothes. I never thought them too young for me — "

"What did she die of, Grandmother? And did we hear from — "

She, in turn, was interrupted. "And Captain Molyneux is very sick, they say. I still have one of his beautiful suits. With all this bad news, at least the Arabs have lifted the oil embargo — " She stopped, as Mr. Vincentia cleared his throat loudly and, picking up his cup, moved to the bay window behind the large, leather-topped desk. Mrs. Worthington reluctantly put the newspaper aside to look at her granddaughter.

"The bread and butter is thin, for once, darling," she said. "And Alice made not only scones but little sponge cakes. Imagine!" She put some of each on a plate and handed it over before she picked up the paper again. "Do you think President Nixon will resign, after all, Vito? This writer seems to think so. If not now, by the summer or early fall."

Mr. Vincentia, still staring down into Mount Vernon Street, cleared his throat again. He then managed a very ineffectual cough.

"What's the matter with everyone?" Elizabeth Lamb had thirstily emptied her cup and was holding it out for a refill. "Alice seems to have got religion and, on the other hand, you don't seem awfully pleased to see me, Grandmother. Do you think I've done

22

something terrible? Honestly, I haven't.

"Did the letter from St. Paul's come? A lot of kids at school have already gotten theirs, from the schools they applied to. A couple of them got into SPS, so I'll know people there, besides Persis. All the parents who pick up their kids told them about their acceptances right away, they were so excited. 'Most everybody got the school they wanted. We're so glad to get out of Greene Country Day; honestly, the teachers there are all bonkers, the old ones, and the new ones are even crazier. We think they're rejects from reform schools, or something. Please, may I see the letter now?"

"Have another scone, dear." Elizabeth Worthington proffered the plate. From the window, came almost a spasm of coughing. She looked over at the erect back and then turned to regard her granddaughter gravely. "They didn't take you, Elizabeth Lamb," she said slowly.

"They . . . didn't . . . take me?" Elizabeth Lamb sank back in her chair. "They . . . turned me down? But why? What did they say?"

"Schools never say why they reject you," Vito put in, his back still turned. "They always write merely that the applicant would be happier, do better, elsewhere. It's happened to a few grandchildren of friends of mine. And no one ever knows why some are taken and others, who would seem to be much more desirable, are rejected."

"But I thought it was a sure thing! My marks are good and the teachers wrote recommendations that couldn't, just couldn't have said anything against me, and you know I wrote a short novel last year and that my English teacher said it was almost good enough to be published! He sent it to St. Paul's before I even had my interview.

"And my father went there, and his father, *and* his grandfather. Oh, how could they have given me such a slap in the face!"

Tears filled her eyes and spilled over. She choked and, with great control, carefully put the cup and saucer on the table. "I know what it was! Oh, Grandmother, how could you have sent Aunt Isabella with me to the interview? She had four or five drinks on the drive up and she just plain batted her eyes at everyone in pants we ran into — even the boy students — and she was worse with the admissions officer. And he talked to her alone before he talked to me. Oh, what could she have said?

"She's ruined my life and I'll never forgive her! If you can believe it, she even had a bottle of rum that stuck out of that big straw bag she carries everywhere. Oh, why couldn't you have asked Aunt Sarah to take me when she took Persis for her interview? She doesn't like me, but she doesn't drink, either!"

"Elizabeth Lamb, Sarah didn't want to try to enter two cousins at the same time. I agree with her that it might have been confusing and could have put the admissions people off both of you. And there was no one to send with you except Isabella: Vito and I were cruising on the *Chianti* and your parents were in Spain, as you know.

"Even though they've accepted girls for three years now, it might have been that they limit the number of girls they accept, or" — she brightened — "perhaps it was that you aren't very good at sports. Yes, that must have been it. I cannot think they would judge *you* by your aunt's behavior."

"Well," Elizabeth Lamb answered with a touch of sarcasm, "I wasn't planning to go there so I could join the Boston Celtics, and as for Aunt Isabella, I just bet that entered into it."

Her grandmother ignored the sarcasm. "You know," she went on, "it may have been because of your father's record there; who knows? He was asked to leave at the end of his Fifth Form year."

Vito was interested. "I didn't know that. Why?"

"Well, his grades were not at all good and he was running a sort of black market operation in competition with the Tuck Shop. He sold, very cheaply, candy bars he got from a boy whose father had an interest in a chocolate factory, and he bribed an underformer to go downtown to Concord every morning, without permission, to bring back doughnuts for his operation, and he made up his own peculiar soft drink — out of what, I dread to think.

"But maybe," she added thoughtfully, "the *dénouement* was when he led some boys in carrying a master's Baby Austin up the steps to the chapel's terrace and leaving it close in front of the main doors, where it froze in the overnight snow and sleet and no one could get through the door the next morning."

Vito almost laughed, but looking at Elizabeth Lamb's pathetic face asked, "Then where did he finish school?"

"At Browne and Nichols, in Cambridge. I wonder if they take girls now? Elizabeth Lamb might apply there.

"Oh, really, dear, why did you apply only to St. Paul's? Everyone, including me, advised you to apply to other schools as well."

"It's the only place I wanted to go. Now *what* am I going to do? It's too late to apply anywhere else, isn't it?"

"There are always accepted students who cancel out in all schools," Vito told her.

"But I don't want to wait around on the chance! That would be nerve-wracking and might destroy my spirit forever," she added quaintly. "Couldn't I go to a public school right here in Boston? At least, I know the territory. Even," sadly, "though I thought I was going to see more of the world."

"You've already seen a great deal of it, more than most people many times your age," her grandmother replied. "But I don't think a public high school here is the answer. Vito says — and he is almost always right about these things — that the order to integrate the schools and, in many cases, to bus students to those far from their homes is going to cause riots next September."

"Well, I don't have to get on the buses. With all the money Daddy would save, I could afford to take the subway, or even taxis."

"You'd still have to walk into the school past the protesters," Vito pointed out. "That's a bit rough for a young girl. It would trouble even one of college age."

"Your father never went to college," Mrs. Worthington observed. "But he got a number of jobs because the interviewers were intrigued by someone who lasted five years at St. Paul's — there was a First Form then, as at most schools, which boys entered perhaps at twelve or even eleven — and then was not graduated."

"You know," Vito said thoughtfully, "Elizabeth Lamb is very young to enter the Third Form anywhere at thirteen, and she won't be that until June. From what you've just said, the average age would be fourteen; sometimes, perhaps, fifteen. And even younger, as I've said, to enter a public high school, even in Boston.

"Now, Persis, being — ah, more docile, more pliable — might work out at prep school, but could Elizabeth Lamb repeat the eighth grade at Greene Country Day?"

Elizabeth Lamb, though inwardly furious at the mention of Persis and her pliability, merely raised her tear-wet eyes to regard him with a mixture of scorn and despair. He looked back, into those young eyes that had seen the truth of four murders — and solved them with bravery and poise as well as an adult intelligence — and was abashed. "Well," he said quietly, "I suppose she can handle anything that comes along. She's old beyond her years."

"I've got to find a *place* to 'handle anything that comes along,'" Elizabeth Lamb said sadly. "Well, I guess I'll go call Persis. Misery loves company and, besides, maybe Aunt Sarah has thought of a school we could get into, even so late. I guess Persis and she feel as bad as we do." She rose wearily.

Elizabeth Worthington straightened her slim shoulders. "Sit down, dear. St. Paul's took Persis — "

"What!" Elizabeth Lamb turned a deadly white. "They refused me and took her? Why, she's a whole week younger than I am, has barely read a book except the ones we were required to read, *and* can't pronounce two words in a row correctly. Oh, I can't stand it!"

"— but," her grandmother went on calmly, "Persis and her mother have decided on Kent. Kent accepted her, too."

"Oh, for the love of the good living God!" Elizabeth Lamb was now beet-red.

"Elizabeth Lamb," her grandmother said sternly, "maybe we could find a very strict church school for you in Boston; what is the Second Commandment?"

Although distraught, Elizabeth Lamb put her mind to it. "'Thou shalt not commit adultery,' maybe?"

Vito smothered a laugh. "That's the only one they ever remember — at least remember the words to. Now, in a strict *Catholic* school — " He stopped, looking thoughtful.

"What do you mean, *Nonno*?" Elizabeth Lamb asked. "I'm not

Catholic; I guess I'm not much of anything. What about 'a strict Catholic school'?"

In turn, he asked, "Have you ever heard of St. Augustine's School?"

Her grandmother spoke for her. "Since I haven't, I'm sure she hasn't. What and where is it?"

"I'm surprised at you, my dear. You pass the brick pillars at the head of its road every time you drive over from The Bungalow to Bar Harbor. It's a school with a great academic rating, as well as a reputation for strict but fair discipline. And it's well-rounded, too: an excellent arts staff and remarkable achievements in sports, all sports.

"Why, its crew teams, both boys' and girls', are neck and neck with Kent School now, and for years Kent's were the best of all the prep schools in the country. Both boys and girls have won in the Head of the Charles many times and the boys have more than once taken the Princess Elizabeth Cup, at Henley.

"And you've never heard of it! I am amazed. It is, by the way, Elizabeth Lamb, no longer officially a Catholic school. It was started in 1902 by a Catholic priest, but now the Episcopalians and other sects outnumber the Catholic students and so it became inter-denominational, but leaning a bit more towards the Episcopal Church. There are a lot of Episcopalians in the world, you know; maybe it's because they say Episcopalians have no need to prepare for heaven because they can do just about anything they want to do on earth." He smiled deprecatingly at Elizabeth Worthington, who had been raised in that faith.

"But it has a Catholic chapel still, as well as the Episcopal chapel, formerly the Catholic one, and priests on its teaching staff, as in former days, and a few nuns. They exert a great influence. It may, you know, be our answer."

His listeners stared at him. "It's on Mount Desert Island, then?" Elizabeth Lamb had finally found her voice. "MDI's cold in the summer, even; I don't think I could take a Maine winter. I hate being cold.

"*And* you say it's strict, *and* I'd have to get into one of those damned — those skinny little boats that I bet tip over a lot. And I'd have to pray to the Virgin Mary? Not that I've got anything against Her, but I'm not used to it. It all sounds too grim for me, *Nonno*."

Her grandmother was more receptive. "Yes, Vito, of course, now that you remind me, I have heard of St. Augustine's and know that it's highly thought of. It's just that I'm on MDI only in the summers, and so never see the students.

"It well might be the answer — but could she get in? They've probably sent out their acceptances, like all the other prep schools. And how do you know so much about it? Have some of your friends' children gone there?"

He smiled. "Not only have my friends' children, and grandchildren, too, who went there been superbly educated, but, over the years, they have all praised it highly. And as for her getting in — well, I happen to be on the board of trustees. That's why I know all about the school."

He smiled again. "Well, 'practically all,' is the way I should put it, I suppose. There must be things the trustees don't hear of, even those of us who contribute generously to the school."

"Like how many kids they lose when the boats tip over?" Elizabeth Lamb asked morosely.

"Elizabeth Lamb, not everyone goes out for crew, or is permitted to. And they're 'shells,' not 'boats.' St. Augustine's is a good, even a great school, not so large that the students lose their identities and not so small that the teaching is not of the highest quality.

"The school is heavily endowed and gets the best instructors. Some of them have even refused offers from 'St. Grottlesex' schools to teach there. There's not one graduate, and this I know for a fact, who was not admitted to the first college he or she applied to, among them Harvard, Brown, Stanford, Yale and many others. All the top ones."

Elizabeth Lamb was becoming faintly interested. "How long have they had girls?"

"They, and Kent, in 1959, were the first to admit them. After the Quaker schools, that is. The Quakers are very progressive. But Kent and St. Augustine's were not long behind. They were way ahead of St. Paul's, in 1971."

Elizabeth Lamb winced at the mention of St. Paul's, but rallied. "So I wouldn't be an experimental case," she added thoughtfully, in the formal manner familiar to her from being so much with adults. Her grandmother, with some remorse, thought that it would indeed be a better thing for her granddaughter to live in a young person's environment. "But," Elizabeth Lamb went on, with a diffidence unusual to her until that afternoon, "would they have me?"

Vito smiled again. "It will take but a telephone call to the admissions officer, Lyman Salton, to get you an interview. Then it will be up to your record at Greene Country Day and to your personality — and to me. I will, I assure you, take no bottle of rum with me when we go up there. Shall I make the call?"

Elizabeth Lamb drew in a deep breath. "Yes, please, *Nonno*. I guess it's my only hope. But I can't stand to hear people talking about me; I'll go up to my room while you do it, or else stay here and put my fingers in my ears and make loud gibbering noises like Woody Allen in *Play It Again Sam*."

Her grandmother laughed her pretty girlish laugh, while she thought again how good it would be for Elizabeth Lamb to be in a young community, the members of which had neither time nor opportunity to see adult movies. Her granddaughter, with a determined smile, left the library.

She did not go to her room, however, but sat on the lowest step just outside the doors she had shut behind her. Her fingers were in her ears until, yielding to her great inborn curiosity, she removed them and listened as closely as she could. But the doors were thick, and she heard nothing.

Presently they opened and Mr. Vincentia put out his hands to help her rise. "We see Mr. Salton the day after tomorrow, at eleven-thirty in the morning. Now come in and I'll convince your grandmother to let me pour us all some sherry, to celebrate."

Despite a reviving sip of her half-filled glass, Elizabeth Lamb was still not her usual confident, happy self. "I'm still angry at St. Paul's," she said in a low voice. "How could they! I'm just terribly down; no pride left."

"Don't show any anger at your interview," Mr. Vincentia

advised. "Or pride, either, if you get it back." He restrained himself from smiling. "You've heard the saying, perhaps: 'Anger and pride are both allies, since anger never catches flies.'"

"Your quotations are usually Sicilian, dearest," Mrs. Worthington observed mildly. "But why should she have to 'catch flies,' Vito? Surely they'll take her, with your influence. And, of course," she added hastily, "they'd take her, anyway; for herself, for what she is." Her granddaughter gave her a somewhat caustic glance.

"No, no, my dearest Elizabeth; my 'influence,' as you say, will have no effect at all on Mr. Salton. I know of several promising students who were not accepted, although highly recommended by one trustee or another.

"What I will do, immediately, is send a copy of her novel by overnight mail. It is short and I'm sure he will read it through before he sees her. I thought it perfectly charming, and clever, too; she worked out the plot most ingeniously.

"And to think she wrote it last year, when only twelve, and in just a few days, as we cruised back to Boston on the *Chianti*."

He was silent, his expression sad, as he recalled the tragic circumstances which had provoked the return trip. Quickly, Elizabeth Worthington said, "I thought it remarkable, too. I have re-read it many times, as I do that delightful little book by a young English child, *The Young Visitors*. But I like Elizabeth Lamb's better."

Elizabeth Lamb was angry again. "Well, I do hope so, Grandmother, since *I* can spell! And since mine had something of a plot, not to mention correct grammar.

"And I've been thinking; why do I have to go to a prep school at all? I know I said St. Augustine's was my last chance, but I still say I could do pretty well at a Boston high school. Does Boston Latin take girls?"

"The reason to go to a prep school," Vito advised her, "is that you'll be certain that when you need to know someone or do something, you'll most certainly have had a schoolmate who knows that someone or who knows a person who knows that someone, or knows the someone who can help you to achieve that something. I hope I'm being clear? Clear or not, what I have said

30

is," he finished solemnly, although his eyes twinkled, "a fact of life, although known only by those who know everything. Like me.

"And it will help you to handle everything else you will encounter when you are out in the real world. You know they say that 'in the battle between you and the world — bet on the world!' Well, a preparatory school education will help you in your battle."

Elizabeth Worthington laughed. "How worldly — although I feel redundant using the word — you are, darling. But I am concerned about the Roman Catholic aspect of St. Augustine's. She won't have to convert?"

"As a Catholic myself, I can say only that it wouldn't be such a bad thing if she did. But, no, of course not. Although, as I have said, the school was originally strictly for Catholics, it is no longer. It has services in both the Episcopal and Roman Catholic religions, but it has, for instance, students who are Jehovah's Witnesses who are driven each Sunday to their service in Bar Harbor; Quakers who are driven to theirs in Ellsworth, and Mormons likewise. The Jews are taken on Friday nights to a synagogue in Bangor, those who wish to go, even though the early start means they must be excused from Friday afternoon classes. Possibly Saturday morning ones, too; I'm not sure."

"Saturday classes?" Elizabeth Lamb moaned.

"All prep schools have them," her grandmother told her. "Vito, who founded the school?"

"A very interesting man, a staunch Catholic in his youth who married a charming young girl, I am told; a Catholic like him. They had much money but no children and when she died a few years later, he led for some years a most dissolute life. But, like Saul on the road to Damascus, the story goes, he received some sort of dazzling vision and, to make the story short, eventually became a Catholic priest, although he was by then in his forties. He identified his life with that of St. Augustine's.

"And, being both wealthy and having summered on MDI, he determined to spend his fortune on founding and endowing a Catholic school there. It has, and I've told you this before, a high standard of excellence. Father Fitzgerald, the man I've been speaking of, insisted on it. He was, of course, the first headmaster.

They've had only three, including the present incumbent, an Episcopal priest, married to a very learned woman.

"There was emphasis on rowing from the beginning, which is why their crews are now so good. Father Fitzgerald had attended a Catholic high school in New Jersey which produced, and still does, the best rowers in the country. He rowed for the school, Holy Prince, when he was a student there."

"I thought you said Kent and St. Augustine's were tops," Elizabeth Lamb reminded him.

"Of private schools, yes, but as perhaps I didn't make clear, Holy Prince is a public high school."

"Well, you won't find me going out for crew," Elizabeth Lamb said firmly. "I'm not at all athletic."

"You could be coxswain on one of the intramural crews. A cox has to be fairly light, if not small, and it requires brains as well as skill. You're good at steering, at least in small sailboats."

"Never! The rowers throw them overboard if they win. Or maybe if they lose? I really haven't concentrated on this. Or probably," she concluded, sighing heavily, "it's if they win *or* lose!"

"Dear," Elizabeth Worthington said, "you needn't apply to St. Augustine's, you know. Vito can cancel the interview. You *could* apply to other schools where there may still be vacancies, or else be put on a waiting list. No one is forcing you anywhere."

Elizabeth Lamb had finished her miniscule amount of sherry and was in the post-alcohol state of depression induced by even a small drink, as her Worthington forebears, heavy consumers of madeira, whiskey, sherry and port could have, were they alive, advised her always followed the first euphoria of liquor.

"No," she said with another heavy sigh, "maybe it's fate. Maybe I was meant to go to St. Augustine's — if they'll have me. Maybe *they* won't take me, either. And maybe they will and I'll forget all the rules — you said it was strict — and end up on bread and water." Another sigh, deep and dramatic.

Mr. Vincentia laughed. Mrs. Worthington did not: "It's not Dotheboys Hall," she said. "And Persis, at Kent, will find it very strict, too. Good schools are. And please, dear, control your sense of theatrics. You are making us feel that you think we're selling you down the river, or something similar."

Elizabeth Lamb, preparing to leave for her room, lingered, finding she could now bear the mention of Persis, especially if Persis, too, was going to encounter severe discipline. "As Aunt Isabella is always saying," she thought, "'Time heals all wounds'—maybe even a little time—'and wounds all heels.' I bet those creeps at St. Paul's will be sorry some day they didn't take me, especially if I end up on the Supreme Court, or something."

Aloud she asked curiously, "Why did Persis decide on Kent over that miserable St. Paul's?"

"Persis has become quite proficient in riding, as you know," her grandmother answered, "and Kent has stables. And, too, her father went to Kent. Hill is very pleased Persis is going there, especially since his son went to—ah, somewhere else."

"I know where Gus went; thanks for not mentioning it. But horses! A school with horses! It might as well be Miss Porter's or 'Farmington' as you have to call it if you're trying to be somebody. *They* probably have horses. What's Kent's motto? 'For the want of a nail' and so on?"

"No need to be sarcastic." Elizabeth Worthington spoke severely. "The students who ride, and only a minority of them do, get up at five, Hill says, to do their stable work before breakfast."

"Speaking of horses, Elizabeth Lamb," Vito asked with a grin, "don't you want to know St. Augustine's motto? It's a quotation from the good saint himself, and I can't give you the Latin, but it translates as 'Will is to grace as the horse is to the rider.' Think about it."

"Huh!" responded Elizabeth Lamb, who was seldom rude. Then she spoke with her usual charm: "Well, I won't see you till breakfast, Grandmother, since I'm eating dinner with Alice and Katie. Good night. Good night, *Nonno*. And I really do thank you."

"We will call Greene first thing tomorrow and ask them to send your transcript home with you," Vito answered. "And then you and I leave for MDI early the next morning. Your grandmother will have you excused from school for the day."

"They'll probably put all the papers in three or four sealed envelopes so I can't peek," she told him. "I know their tricky little ways. But I'll have to remember to ask for them because Miss Greene's so out of it, now that she's going to be married, that she forgets everything." She managed to raise one eyebrow, as her grandmother was adept at doing. "Being engaged makes you sort of unconventional, I guess, not to mention bossy." She smiled and opened the door, casting a quick look over her shoulder to see if her remark had been too subtle for them.

It had not. As Elizabeth Worthington opened her mouth to administer a mild reproof and Vito frowned, she turned in the doorway and smiled again, most engagingly. "Off I go, bravely into the night," she said dramatically, "even though I'm 'rejected of men . . . acquainted with grief.'"

"What!" her grandmother exclaimed. "Where in the world did you get that?"

"Why, Grandmother, I thought anyone who knew the Commandments would know. Isaiah: Chapter 53, verse 3. I'll see you tomorrow."

• CHAPTER 3 •

Accept the place the divine providence has found for you.

— Ralph Waldo Emerson

ELIZABETH LAMB survived breakfast with her grandmother and Mr. Vincentia, who had obviously stayed the night. Aware that the ice under her was thin, after her pert behavior of the previous afternoon, she raised not even one brow at him and was the complete model of a child in whose mouth butter would not melt. She did, though, spread a great deal of it on her toast, having read somewhere that fats stay in the stomach a long time and so give a feeling of fortification.

"Which is what I'll need today," she thought. Her breakfast companions, who, even privileged as they were, had endured rejections and so were aware of how she, a proud child, must feel, made only polite table conversation and wished her well as she set off. Today there was a cruel wind at her back that hastened her to the corner where the testy Miss Milton would pick her up.

At school, she endured the sympathetic embraces of her cousin.

Persis' brown curls were damp with emotion and her hugs much stronger than her once-chubby arms had previously been able to produce. "All that riding," Elizabeth Lamb thought, patting Persis' back in gratitude despite the painful compression of her own ribs, while she realized that Persis was now almost as tall as she.

Persis' round face was as pink and pretty as when the girls had first met five years earlier, her nose as pert and her large blue eyes now made even more brilliant by the genuine tears they displayed. The observant Elizabeth Lamb, though, could detect a slightly smug expression behind the tears. She sighed and gave Persis a final pat.

And she parried the questions of her classmates as to which school she would attend after they were all freed of their present bondage. Wishing she had eaten more butter, she told them she was off the next day to visit St. Augustine's. A few of them were impressed.

"That's a tough one," a boy told her. "Hope you make it. They turned down my brother and he had top grades and was a real jock, too." After word reached her teachers that she needed her transcript for application to a school other than St. Paul's, she endured more sympathy, but on a more reserved level than Persis'.

The day passed. She picked up her papers, suffered through Miss Milton's lack of navigational ability, and ate again with Alice and Katie, her grandmother having left for a dinner engagement. At 7:30 the next morning, after merely pushing about her plate the lavish breakfast a still-agreeable Alice had prepared, she went out to the curb where Mr. Vincentia's chauffeur waited.

"Hello, Antonio," she said glumly as he opened the door of the limousine. "I'm sorry you had to get up so early. Where's Mr. Vincentia?"

"The *padrone* had to make a quick visit to his book company. He will meet us at Logan. Mr. Moselli's Lear jet will fly you to Maine."

Even though she sat in luxury in the plane, with a pleasant young man in the cabin to serve them, she was silent and withdrawn as she stared out the window. Grimy, snowy Boston disappeared as they headed northeast. Mr. Vincentia drank San

Pellegrino water the attendant supplied and frowned as he wrote in a notebook. Finally he raised his head and smiled across the aisle at her. "How I envy your being a schoolgirl with no business worries. Think, in a few hours you will, I am sure, be enrolled at St. Augustine's for four years. And then, probably, college for four more, before you must face the world and its problems."

She nodded soberly as she looked out at the clouds. "All I have to face now," she thought, "is a person who'll turn me down and then I'll have to face another admissions person, and then another and—" Aloud she said, with more than a bit of assumed pathos, "Maybe we'll crash and I won't have to be interviewed, being dead."

Mr. Vincentia smiled into his notebook. "Well, look at it this way: we can't die any younger. That's what my wife used to say to our children when German bombers flew over our English home. Somehow, it cheered them."

"That's what I'd call a half-vast thought," she muttered under her breath. He glanced over at her with a touch of anger and closed his notebook. But he spoke mildly. "Elizabetta was a very wise woman, as well as a brave and beautiful one. I have told you that you as well as your grandmother remind me of her. In a similar circumstance, you might well say the same sort of thing: you would face the reality and have your children do so.

"Now, what can I tell you of the reality of St. Augustine's, to prepare you before you see it?"

She sipped the ginger ale the attendant had brought her. "Well, does it look like St.—like other New England prep schools? And what do they do to you if you break the rules? And is the food like—like that other school's, where I had lunch?" Thinking of her aunt's behavior at that meal, she was silent again.

"The boys' and girls' campuses are separated," he answered, "but only by about a five-minute walk after they cross the bridge. The Abenaki River divides the grounds; the bridge has a gate at either end and, on each side, two houses that are occupied by members of the maintenance staff and their families. The gates are locked at seven each evening, although the teachers' and other staffs' cars have signals that open them. There are faculty homes on both campuses, you see. Any other vehicles must be passed through by the gatekeepers; they alternate on each side each night.

"The students must be on their own campus at seven; if they need to go to the other for music or dramatic practice or anything else, the school bus or a van takes them back and forth. Lights–out for Third Formers is at nine-thirty, later for the older forms. Since students could, possibly, walk to the other campus and get around the gates at night, flashlights are forbidden to them. This is one rule that is very firmly — "

"What! This all sounds like a prison, *Nonno*. And I haven't gone to bed at nine-thirty since I was seven! I can't believe this school is so strict."

"You must remember that it was still a Catholic school when girls were first admitted; the priests and nuns on the teaching staff wanted the separation of boys and girls and the custom has held.

"And since you must get up at six-thirty in the morning, you will find the early bedtime — "

"Six-thirty! Oh, *Nonno*, — "

He ignored her and went on. "Both campuses have their own library, gymnasium, tennis courts, playing fields and so on, but classes are held in the schoolrooms on both and students take the bus to the other, or walk if they have time. They all use all the facilities on both grounds.

"The boys' campus was the first one, and has the indoor pool, football field, indoor hockey rink, boathouse and infirmary as well as the Episcopal chapel, formerly the Catholic one. The girls' campus has the newly-built, smaller Catholic chapel now, and a dispensary with at least one nurse always on duty. There are two doctors on call at all times, and they make regular semi-weekly visits. The chapels are of stone, and very handsome. All the other buildings are of the traditional brick, with white wood trim, except the boathouse, a new one given by the mother of a former student. That is of wood. The girls' dormitories, being newer, are more modern than the boys'; more comfortable, too. Their common rooms have television sets, kitchenettes — things the boys don't have.

"The food? Well, it is not what you are used to, but it is good and it is nutritious. The girls' dining hall is considered to have better food, though, you will be pleased to hear. Or, at least, the boys, who may eat lunch there if their class before or after is on the girls' grounds, say it is better. They often write letters to the school paper, *The Hippo*, bitterly protesting this, as well as their lack of television sets."

"Does anyone pay attention to them?"

"Of course not. You might, by the way, with your writing ability, try to get on the paper's staff, or, at least this first year, submit articles to it.

"And what happens if you break the rules? Well, various things, though you will not be sent to work the potato fields, as I am told happens at Deerfield Academy, nor the blueberry fields, as at Kent School."

"I guess I'll just be put to breaking rocks, with chains on my ankles and a striped suit, like in the movies?"

He laughed. "Actually, it is to building low rock walls of fieldstone, the old New England kind. But there are milder forms of punishment, *cara* — look, we are landing. I have arranged for a hired car to be ready so we will easily get to the school in half an hour."

Elizabeth Lamb gave a desolate look at her hands, possibly soon to be calloused from making fieldstone walls, before she put gloves on them, shrugged into her jacket and scarf and followed him from the plane. She was silent on the drive, not even regarding with any interest the winter aspect of MDI which, even under very little snow, was so different from its familiar summer appearance.

As they drove through the brick pillars at the beginning of St. Augustine's private road, a loud clap of thunder suddenly sounded from the clouds over the low mountain between them and Bar Harbor, although the sky directly above them was a bright winter blue. Elizabeth Lamb started in her seat.

"Did you hear that thunder on our left? Isn't that a bad omen? I don't like this, *Nonno*."

"I am not superstitious, *cara*," he answered easily, "and I was sure you were not. It means nothing."

Elizabeth Lamb, who knew he was extremely superstitious, felt her heart beginning to pound. "Look," he went on, "are not these woods beautiful? St. Augustine's has a remarkable assortment of handsome old trees, both deciduous and evergreen. And look at the moss and the ground dogwood. Did you know, by the way, that the original definition of 'paradise' was 'a park with trees'?"

"No," she answered politely although she was suddenly impatient with his widespread knowledge and also beginning to feel sick. She turned her head away and opened her mouth to breathe deeply through it. Outside her window she saw several boys in heavy sweaters, wool caps, mittens and corduroy pants rolling stones toward the low walls that separated the road from the woods.

"Oh, no; it's true," she said under her breath. "The chain gang!"

The road ended in a large parking area, also bordered by fieldstone walls. Beyond it was a half-acre of grass, lightly covered with snow in places, with groups of plantings of small trees and shrubbery, and brick paths winding through it. Around it, the promised brick buildings formed a quadrangle. On a rise, above the green, woods dark behind it, was a stately tan stone edifice topped by a bell tower.

As they walked toward the nearest building, she glanced to her right and saw the little river, some ice patches on it, across whose wide bridge a number of figures, burdened by piles of books, were walking. Some of them put down their loads on the wooden benches that ran the entire length of the bridge on either side, and scraping up snow from the benches, proceeded to try to thrust it down the backs of the necks of three girls walking in front of them. Elizabeth Lamb shuddered.

"Oh, well, I won't get in anyway," she thought. "Otherwise, if that happened to me, I'd really let those nasty preppies have one or two of the karate chops Daddy taught me."

Inside the door of the admissions building was a short hall lined with closed, glass-panelled office doors that ended in a carpeted, sunken pit, a skylight in the ceiling over it. It held comfortable-looking sofas and chairs, standing lamps among them, around a big, low table of light wood with piles of periodicals. A few students occupied some of the chairs, reading, or slouching with hands in trouser pockets, legs straight out, staring forlornly at the skylight. One girl, though, long-legged, with coal black skin and kinky reddish hair divided into cornrows, as Elizabeth Lamb knew they were called, sat upright, studying a large notebook. She raised her large dark eyes and glared at them as they skirted the pit and proceeded down a hall similar to the first.

"They're probably waiting to see the headmaster for some infraction of rules, serious ones or the deans or the Student Council would handle the discipline," Mr. Vincentia informed her in a low voice. Her heart, partially provoked by the antagonistic glance of the black girl, again began to pound painfully. As they turned right into another hall, he waved toward his left. "Father Farnum's office is that way. I hope you'll never be back in that pit waiting to see him."

He paused at an open office door and a thin, elderly woman with well-coiffed white hair smiled and rose from behind her desk. "Oh, it's good to see you, Mr. Vincentia. And this is Elizabeth? Mr. Salton is ready. You're to go right in."

Before she could grasp Elizabeth Lamb's hand but not before she was told in a subdued but firm voice: "My name is Elizabeth Lamb," the inner door opened and a tall, heavy man stood beaming at them. Elizabeth Lamb stood transfixed.

He gleamed from the top of his completely bald head, that looked as though it were buffed each morning, to the tips of brilliantly-polished tan shoes. His clear blue eyes twinkled behind horn-rimmed spectacles whose immaculate lenses positively glittered. His shirt front and collar were of a dazzling white; his blue silk tie sparkled like his eyes; even his jacket of rough, hand-woven brown tweed had strawlike flecks in it that scintillated under the light of the ceiling lamp.

Across his ample paunch, the sheen of his heavy gold watch chain almost hurt her eyes as he stroked it with a hand whose fingernails glistened. And with all this lustre, he still exuded an air of such terrifying integrity and forceful geniality that Elizabeth Lamb became extremely frightened of him. Her heart beat harder than before.

"How are you, my dear sir," he beamed, displaying large, shiny white teeth as he spoke. "And," to Elizabeth Lamb, in confidence-inspiring tones, "I am *extremely* pleased to see you here, my dear young lady. I have much enjoyed your little book. Please come in." They left their coats with the secretary and followed him.

Seated behind his mahogany desk, the almost-bare top of which shone with polish, Mr. Salton was no less dazzling. He picked up a glossy black pen and manipulated it as he conducted the interview, after praising her book earnestly and in words that showed, at least, that he had read it. He consulted the reports from Greene Country Day and seemed to find no fault or flaw in them. It soon became evident that St. Augustine's, in the person of Lyman Salton, wanted her; now Mr. Salton began to prepare her to desire ardently to be a pupil at St. Augustine's.

Elizabeth Lamb, who had crossed her legs at the knee, uncrossed them at Mr. Vincentia's frown, smoothed down her pleated grey flannel skirt, and assumed an eager expression, now that she saw the wind was blowing from a favorable quarter.

"You know," Mr. Salton confided to Mr. Vincentia but with one bright eye directed at his prospect, "that we have Sancho Pella now as cook for the girls' dining hall, but do you know, Elizabeth Lamb" — he now turned both eyes on her and she smiled, pleased that he had given her her full name — "that he *founded* 'Pella's' in New Orleans and in twenty years made it a world famous restaurant?"

"Oh, yes!" enthusiastically exclaimed Elizabeth Lamb, who had never heard of it.

"We are very lucky to have him. He turned the restaurant over to his sons last year and moved to the quiet of a town outside Boston, where he found the climate more salubrious than the heat of New Orleans. But he discovered retirement boring, put out feelers and we heard of it; our tentacles stretch far, as you know, sir. Ha! He decided St. Augustine's was the place for him."

"Oh, how nice!" exclaimed Elizabeth Lamb, showing more real enthusiasm at the idea that the food might be edible.

"And you will enjoy Miss Melinda Curtain. She teaches drama and creative writing. It is not every school that has a famous actress on its staff. And still a most beautiful woman! You know" —

his voice dropped in awe—"when she first went to Hollywood, she was called 'the young Miriam Hopkins.' Yes, it is *not* every school that has such talent available to its pupils."

"Oh, no!" agreed Elizabeth Lamb, who had heard of neither Miss Curtain nor Miss Hopkins.

His voice dropped further. "And Mr. Timothy Cranston has returned to his old school to teach Third Form English and French Literature. You know his *Marianne*, of course?"

Now Elizabeth Lamb was honestly enthusiastic. "Here? Oh, my goodness! Oh, that's wonderful!"

Mr. Vincentia stirred. "Mary Ann? I didn't know Cranston was married. You know the lady, Elizabeth Lamb?"

Both turned to him in surprise. Mr. Salton dropped his gleaming eyes and toyed with his gleaming pen as Elizabeth Lamb explained.

"*Nonno, Marianne* is a book. It's really called *Marianne l'immortelle* but nobody says all that. It was one of the first books Mummy read me. I've read it over and over, both in the original French and in English. There's been *Black Beauty*, there's been *Old Yeller*; there's been *Sounder*, there's been *Bambi*; but none of them ever made me cry like *Marianne*. It's the saddest animal story ever.

"Mummy told me it was written in France during the German occupation and though it's about a dog, it's really what you call a parable, I guess. You see, the dog stands for the spirit of France."

Mr. Vincentia was still confused. "I didn't know this. I've never heard of the book. And how is it Cranston was writing in France during the occupation?"

Mr. Salton took over. "He and a cousin went to France in the summer of 1939, just after Cranston was graduated from St. Augustine's and his cousin from a Canadian school. They stayed on even after the war broke out in September, and eventually joined the French Resistance. The cousin was killed—their unit was betrayed, I believe—but Cranston and some others survived and, to keep his mind off the continual danger, somehow managed to write the little book.

"It was first published by an underground press in France. After the war, its popularity spread worldwide; it's been printed in at least twenty languages, I believe."

"It has somehow escaped my notice." Mr. Vincentia was a little embarassed. "Although probably my wife introduced my children to it. And I've never heard it mentioned here, before. But why did you cry, Elizabeth Lamb?"

"Cranston is very shy and retiring; puts on no 'side,' so to speak, at all," Mr. Salton broke in to explain. "So you well may not have heard it mentioned here. We think so highly of his teaching that perhaps sometimes we forget that he has written one of the most famous books in the world."

"But why did you cry?" Mr. Vincentia asked again. "I never thought you so susceptible to the written word, Elizabeth Lamb."

"Oh, *Nonno*, it's just so sad. It's about this starved, beaten, black Labrador dog who is befriended by a little girl who's also mistreated and hungry. The girl calls the dog Marianne, after her little sister who died following a whipping. They both have this bully of a stepfather the whole village's afraid of. The dog dies — is killed" — her voice broke — "defending the little girl from the stepfather, but the whole thing makes the village so mad the people just get very brave and kill the stepfather.

"Mummy said that, published during the war as it was, the French people saw Marianne, the dog, I mean, as the spirit of the French nation."

Mr. Salton beamed. "Very well explained," he said heartily. "Now, I'm sure you know rowing is the sport we're best known for, but there are others for girls: field hockey, soccer, tennis, swimming, basketball, volleyball — oh, you'll be extremely happy with our variety." His teeth flashed as he asked eagerly, "Can you row, Elizabeth Lamb?"

"Not very well," firmly answered Elizabeth Lamb, who was adept at rowing.

Hastily, Mr. Vincentia asked, "I've never fully realized, Salton, how, being so far from other schools as St. Augustine's is, you get the crews to meets without their being exhausted from the trip before they even compete. Elizabeth Lamb is not yet thirteen, as you know, and not of a sturdy constitution."

The teeth gleamed again. "Oh, we fly them, of course. The shells are trucked down the day before. The crews are quite fresh when they arrive."

"But sometimes planes don't fly from here in the winter, when there's snow and ice," Elizabeth Lamb observed.

"My dear young lady, there are no meets during the winter. We do practice on the river here, of course, when possible. Mr. Prestwick is firm about that. Besides being a most accomplished coach of boys' crew, he advises Miss McMurtrie with the girls', and both are held to his standards.

"And, do you know," his voice again dropped in studied awe, "he twice won the gold in the Olympic single sculls competition! He was pleased, of course, but chagrined that he never won in Germany. There was a score to settle, so to speak; his great-uncle was Jesse Owens."

Elizabeth Lamb nodded with an understanding she did not possess. Mr. Salton's shining telephone sounded discreetly just then, and he picked it up after a hasty apology and swivelled in his chair, his back half-turned to them. Mr. Vincentia muttered to her: "Jesse Owens won three track and field events at the 1936 Olympic Games in Berlin but Hitler refused to shake his hand."

"Why on earth, *Nonno*?" asked Elizabeth Lamb, who knew, at least, who Hitler was, or had been.

"Mr. Owens was a Negro — a black, as people of color are now called. I've always thought that a misnomer, because not every dark-skinned person has *black* skin. However, one must go with the flow. You'll learn that in school as well as in life."

Mr. Salton put down the phone. "Father Farnum is anxious for you to lunch with him at his house, Mr. Vincentia, as soon as we finish here, and Elizabeth Lamb can lunch at the girls' dining hall.

"Now, what more can I tell you about our little community, young lady? We really are a community you know, a truly friendly group. We do things together. For instance, some of the men teachers, and I with them, take great pleasure in singing plainsong one or two evenings a week on the steps of the bell tower in the chapel on this campus. It's just a little thing we enjoy. And we have a fine group of bell ringers; you might want to join.

"And there's the observatory. Small, but well equipped, if you have an interest in astronomy. And many clubs — the social club, the Bon Vivant Society, is composed of both boys and girls who arrange student social events. Our arts department is well staffed — you can learn painting or sculpture with Mr. Dipietro or Mrs. McFarland in the SEXCA program."

Elizabeth Lamb had thought he might say they had studied under Michaelangelo but her thought was diverted: "Did you say sex-something, Mr. Salton?" she asked.

He laughed merrily. "It merely stands for Supervised Extra-Curricular Activity," he explained, his already ruddy cheeks deepening slightly in color. "All students must have one." Mr. Vincentia kicked her ankle.

"Oh, and I forgot to mention that Mr. Prestwick teaches Scuba Diving. Required for members of crew, but students may elect it as their SEXCA."

"That's where you dive under water. I've read about it. What does *that* stand for, though?"

"Self-contained underwater breathing apparatus," Mr. Vincentia explained, getting ready to kick her again.

Elizabeth Lamb opened her mouth to say she would rather die than voluntarily put her head under water while carrying a tank of air on her back, as she had seen poor misguided souls doing in the movies, when Mr. Vincentia, observing her disdainful expression, really did kick her, this time harder. Instead, she asked, "How cold does it get up here — the weather, I mean, as well as the water?"

"MDI winters are fairly mild, to the regret of our ski team. But the water temperature doesn't matter for scuba since it is taught first in our pool and then done, in fall or spring, in our little lake."

"It's required for crew members because of the new boathouse, isn't it, Mr. Salton?" Mr. Vincentia asked. "I remember some controversy about the school's accepting the gift of the boathouse from Mrs. Proctor with the condition attached."

"Yes, that was the condition of the gift, but the trustees finally decided it a good idea. This was some years ago, before you came on the board, I believe, sir. Since the previous boathouse was in bad shape, the trustees accepted the gift.

"Mrs. Proctor, Elizabeth Lamb, was convinced that her son — a

46

Fifth Former at the time of his death, and stroke of boys' crew — would never have died as he did if he had been properly taught scuba diving."

"He died here?" Elizabeth Lamb was appalled.

"Of *course* not. At their place in the Bahamas, on spring break. We had no scuba instruction here at the time. Few schools do." He grew pensive. "Of course, Groton may; they teach woodworking, of all things, I am told. Young Proctor went diving on his own, and, somehow, drowned."

The telephone rang. Mr. Salton again half-turned to answer it.

"I'm getting a feeling of deja-voodoo, *Nonno*," Elizabeth Lamb whispered. "This is just how Harvard got a swimming pool, Aunt Isabella said. From a woman whose son had gone to Harvard and then drowned when the *Titanic* went down and she thought he wouldn't have, if Harvard had made all students learn to swim the length of a pool, at least, before they graduated.

"She didn't learn, of course. She got, ah, friendly with one of her tutors — probably more than one! — and he turned his back while she was supposed to be doing it. Aunt Isabella still can't swim."

"I know all that, *cara*," he whispered back. "Well, not about your Aunt Isabella's ingenuity. But this interview has gone on long enough; obviously you are accepted. And the headmaster is waiting for me. I'll see if I can — "

Mr. Salton put down the phone. "Where were we? No matter. Well, I think we've said all we need. Do I understand that you wish to enter St. Augustine's, Elizabeth Lamb?"

"Oh, yes, sir," she said charmingly.

Mr. Salton smiled with gratification. "I take it there is no need of financial aid, Mr. Vincentia?" he asked. "I am required to inquire, but only after the applicant has been accepted."

"None at all." Mr. Vincentia rose and extended his hand. "Elizabeth Lamb will lunch with the students?"

"Indeed, yes." Mr. Salton pressed a button. The secretary appeared and was requested to send in Joylene Treble. Almost before she could turn away, the tall black girl who had looked up as Elizabeth Lamb passed was in the doorway.

"Ah, Joylene!" Mr. Salton beamed happily. "You are prompt.

This is Elizabeth Lamb Worthington whom I asked you to show around after lunch. She'll be a Third Former next year."

Joylene nodded coolly to them. Mr. Vincentia shook her hand and made his escape. "I'm prompt because you told me to be here at eleven, Mr. Salton," Joylene said with poise. "And I have my mid-term French exam at two."

"Yes, yes, of course. Elizabeth Lamb, Father Farnum has named Joylene to be Senior Prefect of Girls next year, her Sixth Form year. She knows the school well.

"A pleasure to have met with you, Elizabeth Lamb. Now, I know you must be hungry. I'm happy you're to be joining us."

As she, following Joylene, passed the pit, the one remaining occupant, a handsome curly-haired blond boy, looked appraisingly at her. "The St. Augustine's once-over-tightly?" Elizabeth Lamb muttered to Joylene's back. She heard a smothered laugh.

"That's what you get for your sins, Joylene?" the boy asked. "Though you probably don't have any," he added sarcastically. "A rat to show around?"

Joylene stopped dead. "We're not to call new students that, Harris, as you know perfectly well. Knock it off or I'll see you get stung."

"Yeah?" the boy sneered. "How'll you-all do that? You're not Senior Prefect yet, honey chile."

"Yeah!" answered Elizabeth Lamb, who was recovering from her traumatic morning. "And I'll see our brother beats you up; Joylene's my half-sister and he just won the Golden Gloves." She marched along behind Joylene, who was now laughing audibly.

She turned and took Elizabeth Lamb's arm in a friendly manner. "I'm sorry I gave you a nasty look, before," she said. "But I was pissed at having to wait so long, just because Mr. Salton always messes up. I liked your style with that Harris; he's a real jerk. Only his money stops him from being a total loser."

She laughed. "Or maybe it doesn't. What're the Golden Gloves, anyway, some television award?"

"I'm not sure, but I think you get it for boxing. Are all the boys like him?"

"A few," Joylene admitted. "And a few of the girls. The wealthy curled darlings of our nation' is what my uncle, a Shakespeare freak, calls them. But there aren't many, and I've got an idea you can handle yourself. You're shoe. You go by both your first names?"

"Yes. Always have. What's 'shoe'?"

"Top drawer. Come on; we can make that bus."

They scrambled on just as the bus was starting and fell into a seat behind one occupied by a tall black man who smiled at them.

"Is he a student?" Elizabeth Lamb asked in a low voice. "He looks sort of old."

Joylene giggled. "He is old, sort of. That's Harry Prestwick. He's a master here and my uncle."

"The crew coach? The Olympic champion?"

"How'd you know?"

"Mr. Salton told me about all the stars on the faculty. He went on and on."

"He would. He always does. Has to, to sign prospects up. I guess you don't need financial aid?"

"I guess not." And, with the directness about money her whole family possessed, she asked, "Do you have it?"

"No way. A lot of black kids do, and some white kids, too, but my daddy makes a lot of money now in his factory in Virginia. Ever hear of Miss Bettina's Brittle?"

"I love it! It's the best peanut brittle ever. Do you get samples to bring here? And why's it called 'Miss Bettina's'?"

"That was the name of the woman my daddy's grandmother worked for, way back. She taught my great-granny the recipe. Times were hard and Miss Bettina and Great-granny made it and peddled it around. They never took in more money than just enough to live on but before she died, she told Great-granny she should keep on with it, just in case.

"So she did, and her son did, and so on and now it's doing great. So what else did Lying Lyman tell you?"

Now Elizabeth Lamb giggled, as they got off the bus on the girls' campus, in style similar to the one she had left. "Is that what you call him?"

"Sometimes we say, 'take it with a grain of Salton.' He just can't

49

help it; he gets carried away and tells real lies. And he tells them over and over; he's a guy who doesn't waste a good thing by saying it only once. Did he tell you there's a volleyball team, a ski team, and that some of the masters sing plainsong on the chapel steps?"

"Yes, he did. And he said there's an observatory, and a social club, and bell ringers and I-don't-know-what-all. All lies?"

"There is a social club and there's a bell-ringers group, but no volleyball, no ski team and no one's ever been seen to enter what he says is the observatory. *And* nobody's ever heard anyone singing *anything* on the boys' chapel stairs. I'm surprised he didn't say we're going to have a polo field soon; he actually said that to a girl whose father's a polo player."

"Look out! Don't walk on the hippopotamus! Not till you're a Sixth Former."

Elizabeth Lamb looked down at the large painted animal on the concrete slab at the entrance to the dining hall. As they carefully stepped around it, she asked, "What happens if I do?"

"Well, there have been girls thrown in the river, but don't quote me. And don't worry much; the river's only three, sometimes four, feet deep. The lake, now, that's a bigger deal. It's at least a hundred-fifty feet deep in places. Just be careful not to step on Hilda."

She led Elizabeth Lamb to a thin, distraught-looking woman supervising a girl seated at a small table who was checking names on a list as students entered. "This is Elizabeth Lamb Worthington, Mrs. LeStrange," she said. "She'll be a Third Former next fall. Mrs. LeStrange is the Dean of Girls, Elizabeth Lamb."

Mrs. LeStrange produced a harried handshake and a nervous smile and suggested they sit at her table. "There are two empty places because I'm training Jane and I can't leave here and Jocelyn Morang hasn't shown up. Even a Third Former knows she must appear at all meals." She frowned in warning at Elizabeth Lamb.

"She's probably having lunch at the boys', Mrs. LeStrange," Joylene answered soothingly. "I saw her on their campus just as we got on the bus. Isn't her class after lunch over there?"

"Oh, Joylene, you know everything! Father Farnum was *so* right in naming you Senior Prefect!" She continued muttering names to herself and to her trainee, who raised her eyes to Joylene and rolled them meaningfully.

Joylene smiled agreeably and, as she led Elizabeth Lamb to a table, muttered over the din of shrill voices in the large room, "The LeStrange gets more and more weird. Sometimes she's so out of it she can't remember what day it is. I don't know how she keeps her job."

The table was set for eight. Six girls were already eating, some reading as they ate and some talking. Pitchers of milk, bowls of mixed salad and baskets of rolls and butter were in the middle of the table. Joylene picked up a plate, motioned to Elizabeth Lamb to do the same, and inquired of a red-haired girl, "What's that stuff on your rice, Andrea?"

Andrea, immersed in a book, put a forkful of the substance into her mouth and, without looking up, answered, "It's got black olives so it's got to be turkey tetrachloride. He puts green in chicken critical and pimento in his poison *poisson*. You know that. Anyway, it's Wednesday, so it's turkey, even though LeStrange already made her announcements as if it were Thursday."

Joylene sighed and led the way to a steam table, presented her plate and had a large dollop of rice slammed on to it by a white-uniformed, red-faced, irritable-looking woman of about fifty, who then with the other hand tossed another dollop of what may have been creamed turkey more or less on top of the rice. Elizabeth Lamb presented her plate, saying, "It's nice to see you, Dora."

The woman looked up, frowning, served her, and then recognition spread over her face. If possible, she looked more annoyed than before. "Well, Miss Girl," she announced, aiming her comestibles toward the plate of the girl behind Elizabeth Lamb, "and what're you doin' here? Causin' trouble, I don't doubt?"

Elizabeth Lamb laughed, Joylene with her. "I'm coming here next fall. I didn't know you worked here in the winters. How long've you been here?"

"Third year, this is. Thought you knew. Can't live all winter on what your grandma pays me to cook in the summers. She bring you up today?"

"No, Mr. Vincentia did." As Dora looked blank, which caused her to toss her portions even more erratically at another plate, Elizabeth Lamb went on: "You know; you met him at The Bungalow last summer, when Persis and I came up on his boat. Grandmother and he're going to be married soon."

"It is better to marry than to burn," Dora proclaimed impressively, and then questioning, as she ladled out more of her wares to the next supplicant: "You got a holler leg or somethin'? You been back three times."

Elizabeth Lamb was amazed. "What did you say, Dora?"

"Holler leg? You heard me say that before."

"No, about marrying."

"Oh, what I said's from that there St. Paul. Heard it here in chapel onct and it struck me. Learn a lot here, I do. Hope *you* do. It's strict, this place is. You'll have to watch your step. Take some of the staach out of you, it will."

"Yes, Dora," Elizabeth Lamb said submissively, moving away at Joylene's nudge. "Well, I won't see you this summer because I'm going to Pakistan to be with Mummy and Daddy, but I'll be here in September."

"I jest can't wait," was the reply.

As they seated themselves, Joylene asked, "You know that wombat? She's never pleasant but I thought she was just plain rude to you."

"That's Dora Dorr, my grandmother's housekeeper at her summer place over on the backside of the island. She's always like that. The man who brought me up today, my grandmother's friend — he's Italian — says all New Englanders are rude; they just call it being direct."

She drank some milk Joylene had poured for her. "I hope they don't let her cook here because she burns just about everything. Why do you call her a wombat?"

Joylene looked a little ashamed. "I guess that's as rude as *she* is, but all the help in every school I've ever heard of's called that. Don't know why." She took some salad, held the bowl so Elizabeth Lamb could help herself, and then attacked her plate with a sigh. "The cook's supposed to be from the South, so I don't see why he couldn't give us some decent Southern fried chicken once in a while. And don't say I'm being stereotypical."

"Why should I?" Elizabeth Lamb was gingerly tasting the rice mixture.

"Don't you know black people are supposed to love fried chicken?"

"No, I didn't. I only know four black kids, at my school, and they're all vegetarians."

Joylene laughed. "Then they'd be happy here. His vegetables are okay."

"This turkey stuff has no taste at all," Elizabeth Lamb decided. "I'm hungry, but this is ridiculous." She rose and quickly went to a corner of the large opening in the wall behind the steam table. Joylene raced after her and arrived as she was calling to a tall, swarthy, white-uniformed man in the kitchen: "Are you Mr. Pella? Could I have a bottle of Tabasco sauce, please?"

The man, frowning, turned from a large iron pot on one of the four stoves. "Why?" he demanded.

"To give the turkey some flavor. It's good, but it's bland."

His frown turned to a smile as he reached for a glass cruet on a shelf near him. "You are right. They let me put in no spices. I could make the food very, very good here if it were not for their silly rules. Here's my own sauce I make for myself. Return it to me, please."

As she turned, Joylene was tugging at her arm; Mrs. LeStrange, looking more distraught than before, was just behind her. "No one ever, ever may bother the cook, young lady," the dean said faintly. "Joylene, you must explain our rules."

Mr. Pella's sauce was a great success at Elizabeth Lamb's table. "You're a hoot, Elizabeth Lamb," Joylene pronounced. She introduced her to the others. The red-haired girl nodded politely and continued reading, as did the brunette beside her. Two Asian girls, who were eating chiefly salad, smiled affably and one requested some sauce to put on a roll.

The two others, very blonde and curly and dressed in what were obviously boys' team jackets in the school's blue and green, nodded faintly and continued giggling over a letter one of them held. As soon as a thin, pale little girl, a white apron tied under her armpits, brought a tray of pineapple upside-down cake to the table and they had eaten their portions, they got up, without any farewell to the others, and left, waggling tightly-jeaned bottoms as they did. The red-haired girl murmured, "They get more *nouveau* every term."

"N.O.C.D.," one of the Asian girls responded. Everybody except Elizabeth Lamb laughed.

"What's that mean?" she asked diffidently.

"'Not our class, dear,'" Joylene told her. "Those two are real jock toys. This cake is burned; bet your friend made it. Oh, well, it's something in my stomach to stir me up during my exam. And, look, if I'm to show you around a little, we'd better hurry. It's almost one-fifteen."

"What're jock toys?"

"Well, you know what jocks are — athletes. Those two, and some others like them, just hang around the teams. They've got brains, or they wouldn't be here, but they're pretty dim in some ways.

"They're dressed that way because we don't have to wear uni in exam week. Any other weekday, after breakfast and until classes are over at three-twenty, both boys and girls have to wear uni. They'll send you a book this summer, about uni and all the other rules."

"But what does it *mean*?"

"Short for 'uniform,' of course. Grey flannel or tan chino pants for the boys, white shirts, blue or green ties and navy blazers. For the girls, grey flannel or chino skirts, white shirts or blue blouses — big concession there — and the good old navy blazers. When you're a Sixth Former, the jacket can be anything except plaid."

"What about when it's hot?"

"Same thing, but no jacket for girls. Boys have to wear ties and jackets though, even if it gets to be eighty. Which, in the spring and fall sometimes it does sometimes. It's unfair, because the masters can take off their jackets anytime if it's hot in the classroom, but the boys can't. Women teachers can wear anything. Funny: sometimes the men are referred to as 'masters' — ye olde

54

English school usage, you know — but the women are never 'mistresses'!"

Elizabeth Lamb laughed as expected. "But what's the point of the uni?"

"Supposed to be so the poorer kids don't feel like they look different. But on Sundays, or at dinner or parties when the cashmere sweaters and the Saks dresses come out, of course they feel bad in their stuff from J.C. Penney, or whatever. The system's corrupt here; you'll find that out, but no worse than any other prep school, I guess.

"And it *costs* to buy the uni, so why not let the poorer kids and everybody else wear what they have, is what I say. So does everybody else."

"Have you suggested it?"

"No, I don't rock the boat." She grinned. "Maybe that's why Farback Farnum — Father Farnum named me Senior Prefect. But you can try to change the system. You're intense."

"Thanks," Elizabeth Lamb said uncertainly. "Well, what are you supposed to show me? I'd better return Mr. Pella's sauce first."

They quickly visited several dormitory rooms, Joylene knocking before she opened the doors. "They don't allow keys — say we have to live in 'a community of trust.' That's crap, because a lot of stealing goes on. Remember *Catcher in the Rye?* So just don't bring anything valuable that might get ripped off."

Some of the rooms were luxuriously decorated; some displayed only the essentials. "You can bring anything that the rule book doesn't say no to. Remember, no flashlights or matches. Some of the rich kids bring stuff you wouldn't believe; their rooms look like *House Beautiful.*"

"Oh, well, the really rich are different from you and me. Didn't somebody say that?"

"Yes; they get what they expect," Elizabeth Lamb answered absently. They were in one of the dormitory bathrooms. "Why are the shower heads down so low?"

"Rumor is that once a girl tried to hang herself. I don't buy it; you hear a lot of crazy things. *I* think the workmen just felt all girls were four-and-a-half feet tall."

55

She laughed. "'Yes, they get what they expect.' Elizabeth Lamb, on a scale of one to ten, I reckon you're a twelve. Oh, I forgot; shout before you flush the john if somebody's in one of the showers. The shower water turns scalding hot. Yell 'Flushing!'

"No sense showing you the gym or the library. They're probably just what your school has, and you'll see plenty of both. Or the Catholic chapel. Are you Catholic?"

"No."

"Me neither. But even a lot of the girls who aren't go to the Catholic services. The chapel is right behind the main quad of dorms so you can sleep later on Sunday mornings instead of busing over to the Episcopal chapel. And chapel attendance is also required on Wednesday evenings, after dinner, so that's more convenient, too. And besides, the priest, Father Rogers, is awesome, really hot! He's to-die cute. You just look at him and you feel — well, you'll see. Black, white, yellow or red, we all go for him!

"Let's walk over to the boys'. If we book it, I've got time to show you the swimming pool and their library — it's bigger, though ours is *supposed* to be equal. We use both, you know. And you can look at the outside of the boathouse; it's near the headmaster's house, where I'm supposed to leave you."

"What's 'book it'? And what's 'stung'? You said you were going to get that Harris stung. And why was that girl waiting on us at lunch?"

"'Book it' means go fast. When you 'sting' somebody, and only teachers and Sixth Formers can do it, they get hours of physical work assigned. Sometimes they clean the dining hall, or rake leaves or — "

"Or build stone walls. I heard. Did that girl in the dining room get stung for something? There were a couple of others waiting on table, too."

"Everybody here has a job. The Third Formers wait on table or do other stuff in the kitchen or dining halls. You will, too. Fourth Formers keep the dorm halls clean and scrub the bathrooms every Sunday, before chapel. Fifth Formers see that the grounds are picked up and the chapels neatened and Sixth Formers don't have to do anything, except keep the lower forms shaped up, unless they're one of the Prefects or the Rep to the Student Council."

They were crossing the bridge. Despite the snow on the benches that lined it, a few boys and girls were sitting there, talking with heads close together or helping each other with class assignments. "They're making the scene," Joylene muttered. "That's going steady, sort of; you never sit on the bridge with a boy unless you're serious about him. And vice versa.

"Got a boyfriend?"

"Me?" Elizabeth Lamb was surprised. "I'm twelve years old! *And* I'm from Boston," she added with a grin.

"Enough said. But now I see why you've got manner as well as manners. The really cool Bostonians do, I've noticed."

They looked into the large, high-windowed library where students sat writing at tables, or examined the shelves under the carefully-casual regard of librarians of both sexes, and then walked over to the building that housed the pool and boys' gymnasium.

"I've never seen a pool so big!" Elizabeth Lamb exclaimed. "It's huge!"

"Biggest of any school in the country, they say. You can't use it except with a buddy, remember. If you do, you'll get stung for twenty hours. A kid nearly drowned once, swimming alone. He got awful cramps. My uncle brought him around, but it was close."

They walked up the little hill to the chapel. Again the building was enormous, of vaulted stone with dim hanging lights. There were two beautiful stained-glass rose windows, one high over the altar. The pews, of old carved wood, were not only on both sides of the red-carpeted main aisle but also in tiers along the side walls. The altar, at the far end of the aisle from where they stood, was banked with flowers and tall candles burned on it.

"The wife of the man who founded the school, Father Fitzgerald, is buried now under the altar," Joylene whispered. "He got special permission, after the chapel was built; from the Catholic Church, I guess. It used to be the Catholic chapel, you know. He left enough money so fresh flowers could be put there every week."

They walked up the path towards the river. "Farback Farnum's —

I mean Father Farnum's house is right there." Joylene waved her hand towards a large white house with pillars in front that reminded Elizabeth Lamb of, not that she had ever seen it, the Old South. "And the boathouse is behind it. We've got a few minutes; let's walk down to the river. You'd like to see the shells, I guess, but the boathouse is always locked in term time. Maybe you could look through a window."

As the path led them past the boathouse, only a few yards from the river, Elizabeth Lamb glanced at its heavy double oak doors, hung with impressive wrought iron fixtures. "It looks like the entrance to a castle," she observed. The doors were slightly ajar. "Didn't you say it was always locked?"

Joylene pushed one door farther open, and reached just inside to press a light switch. The building was spacious and rather dark, windowed by only four apertures about one-and-a-half feet wide by three feet high on its ground level and eight more just under its high rafters. The ranks of cedar shells were stacked three deep on triangular supports that jutted out from vertical four-by-fours. "We have eighteen, plus a couple of mahogany kayaks," Joylene told her. "Are you good at rowing? We live near a river down home but I'm terrible."

"So am I," Elizabeth Lamb lied. "Gee, the shells sure are beautiful, though. So graceful. I've never been close to one before."

"Just don't get too close to the ends of the riggings," Joylene advised. "That flat piece of metal supporting the clamp that holds the oar on the rigging could put your eye out if you stumbled into it."

"Is that why they lock the place?"

"No, it's because they keep the scuba stuff in the back. A couple of years ago, two jokers burned pot beside the air compressor my uncle fills the scuba tanks with and then they filled a tank from it — which, of course, put THC in the tank; that's the part of pot that gets you high. They were sitting taking turns breathing it in through a regulator when my uncle showed up.

"They were pretty well baked by then. You get much more effect from pot if you take it in by using compressed air, you know."

"Where'd they get it?"

"Oh, it's everywhere on campus even though, of course, it's strictly off-limits. I know for a fact, and don't ask me how, that many of the teachers use it. The men, anyway, and some of the women. I told you it's corrupt here.

"My uncle's dead set against it, so, after he made them clean out the tank, he slapped them hard a couple of times — that's off-limits, too, for a master — and then he lectured them on what just might've happened if some student in a class had used the tank, and then he dragged them over to the headmaster. They were suspended for a term, but their parents got mad and took them out for good."

"Why?"

"Well, they said it was just boys being boys or something. But, as my uncle told Farback Farnum — I've got to watch that; when his hairline started disappearing a year or so ago we started to call Father Farnum that — as my uncle told *Father* Farnum, if enough air had been left in the tank and another kid used it in a class, he could have got nitrogen narcosis and had an accident."

"I've read about that. Cousteau called it 'rapture of the deep,' I think. It's called something else, too — "

"Well, anyway, that's why Uncle Harry insists that the place be locked in term time. When the school's on holiday, they aren't so fussy. Nobody could really steal a shell and hide it easily, but, still, only he has the keys; well, Mr. Sullivan does, too. He's the head of the English Department and Father Farnum's assistant. He has keys for everything.

"But I wonder where Uncle Harry is?"

"I'm here, my dear child, listening to your profound exposition," declared a pleasantly deep voice somewhere above them. Mr. Prestwick, dressed in a sweatshirt, sweatpants and sneakers was standing on a little balcony at the far end of the boathouse, an open door behind him. "I just went up to my office for a minute," he said, pulling the door shut with a loud click and running lightly down the stairs. "Since I could see and hear anyone coming in, I didn't lock up behind myself."

He put his arm affectionately around his niece. "Recruiting a

59

new crew member for Miss McMurtrie?" he asked. "Can you row, young lady?"

Elizabeth Lamb was beginning to wonder how many times she would have to lie. "No, I'm bad at it. I get seasick even in the swan boats at the Boston Public Gardens."

Mr. Prestwick, turning keys in the two locks on the door, laughed. Joylene looked at her watch. "No! It's five to two," she exclaimed. "Good thing the schoolhouse is practically right next door.

"Mr. Prestwick," she said formally, eyeing two girls who were approaching them on the path to the river, "would you take Elizabeth Lamb to Father Farnum's house? I'm not supposed to call him 'Uncle' when anybody's around," she muttered to Elizabeth Lamb. "Bad for morale, or something.

"Well, see you next fall. Good luck!" She raced away.

Mr. Prestwick had no sooner knocked on the headmaster's front door than it opened and Mr. Vincentia, scarfed and coated, came out and, after greeting the coach, hurried her to his car. "I'd like to reach Boston well before dinner time," he explained as they drove rather fast to the airport.

She said nothing, again staring out at Mount Desert Island, now in late afternoon light. There was a hint of snow in the air. He glanced at her. "Why so silent?" he asked playfully. "We are not even on one of the island's mountains, let alone on a peak in Darien."

"Oh, *Nonno*, maybe I really am too young to go away to prep school. A lot of the girls have boyfriends, and they use all sorts of slang I've never heard, and they smoke marijuana, and there are girls called 'jock toys'—dreadfully tacky-looking girls, Grandmother would say—and I met a nasty boy and if I forget and walk on a painted hippopotamus I might get thrown in the river—oh, I just don't know!"

"You'll be all right. Often, they younger they get you, the better. Remember the Jesuit saying: 'Give me a child until he is seven.' Just keep your head. You're very good at that."

They were boarding the jet. "What's 'until seven' got to do with it?" she asked morosely. "That sounds like what Aunt Isabella would call 'famous lost words.' The Catholics aren't going to 'get me' at thirteen; certainly not the Jesuits, whoever they are — wait, aren't they the ones that carried on the Spanish Inquisition? Oh, Lord!"

Mr. Vincentia ignored the Inquisition. "It just means, to me, that the younger one begins to be well educated, the better for her. And well educated you will be. Remember, fate often hands you what you first thought unseemly and undesirable and you end up liking it. It's happened over and over to me."

"Well, I'm not going to like smoking pot. In fact, I'll never do it again."

Mr. Vincentia, settling into his seat, was, for once, at a loss for words. Finally he asked, "You tried it already — in the few hours you were there? Really, Elizabeth Lamb, it is strictly forbidden. I am surprised at that girl, the Senior Prefect next year! I think I had better forget what you said but I warn you never to do it again. If you had been caught, I couldn't have persuaded Mr. Salton to stand by his agreement. And the headmaster would have named a new Senior Prefect of Girls. You were both extremely foolish."

"No, no, *Nonno*! Of course we didn't! I don't think Joylene ever does! It was a couple of years ago. Persis found some in Gus' room and we figured out how to make a cigarette and we were smoking it when Gus came in. He made us finish the whole joint; just to teach us, he said. My chest hurt terribly — and we both got dizzy and sick.

"I'm through with it forever. Who needs it?"

He smiled. "A wise decision as well as a thrifty one. And what about Gus?"

"Oh, he only smoked his first term at St. Paul's. Then, he said, he grew up.

"I wonder what classes I'll have. Gus studies Russian. I'd like to learn Russian, I think. I read it's the most beautiful of the Slavic languages."

"Another wise decision. Do you know the difference between an optimist and a pessimist? I'll tell you that an optimist is a person who thinks a loaf of bread will cost five dollars five years from now."

"Okay, I'll bite. So what's a pessimist?"

"A person who thinks that in five years a loaf of bread will cost five rubles."

She laughed, and then sobered. "But there's a lot of pretentious kids at St. Augustine's, I'll bet. I won't like that."

"No doubt. There are snobs everywhere. And the very rich are around, and the very poor are always with us, to quote from someone wiser than I. You'll meet them all. The very rich and the very poor talk frankly about money, you'll notice. Only the middle class is inhibited about discussing it."

"Really, *Nonno*! Grandmother would certainly call *you* a snob for talking like that." She sighed. "Grandmother. You know what she's going to ask me, don't you? She's already sure St. Augustine's is a good school; what she's going to ask is do I think I'll be happy there. What'll I say?"

"I doubt she will. Elizabeth is not a shallow person. If she should, tell her that happiness goes with the wind: what is *interesting* stays with you."

"Oh, *Nonno*, I can't see it's going to be interesting. Good for me, you say, but I don't think *interesting*."

"In that," replied Mr. Vincentia, who was usually right, "you may be very much mistaken."

• CHAPTER 4 •

J'accuse.

— Emile Zola

A T LEAST the summer before Elizabeth Lamb was to enter St. Augustine's *was* interesting. She had a joyful reunion with her parents, learned a great deal about the operation of their mine in Pakistan, swam each afternoon in the little pond not far from their camp, hitched a ride on the jeep every time the cook drove to the nearest village for supplies, and there frequented its bazaar.

Perhaps because, as the Muslim cook proclaimed: "Allah protects children and lunatics," in spite of the numerous sirops and fruits and exotic sweets she consumed in the bazaar and the murkiness of the water in which she swam, or perhaps because of the quantity of shots provided by her grandmother's doctor before she left Boston, she contracted no diseases. She did contract a number of friendships with the village children, who taught her their games and tried, with polite hands covering their smiles, to teach her their dialect.

And there was a Catholic mission in a farther town, attended some Sundays by a few of the mine workers, to which her mother allowed her to accompany them. "So I won't do something awful at chapel at school," she explained to her intolerant father, who tried to dissuade her by asking if she intended to convert so she could become "one of those damned sleazy Boston pols."

Her grandmother had shipped her two cases of books, among them Kipling, and Rumer Godden's stories of India, and these occupied her in the long evenings. By the end of August, she was packed to fly back to The Hub of the Universe when the maintenance crews of Air India decided to strike. She fretted for two weeks, knowing she would be late reporting to St. Augustine's.

At last, tanned, tense, and bearing gifts, she was met at Logan by Mr. Vincentia's chauffeur and heard that there had indeed been busing riots when the Boston schools opened. "They throw eggs and tomatoes at Senator Kennedy; somebody say that *if* he has his driver's license back why don't *he* drive school bus!" And then she heard that her grandmother and "the *padrone*" had gone to England and that her Aunt Isabella — Antonio here rolled his eyes expressively — was in residence at the Brimmer Street house and was to drive her to Maine the next day.

"But why, Antonio? I thought you or Mr. Vincentia would take me to the plane for Bangor tomorrow. The school van would pick me up there. What are they trying to do to me, get me thrown out of school before I get in? Oh, no, not Aunt Isabella!"

He shrugged as he carefully maneuvered the large car past the tollbooth at the entrance to the Sumner Tunnel. "I don't know. They don't ask me. Your aunt want to spend time at your grandmother's place in Maine. She having a friend there for a week" — he glanced at her in the rear view mirror and again rolled his eyes — "and I guess they all think it easier for everybody if your aunt drive you right to your school."

At dinner time, Elizabeth Lamb made her descent of the stairs last as long as she could. Her Aunt Isabella, who had retained the title of *Gräfin* along with the surname of her first husband although she had several times subsequently been married and divorced, sat royally erect in Mrs. Worthington's place at the candle-lit old oval walnut table. Elizabeth Lamb noticed that despite her grandmother's injunction of no cocktails in the dining room, her aunt was sipping from the over-large Bavarian crystal martini glass that accompanied her everywhere. She often explained, with her carefully-retained girlish laugh, to those who were interested — few were — that it was the only tangible thing she had salvaged from her first marriage.

Isabella, whose face in her youth had been compared to that of the young Queeen Victoria, produced a regal nod for her niece, who slipped, with a subdued sigh, into the place set for her at her aunt's left and bade her a polite, "How nice to see you, Aunt Isabella." She then pondered which saint a Catholic priest would advise one to petition after saying a deliberate lie, if any such single saint were designated.

With some effort, Isabella produced a dimpled smile of the type that she considered might have appeared (though seldom) on the face of Her Late Majesty. Elizabeth Lamb observed that it was with much more effort that her aunt's foot finally, after much fumbling about on the Persian rug under the dinner table, found the concealed button to summon the maid. Isabella had to step on it several times before Katie, bearing two plates of soup, entered through the swinging door from the kitchen.

"The wine, Katie?" Isabella inquired frostily.

"Alice thought you would prefer water with the lamb curry she's doing, Miss Isabella," Katie replied.

Isabella frowned severely. "Curry?" she asked. "I distinctly ordered salmon. And why cannot you address me correctly, Katie?"

"It's curry, Miss Isabella," Katie replied, "because Alice had that whole roasted lamb leg left from when your friends were here last night. They didn't seem to have much appetite after they'd had all those — after they'd had their cocktails.

"And," making her departure, "I just can't seem to say your title correctly, Miss Isabella." The swinging door closed gently. Isabella muttered something inaudible.

Elizabeth Lamb smiled into her soup, well aware that Katie was a languages major at Boston University through Mrs. Worthington's thoughtful consideration in giving her three free mornings a week, as well as forgoing the traditional 4:30 tea hour two afternoons a week so that serving a very early dinner would free Katie for classes those evenings, as well. "She probably can pronounce '*Gräfin*' better than Aunt Isabella can," she thought.

Aloud, she inquired about her aunt's recent visit to Europe and was told that Isabella had been very disappointed to find that most of her friends, responding to her advance telephone calls, had, almost as one, announced their long-held (so they said) plans for immediate travel. "And *all* of them were going to obscure places in Africa," Isabella said plaintively, forking distastefully at the plate of curry Katie had deftly substituted for her emptied soup plate. "Why Africa, I ask you? The last place *I'd* go!

"And," even more plaintively, "their husbands were all going with them. I was able to visit only a few dreary spinster school-mates. And even some of *them* weren't available."

Elizabeth Lamb thought to herself that her aunt's friends had not been born yesterday. She also thought that if St. Augustine's served curried-anything the next night she would probably die of violent indigestion, "after a whole summer of eating it! And Alice's is hotter."

Salad and cheese followed the lamb curry. Isabella, cheered by the refilling of her martini glass, which Katie did with pursed lips, praised the virtues of her mother's fiancé (with special emphasis on his virtue of having so much money), adding that, "If by any chance Mama should change her mind, I'd be most happy to sub-stitute for her." She then stretched her neck up and sideways in an unnerving manner so that she could practice a few Victorian dimpled smiles, evidently with the future enchantment of Mr. Vincentia in mind, glancing in a queenly manner into the mirror over the sideboard to her right as she did. "Really, why place a mirror so high!" she complained.

"And," she continued, now glancing sideways to her niece on her left, in what she evidently thought was a subtle fashion, "You won't forget to write Mama of my selfless, really, really selfless action in driving you to Maine? And tell her of the fun we're just *bound* to have tomorrow on the trip, just two girls together." She stretched her neck to the right again, giggling girlishly, or so she assumed, as she stared into the mirror. "I'm a bit out of her good graces right now, for some reason," she added.

Elizabeth Lamb, accepting *crème brûlée* from Katie, wondered if she should inquire of Isabella how selfless it was to take along an unwilling person on a trip one was making anyway. "And if Grandmother knows she's having a *rendezvous* with some man up in The Bungalow, no wonder Aunt Isabella's 'a bit' out of her good graces."

She finished her dessert, drank her milk and asked to be excused. Isabella nodded graciously, dimpled, and then her foot fumbled for the floor bell again, this time even more erratically. In an artificially gay voice she said, "See you in the morning, dear child. Very early, remember?"

As Katie, with a slight frown, appeared in the dining room, Isabella called after her niece: "Oh, and I hear sweet little Persis — such a charming, well-mannered child! — is doing very, very well at Kent. I wonder why you didn't inquire about her? Well, good night, dear. We'll get you early to St. Whatever-it-is. What a shame St. Paul's didn't take you, though!"

Upstairs, Alice assured Elizabeth Lamb that her school necessities had been shipped to Maine and that two suitcases of clothes were already packed and in the trunk of her aunt's car. "I seen to that meself. You jest put a couple of things you might need, yer alarm clock and sich, in this little bag, with this money yer grandma left fer you to begin with. She'll send you a check fer spending money ivery month. And ye're to be ready at eight, ter-morrer, remember. Herself downstairs wants an early start."

Muttering to herself, Alice left. Muttering to herself, Elizabeth Lamb made a sketchy attempt at washing and brushing and got into bed.

In dead silence, she sat beside her aunt in the car the next morning, too nervous at what might await her at the end of the journey to have eaten breakfast, as Isabella sang happily in French at times and at others regaled her niece with stories of her "utterly charming" friend who was driving to The Bungalow from Chicago to join her. "He has the most divine house in Chicago; you must see it some time." She giggled and took a sip from a small flask that had mysteriously found its way into her hand.

"I wish she'd keep both hands on the wheel," Elizabeth Lamb thought, but said only: "Why don't you visit him there, then?" She was told that the gentleman's "utterly impossible wife" was being "disgustingly difficult about the divorce" and would not surrender the house. Tales of the wife occupied her for miles.

They reached Portland before noon and Isabella decided on an early lunch. The lunch was preceded by five martinis for Isabella and five Shirley Temples for Elizabeth Lamb, by which time the restaurant was closing until dinner time. They found another restaurant, in a hotel that Isabella had heard was "utterly enchanting — at least for Maine" but, because of the martinis, it took her some hours of driving back and forth around the city before she found it, and now she announced she was "utterly distraught" and needed a drink.

The drink multiplied to several, and now she felt the need of an early dinner. Dinner was slow in coming. Elizabeth Lamb was starving and they both became so fractious that it was decided to spend the night in the hotel. Elizabeth Lamb went to bed ready to scream, rather than mutter. Isabella was too "utterly exhausted" to get their suitcases out of her car.

The next day, after more stops for refreshment, they finally, finally arrived at St. Augustine's. "You drive across the bridge and keep going up to the girls' campus," Elizabeth Lamb directed wearily. "There, see — that building over there. I'll go in by myself." Picking up her small bag, she raced into the Girls' Schoolhouse and down the hall towards the offices, asking directions of a boy wandering along.

Mrs. LeStrange seemed not to realize who she was. "The letter said to come to your office, since I'm late," Elizabeth Lamb protested. "But Elizabeth Lamb Worthington was to have been here yesterday," Mrs. LeStrange replied nervously. "And *that* would have been over a week late." She gave Elizabeth Lamb a reproachful stare. "I'm sure she checked in with my secretary, but Mrs. Jones is gone for a few hours." She peered dubiously up at Elizabeth Lamb who felt that she now might really scream.

Clenching her teeth instead, she said, "Mrs. LeStrange, *I* am Elizabeth Lamb Worthington. My aunt and I were to be here yesterday, but we had — car trouble. I did not get here yesterday. I just got here. My aunt is in the car. Would you like her to explain?"

"Oh, no, no; of course you know who you are." She fumbled through a stack of cards and pulled one out. "You're very late, you know. Let's see; no, you didn't arrive yesterday. I'd better show you your room. Mrs. Jones will know where your class schedule is. I'll give it to you when she finds it. You *did* receive our rule book and are aware of mealtimes and everything else you need to know?"

"Yes, ma'am. I memorized it this summer." Still clenching her teeth, she followed the dean. There was no car outside the school-house; it was turning out of the road that circled the quadrangle of buildings. A graceful hand produced a graceful wave from the driver's window.

"She's taken my suitcases! My clothes are in them! Oh, where can I find a telephone? Oh, but she may not go straight to The Bungalow! She may stop for a — she may stop somewhere! I'm cold and don't even have a sweater!" She was almost weeping.

"Please compose yourself. You are a St. Augustine's girl now. Your trunks should be in the storeroom down the hall from your room. Surely there are clothes in them and surely you have the keys."

Looking as if she would be glad to be rid of this confusing student, Mrs. LeStrange quickly led the way along a path to a brick building on the far side of the green, stopped a good distance from a blue door placed between a yellow and a red one, and gestured erratically at it. "You were put in a triple because you were so late, but I know you will find your roommates — interesting. You need not wear your uni at dinner, you know." She wavered back towards her office.

The late afternoon air was by now cool. The large window to the right of the yellow door was open only a crack but through it came the pleasing sounds of "Take the A Train." "Somebody's got good taste," Elizabeth Lamb murmured, approaching the blue door, the window beside which was shut. She ran up the two brick steps and raised her hand and knocked.

What sounded like a combined chorus of roaring lions and wailing cats echoed from behind the door, punctuated by crashes. She knocked louder. She knocked again, still louder. She opened the door a foot or two.

A short, buxom blonde girl was standing in the middle of the large room, shouting at a thin, black child cowering on the top tier of a bunk bed. The child was clutching a stuffed bear and tears were streaming down her face. "You're a klepto, that's what you are!" the blonde girl yelled. "You worthless little nigra!"

"Excuse me," Elizabeth Lamb said faintly.

The girl turned to her. "Who the fuck are you? Get out of here!"

Someone reached from behind Elizabeth Lamb and pushed the door wide open. As she turned, her mouth parted in surprise. "I never saw a Greek goddess in the flesh before," she thought. "If she were dead white marble, she'd be perfectly authentic."

The tall girl who stood behind her, glaring into the room, was far from dead white. From the top of her head of short, coppery blonde curls to her green enameled toenails, she blazed with color. Her eyes were of the blue sometimes called "Madonna's Robe" and her generous mouth, although unpainted, was bright pink. Her wide forehead, long nose and high cheekbones followed the classic mode. From her face to her feet, her skin was a golden tan and she displayed a great deal of it: she wore nothing but a red towel twisted and tucked under her armpits that reached only to her knees. She opened her mouth to draw in a deep breath. Elizabeth Lamb waited for some divine pronouncement.

"Boston-fried Jesus!" the goddess said loudly. "Shut up! What's it now with you creeps from hell? I could hear you in the shower, and over the Duke, rest his soul, and if I could on our side, so can the Greenwell on hers. You'd better hope to God she's not in."

She regarded Elizabeth Lamb. "And who're you?"

Elizabeth Lamb also drew in a breath. "I'm Elizabeth Lamb Worthington. I'm new. I'm a Third Former. Mrs. LeStrange told me I was assigned to this room."

The girl pushed her inside, shut the door and stood leaning against it. Elizabeth Lamb righted a desk chair that was lying on the floor and sat on it. The small girl on the bed, snuffling loudly through her words, addressed the girl in the towel.

"Miss Lara Jane, I did not either take her money! Miss Faith bess catcherself! I never stold a thing in my life. Arybody who knows me say that. Lady Haslam knows and she's still at the hotel in New York and you can call her. She don' — doesn't fly back to The Rock till tomorrow. The telephone number's right here and you can ax her. She said I could call collect if I needed arything we didn't bring with us." Holding the bear firm with an elbow, she began to pull down a zipper on its back with one hand, using the free hand to wipe across her eyes and nose. The blonde girl sat on a bed and then slumped face down on it.

Elizabeth Lamb was interested. "The way she talks, she's from Bermuda," she decided. "Especially the way she pronounced 'telephone'. Either that, or she's seen too many Inspector Clouseau movies."

Lara Jane sighed. "Josas," she answered gently, "I'm not going to call anybody. And don't *you* call me or any other Sixth Former 'Miss'. I've told you that. Only teachers. This whole mess is going before the Student Council tomorrow night and you'll tell us you didn't steal and Faith'll tell us you did and how can either one of you prove it?

"Now, which is the new girl's bed?"

The blonde girl sat up. Now *she* was crying. "Lara Jane," she asked in a pronounced Southern accent, "you just tell me what I did to deserve this? This place is Rat City. First I get a black klepto rat, and God knows what's the matter with *this* one. I was supposed to be in here with Melanie and Sarah and you know it. Third Formers don't rate what used to be a teacher's apartment, ever, and you know *that*. My daddy is going to hear about this and I hope he takes me out of this damned school. It was ruined for me already, and now these two!"

Elizabeth Lamb was annoyed. "'Fate often sends you what you thought unseemly and undesirable and you end up liking it,'" she quoted coldly. The blonde answered her with a nasty look.

"Faith," Lara Jane said gently, "we all know you're hard hit about Jay. But it happened and he's gone and you can't take out

71

your feelings on these kids or the rest of the school. You'll get booted.

"And the reason you're in with them, as you know perfectly well, is that Sarah's out for a term because she took a bad fall riding this summer. And Melanie got booted for parallel parking — and with a Fifth Form boy, yet! *And* you got here late, remember that. What can you expect? You're lucky to be here with your own bathroom and kitchen even if two Third Formers are in with you. There was no place else to put them. And don't call them rats! I'll sting you if I hear that again."

"And just what'll you sting me *for*, Lara Jane? What've I done? *I'm* no thief. You're mighty uppity. You're not on the Senior Council because Father Farnum named you a prefect or gave you an office; you're only on because the Sixth Form elected you its rep to it. Not," she added in a very low voice, "that my friends or I voted for you."

"I'll sting you twenty hours for 'gross unproper judgement,'" Lara Jane drawled. "You know I can and I certainly will. And you don't have to bring up that Farback Farnum didn't make me a prefect. He couldn't because I got busted in my Fourth Form year for getting caught carrying 'rettes for your buddy Melanie. She wouldn't own up they were for her, and I wouldn't rat, so I took the rap.

"And I got on the Council because the Sixth Form wanted *me* to represent them. That's an honor, more than getting named to it, in case you can't grasp it. I asked you, which is this new girl's bed? And her closet?"

"My name's Elizabeth Lamb Worthington," the new girl said firmly. "I am always called Elizabeth Lamb. And you're — ?"

"I'm Lara Jane Oliver. I room next door on your right with three friends. We've got what they call 'the quad,' the only four-roomer on campus. Not to be confused with the quad all the dorms are built around. Miss Greenwell, the dorm mistress, has the apartment on your left. Watch out what you say in your bathroom because she can hear everything in hers. And vice versa, though she doesn't seem to grasp it. You can use the first floor dorm bathroom down the hall, too, if Faith or Josas is in yours."

She tightened her towel around her breasts with one hand and waved the other towards the blonde. "That's Faith O'Malley. She's from Georgia. And that's Josas Outerbridge. She's from Bermuda and a Third Former like you. As you've gathered, no doubt.

"Now, I've got to get on some clothes. I'm freezing. Just keep it quiet in here. I'll send over one of my roommates to help you get settled, Elizabeth Lamb. Her name's Molly Peale and she's the prefect of Falls Dorm. That's where we are, if LeStrange forgot to mention it.

"Now, Faith — "

"Look!" Josas had got her bear unzipped and her face wiped, although somewhat streakily. "Just look, please, Miss — I mean Lara Jane. Look how much money Lady Haslam left wif' me! I don't need to steal!"

She clambered down from the top bunk and timidly proffered a thin, neat packet of crisp currency, held together with a rubber band. "Please count it."

Lara Jane sighed, but she took the bills and flipped through them. "You've got over eighty dollars here, Josas. You shouldn't leave it in that bear. Don't you have a little purse you can carry with you? There's no way to lock money up, you know."

"She knows all right," Faith put in bitterly. She stood up and went to one side of a double dresser beside the bed she had been lying on. She pulled off her blouse without unbuttoning it and threw it in a drawer, taking out a pink short-sleeved cotton knit shirt with a plain round neckline and a design of peach trees on the front. She slipped it over her head and then slung a pink sweater around her shoulders.

"Oh, that's beautiful, Faith," Elizabeth Lamb exclaimed. "What is it? That pink thing under your sweater?"

"It's peach trees, of course. My daddy grows them."

"No, I mean the top. I've never seen anything like it except those plain white Fruit of the Loom undershirts my father wears."

"It's a T-shirt, for God's sake! They're all the rage, have been for months. The Gimbel's chain — I have a cousin who buys for it — says they'll be around forever. Where've you been all summer?"

"Pakistan."

"Oh." Faith was somewhat impressed. "Look, Lara Jane, I'm out of here. I'm going to go somewhere with Dan and light up a few. Maybe we'll hitch to Bar Harbor and get some beer." She got a handbag out of the dresser and fumbled in the back of the drawer for a handful of crumpled bills. "I'm not taking it all," she said, poking the remaining confusion of bills into a corner and piling underwear on them, "so just tell these two to stay out of my things. Totally."

Elizabeth Lamb frowned. "Of course we will." Lara Jane frowned, too. She sat on the bed and addressed Faith sternly: "You really do want to get tossed, don't you? And in your last year, too. What school would take you, then, do you think? You know we're not allowed to hitch, have beer, or smoke — and I hope you mean 'rettes, not joints. You get caught with grass, you're definitely out. And Dan, too.

"Why're you dragging him into this? He feels bad about Jay, so he's doing all he can for you. But you don't want to get him booted, too, do you? He's serious: he's applying to Brown and Harvard and Yale and he'll get accepted by all of them, I bet, if you don't make him mess up."

Faith's face crumpled like her stock of currency. "Let him suffer. He could've saved Jay and he knows it!"

"He could not! He tried everything and then he ran like hell for Mr. Prestwick. And *he* couldn't do anything, either. Jay was too far gone. Be reasonable."

"You weren't even here yet, Lara Jane. How do you know how hard that nig — " she glanced at Josas — "how hard Mr. Prestwick tried? He always hated Jay, just because Jay quoted what Professor Shackley — Shockley — something like that — said about blacks being inferior to whites."

"Faith, you'd better watch your mouth. Just be back for dinner, sober to the max."

Her voice softened. "Faith, you shouldn't take this so hard. What was Bogie's line in *Casablanca* — something about the troubles of two little people in this crazy world not amounting to a hill of beans? I forget, exactly, but you know what I mean.

"My God, Ford just pardoned Nixon; they're going to move

the Doomsday Clock from twelve minutes before midnight to only nine minutes; the stock market hasn't been so shaky since twenty-nine; France's got 'les MIRV' — whatever that means — "

"Multiple Independently Targetable Re-entry Vehicles," Elizabeth Lamb put in helpfully. "My daddy told — "

"Shh," Josas whispered. "You musn't interrupt when the Big Girls talk." Lara Jane glared at both of them.

" — and Mama Cass and Lindbergh and The Duke all just died. I'll never hear him play "A Train" again except on records. At least you're alive, Faith. Wake up and smell the flowers!"

"I'm history," replied Faith, leaving. "Just forget about lecturing me." She slammed the door.

Lara Jane rose and stretched, shaking her head in disgust. "Josas, you show Elizabeth Lamb the layout. Molly'll be over in a minute. And don't worry about that damned missing money. If only you hadn't used a two-dollar bill at the Snack Bar and if only Faith hadn't said she'd had one that was missing from her drawer, along with all the rest she *says* is gone. I don't see how she can count that mess; she just throws everything around like her clothes and books. Good thing 'Daddy' is so rich. But two-dollar bills aren't all that common. Still, there's no proof the one you spent was hers."

"It wasn't, Lara Jane!" Josas wailed. "It was just in the money Lady Haslam gave me. She say to keep it for luck but I never saw one before and I paid with it by mistake and with all the actin' up about her money Faith was doing all over the school, the man at the greeze place told Mrs. LeStrange where he got one.

"And Faith says she knows the numbers on it. Even if she just guesses some right, they'll believe her. And after all Lady Haslam's afferts to get me here! Faith says I'll be put right out for stealing. And" — Josas wailed louder — "I didn't! I didn't! She's one stupid fatten Arab!"

"I don't know what that means, but it doesn't sound complimentary. Just cool it." Lara Jane made for the door, then compunction made her turn back to the sobbing Josas. "You're entitled to have a faculty member appear with you at the Council meeting. Who do you want? I'll ask him, or her, for you and if he agrees, you tell him everything you've been telling me."

Josas thought. "Mr. Prestwick?" she said hesitantly. "He's been to Bermuda. He lived there a while and he don't laugh when I say Bermewjan things like I do when I get upset. Mostly I talk properly, you know."

"I know. Stay cool and tell Elizabeth Lamb what to do with her stuff. I'll see if I can get over to Mr. Prestwick's house before dinner. Or I'll talk to him then."

"*What* is the matter with Faith?" Elizabeth Lamb asked as soon as the door closed. "Who is this Jay? What happened to him?"

Josas zipped up her bear and put him carefully under her pillow. "Here," said Elizabeth Lamb, fumbling in the small bag she had with her. "I bought a little wallet in the bazaar for Antonio—he's someone I know in Boston—but I forgot to give it to him. Take it and put your bills in it and keep it in your pocket." Josas grinned with pleasure, expressed her thanks and did as she had been told.

"Your bed's the bottom one. Lara Jane might have known that, because it's not made up. Faith took the separate one and I took the top bunk to get away from her. She wasn't around when I got here, but they said she was a Sixth Former and so I didn't dast take the separate bed.

"We'd bess go find your trunks and get the sheets and blankets. They give you a pillow, but the rich kids bring big fluffy ones. Faith did. Your dresser's right here by the bathroom door and you get the desk and chair over by the hall door. Faith got the desk by the window and mine's on the other wall beside the double dresser. You got your keys for the trunks? Don't you have a suitcase?"

"I had two but my aunt drove away with them. I've got to try to call her later."

They had made up the bed, arranged the desk lamp and school supplies, and put away the clothes that had been in the trunks before Elizabeth Lamb realized no pajamas, robe or slippers were among them. "They must be in my suitcases; of course that's where Alice would have packed them. I had to sleep in my underwear last night and now I'll have to keep on doing it till I find my darned aunt! And there's no clothes except the uni ones here,

76

either. I hope they're in the suitcases; I have a really pretty dress for best."

"I can lend you pajamas," Josas offered. "I have three whole pairs! Lady Haslam and my mama bought me all new things at Trimingham's. Look!"

She opened her dresser drawers and proudly displayed a modest amount of very nice underwear, sweaters, socks, woolen gloves, hat and scarf, and then opened her closet to show a winter jacket and the skirts and shirts and the rest of the required "uni." She had many fewer clothes than Elizabeth Lamb but there was one beautiful dress of black velvet, with a lace collar, that surpassed anything in Elizabeth Lamb's wardrobe, much of which her grandmother had assembled, with proper Boston thrift, from Filene's Basement.

"My mama designed it. Lady Haslam let her make it in the workroom. It's for Sundays and best. Isn't it dickty, though!"

"It's perfectly lovely. Who *is* this Lady Haslam?"

"She's not what we call an 'onion,' down home. She moved to Bermuda from England when her husband died, and she wanted something to do so she opened a little shop and she designed clothes for it and got some ladies to sew them up. My mama's her best sewer and now Lady Haslam lets her design some of the clothes. She pays my mama big money because the longtails just love what my mama makes. Lady Haslam's going to make the shop bigger."

"I've been to Bermuda. I lived there for six months while my mother had a job as secretary to a writer who stayed there one winter. A longtail's a bird."

Josas giggled. "It's what some call the young lady tourists, too."

"Look, you've got to watch the Bermuda slang or I'll never understand you. Lady Haslam's certainly been good to you. She brought you up to school, you said?"

Josas sobered. "Well," she said hesitantly, "she thought I should get away from Bermuda and so did my mama. Lady Haslam got me in here. Her brother went to St. Augustine's for a year, a long, long time ago, on some exchange program they had with England, and that's why she thought of it. She's Catholic, and so are we. She arranged to come to New York to buy materials for her shop at the right time to bring me."

"But why did they think you should leave Bermuda?" Elizabeth Lamb vaguely thought that perhaps the unpleasant Faith might be correct in saying Josas was a "klepto." Then she felt ashamed of herself. "I really can't see this little kid shoplifting up and down Front Street," she told herself.

Josas bit her lip. "You won't tell?"

"Cross-my-heart-and-hope-to-die-I-won't."

Josas dropped her voice. "My deddy—my daddy—he's been dead a long time. My mama had this friend who lived with us and wanted her to marry him but she just kept putting it off. She says now she must have seen something in him but didn't realize it."

"Seen what?"

Josas looked as if she were going to cry again. Then she drew in a deep breath. "It helps to talk about it, and then you can deal with it, the doctor said."

"*What* doctor, for heaven's sake? The doctor here at school? Why?"

"See, my mama came home early one day and she found him trying—he had pulled my dress off—it was the first time he'd tried—he'd always been nice to me—he didn't have time to, to do anything—anyway, she picked me up and drove me to the doctor and then she went to Lady Haslam and she knows a magistrate and that pawn dog had his chocklits all right —"

"Who *what*?"

"He got sent to Channelview—that's what they call the maximum security prison. But everybody knows everything about everybody else down on The Rock and some of the byes—boys—at my school last spring were like cuttin-their-eyes at me —"

"Doing what?"

"Giving me nasty looks and saying sort of dirty things. So that's why Lady Haslam and my mama sent me here. Now, you promised not to tell, Elizabeth Lamb."

"Of course I won't. But now your mother's all alone."

"No, I have a big sister. She's with her."

"Why didn't that—ah, pawn dog try anything on her?"

"She goes to De College—I'm sorry, I mean the Bermuda

College, Department of Academic Studies. She used to get home after my mama did. Anyway, she's very strong and she's studied The Arts — that's karate. She'd have given him a slap that sent him ringin'."

Elizabeth Lamb decided that, although St. Augustine's might not, in general, turn out to be very interesting, this roommate certainly was. And nice, too, and maybe even coherent once she substituted the school's slang for her Bermudian expressions. The other roommate was interesting, too, although she as yet had exhibited no signs of being at all nice.

"You never did tell me what's the matter with Faith," she observed.

Josas looked apprehensively at the door. "The dorm prefect's coming over, Lara Jane said. The Sixth Form doesn't like the underformers talking about them."

"We'll hear her coming. Who was this Jay? He's dead? And did he die here?"

"It happened before school really opened. Even before the Third Form got here, and we were here earlier than the other forms. You're going to have lots of work to catch up on but I'll help you. We're bound to have much the same classes. You see how I don't talk Bermudian when I'm not nervous?"

"I see. Keep it up. But what happened?"

"Well, the crew team comes early, in the last few days of August, to practice. 'The Augies of August' they call themselves. There's jackets with that on it, for them. They have to practice a lot because there's some race somewhere in October that they win almost every year. Boys and girls, too, but it's only the boys' team that comes here in August. Lara Jane — she's on the crew — says it's discrimination against women, but the girls don't really want to come early. Lara Jane says it's the principle of the thing, though."

"'The Head of the Charles' is what the race must be. It's in Boston. But what happened? You're driving me crazy, Josas."

"My mama and sister call me Josie. You can, if you want. I like it.

"Well, this Jay, Jay Colket, was one of the crew members. He was stroke, or something very large — that means important, but

I'll try to stop the Bermudian. Faith and he went steady, for all the time they were here, since Third Form. I heard" — Josas dropped her voice — "she'd lost her divinity to him. There's some girls here that brag when they 'lose it,' as they say. A Fourth Former told me. I certainly don't intend to lose my divinity!"

Elizabeth Lamb tried not to smile. "Me either. Not quite yet. So what happened?"

"So this Jay Colket was here, and some of the teachers as well as the crew, and he and a friend went scuba diving one evening after crew practice. They did it most evenings and they were allowed because they were good. They had all sorts of degrees or papers or whatever you get when you're experienced. Then you can dive without being in a class, as long as you have a buddy with you.

"So Mr. Prestwick always let them. Sometimes Jay had another buddy but this time it was Dan Garde — he's the one Faith was going to meet. He was even better than Jay. He was qualified as a scuba instructor. But Jay drowned even though Dan tried to save him, and Mr. Prestwick, too. You heard Lara Jane.

"But Faith's all the time actin' up about it. She can't get over it. And Dan's always hanging around, even in here though it's not allowed. No boys can ever be in girls' rooms, or girls in boys'. He's just all the time trying to make her feel better. I guess she was really in love, but it certainly turned her mean!"

"She'll get over it. My grandmother has a French saying: 'Love makes time pass. Time makes love pass.'"

There was a loud knock at the door. It opened and three girls came in. One was very tall and strongly built, with long blonde hair pulled back into a ponytail; the second was taller even than the first, with a similar body, her black wavy hair hanging to her shoulders. The third, who sidled in behind her companions, was of average height, her hair red and curly, and she was very slim and delicate of form. The first two wore shabby plaid shirts and faded blue jeans, but the redhead was dressed in black from the velvet ribbon tied around her forehead, red roses embroidered on it, down to a turtlenecked jersey and matching jeans ending in black socks worn under black kid ballet slippers.

"I'm Molly Peale, your dorm prefect, Elizabeth Lamb," the tall blonde said, "and these are two of my roommates. You've met Lara Jane. This," indicating the brunette, "is Liz Fyordberg and the Deadhead here is Leigh Urson. We went over and got your class schedule before LeStrange lost it, or something. I'll explain it to you. You do have the map of both campuses with all the rooms marked, and so on, so you know what the numbers beside the class assignments mean?"

Receiving a nod, she pulled Elizabeth Lamb down on a bed and sat beside her, consulting the schedule. Elizabeth Lamb was still looking at the exotic Miss Urson. "Deadhead?" she asked timidly, and then was terrified, thinking Molly must have said "redhead."

But Leigh smiled. "I'm a Grateful Dead fan," she said in a barely audible voice. "That's all Molly means. She and my other two roommates aren't into them yet. They haven't even reached the nineteenth century, so far."

Elizabeth Lamb laughed. "At least we have sense enough not to keep a tarantula for a pet," said Liz, the brunette. "If it gets loose one more time and I wake up to find it sitting on my face, I'm turning it in."

Leigh began to expostulate in a voice no one could hear except, possibly, Liz when Molly exclaimed sharply.

"Hey! Do you know that idiot's given Elizabeth Lamb six subjects? I've never heard of a Third Former having more than five. Four's average."

"LeStrange didn't do it," Leigh whispered. "The schedules are figured out by some mathematical genius in the office before school opens. LeStrange certainly should have checked it, though. If Elizabeth Lamb had got here when she was supposed to, she could have got it straightened out."

"She still can," Liz declared. "Maybe she'd better go to them all tomorrow, though, and see which one she wants to drop. If they let her. LeStrange has okayed it, so they might not. This place is getting crazier and crazier."

"How's she going to get to six classes in one day?" Molly asked.

"If the first one starts at seven-forty, she can, since the classes are only fifty minutes with a ten-minute break between and a half-hour for lunch. Do they run consecutively?" Liz began to count on her fingers.

They do," Molly admitted. "No gaps in between, except the ten minutes to get to the next one. But taking six classes, how could she do any sports? Lara Jane thought she might make a good cox for the intramural crew."

"Crew?" Elizabeth Lamb asked faintly. "I don't see how I could. I'm here to study."

"Well, you have to have a sport. Of course, this term you could do a SEXCA. That's — "

"I know. Mr. Salton explained it. I'd like one." Anything, she thought, to get out of that damnable crew everyone was pushing on her. "Are you all in crew?"

"Lara Jane's stroke. And Molly and I row powerhouse," said Liz.

"Not I," Leigh was so definite that she could be heard clearly. "I run around the quad once or twice a day and do sculpture and drawing for SEXCA each term. Have since I was a Third Former."

"And she gets away with it," Liz said. "Maybe you could, too, with a swim once a week, to pacify McMurtrie. She's as nuts on swimming as she is on coaching crew. But what classes have they given this kid, Molly?"

"First is Foundation in Learning. That's taught by Mr. Sullivan and all Third Formers have to take it. You can't get out of that. It's to teach you how to study, and so on."

"It's a blow-off course," Liz said. "Sullivan's entertaining and you don't have to do much prep for it."

"I know how to study, anyway. I guess I could take six classes and a SEXCA thing." She looked at the schedule. "Next is Latin I with Miss Greenwell, then Biology I with Miss McMurtrie then Algebra with Mr. Prestwick. Then lunch."

"All those classes are on the boys' campus," Molly told her, "so you can eat lunch over there, if you want. Or you could come back, because the last two are here: Biblical Literature with Mrs. Farnum and French I with Mme. Hofferman. You're lucky to have Bib. Lit. in the afternoon because Electra is usually hung over in the mornings. And mean."

"Who's Electra?"

"Farback Farnum's wife. Mrs. Farnum is a brilliant woman, a graduate of one of the women's colleges at Oxford, and they really should show her more respect," Leigh whispered. "But she drinks too much and embarrasses him, poor man, though she minds her step when the trustees are around and she's pretty well sobered up by the afternoon. Lara Jane put it very well the other day: 'Morning does not become Electra.'" Everyone laughed and Molly stood up.

"I see Josas got you all squared away," she said. "Good, because it's almost dinner time. And it's Wednesday, when Lara Jane gives the work assignments for the coming week and makes the announcements. Now, Elizabeth Lamb, you've read the rule book but let me repeat some things and tell you a little about your dorm: no smoking — anything, and no matches or lighters, either. No liquor. No flashlight. Don't ever step on the hippo outside the dining hall. You must go to chapel on Sundays, either here or on the boys' campus, and on Wednesday evenings after dinner, unless you get excused. You must show up at every meal, whether you eat or not. If you're sick, go to the nurse. At once.

"You can cook in your kitchen. On Saturdays, the classes run only till twelve-thirty, so there's a bus that takes us to Bar Harbor. You can buy groceries there, if you've got the money and the desire to cook. You keep your kitchen clean and your bathroom, too. I'll inspect the whole dorm on Sunday afternoons and any other time I think I've got a reason to, and Miss Greenwell might inspect at any time.

"Your door out to the quad locks from the inside, but not the out. Your door to the corridor doesn't lock. If you've got a lot of money or valuables you don't want stolen, take them to the safe in the Dean's office.

"You Third Formers will have dining room and kitchen duties; not every one of you every day. Look at the list Lara Jane will post after dinner, just outside the dining hall. Outside your door to the corridor, a little way up the hall, is a bathroom for the rooms on this floor. You can use it if you have to but it may cause resentment from the girls who don't have their own. You two and a couple of Fourth Form boys, I hear, are the only underformers who do. You lucked out. Even most Sixth Formers don't. But *don't* forget to yell 'Flushing,' if you use the john when someone's in the shower.

"Just before the hall bathroom, there's a door that leads out to a road at the back of the building. There's one at the far end of the hall, too. Don't ever use them unless there's a fire and you can't get out your door to the quad. An alarm goes off if they're opened, and you'll get stung forty hours. Don't use the road they open on for *anything*." Molly paused for breath and frowned, wondering what she had omitted. Elizabeth Lamb was surprised to see Josie winking at her, quickly, before the three Sixth Formers noticed.

"What's on the road that makes it so important?" Elizabeth Lamb asked.

"Three of the faculty houses. They've got their own little gardens just back from the road and they don't want students looking over the walls when they're out in them gardening — or doing whatever they do." There was a snicker from Leigh. Molly gave her a severe look.

"Which teachers live there?" Elizabeth Lamb asked hastily, not that she really cared.

"Mr. Cranston, Miss McMurtrie and Mr. Prestwick. They're just little houses, but private. Miss McMurtrie has a Labrador that's very defensive of her. He's nothing to fool around with until he knows you. The married faculty have bigger houses, all around the grounds, both here and on the boys'; and some of the unmarried women teachers have the whole top floor in the dorm across the quad. Same over at the boys', for the unmarried masters. And NO boys in this room, ever. They wait outside, and they've got to be on their own grounds by seven P.M., unless there's a party or something. A school party, that is. The plays and concerts and movies are held over at the boys' and we can go to them.

"Oh, there's a common room upstairs. It has a television set and a kitchen for the kids who don't rate like you three in here and us, next door. Miss Greenwell has the apartment on your other side so watch it. She has ears like a lynx."

Liz giggled. "And so does Mr. Alsop."

"Is there a man teacher living in this dorm, too?"

Molly gave Liz a hard look. "No, but Miss Greenwell sort of, ah, goes with him. He comes over for — dinner, sometimes. You have her for Latin. He teaches Greek. They have a mutual interest in — the classics, you might say.

"Well, I guess you're all set. It's funny they didn't give you English I, though. Maybe you should check. Dinner's in fifteen minutes. I hope you have a watch, because you'll need it. We'll see you later."

They left, Molly giving Liz a hard pinch as she passed her. "Ow," Liz exclaimed, none too low, and, before the door closed, Elizabeth Lamb's sharp ears heard: "That kid'll find out soon enough about the Greenwell liaison. She doesn't look stupid to me." Elizabeth Lamb rushed over and put her ear to the closed door. "So okay," Molly was responding, "but she's not hearing it from me. The dorm prefect, at least, has to act as if nothing in the dorm, or the school, either, is at all corrupt." There was a low laugh, probably from Leigh, before their door closed.

"I'll lend you a sweater, to wear to dinner," Josie offered. "It was nice this morning, what we call a 'real Bermudaful day,' but it's cold in the evenings. We can go down to the phone at the end of the hall and call your aunt so she brings your stuff over tomorrow."

As they walked to the phone, Josie carrying her bear even though her bills were safely in the new wallet in her pocket, as Elizabeth Lamb had put her own small purse into hers, she asked Josie, "Why did you wink at me?"

"Oh, because Faith's got the door back there" — Josie turned and pointed to the exit door almost directly opposite the hall door to their room — "disconnected. Dan got some friend of his who knows all that stuff to do it. And Dan helped; he's going to be an engineer or a physicist or something. And she props it open just a little bit so he can get in but nobody notices it's open. He comes to visit. Miss Greenwell hasn't caught on yet."

"Where do you go when he visits?"

"Up to the common room. You can study there, or over to the library. Here's the phone. Have you got change?" She zipped open the bear, which still held some coins.

The call was made, Isabella sounding very jovial and promising faithfully to produce the suitcases the next day. A man could be heard singing happily in the background. "You can just leave them in my room," Elizabeth Lamb told her. "It's the blue door across the lawn from where you left me, and it's got a number on it. What's the number, Josie? I didn't notice, Faith was yelling so loud."

"Oh. It's thirteen."

"I might have known."

• CHAPTER 5 •

Sweet food of sweetly uttered
knowledge.

— Sir Philip Sidney

A S THEY WALKED across the green to the dining hall, a young man got out of a van stopped near it and asked, "Could you tell me where I could find a Miss Faith O'Malley?" He was wearing a cap with the emblem of a hand with a green thumb on it and carried a long, conical package wrapped in stiff white paper.

Josie pointed. "That blue door, number thirteen. She stay there. But she's not in. You could leave it on the desk right by the window." As he nodded thanks and walked away, Elizabeth Lamb called, "What is it?"

"A dozen roses."

As they went on, Josie said, "I guess her daddy sent them to cheer her up. He did before. He has so much money he bought her a Volkswagen 'Love Bug' when she got on the honor roll last year. It cost twenty-four-hundred-and-ninety-nine dollars! I heard her talking about it. 'Bye-no-bye' I said to myself: 'down on The Rock I know peoples work half a year for that money.' Still, I guess she didn't lie. She's asshey but she's too dumb to lie." Josie brooded. "Except about me taking her money!" She looked ready to cry again.

"What's 'asshey'?" Elizabeth Lamb asked quickly. "And you said you'd cut it out."

"I'm sorry. It means 'no good.'"

They checked in with the attendance prefect and Josie led the way to a table of younger girls where there were several empty places. "They're all in our form," she told Elizabeth Lamb in an undertone after she had announced her name to the table, "but I don't know them all."

They sat down and Josie folded her hands together. There was a table on a dais at the far end of the hall at which sat two masters and some older girls, among them Joylene Treble and Lara Jane. Three or four other teachers, both men and women, were seated at various other tables. The din in the hall quieted as Mr. Prestwick, on the dais, stood up.

He spoke loudly. "Our hearts are made for you, O God, and they are restless till they rest in you. For what we are about to receive, we ask you to make us truly thankful. Amen."

"Now we can get our dinner," Josie whispered. "But let the older girls go first."

"Why's Mr. Prestwick here? I thought he'd be eating at his house, or over at the boys'. And I never heard a grace like that."

"The teachers get assigned dining room duty at night, followed by hall duty, every so often, no matter on which campus. But they can eat in the dining rooms even if they're not on duty. And they always say something from St. Augustine at the beginning of grace. It's a rule."

"I guess he wrote a lot of stuff, too," Elizabeth Lamb replied gloomily. "And I don't think it was very cheerful." The girls ahead of them were accepting without enthusiasm portions of some sort of meat and gravy and scoops of mashed potatoes. Most refused the broccoli in a cheese sauce that was offered them and departed to the salad bar next to the steam table that also held a coffee urn and cups.

Elizabeth Lamb took whatever she was given by a small dark woman, wondering if Dora ever served at dinner. The girls at her table poured milk for themselves and passed plates of buttered bread. The bread was warm and obviously homemade. "Mr. Pella's touch," she thought. "And the broccoli is great."

"I wish to God they'd put butter on the bread every day and not margarine every other," one girl muttered.

"Cheer up," another answered. "The mystery meat is absolutely awesome tonight; it actually tastes like something."

"I can't tell what it is," Elizabeth Lamb confessed, though she was eating avidly after the two-day Spartan regime, as food went, she had suffered at the hands of her aunt. "That's why it's 'mystery meat'!" three girls said in chorus. Everybody laughed. "At least, when it's mystery meat night, the dessert's ice cream," Josie said happily. "Sure, and we only get mystery meat four times a week," another responded sarcastically.

Elizabeth Lamb looked at her with interest. The sarcastic one was blonde and petite, with a narrow, aristocratic face. Her intelligent brown eyes were only very slightly obscured by the large, tortoise-rimmed spectacles perched near the tip of her thin nose. She winked at Elizabeth Lamb as she made a dramatic show of forcing down her 'mystery meat,' producing exaggerated but somehow inoffensive choking sounds as she did.

"You're supposed to be truly thankful, my dear girls." A chubby, round-faced, curly-haired young woman, carrying two plates of food, took one of the seats at the table and began to attack her dinner with appetite. "Good evening, Miss McMurtrie," a girl said politely. "This is Elizabeth Lamb Worthington, a Third Former. She just got here."

Miss McMurtrie and Elizabeth Lamb, their mouths full, nodded at each other. Faith appeared, very red in the face, and slumped into a chair beside Miss McMurtrie after, Elizabeth Lamb noticed, a searching glance to see if there was a vacant place at another table. "Somebody sent you a dozen roses, Faith," Elizabeth Lamb informed her. "We told the delivery man to put them on your desk."

"A dozen?" Faith spoke ungraciously. "They're from Dan, then. It's bush to send a dozen flowers." A deep sigh. "Jay — Jay and my daddy always sent ten, or maybe fourteen." She drank some milk, her hand unsteady on the glass. Miss McMurtrie responded cheerfully: "'The gods give breath, and then they take it away.' You must come to accept that, Faith."

Faith glared at her and had opened her mouth to reply when a semihush fell over the hall. Elizabeth Lamb looked around. Lara Jane was standing up.

"Announcements!" she shouted, over those still talking quietly. There followed a string of quickly-spoken messages: something about a silver bracelet someone had lost and would the finder please return it to the dean's office, something about the buses for Bangor for the girls' hockey game with John Bapst High School on Saturday, something about absolutely NO PETS for students — whoever had the kitten seen in Acton Dorm was to turn it in IMMEDIATELY, that the work schedules for next week were now posted outside the hall and check them when you leave or else before breakfast.

And the first Student Council meeting would be in the boys' library at five P.M. tomorrow. Then, very clearly, that all Third Form girls were to meet with Dean LeStrange in the girls' gym right after dinner; any Third Former on dish crew was excused for the evening. There were a few sighs of relief at Elizabeth Lamb's table. "That's all!" barked Lara Jane, who sat down, leaned toward Mr. Prestwick, and began to talk earnestly.

Girls passed out trays of dishes of mixed chocolate and vanilla ice cream. Miss McMurtrie hastily deposited the contents of her second plate of food in a small carton she produced from a capacious handbag before surrendering the plate to the steam table server, who was collecting them. Then she took her dessert. The observant Elizabeth Lamb noticed that Mr. Pella was peering at Miss McMurtrie from the opening in the wall of the kitchen, his mouth tense. He emerged from a door and was halfway to their table when an absolute quiet fell over the room, broken only by Josie's whispering, "That was good, innit?" as she licked her ice cream spoon. Elizabeth Lamb looked around.

A tall, tanned man wearing grey flannel slacks and a black clerical blouse below a Roman collar, topped by a worn tweed jacket, was walking about the room, stopping at tables and greeting students graciously. He was tanned even on his high forehead, which extended far down the back of his head, with only a thin fringe of blond hair separating it from his white collar. "Working the house, as usual," said Miss McMurtrie, with an irreverent grin. Mr. Pella, whom she seemed not to have noticed, disappeared back into his domain.

"Well, Cerberus is waiting," Miss McMurtrie told her table. "And so are the biology quizzes I must grade for you dears before rehearsal." She smiled and left, swinging her bag and making a large circle around the tall man.

"Who's Cerberus?" Elizabeth Lamb asked.

"Her dog," a girl answered. "A black Lab, very nice once he knows you. Miss McMurtrie cops dinner for him whenever she eats here. The cook's getting ready to kill her. Or, at least, make a scene."

"Why should he care?" asked the blonde girl who had choked down her 'mystery meat.' "He doesn't pay for the food. Our parents do. If we don't mind a sop for Cerberus, why should he?"

Elizabeth Lamb recognized a wide reader and therefore a kindred spirit. "What's your name?" she asked.

"Caitlin Connor," the girl answered. "And you're Elizabeth Lamb Worthington, right? In full. Hey, where're you going? We have to be dismissed."

Elizabeth Lamb was making for the coffee urn. She came back with a half-filled cup and poured milk into it. The girls at her table stared at her, open-mouthed. "Elizabeth Lamb," Josie finally whispered, "only Sixth Formers and teachers can have coffee. Ever. Maybe you'd bess take it back before you get stung."

"She's got it now, all secure," a jovial voice said behind them. Her hand was firmly shaken. "I'm Father Farnum," the voice announced. "I don't think I've seen you before."

"I just got here today. That's why I didn't know about the coffee. I'm Elizabeth Lamb Worthington."

"Oh, yes. Mr. Vincentia's young friend. Enjoy your coffee; it's the last you'll get here for three years." With a grin and an avuncular pat on the head he went on working the house. The other girls at the table still stared at her.

Mr. Prestwick rose. "Dismissed!" he shouted. Elizabeth Lamb gulped her coffee before she joined the mass exodus. All of their tablemates walked along to the gym. There were now softly glowing lamps along the paths and around the buildings.

"It's so pretty here," Josie whispered. "At home we live back-atawn and it's not like this. I liked it before you came and now I like it better." Holding her bear with one hand, she slipped the other confidingly into Elizabeth Lamb's, after checking her pocket to be sure her new wallet was secure.

The Third Form girls seated themselves on the lower rows of the tiers of benches around the gymnasium floor. Mrs. LeStrange came in and stood before them, looking, as usual, distraught. "I always feel she'll come apart before our very eyes," Caitlin murmured, pushing back her spectacles to better observe the Dean.

The Dean looked around vaguely. "The whole form should be here. Are there fourteen of you?" A girl stood up and made a performance of jabbing a finger at each of the others while counting aloud. "Yes, Mrs. LeStrange. Fourteen," she said with mock politeness.

"Well, now." Mrs. LeStrange drew in a deep breath. "The Student Council meets tomorrow, earlier than I thought it would, and your form still has no representative. The Third Form boys voted today. You will vote for your representative in the dining hall before breakfast tomorrow, by secret ballot, after you have had the night to consider. The other forms, of course, voted last spring for their reps.

"Some of you know each other; some may not. Will you all stand up, one by one beginning with the first row, and face the others and tell us your name, slowly and clearly."

This accomplished, the Dean adjured them to be in the dining hall at 6:40 to eat and vote before breakfast for the others began at 7:00. There were subdued groans.

"Now," she went on. "About tomorrow night. The Headmaster

is giving a reception at his house for all Third Formers and all the teachers so you can get to meet the staff and they can get to know your form, those of them who are not your instructors. It should have happened in the first week of school but Mrs. Farnum was not — feeling well." Subdued giggles came from the benches.

Mrs. LeStrange raised her voice. "Now, you girls are to help set up the refreshments for the reception. Since it is at seven, all of you will be on dining hall duty to set up for dinner at six-thirty. You will be there at six, do the usual pre-dinner preparations, have your own dinner early and a van will take you and some of the refreshments at six-thirty-five."

Elizabeth Lamb raised her hand. "What do we have to do at Father Farnum's house?"

"Assemble the sandwiches and desserts on trays, fill the punch bowls, put out napkins, ashtrays for those who smoke, set up the coffee urn and put out the cups, sugar, cream and so on *and* do whatever else Mrs. Farnum tells you to do."

Elizabeth Lamb raised her hand again. "In twenty-five minutes? I don't see how we can, especially since it will take four or five minutes to get there. Say twenty minutes. And we have to unload the food, too. And I don't see how we can set up the dining hall, eat dinner and get over to Father Farnum's house in time, either."

"Oh, dear." Mrs. LeStrange was disturbed. "Perhaps I didn't allow enough time? Oh, dear."

"No, ma'am," several voices agreed.

"Aren't the boys going to help?" Elizabeth Lamb asked.

Mrs. LeStrange frowned. "That hadn't been planned on."

"Why not?" a tall black girl asked. "Is it just women's work?"

There was a murmur of assent and a girl next to the questioner patted her on the shoulder and said, "Right on!"

Mrs. LeStrange seemed about to cry. Everyone sat silently until Elizabeth Lamb raised her hand again. "If we were excused from dining hall duty — maybe some of the Fourth Formers could do it, since they must remember how — and ate dinner at six, then at six-twenty-five or six-thirty or whenever we finish, were driven to Father Farnum's *and* if the Third Form boys were there to unload the van and help us, we could all be done by seven. Or shortly after; people don't always arrive just on time. The teachers who have dining hall duty certainly won't get there till seven-fifteen or later."

There was loud applause. Mrs. LeStrange wrote frantically in her notebook. "That is an excellent plan — ah?"

"Elizabeth Lamb Worthington," advised Caitlin.

"Oh, of course. I'll arrange it with the Dean of Boys. Very well, you may all go to your dorms and your studies. Chapel has already begun so you are of course excused."

The black girl raised her hand. "Can't we go to the library, as usual, if we want to work there?"

"Oh, of course, Mary. Of course. I will see you all in the dining hall tomorrow morning for the election at — at — "

"At six-forty," several voices chorused.

"Yes, yes. Good night." She left, talking to herself as she consulted her notebook.

The roses were in a vase on Faith's desk and several articles of clothing were strewn on her bed but she was not in Room Thirteen.

"I've just got a little Latin homework to finish," Josie said. "Then we could go to the library or take a walk or go to the Snack Bar. It's open until eight-thirty. Or whatever you want.

"We don't have to be in bed till nine-thirty. Faith doesn't have lights out till ten-forty-five. She always wakes me up when she comes in late. I don't know when she studies. And sometimes she comes peezin in around midnight. My mama got me a watch that shows in the dark. Sometime's she's tapped, too. If Miss Greenwell or Molly or Lara Jane ever catch her, she'll get her chocklits all right!"

"Peezin? Tapped? I get the chocklits thing. From before."

"Sneaking. Drunk. I'm sorry; I forget. It'll wear off, though."

There was a loud bang on the hall door. Lara Jane put her head in. "Good; you two are here. I need you. We've got a crucial rehearsal of *Penzance* in fifteen minutes and Miss Curtain just found out two of the daughters are out. Both damned fools sprained their ankles today in field hockey practice."

"What's *Penzance*?" Josie asked.

"Whose daughters?" Elizabeth Lamb asked. "What do you want us for? And why's this rehearsal so crucial?"

"Crucial means very nice — dickty — down home," Josie told her. "Is this thing very nice?"

"It's crucial — it's critical — because Curtain wants the performance all lined up by Sunday. She's taking five days leave of absence to go to some actors' society fund raising thing in California and we're doing *Penzance* for Parent's Weekend. That's in two weeks. And you guys can play two of the daughters as well as the Ankleless Twins. All you do is stand around looking winsome and sing a little and sort of cavort about.

"I'll help you. I'm 'Ruth,' 'Frederick's' old nurse. You need a SEXCA, Elizabeth Lamb, and, Josie, basketball doesn't take much time."

Light began to dawn on Elizabeth Lamb. "The school's doing *The Pirates of Penzance*? I saw it once. But I can't sing. I'm awful. And isn't Josie the wrong color for one of the Major General's daughters?"

"Oh, yes, Lara Jane," Josie spoke hopefully. "I just am not light enough. I'm sorry. And I've got some Latin to do, anyway. We just can't."

"I'll help you with the Latin after rehearsal. Elizabeth Lamb, the others will cover your voice, if it isn't *too* awful. And color doesn't matter. We've got a Chinese girl and a Korean girl and a fairly dark Jamaican one. You just need stage presence, Miss Curtain says."

"We don't have any." Both Josas and Elizabeth Lamb spoke loudly and quickly.

"Look, no more arguing. Come on; we've got to tell Miss Greenwell where you're going."

The hall door next to them opened to her knock, revealing an interesting scene. A slim, pale, dark-eyed young woman with black hair pulled back into a bun, dressed in a long, blue heavy silk kimono stood there with a thin green snake draped around her shoulders. Both Josas and Elizabeth Lamb moved behind Lara Jane. Though an archway they saw a small kitchen in which a man stood at a table with his back to them, chopping something in a bowl. A speckled brown serpent was coiled around his white-shirted torso just below his neck, above which was a sparse amount of greyish-brown hair.

"Good evening, Miss Greenwell." Lara Jane was calm. "Rome and Carthage look well. This is Elizabeth Lamb Worthington. She's a new Third Former and rooms next door with Josie and Faith. I want to take these two to a *Penzance* rehearsal. We'll be back by nine-thirty. Okay?"

Miss Greenwell nodded slowly, several times. Then she extended a hand toward the half-hidden Elizabeth Lamb, who moved a little way from behind Lara Jane to take it. The hand was very cold. "Of course, I have been expecting you," said the house-mistress. "And you are on my list for Latin I. I am glad to see you."

The man turned, brandishing a cleaver in a wave. His face, though pleasant, was lined. He seemed much older than Miss Greenwell. "Her father?" Elizabeth Lamb wondered.

"Hey, there, Lara Jane," he said. "I caught a few minutes of rehearsal last night. You were terrific in 'When Frederick Was a Little Lad.'"

"Thank you, Mr. Alsop. I can't sing very well, so I just wing it. And Sam covers up for me in 'Paradox.' Miss Curtain said she gave me 'Ruth' for my —"

"Stage presence," both Miss Greenwell and Mr. Alsop supplied, with smiles. Closing the door, the three girls ran across the green to the waiting van, in company with a few other students and one master.

"Who was that man?" Elizabeth Lamb fell into her seat, breathless but still inquisitive. "And why does Miss Greenwell have snakes?"

"Mr. Alsop," Lara Jane replied. "Theodore Alsop. He visits Miss Greenwell frequently. He's married but his wife lives in their house in Bangor and he stays here, in term time. And she has snakes because she likes them, I suppose. I think he gave them to her."

"Does Mr. Alsop live on the boys' campus?"

"Well, of course. There's a whole top floor of one of the dorms that's made into apartments where other single masters live, those who don't rate houses. They call it 'Writer's Block' because most of them are writing The Great American Novel. One of them's a poet, though, I think. Not published yet."

"*The Great American Novel*'s been written," Elizabeth Lamb told her. "I thought Mr. Wolfe was very clever to call his book that. Nobody else ever thought of it."

"Well, you know what I mean. They're some of them very 'precious' as my mother would say or as Molly, who lived in France awhile, describes them: *les tapettes*. But they're all good teachers or they wouldn't be here, and very civilized, too."

Elizabeth Lamb giggled. "What's that mean, what you said?" Josie asked. "Oh, now I get it. Back home we say 'qwer' or 'backin' up.'"

"The things I learn from Third Formers," Lara Jane told them as the van deposited them in front of a large building. "Madison Hall," she said, running quickly through the darkened auditorium, followed by her recruits. There was already action backstage, from the subdued sounds coming through a realistic-looking Cornish seacoast backdrop. "Great rocks!" Elizabeth Lamb exclaimed. "But there aren't many."

"Is that you, Lara Jane?" called a woman in a dark pink dress who was standing on the edge of the stage, one hand shading her eyes as she peered toward them. "You're late. Sam is ready to do 'Paradox' with you. It needs a lot of work." She blinked at them through pink-framed spectacles.

"I'm sorry, Miss Curtain," Lara Jane gasped, running up the four steps beside stage right. "But I got you two daughters. They're Third Formers and I had to get their dorm-mistress' permission."

"Oh, very well done!" beamed the woman, her round rosy face crinkling with approval. As she and Josie arrived on stage, Elizabeth Lamb was reminded of a full-blown pink peony, if peonies were ever topped by a head of platinum-blonde hair done in the pageboy style of the late 1930s.

"Now," Miss Curtain went on, after Lara Jane had introduced her victims, "you girls go backstage and Joylene will give you copies of the song we're going to run through presently and tell you the action and placement. Mr. Emerson," — to a man sitting patiently at the piano in the orchestra pit — "let's have 'Paradox,' please, now that Lara Jane is here."

A boy sitting at her feet rose wearily and Lara Jane ran to stand beside him. Another boy appeared and inserted himself between them. Mr. Emerson began the introduction to the song and Josie and Elizabeth Lamb fumbled their way behind the backdrop.

"Backstage" was an enormous area. Eight girls were lounging on folding chairs, amidst pieces of scenery, being addressed by Joylene Treble, who greeted Elizabeth Lamb with pleasure and Josie with courtesy. "Although the backdrop is thick, we must sing very softly," she admonished them. With scores in hand, they attempted to follow Joylene and the others. "Climbing over rocky mountain, skipping rivulet and fountain," trilled Joylene and the rest of the Major General's daughters, straggling about in single file and flourishing their parasols.

Somehow they all finished the song together, in spite of a loud "Ow!" from Josie who had been poked in the back of the neck by the tip of a parasol aimed by an over-exuberant daughter. Joylene sank into a sofa and sighed. "Alice," she said tiredly, "that thing is a deadly weapon in your hands. That's the third 'Ow!' I've heard tonight. I don't want you to wave it anymore. Keep it folded and swing it *only* at your side. The next time you're likely to get somebody in the eye.

"You two," to Elizabeth Lamb and Josie, "come over here and I'll try to show you a few maidenly Victorian ways of tripping over rocks. And I don't mean 'stumbling' when I say 'tripping'; that's what you've been doing and there aren't even any rocks back here! You both looked as if you were chasing criminals, not butterflies, or pulling up weeds, not daintily picking daisies."

She labored with them a while as the other daughters went through their maidenly Victorian steps, singing under their breaths. Loud sounds from Lara Jane of "a paradox, a paradox, a most ingenious paradox" came through the backdrop interspersed by loud cries from Miss Curtain asserting she was, again, off-key. The Pirate King could be heard sighing with heavy patience.

Joylene told Elizabeth Lamb, who had memorized the daughters' song by now, to join the others while she continued with Josie, whose face was several shades paler from fright although she had yet to get on stage. Instead, she melted away to peer through the open door of a well-lighted room at the side of the backstage area. Costumes hung around the walls, a woman was operating a sewing machine and another was fitting a bustled costume on to Faith, who was standing in the middle of the room with clenched teeth. "You're swaying again, Faith," the fitter was saying. "Don't you feel well? Only a minute or two more and you can join the others, but Miss Curtain wants your dress finished tonight."

Josie had escaped from Joylene who was at the drinking fountain at the other end of backstage. She peered around Elizabeth Lamb. "That girl," she whispered, before Joylene captured her again, "has got one girt big bumpy. Last thing she needs is to have it padded."

Elizabeth Lamb looked into another room beside the first. It held long tables on which scenery was being painted and others on which several boys and girls and Miss McMurtrie were shaping rocks out of large lumps of papier-mâché. "No!" one boy reprimanded another as he scooped the last of a mixture out of a large tub. "That's all that's left and Miss Curtain wants a *flat* rock for 'Mabel' to stand on when she does 'Poor Lonely One.' You crumple that up, with the glue already in it, and we'll never get the wrinkles out and I'm damned — sorry, Miss McMurtrie — if I'm going to mix any more of this glop. Here, smooth it over this hunk of foam rubber."

"Faith'll bounce when she steps on it," a girl demurred. "You ought to put pieces of plasterboard on the top and the bottom of the foam."

"She'll bounce anyway," a girl giggled. "A tighter corset's what she needs, not a rock to stand on."

A loud argument ensued between Faith's friends and the others. Miss McMurtrie called softly for silence and a boy quickly ran over to shut the door. Elizabeth Lamb wandered back to the daughters. "Paradox" finally finished, more or less to Miss Curtain's satisfaction, and Lara Jane, red-faced, came backstage for water. "She wants you to make your entrance now," she told Joylene and the others. "For God's sake, don't anybody fall down the staging this time. She's in a fit as it is. Can I help it if I'm getting laryngitis?"

Several girls murmured sympathetically. "And," Lara Jane went on, "just remember it'll be worse when the 'rocks' cover half the staging *and* you've got long dresses on." After her encouraging words, she sank down and began to mumble over the script she carried.

Mr. Emerson began playing their song. Faith, again in jeans, joined the daughters who one by one climbed a ladder and began to descend through an opening in the backdrop, with many virginal squeals and dainty gestures, singing between the squeals and helping each other descend. Josie and Elizabeth Lamb were the last. They managed to clamber down to the stage and skip among the rocks already placed there when Elizabeth Lamb stumbled and fell flat, face down. Josie staggered and fell on top of her. They lay there, half-stunned, as the piano stopped and Joylene ran back to help them up. Faith laughed loudly. There was an exclamation of disgust from the front row of audience seats. "You two," came Miss Curtain's voice, "go backstage and come down again."

Although Josie was limping and Elizabeth Lamb bleeding from a scraped forehead, they made a more-or-less graceful descent. Three more times Miss Curtain made the twelve girls go through the performance before she came on stage and directed Joylene to do something about the blood now running into Elizabeth Lamb's eyes. "A good thing you're not in costume," were her only words of solace. "And, Joylene, take the other girl and do something about her limp."

There was a first-aid kit in the prop room. "What are you in this epic?" Elizabeth Lamb asked Joylene as alcohol and a large square of gauze were applied to her forehead and tape bound around Josie's ankle.

"I'm assistant director, stage manager, one of the daughters — as you saw — *and* one of the policemen. They're short on boys and Father Farnum won't let any of the masters take a part. They often do, in Miss Curtain's productions, but this is for Parent's Weekend and he wants only students.

"Why she ever decided to do a musical with only half the cast able to carry a tune is beyond me. I guess because Father F. is a Gilbert and Sullivan freak and she's a gunner if there ever was one. God, since I, for one, can sing, she was even considering putting me in whiteface to do 'Edith,' the second female lead — no, I guess 'Ruth' is second. Anyway, Mr. Emerson talked her out of it. He's head of the Music Department. He'll have a full orchestra here when the show actually goes on. Tonight, the teams got back late from their off-campus games, and some of the members are in the orchestra."

"What's a 'gunner'?" Elizabeth Lamb asked.

"Oh, somebody bucking to be a prefect, or to get some office or honor. A would-be 'teacher's pet.' It's usually a student, but there's a couple of the faculty who could teach us a thing or two about gunning.

"You two'd better just sit here a while. Here's the daughters' score for the 'Talk About the Weather' number. You can learn it while the rest are doing it. It'll be over soon and that's all Curtain has on for tonight. Some kids had to skip dinner to get here early, but she had sandwiches sent in."

Instead of following her directions, they slunk to a side of the backdrop and peered around it. The characters of 'Frederic' and 'Mabel' — and they saw with surprise that Faith was 'Mabel' — were doing a duet with the daughters singing their 'Weather' song as —

"Counterpoint?" Josie asked.

"I guess so," Elizabeth Lamb answered glumly. "I don't know one thing about music. Most of them sound as bad as we do, though I'm surprised that Faith can sing so sweetly. It doesn't fit her personality. But if you ask *me*, 'this is going to close in New Haven.'"

They hadn't noticed that Miss Curtain had moved to the side of the stage and was right in front of them. Her face turned a darker shade of peony pink. "I heard that!" she said. "Young lady, you had better remember that famous quotation from Winston Churchill: 'It is better to be an actor than a critic.' Think about it while the both of you get out here and try, *try* to be troopers! And show some stage presence, if you know what that is."

Chastened but giggling, they obeyed. Three times they rehearsed the number. "Oh," Miss Curtain moaned to 'Frederic,' "if only you had more range, Dan! I do wish the faculty could perform in this; Mr. Cranston is the finest tenor I have ever heard!"

"Sorry, Miss Curtain," Dan said stiffly. "I *am* trying to extend my range, but if you think someone else would be better — "

"Oh, no! No, we have no time for substitutions. I want you and Faith to do this number together all you can, though; not just at rehearsals." Dan appeared pleased. Faith, as usual, looked sulky. "Now," Miss Curtain went on, "I want 'Edith' to introduce 'Weather' just once more. You daughters get ready."

"Miss Curtain," Lara Jane said deferentially, "I promised Miss Greenwell these Third Formers would be back at Falls before nine-thirty. Could we leave?"

"Yes," Miss Curtain answered, with a bitter look at Elizabeth Lamb. "But have them here tomorrow just after dinner. They need a great deal of practice. And you need more on 'Paradox.'"

Elizabeth Lamb raised her hand. "Josie and I have to help at the Headmaster's reception tomorrow, Miss Curtain."

Miss Curtain clutched her platinum hair histrionically. "Is there no respect for Art at this school? God, I suppose I must be there, too. Very well, but you will come back here with me as soon as we can decently leave. Joylene will direct the rest of you until I get here. Now, 'Edith' — "

"I don't think she likes me," said Elizabeth Lamb as they walked to the van.

"You're right," Lara Jane answered. "And she never will. She takes dislikes and holds them forever. Likes, too. She's doing *Earnest* after this. Maybe you'd better not try out for it. You can keep drama as your SEXCA by doing makeup for it. Are you any good at makeup?"

"I've been backstage at the *Folies-Bergère* lots of times. One of the principal dancers was our landlady. She owned a big apartment house. I used to watch them put on their makeup," Elizabeth Lamb answered as Josie asked "What's *Earnest*?"

"Oh, that Oscar Wilde thing. A lot of drawing-room talk and two guys pretending to be someone else and simpering girls and a terrible old woman, Lady Bracknell — I think Curtain's going to

102

cast me for her — and then the guys are really cousins or brothers or something. The old mistaken identity plot."

Josie did not appear enlightened but asked no more. Miss McMurtrie and another woman were already seated in the van. The three girls sat several rows behind them, Josie and Lara Jane together on one side of the aisle going over the Latin textbook Josie had hopefully brought to rehearsal. The driver got out, announcing he would have to wait five minutes more since it was the last van of the night.

In spite of the loud conversation from the back seat and the *Sicilia est insula magna in Europa. Magna est fama Siciliae, sed fortuna Siciliae non bona est* from Lara Jane followed by a stumbling translation into English from Josie, and then more Latin sentences and more translations, Elizabeth Lamb's attention was caught by Miss McMurtrie's saying something about "Faith and Dan" to her companion. They were speaking quietly but Elizabeth Lamb had excellent hearing, which had been a great help to her in her childhood occupation, still continuing, of eavesdropping.

"It's just too bad," Miss McMurtrie went on, "that Melinda gave Dan the part of 'Frederic.' If Jay hadn't died, she'd have undoubtedly given him the part, if he'd wanted it. He had a good voice and she was terribly fond of it — or him. Always deferred to him, I noticed. And now Dan feels he's standing in a dead man's shoes, so to speak."

"I don't think he's that sensitive," her friend answered. "And he *could* have refused. Melinda's a dragon, but one can stand up to her. She's not the Lord God Jehovah, though she acts as if she were."

"He didn't try out for the part; didn't want it. But Melinda couldn't find a suitable 'Frederic' so Faith volunteered Dan and forced him into it."

"That brat!" Miss McMurtrie's friend gave a quick glance over her shoulder but the Latin coaching and the talk from the back were still going on and Elizabeth Lamb now had her head resting against the side of the van with her eyes closed and one hand covering her bandaged forehead.

"Yes, she and Jay were well suited. Not to speak ill of the dead, but he really was the most arrogant student we've had here in a long time. Oil money, lots of it, I believe. But no manners. I always come back early, when the 'Augies' come, because just watching Harry with them gives me many tips for my coaching of the girls. He is one superb coach!"

"Of course he is," the friend agreed, smiling a little, but very politely.

"Well, after the Augies' first week of practice, they made an incredible showing one day — broke all their previous records on the Abenaki — so Harry invited them to his house and ordered tons of pizza. I brought a case of Coke. And Tim Cranston, who helps Harry on occasion with the crew and who had seen the practice, had just got back from a month in France, with his usual supply of champagne. He brought over two bottles."

"Champagne! But Harry's so strict! And what would Father — "

"It wasn't term-time yet. Another week to go. And I guess Harry thought they really deserved a treat. You're no fool, Agatha; you realize the crew and just about every other student here, even a few Third Formers, sneak beer in quite often, not to mention vodka. Some get caught, but most don't. And Harry's no fool, either. He knew it wasn't the *first* time they'd had liquor!"

"But — "

"Well, anyway, we drank it. Just *don't* you tell *anyone*. And I think Jay had been drinking before he got to Harry's, because just one glass of champagne, which was all anyone got, put him right over the edge."

"How?"

"Well, he made slurs about almost every other crew member — they ignored him; probably used to it — and then he started rummaging around Harry's bookshelves. Harry's a Shakespeare enthusiast, you know. Some of the volumes are quite valuable, and Jay handled them very roughly. Harry was about to go over to him when Jay suddenly sat down quietly with *The Merry Wives of Windsor*, saying it was his favorite play and he knew it by heart."

"I didn't think he read anything but *Playboy*. Not that I knew him; I only had him for one class, thank goodness."

"Well, he really began ranting. He was paging through it and shouting out stray sentences. I was so appalled, I remember some

104

of them clearly. 'Like a fair house built on another man's ground,' was one. And 'I cannot tell what the dickens his name is.' And 'Faith, thou hast some crochets in thy head now.' And 'I am almost out at heels' and then he laughed nastily and looked over in a mean way at Harry who was talking quietly to Tim, but with one eye on him, and said, 'Or out of heels. Or out to get heels.' He was dreadful. Just acting up for no reason."

"What happened?" Agatha raised her voice as several more girls got in and the driver returned and started his engine.

"Oh, everybody was talking loudly, too, and playing records. There wasn't a scene. They all soon left; they'd been there a couple of hours and Harry insists on an early lights out for crew. It was just so insulting to him. Jay really resented him, I suppose, for being so talented *and* for being black, *and* for having to do as he said. But he was practically implying Harry was a cheat; cheated to win the Olympics, I guess."

"And Harry detested Jay," said Agatha. "But no use talking over dead issues. Silence is golden."

"Mmm. Sometimes it's guilt." Miss McMurtrie spoke louder, too. "But you're right. I was somehow reminded of it tonight. Something in *Penzance*, maybe."

"How Gilbert and Sullivan can remind you of the immortal W.S. I cannot imagine!"

Miss McMurtrie laughed. "Well, you teach English. I'm only an uncouth biology teacher. Speaking of biology, did you hear that over in Bar Harbor, at the Jackson Lab, they've managed to get virgin mice to produce embryos for six days of a thirty-day gestation period? As a good Catholic, I've always had to believe in parthenogenesis, but this is amazing. No Holy Spirit involved. A couple of years ago, though, *The Lancet* ran an article about several British doctors who swore they'd delivered babies from virgins."

"What happened to the mice after the six days?"

"As I read it in *Time*, they went haywire."

Both teachers were laughing as they got off the bus. Josie went to Lara Jane's room to finish her Latin and Elizabeth Lamb decided to have a shower and then take advantage of Josie's offer of pajamas. "Good thing my toothpaste and brush were in my little bag," she thought, gingerly removing her bandage. The damage appeared to be minor and she delicately washed off the dried blood.

Josie had kindly hung Elizabeth Lamb's towels and washcloth next to hers on a long bar above the bathtub. Faith's, thick and soft and of a peach color trimmed with rows of white lace, were in solitary grandeur on a bar on another wall. As Elizabeth Lamb, although disappointed that there was no shower, lay luxuriantly in the huge tub that could have been manufactured for the Paris Ritz, voices, accompanied by playful splashes, came distinctly through the wall to her left.

"Ah, my Juno, my Minerva, my Venus," said a man, "as heavenly as this has been, I must get out of this wet tub and into a dry martini."

"I'd be more flattered if you'd mentioned Venus first," Miss Greenwell's voice answered. "Still, we spinsters must take compliments as we get them. There's a small pitcher of martinis already mixed in the fridge, but I've never known you to drink them after dinner. Besides its being *déclassé*, you'll get argumentative."

"One can no more keep a martini in the refrigerator than one can keep a kiss there. Speaking of which —" There was silence for a time, followed by more splashes and laughter. "And it isn't the gin in martinis that makes one mean; it's the vermouth. Anyone as learned as you, my Minerva, should know that. I'll mix some more, with very little vermouth."

"Not for me," said Miss Greenwell. "I'm still feeling the three I had before dinner, and then all that wine! No wonder I felt so —"

"Ah, the martini effect! On you, darling, it only makes you more pliable to my wishes. Let me dry you off."

"My God," Elizabeth Lamb thought. "I wonder if I should cough or sneeze." She managed a loud, strangulated cough and a loud splashing of water which produced nothing from Miss Greenwell's bathroom but more giggles and murmurs.

"I wonder what Josie makes of this," Elizabeth Lamb said aloud as she towelled herself. "As for Faith, I wonder she doesn't try blackmail. Maybe she does." She thought a moment. "Maybe she told her friend Jay and he — no, I'm being silly. And, anyway,

Faith probably didn't have this room last year. But maybe — no, forget it!"

She was in her bed, half asleep, when Josie came in, whispered "Good night" and, after washing quickly, got into bed and pulled the sheet over her head. Neither of them was awake when Faith came back to the room.

• CHAPTER 6 •

With shining morning face, creeping like snail, unwillingly to school.

— William Shakespeare

FAITH WAS ASLEEP in her bed when Josie's and Elizabeth Lamb's alarm clocks sounded at 6:15 the next morning. She raised her head, opened her mouth to shout a protest, then fell groggily back on her pillow. Elizabeth Lamb awakened with a start, wondering why she had been dreaming of rocks.

She had spent a restless night, waking often from dreams. In one, her grandmother was sitting on a chair in the middle of the quad, her slippered feet resting on a pile of flat stones, engaged in unravelling a sweater that showed a number of dropped stitches. Since Elizabeth Worthington had never been known to knit, Elizabeth Lamb had questioned her about her activity and received no reply. Then she had asked why Miss Greenwell was having an affair with Mr. Alsop. Her grandmother smiled and answered that "the old can be attractive to the young, if what they offer is what the young seek — not necessarily financial security but the security of love."

In another dream, she was arguing with Miss Curtain, who again quoted Winston Churchill, and Elizabeth Lamb, in return, told her that part of Mr. Vincentia's advice, after she had been accepted at St. Augustine's, was something from a speech the great man had given at Harrow School in 1941: "Never give in, never, never, never — in nothing, great or small, large or petty. Never give in except to convictions of honor and good sense." Miss Curtain had snarled.

In another, she was climbing a huge pile of grey rocks, a lowering grey sky above her and a cold grey sea visible on the horizon. She stumbled and fell, and as she did, the clock woke her up. She mumbled, "Remember rocks." She and Josie washed perfunctorily and put on their school uniforms, Elizabeth Lamb tripping over some objects on the floor between Faith's bed and her own closet.

"Why in the world did she bring these things?" she asked Josie quietly, holding up a black rubber hip-wader. "Does she fish?" Josie answered that many of the girls had them, and probably boys, too, for wading the shallow Abenaki after hours. "Faith had bess wake up and put them under things in her closet, the way she always does, in case Miss Greenwell looks in. Why were you saying 'remember rocks'?" she asked softly.

"I don't know," Elizabeth Lamb answered confusedly. "I can't think — it's gone now." They pulled on sweaters and ran across the wet grass to the dining hall.

A sleepy Dora was in place at the steam table, serving Mrs. LeStrange with scrambled eggs, grilled sausage patties and what looked like homemade biscuits. The Dean took a large cup of coffee with her to one of the two tables that were already prepared for Third Formers. Other kitchen workers were setting the remaining tables for the seven o'clock breakfast.

Elizabeth Lamb looked wistfully at the Dean's coffee as Dora, with a loud, "Humph! Thought we was going to miss the pleasure of your company," threw the food on to her and Josie's plates, and then on to those of the rest of the form, who had straggled in behind them. There was silence as the girls ate, interspersing their forkfuls of eggs and sausage with yawns. Elizabeth Lamb, who had had *café au lait* for breakfast for as long as she could remember, found that orange juice and milk were unsatisfactory substitutes. She yawned with the rest as Mrs. LeStrange walked around the tables, presenting each girl with a small piece of paper and a pencil.

Each girl wrote on her ballot and folded it before Mrs. LeStrange collected them. Elizabeth Lamb was hesitant, debating whether or not to vote for the prepossessing Caitlin or for Josie, to give her confidence. She finally printed, "Josie Outerbridge" and put the paper in the Dean's impatient hand.

They watched as Mrs. LeStrange made a long and impressive performance of putting on her spectacles, unfolding the ballots and slowly putting them in one pile. The last ballot was placed to the side of the pile. She cleared her throat and looked at the expectant faces.

"Elizabeth Lamb Worthington is your form's rep to the Student Council," she said impressively, and then, less impressively, searched their faces, obviously to determine which face belonged to the victor. Twenty-six hands clapped loudly and Josie threw her arms around Elizabeth Lamb, who was wondering why in the world she had received every vote but her own. She decided, with more than her usual amount of modesty, that it was because she was the only girl who had not been there long enough to arouse any antagonism, quite forgetting her handling of the Dean in the gym the night before.

She blushed and said, "Thank you," as Josie loudly cried "Congratulations!" and then whispered, "You *very* large now, Elizabeth Lamb. I proud to be your friend." The tall black girl, Mary, made a "thumbs up" sign and a little brown-haired girl, not to be outdone, held up her hand, fingers separated, in the Vulcan "live long and prosper" greeting. Mrs. LeStrange reminded Elizabeth Lamb, of whose identity she was finally aware, to be at the Student Council meeting in the boys' library at five that afternoon. Josie sobered at this, but then looked at her roommate and her face brightened. The girls dispersed, as the others arrived for breakfast, some to get more food and some to go to their rooms.

Josie and Elizabeth Lamb met Faith running across the quad. "Elizabeth Lamb got herself elected S.C. Rep!" Josie told her. A muttered "Christ!" was the only response. Josie made a face at the departing back. "I wonder who got the other vote?" she said.

"You did," Elizabeth Lamb told her, and received another hug. They had time for Josie to collect her books and Elizabeth Lamb to gather up a pen and notebook and for both of them to brush their teeth before leisurely leaving for the first bus to the boys' campus. Josie looked at Elizabeth Lamb's schedule.

"I have Biology with Miss McMurtrie on the boys' when you have your first class, Foundation in Learning," she said. "Then I'm with you second period for Latin and fourth period Algebra. I have English when you have Biology third period. But we can't eat lunch together because I have Foundation in Learning over there when you have Biblical Literature here. I have to eat at the boys' because all my classes are there. And I only have five classes. Then I practice basketball, usually. After that, I do homework."

While Elizabeth Lamb was trying to explain that Molly had said she could eat on either campus, they opened the door to the quad to find two suitcases reposing on the top step. Elizabeth Lamb thankfully put them in the room, wondering out loud if her Aunt Isabella's latest love was a cat burglar by profession. "He was so quiet," she said. "I know my aunt didn't bring them because she never gets up until eleven. I guess she sent him over to Bar Harbor for something. Like breakfast!"

Josie giggled and pursued the idea of her friend's aunt's bye — "I mean *boy*" — being a burglar. "Down on The Rock, in the old days, they used to get put to cutting up limestone rock into bricks for building houses if they got caught robbing. What happens to them in the States?"

"Rock. Rocks." Elizabeth Lamb stopped walking and looked at Josas. "Now I remember."

"What's the matter?" Josie asked uneasily. "Come on. The bus is waiting." They walked faster, Josie favoring her taped ankle only slightly.

"Did Lara Jane get Mr. Prestwick to go with you to the Student Council meeting this afternoon?" Elizabeth Lamb asked as they found an empty seat amidst a couple of dozen of girls, some talking, some consulting notebooks, and some with their eyes closed and their heads resting on the back of their seats. "Yes. She said he say I'm to go to his house and tell him my side right after his last class. That'll be at ten to three. He said tell me be there on time because he has crew practice at three-fifteen."

"I'll meet you in our room before three. There's something I thought of. I think he'll let me tell him and I think he'll believe I've got a point. And I wouldn't worry too much, if I were you. But wait till you hear what I say to Mr. Prestwick. Don't ask me now. I'm scared to death at the thought of my first class at St. Augustine's."

Josie reassured her, or tried to, as they got off the bus and parted. Elizabeth Lamb found Mr. Sullivan's classroom without difficulty and looked in apprehensively. Three boys were already sitting at a large table in the middle of the room, comparing passages in their notebooks. She sat down timidly, leaving a space between herself and one of the boys. Five more boys entered, followed by three girls, Caitlin among them. She beamed at Elizabeth Lamb and sat down in the empty place, putting her arm affectionately about the shoulders of the boy Elizabeth Lamb had not dared sit beside.

"I hear you're the boys' Third Form rep to the Student Council, B.B.," she said to him. "Way to go! This," indicating Elizabeth Lamb, "is ours, Elizabeth Lamb Worthington. Elizabeth Lamb, this is my cousin, Will Dickinson. But he's been called B.B. since we were in nursery school."

B.B. rose and smiled and reached around his cousin to shake Elizabeth Lamb's hand. His own hand was thin and brown and his clasp was firm and cool. Elizabeth Lamb felt a strange sensation, a sort of tingling from her palm up to her elbow. Observing B.B. closely, she murmured, "Hello."

He was fairly tall and angular, with a narrow face but a square jaw. His nose was beaked, his mouth well-shaped and his eyes a dark brown that set off his hair, the color of wheat and only a little longer than her father would have approved. Elizabeth Lamb felt warm all over. "It can't be," she thought. "Am I getting what Grandmother calls a 'crush' on this kid?" She grinned to herself. "But I'm too young and I'm from Boston!"

"Why 'B.B.'?" she asked, her voice a little unsteady.

Caitlin answered for him. "He was the only blond boy in nursery school and the teacher would say 'Hand this to the blond boy,' things like that, for the first week or so. The rest of the kids began to call him 'blond boy' so the teacher shifted it to 'B.B.' and it stuck."

A spry, bald elderly man with a white goatee and wire-rimmed glasses entered briskly and sat in the chair at the end of the table, the chalkboard behind him. He looked around, checking names in a little book. "And you," he said to Elizabeth Lamb, "must be the until-now-missing Miss Worthington. Mr. Salton gave me your book to read. Pretty good. I'm a writer myself and I'm always glad to meet a fellow scribbler. I told the Powers-That-Be that English I would be wasted on you so you won't get an English course till next year."

Elizabeth Lamb blushed and smiled as everyone looked at her. "What's your book about?" a chubby boy at Mr. Sullivan's right asked her.

"It's sort of a mystery," she answered, still blushing and very much aware of B.B.'s approving regard.

"Mr. Sullivan writes poetry; novels, too. Very good ones," said a dark-haired girl, obviously what Joylene called a "gunner."

"Who's your publisher, Mr. Sullivan? I never knew," asked another boy, rather smugly. "My father's in publishing."

Mr. Sullivan produced only a thin smile in answer and got up, turning to the chalkboard. "Privately printed," Caitlin whispered to Elizabeth Lamb. "Mark knows that. He's a real jerk and just asking for trouble."

Mr. Sullivan cleared his throat. "You see your assignment for tomorrow," he said, indicating the board. "But, before we go over today's assignment and start talking a little about poetry and verse, let me tell Elizabeth Lamb what the course is about." He indicated the board again. "I've outlined its main objectives. And some of the rest of you could use a little reminding."

He pointed to the board. "The course is designed to help you develop study skills. It will teach you to concentrate your time, listen well, pick out what is important in what I say or in your reading assignments, and teach you to remember and use critical information and express it succinctly.

"Reading and using critical information can be called 'research.' It's been said that if you steal from one author, it's plagiarism, but if you steal from many, it's research. Research leads to knowledge; now, knowledge comes in two forms, as Samuel Johnson said: 'Knowing a subject or knowing how to find information on it.' In this course, you'll learn the latter which, of course, leads to the former.

"And you'll learn to skim an assignment before you read it, and summarize it after. You will learn to read more effectively and your learning will teach you to recognize the key ideas that are the essence of note taking, a skill you'll use all your life. Your assignment for today was to describe poetry, what it is, in one brief paragraph. Mark, suppose you read yours."

Mark, still looking smug, got up and read from his notebook. After about a minute of his reading the same thing, said in various ways, Mr. Sullivan stopped him. "My boy, as Thoreau said, 'Simplify! Simplify!' Do that assignment again, keeping it to one paragraph. You, Caitlin."

Caitlin obliged. Mr. Sullivan beamed. "I would almost think you expected to be hanged in a fortnight. Samuel Johnson, whom I was reading last night, wrote: 'The certainty of being hanged in a fortnight concentrates the mind wonderfully.'"

Everyone but Mark laughed, the gunner loudest of all. Mark murmured, just loud enough, he thought, to be heard by those nearest to him, "Are my parents paying just for me to hear what Samuel Johnson said? Even though *he* was published."

Evidently Mr. Sullivan had keen ears. "No, Mark, they are paying for you to think and remember. Dr. Johnson could think and remember. I hope, on you, that money is not being wasted. Now, Peter."

When a few more assignments had been read aloud, and all of them handed to Mr. Sullivan, he began to explain the difference between poetry and verse:

"'Will no one tell me what she sings? —
Perhaps the plaintive numbers flow

For old, unhappy, far-off things

And battles long ago' — now, that is poetry. I want you to find the poem from which I quoted and copy it in your notebook. If you don't know how to begin, consult a librarian on how to do your research. And here's two lines from the second poem I want you to research — you'd better be noting these, you know:

'Charm'd magic casements, opening on the foam

Of perilous seas, in faery lands forlorn.'

Someone once said that those six lines are the only truly poetic ones in the English language."

A boy raised his hand. "What about some of the Psalms?"

"Not originally written in English, but you have a point. But, you know, Robert Frost said that real poetry must rhyme as well as scan. People who write what is called 'free verse' were, he said, 'playing tennis without a net.'" More laughter, again loudest from the gunner.

"Now, something that both rhymes and scans can be verse, and yet not poetry. Dorothy Parker, for instance, wrote remarkably witty and able verse but not, or so I feel, a poem in her entire life. By tomorrow you will know the difference between poetry and verse — "

Both Elizabeth Lamb and B.B. had raised a hand. "Ladies first," Mr. Sullivan said.

"What about her 'War Song'?" Elizabeth Lamb asked and B.B. said, "I was going to say 'The Maidservant at the Inn.'"

"Hmm. I think I must agree that both are, indeed, poems. I am getting encouraged: this class, on the whole, is literate beyond the usual Third Form class. Let me recite you two lines from Miss Parker:

'Razors pain you, rivers are damp.

Acids stain you and drugs cause cramp.'

"Research the rest of the verse and bring it in. And" — pointing to the board — "each of you will produce by tomorrow your own original poem or verse. Of at least eight lines. With such a heavy assignment, there will be none the next day. I see our time is over. Elizabeth Lamb, this is the book you will need to get at the book-store for this course."

He wrote in his notebook, tore a page out and shook her hand. Mark made a face. She waved at Caitlin, who was running for the stairs, quickly found a washroom, murmuring, "I didn't know prep school made you so nervous," and then went into the classroom next to Mr. Sullivan's. Josie was already there, as was B.B., and several other boys from Foundation in Learning. Two Third Form girls who had not been in Elizabeth Lamb's first class came in.

Miss Greenwell was even more pale than she had been the night before. "The 'martini effect' must have been extreme," Elizabeth Lamb thought. There was a sign at the end of the room: "Welcome to Latin country." Miss Greenwell smiled at Elizabeth Lamb and gestured at it as she took attendance.

She directed them to open their copies of *Latin for Americans* to the second chapter. Elizabeth Lamb shared Josie's book, quickly entering the title on the paper Mr. Sullivan had given her.

"Well, Elizabeth Lamb," Miss Greenwell said, "the purpose of this course is to enable students to read connecting Latin passages with comprehension of the Latin as Latin. You have missed our discussion of our Roman heritage and the Roman world, the Latin dipthongs, vowels and consonants and some of the pronunciation exercises. If you cannot master them yourself when you get your textbook, come to me for help. I am usually in your neighborhood in the evenings," she added with a smile.

"I see you have a notebook. The nouns in Latin should be easy, as should the predicate nominatives, and you will have some verbs to learn. The principle of the change of word endings — inflection — as we discussed yesterday in class is the most important thing for the beginner to master.

"Today we are going on to adjectives and the accusative case and word order, after a little exercise in derivatives that will take a bit of guessing. It should start our class on a light note." She turned to the chalkboard.

B.B. leaned across to Elizabeth Lamb and whispered, "My brother said all he learned in Latin I is that 'v' is pronounced 'w' and there wasn't any 'j'. But he passed." Elizabeth Lamb smiled, blushing only slightly.

Although she had thought Miss Greenwell might have a hearing deficiency, since her splashings and coughing had not deterred the pursuits in the tub beyond the wall last night, evidently she could hear well when, Elizabeth Lamb thought, "there are no amatory distractions."

"Now, B.B.," the teacher said, turning, "you're bright and vocal this morning. Suppose you tell us the English word we derive from the first three Latin words I have listed, first translating from the Latin. These are Latin words we learned last week."

"*Amant*," read B.B. "It means 'love' or 'like.'" He paused.

"Class?" Miss Greenwell asked. "It's an adjective."

Elizabeth Lamb raised her hand. "Amatory?" she asked, and then smiled to herself.

"Good. Go on, B.B."

"*Bona*," he read. "It means 'good.' The derivative would be 'bonus.'"

"Very good. But there's another. We got it from the French. Sweet."

Elizabeth Lamb raised her hand again. "'Bonbon'?"

"Good. B.B."

"*Fama*. It means 'report' or 'fame.' The English would be 'famous.'"

"And the derivative word?" B.B. shook his head.

"'Defamation,'" several students said loudly, Elizabeth Lamb among them.

"You, Mark. *Familia*?"

"Family," Mark said, in a superior manner.

"And the English derivative?"

Mark frowned. "'Family,' of course."

"That's the translation. The word we *derive* from it."

"'Familiar,'" said Elizabeth Lamb quickly.

Miss Greenwell looked at her. "You're sure you haven't read ahead?"

"No, ma'am. I'm looking at page sixteen in Josie's book, where you said to."

"Well, I think you may have no difficulty in catching up, although the grammar and pronunciation are more difficult than the vocabulary. *Magna*, Josas?"

"'Big,' 'large,'" Josas gasped, but was unable to furnish 'magnitude' or 'magnify.' Another girl obliged, Elizabeth Lamb thinking it better to be quiet for a time.

The lesson went on. Miss Greenwell was a sharp, coherent teacher. They began to translate Latin sentences from the textbook and Elizabeth Lamb was totally confused. At the end, Miss Greenwell gave them their assignment for the next day and quickly walked out, looking less pale than she had fifty minutes before. The students rose, some stretching their arms as they did. Josie patted Elizabeth Lamb's hand and left, saying, "See you in Algebra."

"Where are you off to now?" B.B. asked.

"Biology, Miss McMurtrie," she answered, feeling her face flush again and angry with herself for it.

"Me, too," he said. "I'll show you where."

With some others from the class, they climbed up two steep flights of cement steps, Elizabeth Lamb, encumbered only by a notebook, having an easier time than B.B., who carried a pile of books and a knapsack.

Miss McMurtrie looked as cheerful as ever. Her room, on the fourth floor of the Schoolhouse, was also cheerful. It overlooked much of the boys' campus, and through the trees, even some of the girls' buildings were visible, as well as the little Abenaki River.

B.B. let Elizabeth Lamb share his textbook, *Biological Science, An Inquiry into Life*. Miss McMurtrie handed back marked quizzes and he was gratified to find an "A" at the top of his. She appeared not to notice her new student as she began her dissertation on "Water in Cells."

Caitlin raised her hand. "Excuse me, Miss McMurtrie, but would you like me to take attendance?" she asked tactfully. "And here is a new girl, Elizabeth Lamb Worthington. She lives in Falls. She was elected girls' Third Form rep to the S.C. this morning."

"Then she must have already made quite an impression on your form. Thank you, Caitlin; here's the attendance book. Elizabeth, did you have any biology in your previous school?"

Receiving a negative, Miss McMurtrie told her what textbook

to get and that she lived just behind Falls and would help her catch up on what she had missed. Miss McMurtrie then began to sketch the structure of molecules on the board, explaining how they moved in a water element.

Elizabeth Lamb endured the class in a state of bewilderment, wondering how she would ever master biology. She decided to avoid the issue of being addressed by her full name in the hope of becoming more or less invisible and at the end of the class told B.B. she hoped that maybe Miss McMurtrie wouldn't notice her for the rest of the term. "Or maybe I can drop Biology. They gave me six subjects."

"No way," he answered. "It's required in Third Form year. But it's the only science course you have to take unless you're going to be a science major in college. Which I am. If I ever get there, that is. My mother has to support both my brother and me and do you know some colleges now charge three to five thousand dollars a year for room and board and tuition? It's out of sight!"

They were walking down the stairs. "Couldn't you get a scholarship, or something?" she asked.

"Well, beginning this year it's easier to get financial aid if you're poor, because they've started to weed out the crooked parents who understate their income. From now on, parents have to send copies of their income tax returns. Before it was on the honor system, for years and years. So maybe I'll be a science major after all. What about you?"

"Are you kidding? Never! And I can see right now I'm going to flunk Biology."

"No, you won't. Caitlin's terrific. She'll coach you. But go to Miss McMurtrie, too. What's your next class?"

Elizabeth Lamb, thinking of the Air India maintenance crews had caused her to miss so many classes, didn't hear him. "May they live in interesting times," she murmured.

"Who?" B.B. was startled.

"Oh, I was in Pakistan this summer and I would have gotten here on time if Air India hadn't been struck. I was just cursing them. It's an old Chinese curse my grandmother uses. She's too ladylike to *really* curse."

B.B. laughed. "You're a blast. Where are you this next period, I asked. I'll tell you how to get there."

"Algebra. Mr. Prestwick."

"So'm I. He's in the basement. We'd better hurry." They ran down the four flights of stairs. As they reached the bottom, a book slipped off the top of B.B.'s pile and fell in front of him. He stumbled over it and crashed against the white concrete wall. When he stood up, his forehead was bleeding profusely. He pulled a spotless white handkerchief from his blazer pocket and held it to his head as they hurried into the classroom.

"Now I know I'm in love," thought Elizabeth Lamb — boys at her former school had never carried a clean handkerchief (or even a used one). Mr. Prestwick was taking attendance. Some of the students were obviously in forms above the Third. He glanced at the two of them as they entered.

"Hello, Elizabeth Lamb," he said with a smile. His memory was excellent, she thought, since she had been introduced to him many months before. "But he's got my name in his book," she remembered. He looked searchingly at her forehead, which was fairly well healed but still showed red scratches.

Then he regarded B.B., who took his handkerchief from his face as they found chairs. "Someone out there attempting mass infanticide?" Mr. Prestwick inquired. "I've often been tempted, but — oh, well. To work."

Elizabeth Lamb shared B.B.'s copy of *Algebra, Structure and Method*. They started with a diagnostic test in arithmetic before beginning the chapter they were studying, on factors and exponents. Elizabeth Lamb sighed. Mr. Prestwick heard her.

"You've missed our discussions on the history of algebra, introduction of numerals and expressions, variables and expressions, and order of operations, Elizabeth Lamb," he said. "You'll be confused today." He handed her a textbook. "Read up to where we are now — you can get your own text this afternoon — and I'll go over what you've read if you'll be at my house at three. No, wait; I have an appointment at three. How about four-thirty, after crew practice?"

"I could, but there's a Student Council meeting at five, and

I have to be there."

"Well, we'll see how much we can cover in thirty minutes. Now just read. Elsa, give me the formula for the sum, S of the first n positive integers."

Elizabeth Lamb, reading, was interested to find that "algebra" came from a Moorish word, *al-jabr*, meaning — "reduction?" she wondered. That and the explanation of how the equal sign originated were more interesting than the mathematical formulas. "I'm just more verbal than mathematical," she murmured. She struggled though the assigned pages, finding that what small amount of algebra she had studied at Greene Country Day was helping her, but only at the beginning. "This will be impossible," she thought gloomily. "It will take a lot of prayers to St. Jude" — her visits to the Catholic mission in Pakistan had given her some orientation in the faith — "to get me through this. No wonder those upper-formers waited till now to take it." She was relieved when the class ended, and also hungry.

She hurried to the boys' dining hall, waving a welcome to Josas who was approaching across the green. B.B. ran to catch up with them and Caitlin joined him. They found empty seats at one of the long tables and put their possessions on them. Elizabeth Lamb looked around her.

The room was very large, with light plaster walls between oak beams. The hanging chandeliers were of old brass. The floor was of ancient wide dark planks, and the heavy refectory tables and chairs matched them in color. The long windows were curtained with faded English chintz in pleasing floral patterns. There was an enormous fireplace in the wood-panelled wall at the far end of the room, above which hung a large portrait of a man.

"Much more a traditional school dining hall than the girls'," she thought, "And I like it better." Caitlin, Josas and B.B. were already getting food from a steam table in the middle of the hall that was presided over by two short, dark men in white shirts and aprons.

As she took a plate and dubiously surveyed a large platter of something covered with a layer of mashed potatoes, Mark appeared at her side. "First time a girl eats here, she has to pay respects to Father Fitzgerald, Our Founder," he told her impressively. He took her arm and started to lead her to the fireplace. B.B. looked up from the food and said, "Hey, wait a minute," but Caitlin put her hand on his shoulder and firmly shook her head. She and B.B. followed the two, who now stood gazing up at the picture.

It was a three-quarters portrait of a middle-aged man with tonsured head, stern, lined face and a tight, thin mouth. He wore a black cassock and was seated in a chair placed in front of a wall of stone, his hands resting in his lap. His right hand covered his left, and its index finger was extended in a relaxed fashion. Behind him was a large open window that displayed, far below, the grounds of the school, with the Abenaki River, several crewed shells on it, prominent in the landscape.

"Handsome, isn't it?" Mark asked. "And you see how he's indicating the source of his greatest pride and pleasure?" He smirked, waiting for her to blush.

The forefinger, Elizabeth Lamb had quickly realized, through some vagary of the artist, could be thought to be directed at the sitter's groin. She followed the line of the finger. "Oh, yes; I see," she said brightly. "He's pointing at the shells. I was told crew was his favorite thing. Thank you, Mark, for showing the portrait to me." Several boys eating nearby laughed loudly in appreciation. Mark, with an exclamation of disgust, turned away.

Back at the table, Caitlin told her, "That's an initiation rite, sort of. Most girls get all upset and turn red. The boys love it, the jerks."

"I didn't," said Josas, who was still hesistating between green beans and a bowl of salad. "Not that I *could* blush" — Caitlin looked embarassed — "but one of the chandeliers was out and it was rainy and dark and I couldn't see what the boy was talking about. He was Bermewjan, too; some stupid fatten Arab of a Fifth Former! So I just said, 'Enh-ennhh; just what I'd axpact,' and now every time he sees me, he's real gribble to me."

She laughed happily after they all sat down and she began to eat her shepherd's pie with appetite. Elizabeth Lamb sighed, not only at Josas' lapse but also at the dish, which she detested. "I wonder if

Father Fitzgerald's mouth was really so mean," she murmured as she gingerly tasted her lunch.

"You know how Sargent defined a portrait," Caitlin informed her. "He said it was a painting of a person in which there was always a little something wrong with the mouth."

"What's 'gribble'?" B.B. asked Josas.

"Oh, 'mean' — 'disagreeable,'" she answered. "If all the new girls were warned by the old ones, they wouldn't be humbugged and the boys wouldn't do it just-for-the-purpose."

"Just for the what?" Caitlin asked.

"Just to cause trouble, be difficult," Josie answered. "And 'humbugged' is 'bothered' *and* I absolutely will stop it, Elizabeth Lamb. I just get carried away."

"I like to hear new expressions," B.B. said pleasantly. "Tell me some more, Josas." Josie obliged. Elizabeth Lamb found the pie surprisingly good. "It's got garlic in it," she told Caitlin.

"Garlic's only good for keeping out vampires," Caitlin told her. "But it's not as bad as usual. I think Mr. Pella up at our kitchen is having some influence down here."

"What do you know about vampires?" asked Elizabeth Lamb, as Josas came back with another plate of food.

Vampires and Bermudian slang entertained their group for the rest of the meal, which ended with rice pudding, eagerly taken by Josas and B.B. and disdained by Caitlin and Elizabeth Lamb, who handed over their portions. "That shows you two were properly brought up," B.B. told them. "Children raised on wholesome nursery food hate it, but I never got rice pudding. I grew up on cheese and biscuits and apples for dessert."

"For me," Josie told them, "it was potato crisps and bananas." She and B.B. grinned at each other.

There were several boys at the table who had joined in the discussion of vampires and also listened with interest to Josas' slang explanations. Now they went back to talking about their early-morning scuba lesson.

"Mr. Prestwick is terrific," one said. "He's so good he makes me dizzy," a black boy answered. "That guy knows everything and says it so fast I can hardly follow. My head was just about floating this morning."

"That was a curse, Joe," another said, not entirely joking. "Not Prestwick's fast talk. You were using Colket's special million-dollar gear and you know what they say about 'dead men's shoes.' I thought they'd sent it back to his people with the rest of his stuff. But you know Colket was no buddy of yours."

"No, he called me 'damned nigger' more than once," Joe said calmly. "Still, I think Mr. Prestwick is too fast with us novices."

"That's because you're of an inferior race," a Scandinavian-looking boy told him. "*I* had no trouble." Joe drawled: "That's because you're a thick-headed Swede." Elizabeth Lamb gasped with fright, but evidently Joe and the blond boy were friends; they exchanged mock punches and departed with Joe's arm on the other boy's shoulder.

The bus made a fast trip to the girls' campus but Elizabeth Lamb had difficulty finding Mrs. Farnum's first-floor Biblical Literature classroom. It proved to be somewhat hidden at the end of a short hall whose entrance she had twice run past. The door was open so she entered quickly, and breathlessly took a seat beside a girl she finally recognized as Leigh Urson, the redhead from the dorm next to hers. Leigh looked different in her uni and she was slumped despondently in her chair. The circles under her eyes matched her favorite color.

"What're you doing here?" Elizabeth Lamb asked. "I thought this was a Third Form course." Despite her low tone, several students turned and frowned at her.

"Their asinine scheduling kept it till my last year," Leigh whispered. "So I've got six courses this year and they're all tough, especially this one, because the teacher's berserk. There's two Sixth Form boys here they messed up on, too."

She yawned. "God, I'm tired," she muttered.

"Why?"

"Jerry Garcia got loose somehow and I was up all night looking for him. Lara Jane and Molly and Liz say they're going to sleep with the lights on till I get him back in his cage. They're furious."

"Cage? Who's Jerry Garcia?"

"My tarantula. He's perfectly harmless. They're just neurotic," —

and in a louder tone — "Porter, stop glaring at me. I can hear Electra's thunderous approach — quiet; she's coming now." She murmured to Elizabeth Lamb: "She waits till we're all here, so she can catch us talking, or breaking the light fixtures, or having intercourse, or something. She loves giving hours. She's brilliant but utterly weird."

Mrs. Farnum shut the door quietly behind her and strode heavily in a slow, stately manner to her desk. She was a tall, massive woman with a large, white, perfectly expressionless face which was devoid of any cosmetic. She wore huge tortoise-shell-rimmed spectacles, their glass so thick that her eyes could scarcely be discerned behind them. Her long, coarse black hair, widely streaked with grey, was pulled severely back into an untidy knot.

She swept the room with one glance and marked her attendance book. She then directed the spectacles at Elizabeth Lamb.

"The Headmaster" — she spoke her husband's title in a suitably hushed and impressive tone — "told me you had arrived, Miss Worthington. I am very glad to meet you.

"The class' assignment for today was to read the story of Cain and Abel, the mythic 'first murder' of the many related in the Bible." She walked to Elizabeth Lamb and presented her with an open book. "Read these two pages before we begin our discussion. The rest of you may take the time to re-read." She went to a window and stood with her back to them.

"She's not usually so gracious," Leigh murmured. "You related to those Lambs who gave the infirmary, or something?"

"No way," Elizabeth Lamb murmured back. "Please don't talk. She turned her head and looked at me. I don't need any hours building rock walls."

"Now," Mrs. Farnum said presently, "this is a short and deceptively simple story. There is a murder; it is fratricide but the writer does not emphasize that. It is irrational: Cain does not kill for hire, nor does he expect to get his brother's sheep. Nor has Abel wronged Cain. And the murder is not punished by man, but by God and nature.

"So, Miss Urson. Why did the murder occur?"

"The first son syndrome?" Leigh ventured. "Cain was jealous of

Abel because he was ignored after his brother's birth?"

"Possibly. Mr. Andersen?"

"I say the same."

"A cop-out, Mr. Andersen. I would guess you and Miss Urson are only children — no siblings to relate to?"

Both Leigh and the Andersen boy nodded in agreement.

"Miss Worthington. Was Cain his 'brother's keeper'?"

"God and the Bible seem to think so. But, Mrs. Farnum, although I sort of agree with Leigh and — ah — Mr. Andersen, I really think the reason for the murder was just plain envy. For some reason, Cain believed Abel was *really* better than he, not just that he thought he was treated better. God seemed to be telling him to buck up and do the best he could and not feel inferior and it would all be okay."

"Very perceptive. Yes, envy. One of the Seven Deadly Sins. Can anyone tell me the other six?"

A girl raised her hand. "Anger, avarice, gluttony, lust, pride and sloth."

"And how do you know them? Most people can name only five or six."

The girl blushed. "I read an old novel whose plot was based on them."

"Ah, well; knowledge comes from many directions. Suppose you all look up the Seven Deadly Sins and learn them by tomorrow."

Since everyone in the class had obviously written them down as they had been recited, Leigh murmured to Elizabeth Lamb: "You'll find she's a woman known for never taking 'yes' for an answer."

A large, muscular boy with hair cropped very short raised his hand. "Why isn't murder one of the Seven Deadly Sins? To get back to the lesson," he added pointedly.

"Perhaps because sometimes it is justified," Mrs. Farnum answered casually. All her students gasped increduously. "Murder is ever justified?" the boy asked, frowning.

"Yes, Mr. Garde — well, perhaps I should qualify that by saying that murder when it is the assassination of a heinous being or committed because the victim might intend to harm you in some way, may be justified." She smiled calmly around at the amazed faces.

"But it's forbidden in the Ten Commandments," Mr. Garde protested. Mrs. Farnum ignored him and nodded to a girl who raised her hand. "Yes, Miss Cassidy?"

"You might say Judas murdered Jesus, but Jesus set himself up for it; He intended His death should happen. Do you suppose Judas went to heaven?" Leigh giggled inaudibly and whispered, "She's trying to get Electra off the subject — whatever the subject *is*."

"You would have to ask a clergyman," Mrs. Farnum answered the girl. "It would also be a factor if Judas believed there *was* a Heaven. We don't know that."

"I said she had a good mind," Leigh whispered. "She's saying that if you don't believe in something as a reality, it can't exist for you." Elizabeth Lamb pondered this, and also pondered why Mrs. Farnum never seemed to hear Leigh's whispers. "It's because you can barely hear her when she speaks normally," she decided.

The boy sitting next to Mr. Garde, who was so like him in appearance he might almost have been his brother, had been quiet, his forehead furrowed in thought and his mouth tense. Now he spoke, seeming to want to get off the subject of murder and/or Heaven. "There are clergy*women*, now, too," he observed. "Four women priests were ordained in Philadelphia in July, by the Episcopal bishop. As you know, of course, Mrs. Farnum," he added politely. His voice was very deep.

This was surprising news to Elizabeth Lamb, who had, in Pakistan, heard little of the world that summer. "Those things called T-shirts and now women priests," she thought. "I wonder what else happened." Aloud, she asked curiously, "Will they preach, do you suppose, Mrs. Farnum?"

" 'A woman preaching is like a dog's walking on his hind legs,' " she was answered. " 'It is not done well but you are surprised to see it done at all.' Tell me tomorrow who said that, Mr. Cornwall. Since you brought up the subject, you, especially, should be interested.

"And, by the way, Mr. Cornwall, the Episcopal House of Bishops declared the ordination of the women priests invalid

127

a month later, so we must wait and see."

The other members of the class also made a note of the quotation, all except Elizabeth Lamb who had decided that Biblical Literature was the course she would try to drop. "Her mind goes back and forth too quickly," she thought. "I can't cope with this my first year here. I can understand what that boy at lunch meant when he said Mr. Prestwick's fast talk got him all confused."

Mrs. Farnum's mind now returned to the day's assignment. "Murder," she reflected. "We began by speaking of the murder of Abel by Cain." And then it wandered off again: "Do you know," she asked, "that it has been said the promise of people, or tribes, or nations must be judged on how they use force against those weaker than they?" "'Cut the cackle and come to the 'osses,'" a boy behind Elizabeth Lamb murmured almost inaudibly. Aloud, he asked, "Do you mean how they use force against murderers, Mrs. Farnum?"

She only frowned thoughtfully. "But the tribe, or the family, of Cain didn't use any force against him," a girl offered, in bewildered tones. "And God didn't either. He just put a mark on him so no one would kill him. He protected Cain."

"I was thinking of the Philistines," Mrs. Farnum replied, with absolutely no pertinence that Elizabeth Lamb could see. "I have British acquaintances among some archaeologists who are exploring three-thousand-year-old ruins in southern Israel. They say the Philistines — and you know the term 'philistine' means someone who lacks culture and refinement — actually were the creators of a sophisticated society that endured for six centuries."

"But you were talking about force, Mrs. Farnum," Mr. Cornwall protested. "The Philistines killed King Saul and stole the Ark of the Covenant, didn't they?"

"But they dominated the Holy Land," Mrs. Farnum answered vaguely. "They had a monopoly on iron-making and they controlled olive oil production. Olive oil was vital in those days." She paused. "I don't think they produced any literature, though," she added.

A girl raised her hand. "Are we supposed to be taking notes on *this*?" she asked, somewhat disrespectfully. "Did Cain kill Abel for olive oil, maybe? It's not in the Bible."

Mrs. Farnum's mind returned from the Philistines. "We'll continue the discussion tomorrow," she said. "For tonight, read your next chapter, the story of Noah, which is a mythic reality, *not* an historical reality, as you must realize."

Ignoring a hand raised in protest, she looked down at the old-fashioned watch pinned to her capacious bosom. "We have a half-hour to go, but I'm dismissing you now, since I have a great deal to do to prepare for the Third Form reception tonight." She rose and thundered towards the door, where she turned and said: "You may remain here and do your reading or go to the library."

Leigh slumped farther down in her seat and closed her eyes. Then she shook herself and got up, saying, "No rest for the wicked. I'd better go look for Jerry Garcia."

As she left with Elizabeth Lamb, the two look-alike boys stood aside to let them pass. "Oh, Dan," Leigh said to the boy who had asked why murder was not one of the Seven Deadly Sins, "this is Elizabeth Lamb Worthington. She's a Third Former but she's rooming with Faith, so you'll be seeing her. Dan Garde, Elizabeth Lamb." The boy and Elizabeth Lamb nodded politely.

Leigh coldly regarded the other boy. "And, Porter, don't you ever look at me again that way as if *my* voice were loud. Why, in our room I often hear Dan, here, sounding as if he were right in Faith's room. Which," she added sweetly, "I know he can't be; or you either, sometimes. You're both just outside waiting for her, of course." Dan blushed. Porter looked at Leigh with dislike.

"Or at least I hope you are," Leigh went on in her thin, light tone. "If Molly, our dorm prefect, or Miss Greenwell, who's on the other side, should ever hear anything, it could be rough. For Faith, too.

"You're Senior Prefect of Boys, Porter. A word to the wise." She smiled sweetly and took Elizabeth Lamb's arm as they walked rapidly away.

"That boy, Dan, is 'Frederick' in *Penzance*," Elizabeth Lamb said. "I saw him at rehearsal last night. Josas said he sort of goes with Faith. Who's the other one?"

"Oh, sorry. A class with Electra blows my mind and I forget

my manners. He's Porter Cornwall, Dan's best friend *and* Senior Prefect. As you heard. His bass voice got him the role of Sergeant of Police in *Penzance*. Also a top rower. A BMOC."

"So's Dan, isn't he? Lara Jane said he was brilliant."

"He is. And stroke on Boys' Crew. But if he doesn't smarten up, he'll be booted, along with lil' ol' Faith. See you." She raced towards Falls Dormitory.

Elizabeth Lamb ran for the Dean's Office. An efficient-looking middle-aged woman sat at the desk looking through a manila folder. Elizabeth Lamb read the name on a standing plaque on the desk. "I'm Elizabeth Lamb Worthington, Mrs. Jones," she said, "and — " She rapidly explained her predicament.

"As a matter of fact," Mrs. Jones replied, "I was just checking your records. Of course you may drop Bib. Lit. and take it next year. I'll speak to the Dean and the people in Scheduling, who seem to be getting more and more disorganized.

"And I would advise you to take only four courses, this first term. What about dropping French I? From your record I think you could take an exam in it and possibly go to French II next year."

"I think I'll keep French I. I know some French, so it won't be really hard, but there's probably stuff I don't know. Oh, thank you, Mrs. Jones! Could you tell me where the bookstore is? I think I have time before French to get my textbooks. Mrs. Farnum let us go early."

Mrs. Jones smiled wryly, nodding her understanding, and sped Elizabeth Lamb on her way. Her purchases took longer than she had anticipated and by the time, burdened with four heavy books, she reached the French classroom, she was late. The teacher, a strikingly attractive young blonde woman dressed with more chic than Elizabeth Lamb had so far observed of any female at St. Augustine's, turned from the chalkboard, raising inquiring brows. Elizabeth Lamb blushed.

"I'm Elizabeth Lamb Worthington," she blurted. "I got here only yesterday and I'm sorry to say I took longer just now getting my books than I thought I would."

The young woman motioned her to a seat. "I am Mme. Hoffer-man," she said. "Have you studied French before, Elizabeth?"

"Je vivais à Paris de l'âge de deux jusqu'a huit et j'allais à l'école là-bas. Avant cela, le concierge ou nous demeurions me garderait pendant que ma mère allait au travail. C'est lui qui m'a enseigne à lire. Il m'amuserait en me lisant les livres de ses enfants." She had answered rapidly; she stopped, out of breath, wondering if living in Paris from two until eight, going to school there and being read children's books by the concierge, while her mother was at work, qualified as "studying French."

Mme. Hofferman sighed. She spoke as rapidly: *"Ces imbéciles au bureau de cette espèce d'école! Ils m'envoient une élève qui parle français mieux que moi. Je leur conseillerai que vous serez mieux dans la classe de littérateur de M. Cranston. Mais, pour l'instant, afin de ne pas perdre un moment, je vous y enverrai. Allez à la salle numero 226, tout droit dans le couloir. Passe ce petit mot à M. Cranston, je vous en prie."* She quickly wrote a brief note, passed it to Elizabeth Lamb, and, with a friendly smile, waved her out.

Elizabeth Lamb walked slowly down the corridor to room 226, in complete agreement with Mme. Hofferman as to the imbecilic quality of mind that seemed to predominate in the scheduling office, and in hope that Mme. Hofferman could communicate with those in it. She doubted, though, that her French grammar and pronunciation were "at least as good" as the teacher's. "Although maybe it's so," she decided, "since Grandmother said once she'd read that no foreigner who had been *expensively* taught French ever spoke it correctly. And I wasn't 'expensively taught'; I just picked it up as I went along. But do I know enough to handle this French literature class?"

Just as she reached the designated door, she remembered that Mme. Hofferman had said that the class was taught by "Mr. Cranston." Before she knocked, she peered through the glass pane for a look at the author of the acclaimed *Marianne*.

A broad-shouldered man in his fifties slouched easily in his chair behind a desk at the front of the room. His eyes, below bushy grey brows, were narrowed in amusement, evidently at something one of his students, who sat in casually-arranged armchairs scattered about, was saying. His face was wide and pleasant, with laugh-crinkles around the eyes and his turned-up mouth. "He has a sort of Truman Capote smile," she thought, "very appealing, though something about his chin reminds me of Kirk Douglas, and I never liked him."

He stood up, stretching as he answered the student, and she noticed that not only was he very tall but that he was one of the masters who chose to teach in a shirt and tie although his male pupils were forced, by rule, to retain their blazers. "A non-conformist," she thought. "Maybe he'll let me in the class, although everyone else seems to be at least seventeen."

As he laughed and finished speaking, he glanced toward the door. He strode quickly to it and opened it. Wordlessly, Elizabeth Lamb handed him the note, which he held with one hand while with the other he ushered her into the room. Still reading the note, he picked up a book from his desk and handed it to her. His voice was slow and pleasing: "*Ah, je comprends. Lisez cette page ci à haute voix, commencant ici.*" His finger indicated a paragraph.

Her voice shaking, she began to read from the French text. As she read, her confidence increased and she was actually beginning to enjoy the performance when, after a paragraph, Mr. Cranston interrupted.

"*Alors, mademoiselle. Arrêtez-vous là. C'est bien. Et maintenant traduisez ce que vous avez lu en anglais.*"

Producing the English translation of the French she had read was a little harder, but she went through it with her customary *élan*.

Mr. Cranston motioned her to stop. "*C'est assez, mademoiselle. Madame Hofferman, comme toujours, avait raison. Prenez cette place-là. Nous avons commence ce cours en lisant 'Le Petit prince,' comme vous voyez, mais nous allons lire des oeuvres de Moliere, de Baudelaire, de Sartre et des autres.*

"*Hélène, continuez la lecture ou Mademoiselle Lamb l'a laissée.*"

Elizabeth Lamb sank thankfully back into her chair, aware that Mr. Cranston's standing, added to Mme. Hofferman's recommendation, would insure that her French course was changed. "But this is going to be hard," she thought, as the girl called Helen continued translating. "Maybe I should just go to the office and get down to only four courses, as Josie has."

But as the class continued, she changed her mind. Mr. Cranston was a brilliant teacher and also something of a wit, both in French and in the English to which he often switched, the class with him. When a reader could not translate *la poulie* and another student, although also unfamiliar with the word, facetiously suggested "the chicken," Mr. Cranston clutched his hair and announced, "There is a low threshhold of wit in this class. And that 'chicken' is an idea whose time is dumb! Miss Lamb, would there be a chicken in a well?"

Elizabeth Lamb's mind had been wandering, as evidently he had realized. She had, as he strode about the room, been observing his clothes. "Handmade shoes," she had been thinking, "or, as Grandmother would say, 'bespoke.'" Now she jerked her attention back to the book he had lent her. "*Non,*" she stammered, and in English: "I don't know, but — maybe — 'the pulley'?"

Mr. Cranston beamed. "Now, that is an idea whose time has come. And who said — "

"Victor Hugo," finished Dan Garde's bored voice. Mr. Cranston had obviously used the quotation before and inquired as to its origin. She turned and smiled at Dan.

Mr. Cranston was not smiling. "I have noticed that you have, Mr. Garde, an air of *je ne sais quoi.* Although on me, it has the effect Woody Allen might express as *je ne peau pas.* Can you translate the latter phrase?"

"*Je ne sais pas,*" Dan muttered. "I don't know." Another student volunteered, "Something about skin?" Elizabeth Lamb raised her hand.

"I heard people say it when I lived in Paris," she offered. "It doesn't translate exactly but it sort of means 'I don't care' — 'I don't get you' — 'I can't put up with' — but it would be followed by — ah, I forget. Maybe we get 'no skin off my nose' from it."

Mr. Cranston produced his elfin smile. "I see you don't belong to the Anti-Defination League, as many of my students do."

"Sometimes you confuse us," Dan said, and then blushed as the smile was directed at him.

"If I confuse you, then I'm a good teacher," Cranston replied.

Porter Cornwall, beside whom Elizabeth Lamb was sitting, murmured under his breath, "Our parents pay you to teach us, not confuse us."

Mr. Cranston, who had been writing the next day's assignment on the board behind him, turned, smiling. "Not enough, Porter," he murmured in return. "Not enough.

"Now, Miss Lamb, as I have told the rest of the class, when you are given a written assignment, it must be produced exactly when due; it must be typewritten or clearly printed; it must be completely correct as to punctuation and spelling. Or else the paper is not accepted. As to spelling, I am aware that it cannot be taught since I have been a hopeless speller all my life, but I have learned to use, in correcting papers — and you can use in writing them — a wonderful work known as *le dictionnaire. Comprendez-vous?*

"*La classe est fini. Bonjour.*" He was first out the door, after swift, conciliatory pats on the crew-cut heads of Dan and Porter. Elizabeth Lamb was close behind him. She went to the store for a copy of *Le Petit prince* and then raced to her room where Josie was anxiously waiting. "Be sure you have your wallet in your pocket," she directed Josie, throwing her books on her desk and quickly smoothing down her hair.

"You're not very late," Josie gasped as they ran down the corridor, out its far door and around the north end of the dormitory. "You think it's okay to come with me?"

"We'll soon see," Elizabeth Lamb gasped back. "If only we could use the hall door by our room, we'd be there now. Stupid rule! Is this his house, I hope?"

Josie nodded as she knocked timidly on the white-painted Dutch door, the upper half of which was open. "And Miss McMurtrie is next and the last, down near our end of the dorm, is Mr. Cranston's."

Through the open half of the door, a neat, masculine-looking living room was visible at the side of the small hall. Mr. Prestwick, wearing a sweatshirt, sweatpants and sneakers, came running down the stairs. "You brought a friend?" he asked Josas, indicating that they sit on a small beige linen sofa. He drew up a brown leather chair and sat facing them across a large light walnut coffee table on which were several figures of elephants in ebony and an ancient-looking volume bound in tattered crimson that was protected by a glass case.

Both Elizabeth Lamb and Josas opened their mouths to speak, but before they could, Mr. Prestwick raised a calming hand. "Josas," he said, "you first. Lara Jane told me you say you didn't take Faith O'Malley's money, any of it. Is that so?" Josie nodded, swallowing nervously.

Elizabeth Lamb, producing the uneasy smile she used when she was ill at ease and that her grandmother had dubbed her "society smile," said: "Josie, show Mr. Prestwick your wallet. Please look through it, Mr. Prestwick."

Before he could do so, steps approached from outside and a woman's voice called clearly, "Harry, I wanted, darling, to tell you — "

Mr. Prestwick rose hastily and went to the hall. "No, Theo," he was heard to say loudly, "Darlene's finished and gone. I believe she's over at Tim's house. Please excuse me; I'm conferring with some students."

"What — " began the woman, and then dropped her voice. Mr. Prestwick spoke softly and although Elizabeth Lamb strained to hear, the words were indistinguishable. He returned and sat down saying coolly, "Miss McMurtrie is looking for the woman who cleans some of the faculty houses. Now, what about Josas' money?"

Josas and Elizabeth Lamb had exchanged knowing glances but now they composed their faces and Elizabeth Lamb spoke slowly and calmly. "I must have realized last night at the *Penzance* rehearsal that Josie couldn't have spent Faith's two-dollar bill at the Snack Shop; or, at least, you could prove there's a strong doubt she did. I guess Lara Jane's told you that that's what makes Faith suspect Josie.

"But I didn't really get it straight until this morning. I wondered if you could ask the man at the shop — " She went on confidently.

When she finished, a relieved Josas was smiling widely. Mr. Prestwick asked one question and then he, too, smiled. He handed back the wallet. "Well," he said, "that was a quick and concise deduction. To quote my favorite author, Miss Lamb, you are 'Young in limb, in judgement old.'

"There are," he went on, "or so Lara Jane tells me, two cases to come up before the Student Council hears yours. I'll be there a little after five, Josas, to go in with you and I'll speak for you."

He picked up a textbook from the table beside his chair. "Now, Elizabeth Lamb, I'll go over a few things with you to set you up for class tomorrow, but you'd better come over here at six-thirty tomorrow night, when I'll have more time to get you up to date on what you've missed. You, Josas, can stay; even fifteen minutes of review can only help you."

He had explained for twenty minutes — with Josas only half-listening as she gazed at Elizabeth Lamb with large, grateful eyes — before he shut the book and, with them, made a hasty exit, saying he was already late for crew practice. "Come over tomorrow, remember, Elizabeth Lamb," he said as he got into his little VW that was parked at the end of his driveway. Josas patted Elizabeth Lamb's hand affectionately and annouced that, although her ankle still hurt, she was going to the girls' basketball court to work out her relief before she started studying.

"It's not over yet," Elizabeth Lamb warned, "but I think it'll be okay. See you there. The meeting's at five, remember." She attempted to enter Room 13's bathroom but Faith's voice loudly advised her to get lost. She snatched up her notebook and some books and ran to the bathroom down the corridor.

A girl was at a washbasin cleaning her contact lenses, and a happy voice sang calypso above the rush of water from one of the shower cubicles at the far end of the room. As Elizabeth Lamb flushed the w.c. and ran to another washbasin, the singing turned into piercing screams. She quickly dried her hands and ran out the door wondering why the girl at the other basin was staring at her in near-sighted horror and why the girl in the shower had turned it off and begun shouting imprecations.

A corner in the boys' library gave her seclusion while she quickly did Mr. Sullivan's assigned poetry references. She struggled as best she could with the Latin and algebra and biology and read ahead in *The Little Prince*. The "original poem or verse" required by Mr. Sullivan caused her then to sit for fifteen minutes staring into space.

In desperation, she began to look up the definition of "poetry" in a dictionary, but the first word she came upon, as happens so often when one consults a reference book, was another: "parody". She read the definition. "This studying at St. Augustine's is so hard," she murmured aloud in despair. "How will I ever make it through here?"

She glanced at Dorothy Parker's "Resumé" which she had copied into her notebook, as assigned, and inspiration hit. "She names all the methods of suicide as so unpleasant 'you might as well live,'" she said aloud. "Maybe I could do a parody of her 'Resumé.'" She thought. She began to write.

When she was finished, after having made many changes and corrections, she was pleased with herself. She looked around the library, hoping to find B.B. to show him her masterpiece, and did indeed spot him. He was standing in the front of a large alcove beside a long rectangular table, which was surrounded by chairs in which a few boys and girls were seated. As he beckoned to her, others came in and took chairs. One of the librarians, in a firm, carrying voice, announced: "All except members of the Student Council will please leave. The Council meeting will begin as soon as the room is cleared."

As Elizabeth Lamb seated herself beside B.B., she glanced through the double glass doors, through which students and the staff were leaving, into the library's little anteroom, which had benches on which three slumped figures were sitting, staring forlornly at the Council table. Mr. Prestwick and another man joined them.

Porter Cornwall and Joylene Treble were side by side at the head of the table, conferring with Lara Jane who, at Joylene's left, was consulting a large journal. Elizabeth Lamb glanced around at the almost two dozen members, most of them unknown to her except her dorm prefect, Molly Peale. "Who are they all?" she asked B.B. "I know Joylene and Cornwall are the two Senior Prefects."

"Dorm prefects, elected form prefects, the boy and girl who head the social club, the vergers of both chapels, the dining hall heads — Father Farnum picks *them* for their loud voices, I hear — and — " He stopped as Porter banged a gavel on the table and

137

announced that the Council was now in session.

"After the minutes of the May meeting last term are read," he said, "we have no business today except three disciplinary cases. Lara Jane, would you read — " He stopped as Joylene gently placed her hand on his.

"I know Porter," she said sweetly, "that, by ancient custom or masculine right, or some such thing, it is the prerogative of the Senior Prefect of Boys to conduct the first meeting, but don't you think perhaps you should ask everyone to identify himself, since some of our members are new? Himself *or* herself," she added with a wry smile.

Porter mumbled that he guessed it was okay. It having been done, Lara Jane then read the minutes of the previous meeting, speaking in a strained voice and clearing her throat frequently. Porter, who seemed to delight in doing so, banged his gavel again and requested that someone show in George Curtis, the first case.

A small, pale, bespectacled boy entered, accompanied by the man who had been in the anteroom with Mr. Prestwick, and who was evidently Curtis' faculty advisor. Joylene announced that Dean LeStrange had been informed by the prefect of Hope Dormitory that George Curtis had been seen by her in the room of one of the dorm's members. A murmur went around the table. "Very serious," B.B. muttered to Elizabeth Lamb, "to be in a girl's room. Could be they'll — we'll — recommend to the Headmaster that he get booted. And I'm told Father Farnum usually does what the Council recommends."

It was soon established that the hapless Mr. Curtis, a Third Former who looked about to faint, had gone to the dormitory to see a Fourth Form girl who was a friend of his in his home town, that he had asked where her room was and had gone to await her. He had then been observed, through the left-open door, by the Prefect, who had been summoned by the girl who had told him which room was his friend's.

His advisor argued poignantly that Mr. Curtis had had a distressing summer — he went into details — had not completely read the rule book and so was unaware of his heinous offense. Mr. Curtis, gasping, confirmed this and was lead, trembling, from the library.

A long discussion ensued. A girl obviously destined for the Bar maintained that ignorance of the law was no excuse while a round-faced boy with a sweet, saintly expression argued for mercy. "Verger of the Episcopal chapel," B.B. murmured. "Prays there a lot."

Mercy prevailed and it was recommended that Mr. Curtis be given two hours dishwashing duty in the boys' kitchen and be put on Social Probation: no appearances on the girls' campus for the rest of the term except at the classes he had there.

The second culprit came in by himself, a tall boy swaggering a little and nodding in a familiar manner to Porter, who sternly ignored him. "He's a big buddy of Cornwall's, and a member of crew," B.B. whispered.

Porter announced that Father Farnum had seen the boy hitch-hiking to Bar Harbor the previous Wednesday. The boy firmly claimed that he was only attempting to see *Macbeth*, which was playing at the movie theatre there. Since Miss Curtain planned to put it on in the spring, he said, and had promised him the part of Macduff, he was trying to enlarge his experience of acting. He handed Porter a note from Miss Curtain verifying that she had made the promise.

The note was handed around and made quite an effect on what were obviously theatrically-minded Council members, including Joylene. "Wait a minute," said Lara Jane, frowning. "On Wednesday? No way, Stewart. In late September, the Criterion Theatre is closed except for weekends. We did play *Macbeth* on a Wednesday in late August and — hey — you saw it when Mr. Prestwick brought the crew over.

"I remember because you, as usual, threw your weight around at the candy counter. Nice try, though," she added admiringly, raising her brows and smiling slightly. "She really is getting awfully hoarse," Elizabeth Lamb thought.

"The plot sickens," B.B. said to her. "You sure the movie is closed on Wednesdays now, Lara Jane?" Porter asked heavily. "How do you know so much about it?"

"Because I worked at the counter all summer," she answered. "I'm a local, you know. And I remember their schedule. Didn't you see Stewart there with the rest of the crew, Porter?"

"No, I didn't," he answered curtly. Elizabeth Lamb raised her hand. "Lara Jane's right," she said. "My cousin Henry owns the theatre, so I know. I worked there at the counter two summers ago."

Lara Jane grinned at her. "Fellow travellers through hell," she said dramatically though huskily. Porter banged his gavel. A downcast Stewart was shown out.

His offense of lying to the Council was considered almost as bad as being AWOL, at least by the Council. It quickly decided that Stewart not only be confined to campus and be put on Disciplinary Probation for the rest of the term, but also be given 20 hours building walls. Elizabeth Lamb determined to be prudent and avoid getting near him for a while, and Lara Jane's thoughtful expression as she wrote down the recommendation indicated she might be making the same decision.

"The third case," Joylene said, "is a matter of suspected theft, and the accuser wishes to be present, if the Council permits." After discussion, it was permitted and Faith came in, followed by Josas, whose hand tightly clenched the sleeve of Mr. Prestwick's sweatshirt.

Faith was directed to speak first and said that a substantial sum of her money had disappeared, that among it was a two-dollar bill, that two-dollar bills were not all that common, and that, after she had reported her loss, Dean LeStrange had made a search and held inquiries. "And she found," Faith said looking at Josas with dislike, "that this roommate of mine had spent a two-dollar bill at the Snack Shop."

Josas tearfully denied that she had ever touched any money of Faith's, "or ary other thing," and maintained that she had spent a two-dollar bill given her "for luck" by mistake, thinking it was a dollar until she received her change. Asked by Porter why she hadn't asked for the bill back, she began to weep and could be heard to say only that she was afraid to because "the man was so gribble."

"Unpleasant," Mr. Prestwick translated, stepping forward. "If the Council permits, may I ask Faith to show us the money she

140

has with her — the bills, that is."

Surprised, the members nodded at Faith, who was ostentatiously holding a handbag tightly with both hands, while she glanced sideways at Josas. Surprised in her turn, she opened the bag and threw a heap of crumpled bills on the table, keeping her eyes firmly on Josas.

Mr. Prestwick asked Josas for her wallet, and withdrew her slim pack of crisp bills, which he spread out and held up. "Joe, at the Snack Bar, tells me," he said, "that the bill Josas spent was just like these. He particularly noticed it because he gets so few two-dollar bills, and it was completely unwrinkled.

"And Faith's other roommate" — he nodded at Elizabeth Lamb — "tells me all Faith's bills she has seen have been crumpled. It was she, who hearing last night at a rehearsal in Madison that papier-mâché crumpled up to make real-looking rocks couldn't easily be smoothed out, realized that currency was much the same."

He took one of Josas' bills and crushed it in his hand. He put it on the table and asked if anyone could straighten it out so that it looked crisp and new. No one tried. "So," he finished, picking up the bill and attempting himself to unwrinkle it, "although the evidence is, and must be, circumstantial, it would seem to prove that it is impossible that Josas paid with a bill of Faith's."

"Unless, Mr. Prestwick," Porter said hesitantly, "Faith kept her two-dollar bill specially apart. Faith?"

Although Faith was red and furious, staring intently at Elizabeth Lamb, her mouth grim, she turned readily to Porter. "No, I didn't," she said firmly. "I didn't. I could lie and say I did, but *I* don't lie." She gathered up her money.

"But," she said more softly, "*somebody* stole it. That I know. And somebody's going to pay for it." She walked rapidly to the door. Molly Peale rose and ran after her.

"Of course someone stole money from her, if she says it is gone," Mr. Prestwick agreed. "But I don't think there's any proof that Josas took it." He gently placed his hand on Josas' shoulder and led her out. Molly returned to her chair. Porter looked around at the Council members. He sighed. "Anybody got anything to say?" he asked. No one answered. He tried again. "What did *you* say to Faith just now, Molly?"

"I told her to watch it," Molly answered readily. "In *my* dorm I won't stand for any ragging of underformers and, whatever we decide, Faith is the type — Faith is in such a state these days that she might take some action against her two roommates." She looked reassuringly at Elizabeth Lamb.

"She may be so upset about — well, we know it's about Jay — that maybe she only *thinks* her money was stolen," a boy suggested.

"It's possible," Porter agreed. "Dan Garde told me — he was Jay's roommate, you know — that the very day school opened somebody went through their room. Tore it all apart. Nothing was taken, that he could see, but he figured it was Faith looking for something to remember Jay by. She certainly was hit hard by his — accident."

Joylene was appalled. "But Dan should have reported this to his dorm prefect. Did he?"

"No, because, as I said, he thought it was only Faith."

"Maybe it was the same person who took Faith's money," someone suggested. "Maybe we've got a wave of ripping-off going on."

"Maybe so," Lara Jane said, coughing. "But it's not before us at this meeting. What do we do about what *is*?"

"I think the Third Former should get some hours," a girl decided. "If there is stealing going on, it's probably someone in the Third Form, and maybe making an example of her would deter it."

"Making an example of her for what?" asked the boys' verger. "It's not proved she took any money; it's really not certain any money *was* taken. Making an Isaac — a scapegoat — of her is more what you're asking for."

Everybody began to talk at once. Porter banged his gavel loudly. He looked at Elizabeth Lamb. "It seems to me," he said, nodding at her, "that Miss, ah — that this new person on the Council has pretty well proved that the Third Former couldn't have spent Faith's damned — miserable, I mean — two-dollar bill. So there's no proof against her. So let's forget it and it needn't go to Father Farnum. Okay?"

It was eventually so decided, although one recalcitrant voice pronounced that *both* Faith and Josas should be given hours, since all this had taken time and he, for one, had commitments — he was shouted down. Porter exercised his gavel again and declared the meeting closed.

"You were really awesome," B.B. told Elizabeth Lamb as they walked out together. He patted her shoulder. Much to her relief, she did not blush. Josie appeared from her hiding place behind a stone pillar on the library portico and ran up to them, her eyes eager.

"It's cool," B.B. reassured her. "They decided you didn't do it." Before Josie could do more than gasp, Molly appeared behind Elizabeth Lamb and told the other two she wanted a minute alone with her. Josie melted away but B.B. moved only a few feet and stood waiting.

"I know you didn't mean to do it, Elizabeth Lamb," Molly began, "but it's very serious. Mary could have been badly burned. And I remember reminding you myself and Joylene says she told you too, last spring. But Mary doesn't want to make a case of it — reporting it to LeStrange and so on — so Joylene and I think it'll suffice if I just sting you for two hours kitchen duty."

Elizabeth Lamb was bewildered. "Who's Mary? What'd I do?"

Molly sighed. "I know it's your first day and you've been rushed but you forgot to yell 'Flushing' and Mary was taking a shower. As we told you, the water turns scalding hot then, but she got out with only a slight burn on her shoulder."

"Oh, no! Yes, I remember I did. I just completely forgot to yell. But who's Mary? And what should I do?"

"Mary's that tall Jamaican, a Third Former. The other girl in the washroom told her who you were when Mary came out of the shower boiling mad, and when she heard it was you, Mary just laughed. But the other kid reported to me because it's a rule.

"All you have to do is tell Mary you're sorry. And don't forget again. You have to have some punishment, though, so report to the kitchen tomorrow morning at five-thirty. Tell Mr. Pella you have two hours to work off.

"And you showed up as just great in the meeting. Very impressive. Gunning to be the Third Form's Nancy Drew?"

With an affectionate hug and a laugh, she was off. B.B. returned.

"I heard," he said. They walked glumly towards the bridge. Elizabeth Lamb sank down to the bench running along it. She stretched out her legs, folded her arms and declared she just might jump into the Abenaki and end it all. "We've got to do that reception tonight; then I've got play rehearsal; I have more prep to do *and* now I have to get up at five tomorrow morning. I'm dead."

B.B. hesitated. He glanced around, then drew in a deep breath and sat beside her. He reached for her hand. "No, you're not," he said calmly. "A bad beginning makes a good ending, my mother says. And you've already made yourself quite a rep here, and in only a day and a half." Joylene, walking by with two other girls, looked casually at them, looked again, then flashed a grin at Elizabeth Lamb.

"Well," B.B. was still calm, "we've been observed. Now we're 'going out' together."

"Going out where?"

He laughed. "Actually, there's practically nowhere to 'go out.' But I guess we're set for the second Thursday in November. You'll have to ask me. And I'll accept."

"Ask you what? What happens the second Thursday in November — oh, that's right: it's the day they'll open the 1974 Beaujolais, the Nouveau Beaujolais, in France."

"You're confused, and no wonder. No, that's the *third* Thursday. My mother works for a wine merchant; that's why besides the cheese and apples I admitted, today at lunch, having for dessert, my brother and I always got a glass of wine, too. My mother figured, that way, we'd never be heavy drinkers.

"The second Thursday, here, is Sadie Hawkins Day. There's a dance, and girls ask boys."

"All right, I will. But why?"

He sighed. "I guess you never read comic strips. You've got a big hole in your education. Although, in the strip, I think Sadie Hawkins Day was in February. I forget."

"Well, I'm honored to ask you, B.B. You know, I like that name for you. 'Will' is nice, too, though."

He spoke with a pronounced British accent: "Well, really, Gwendolen, I must say that there are lots of other much nicer

144

names. I think 'Jack,' for instance, a charming name.'"

She stared at him. "Now," he prompted, "you say, sounding English: 'Jack?' No, there is very little music in the name Jack, if any at all, indeed. It does not thrill. It produces absolutely no vibrations. . . .'"

She did so. "What was that all about?" she asked. "Are you in a play?"

"Miss Curtain's doing *The Importance of Being Earnest* just before Christmas. I played 'Jack' in it at my old school. Why don't you try out for it, too? I'll tell you when."

Elizabeth Lamb had been conscious of steps crossing the bridge as he had recited. The steps had stopped behind her. She half-turned her head and was aware of a cloud of peony pink mohair on the bench, just a little away from her.

The mohair rose and moved to face them. "No need to try out!" Miss Curtain proclaimed. "I have found my 'Jack' and 'Gwendolen'! And both blond, too!" She peered intently at B.B. Elizabeth Lamb thought it was as like Miss Curtain to address a boy first as it was for her to walk about without the spectacles she obviously needed. "And you are?" he was asked.

"Will Dickinson. I'm a Third Former. I've played 'Jack' before, though, Miss Curtain."

"And successfully, I am sure, from what I just heard. And this young lady will be as superb as you. My first impressions are never, never wrong." She paused doubtfully. "Well, seldom wrong, I mean. You both will have delightful stage presence as well as the right accent and voice. And you thoroughly *look* the parts!"

She turned to examine Elizabeth Lamb closely. "Oh," she said glumly. Both had risen at her appearance. Elizabeth Lamb now stepped forward. "I'll be good and I won't fall down," she promised. "It was only that last night I was so tired after my terrible trip here with my aunt. I'm not much of a singer or dancer at any time, though."

Miss Curtain nodded sad agreement. "I'll still use you in *Penzance* but just for tonight, and your friend, too. Both the girls you were replacing have recovered amazingly quickly, so after tonight you'll be able to concentrate on *Earnest*, reading Will's and your parts together for a few weeks before we start rehearsals."

"Oh, thank you, Miss Curtain!" Elizabeth Lamb was enthusiastic as well as polite.

Miss Curtain took B.B.'s hand warmly, and nodded courteously to Elizabeth Lamb. "I'll see you both at the Headmaster's reception, won't I?" She turned away, but over her shoulder she said the first, and last, humorous thing Elizabeth Lamb ever heard from her: "Just *don't* tell me *Earnest* will close in New Haven. Hertford, Hampshire and the other one I can never remember are more likely."

Elizabeth Lamb laughed happily. "Well," she said to B.B., "I'd better catch that bus. See you tonight. Maybe Third Formers should show up in aprons, since we have to do all the work at this revelry."

• CHAPTER 7 •

There was a sound of revelry by night....

— Lord Byron

THE THIRD FORM GIRLS, feeling half-sick from a hastily-gulped dinner and a jolting van ride, disembarked at the back door of the Headmaster's house to find that the boys were already toiling under the whip of Mrs. Farnum. Elizabeth Lamb, whose apology to Mary had been graciously received, entered the kitchen with her and was amused to see the boys were swathed in large aprons above their regulation shirts, ties, and blazers.

"Welcome to Tara," a black boy murmured to them as he assembled little triangular sandwiches on a large silver tray. "Us field hands needs a few mo' helpers." The other boys headed out to bring in the supplies the girls' van had brought, but Mrs. Farnum seized the ties of B.B.'s apron and directed him to carry an enormous filled glass pitcher into the dining room and empty it into the bowl of pink punch.

"The *pink*," she emphasized, hastening after him. "I put a bit too

147

much grenadine in the adults' punch so we must dilute it with this water. The orange punch is for the students; remember that. There's too much alcohol in grenadine for young people.

"You," to Elizabeth Lamb and Mary, "get another pitcher of water and put it into the students' punch, and also some of the sliced oranges you'll find on the kitchen table." As they obliged, Mary muttered to Elizabeth Lamb: "There's no alcohol in grenadine, is there? I thought it was made from pomegranates. I bet the punch *we* get is mostly Kool-Aid. She's so stingy she won't give us a half-cup of grenadine to give it some taste!"

"I think it is only pomegranates," Elizabeth Lamb answered, staggering under the weight of a huge flat pan of frosted cake from the van that she was to cut into pieces. ("Very *small* pieces," Mrs. Farnum had directed.) "Don't they put it in Shirley Temples?"

"No talking," Mrs. Farnum shouted. "We must be brisk! Everything must be ready in the next ten minutes." Her crew rushed about as she stood commandingly in the midst of the melee, draped in what appeared to be a couch-cover made of silver metallic cloth. At times she raised one hand regally to point an admonishing finger at a clumsy helper.

"She looks like the Statue of Liberty in drag," Mary muttered, passing Elizabeth Lamb and Josas with a tray of red, white and amber decanters she had filled from jugs with labels that read only "wine."

"But wouldn't she be wearing men's clothes, in that case?" Elizabeth Lamb rejoined, pronouncing the last word as if it ended in "sh." They began to laugh helplessly and were banished to the living room to distribute paper cocktail napkins, coasters and ashtrays among the many little gilt-trimmed tables.

As she worked, Elizabeth Lamb observed the room. Josas had said that "on Sunday afternoons, sometimes, they have a few of us in for tea. There's music, and flowers, and the room is just awful dickty." Elizabeth Lamb thought that Josas' standards of what was "awful nice" were a bit generous. To her, the room was a mixture of what her caustic father would have described as "seventeenth century Spanish monastery wormwood combined with early twentieth century Chinese whorehouse."

Mary, who was now in the dining room slicing another cake, assisted by B.B., beckoned to them. She then walked over to the swinging door from the dining room to the kitchen and closed it just as an uproar followed a series of crashes from behind it. Mrs. Farnum could be heard screaming at her captive horde about carelessness, and "quickly, quickly, a mop, and some cloths. Sweep up that glass! Here, give that to me!" A loud hiccup followed her last words.

"I'm dying of thirst," Mary whispered, filling four cups with pink punch. "That creamed dried beef for dinner plus the heat in here is killing me. If only our dorms were half this warm!"

"We had dried beef, too," B.B. told her, draining his cup and refilling it. The three girls emptied theirs rapidly and he gallantly ladled more punch into them. This time they drank more slowly, but when B.B. proffered the ladle again — the war in the kitchen still happily continuing — Josas shook her head. "I feel half-hot," she said, as the other three emptied their cups a third time.

"It is hot in here; I just said so," Mary answered, reaching for the ladle. "No," Josas answered softly, "I mean I'm like done." Mary looked closely at her. "Done?" she asked. "Done what?"

"I've got to go sit down," Josas replied, without explaining. "I'm just done. Like when I was little and drank some of my mama's glass of dark 'n stormy before she saw me."

B.B. led her through the living room to a small study off the front hall. As he shut its door, the entrance door beside it opened and three smiling figures garbed in black came in. "The Three Fates?" asked Mary, beginning to giggle. Elizabeth Lamb took her cup from her and put all their cups on a tray on the sideboard.

"Dark 'n stormy's what they call rum and ginger beer in Bermuda," she said softly. "I've got a feeling that wasn't water Mrs. Farnum told B.B. to put in the punch. And I'll bet it wasn't the first pitcherful."

"But it looked like water — oh, my God, vodka!" Mary answered. She straightened her shoulders. "Breathe slowly through your mouth and try to shape up. We've got to help B.B. And then we'd better put ourselves outside some food. I'm getting dizzy. Oh, God, we could get booted for drinking that stuff."

B.B. did not seem to be in immediate need of help. He was talking easily to the three guests, who wore black headpieces that displayed about an inch of hair above their pleasant faces and to the back of which short black veils were attached. Each wore an exceptionally beautiful crucifix on a silver chain around her neck. The skirts of their black habits reached between knees and ankles, revealing black hose and comfortable-looking black pumps.

"Ursulines," Mary whispered. "They always have wonderful crosses. And these three are awfully learned; they all teach in the science department. Only teach girls, of course."

"Why not religious education?" Elizabeth Lamb whispered back. "Like Mrs. Farnum?"

"I said they were smart," Mary answered, beginning to giggle again. She got a grip on herself and started a bit unsteadily towards the living room, whispering, "I'll send B.B. to tell Mrs. Farnum guests have arrived. On his way by, tell him about the punch and have him warn the others."

Mrs. Farnum was summoned and, after firmly shutting the door to the kitchen, in which the uproar had only slightly subsided, trailed graciously towards the living room, where other faculty members were arriving. Elizabeth Lamb, gulping, ran to the kitchen for a glass of water and whatever dry crackers she could find. B.B., who did not appear to have been affected by the liquor except that his brown eyes sparkled extraordinarily brightly, quickly advised the rest of the Third Form of the lethal effects of the punch. Two boys and one girl immediately headed for the faculty punch bowl, before Mrs. Farnum could observe them. The others shed their aprons, picked up their assigned comestibles and went to fulfill their duties.

Turning from the sink, Elizabeth Lamb took B.B.'s arm and said, "If you'll help me walk straight, I think I can make it into the party." Instead of leading her out, he took her by the shoulders and pulled her to him, bent his head and kissed her long and firmly. She finally pulled away, her mouth open in surprise, and stared at him. B.B. burst into riotous song: "'If this isn't love, then winter is summer; if this isn't love, my heart needs a —'"

"Hush!" shouted Mrs. Farnum, inserting her large white face

in the kitchen doorway. "Stop that noise and get out into the presentation line! At once! When I discover your names, I shall report you to the Headmaster."

"She'll forget," B.B. assured Elizabeth Lamb as they hastily followed the wavering trail of silver-grey draperies. "I'll bet she's been sampling the punch for hours." Elizabeth Lamb, whose mouth was still open, began to breathe deeply through it, as Mary had instructed. Focusing her eyes was harder, since she was now confused and excited by more than alcohol.

The Third Form was lined up, two deep, against a wall of the large living room. As B.B. inserted Elizabeth Lamb into the foremost line and stood beside her, she was surprised to see Josas on her other side.

"I felt awful bad," Josas said quietly. "I had to go Europe the worst way so I found a bathroom and I'm much better now." She saw Elizabeth Lamb's puzzled look. "I mean I threw up," she explained, just as the Headmaster began to announce the names of the students, graciously indicating each as the name was spoken. The assembled faculty, who numbered about forty — "not everyone's here, I'm sure," B.B. whispered — applauded politely, the lines dissolved and little groups formed.

B.B., Mary, and Elizabeth Lamb wandered around in a common state of blurred euphoria, speaking when spoken to and later having little remembrance of what they said or what was said to them. Josie, though shy, was in much better shape and diligently walked around proffering platters of food to the guests. Mr. Salton, who was shimmering as impressively as ever although he was discreetly attired in a dark suit, consumed a great deal of her offerings and then made his way to the rest of the refreshments on the dining table. He was followed by a drably-gowned, grim-looking woman with a mouth so thin it barely showed in her sallow face. Even under the crystal chandelier over the table, her lank brown hair showed no highlights.

"Let me get you some punch, my dear," said Mr. Salton, flashing his gleaming teeth at the woman, who merely frowned at him. She gingerly tasted the pink concoction and returned it. "You may finish this, Lyman, but absolutely no more. It has Electra's usual touch," she said in a definite manner. She then turned away to compliment a woman on her appearance; the woman returned the lie. Mr. Salton immediately filled his cup again, drank it down, and took more. He wandered off, smiling more dazzlingly than before.

Father Farnum circulated with the tray of decanters. "'A little wine for thy stomach's sake,' Sister Mary Anne?" he jovially asked of the youngest of the Ursuline nuns, whose pretty face bore a calm, assured expression.

"No, thank you, Father," he was told with a charming smile. "I always like to know my vintages." Unabashed, he tried another guest, and another, with no success.

A tall handsome man wearing a Roman collar came over to the young nun and shook his head. "Having taken vows of poverty, as well as chastity and obedience, Sister," he reproved her gently, "we, at least, should encourage economy." They both laughed heartily.

As the priest passed Elizabeth Lamb to get punch for the sister and himself, she noticed, even through the haze in which she was moving, his extreme good looks. "Must be Father What's-his-name," she thought. "The one Joylene said all the girls are in love with. When he took his vows, what a waste it was for womankind!"

This struck her as so funny she began to laugh until she saw B.B. looking at her. He shook his head, but then smiled and indicated a small chair that, accompanied by a table with a reading lamp, was in a secluded corner shielded by a right-angled free-standing bookcase that was at least six feet tall. It was made more impressive, in the high-ceilinged room, by an assortment of handsome plants placed on its top.

Elizabeth Lamb wavered to its seclusion and fell thankfully into the soft depths of the little chair. She closed her eyes and half-dozed, conscious nonetheless of people who paused on the other side of the bookcase to talk, some putting their glasses or cups on it as they lit cigarettes.

"Is this Wednesday?" she heard a voice ask jovially. "No, Salton," a man answered, "it's Thursday." There was a laugh. "So am I;

let's have a drink. I had the forethought to put a flask of Scotch in my pocket. Here."

Someone with a sorrowful voice complained that she could never think of anything to say to her psychiatrist until just before her 50-minute hour was up. "I only sit there, wasting her time and my money," she said mournfully, "and then just when it's almost too late, I can talk."

"But that's a universal fact," her companion answered cheerfully. "I've known a few shrinks and they say people blather on, or sit sullenly silent, until the last few minutes, when what's really troubling them — what's really vital — all comes out. They're trained to spot it.

"I gather, too, that they have be more than usually intuitive. It's funny — I'm told a great many psychiatrists are born Sun in Cancer. Cancerians are known for their intuition. I bet all great detectives are Cancerians."

"There aren't any great detectives any more, except in books or on TV," she was answered scornfully. "Although before dinner, Harry Prestwick was talking in the lounge about a Third Former who deduced that a theft that came up before the Student Council today couldn't have been done by the kid who was accused. He was very impressed by her.

"I said I'd bet she was a Cancerian, and Harry agreed, but Tim Cranston and Melinda and Lyman and Theodosia, and Sally, and Ted Alsop, too, shouted me down. So I raced over to the office and terrified poor Olivia LeStrange by demanding to see the sleuth's records. Sure enough, she was born on June 22nd. Just made it into Cancer."

"A Third Former? She's here tonight, then? What's her name? The Third Form is usually pretty pitiful — chicks with their down still damp."

"I don't remember her name. But I wish she'd use her talent to figure out what happened to Jay Colket. I was at school with his mother, you know, and I got another really distraught letter from her today. They still can't believe he drowned, with all his diving experience. I think the family will pursue the thing further."

"But of course he drowned. That's what the Medical Examiner

said. It was so obvious he didn't request an autopsy. The boy was down too deep in the lake, ran out of air, and drowned. His lungs were full of water. It just gushed out when they tried to resuscitate him.

"I don't understand why he ate so much before diving, though; Harry or Tim or Lyman or somebody who was with the crew that night said they all ate as if they'd never seen roast beef before. I wasn't here yet, of course, but Theodosia told me all about it; she'd arrived early."

A laugh. "Naturally she would, if Harry had. Let's go get some cake and coffee, speaking of food. And I think I saw sandwiches. Dinner was pretty pitiful tonight; God, I hate dining hall duty."

Two women's voices: "How can you drink that poisonous stuff? I swear Electra makes it in the cellar, trodding the grapes with her own size elevens. And I mean shoes, not bare feet."

"Oh, the white's not so bad. Rather this than the punch that always makes me sick. Why she serves it every time she's required to entertain, I cannot imagine."

"Well, be my ghost! That wine'll get you sooner rather than later. Oh, my God, Melinda's draped all around that blond boy! And a Third Former, too! She'd better watch it, after what nearly happened with that rotten Colket kid a couple of years ago."

"The one who drowned? What happened? You don't mean she actually seduced him; or, rather, knowing something of him as I did, let him seduce her?"

"God, of course not! But evidently she'd had him at her apartment one night, going over some part, and got carried away because he was reading so well and just seized him and kissed him. She was a fool to have had him there alone, although I, and you, and everyone else tutors students alone, but with doors open or someone doing something in the kitchen, for instance."

"So?"

"So she came over to me in a state of hysteria a few nights later. The boy had coolly informed her that unless he got all the parts he wanted in all her plays, he'd go to Farnum and tell him she'd made advances."

"What'd you say?"

"Told her she was an idiot to get in such a predicament because Father Farnum just might take the boy seriously. Told her to go along with it — after all, he *was* a good actor and in three years he'd be out of here. So she sobbed a bit, wept all down her pink satin blouse, and then agreed.

"And *now* she's clutching that Third Former and praising him to everyone as her new find! Honestly, some people are too dumb to live."

"If the Colket boy tried blackmail, it's a wonder he didn't tackle Sally. Or Ted Alsop. Or both. His girlfriend, the blonde Georgia bombshell, has been in the apartment next to Sally's since her Fourth Form year. And those faculty apartments in Falls have paper-thin walls."

"Maybe he didn't want anything from them. Or maybe he was never in the girl's room and had nothing to hold over them."

"Now that second idea, as Tim is always saying, is one whose time is dumb. Well, come on. Let's go rescue Melinda. You'd better have her on the carpet again, too."

Two men's voices: "It is just too ridiculous the way Cranston's always showing off. He's over there holding forth to those young men from the Writers' Block as to how somebody said 'public psychoanalysis of writers is almost certainly an invasion of privacy,' and telling them the much desired 'Author's Reward' is nothing but a terrible feeling of depression, wondering if your stuff is really any good. And even if you know it's good, that at least one critic will carp about it.

"And it isn't as if any of *them* are ever going to be published, anyway! They not only put off writing; they put off having writer's block!"

The answering voice was mild and pleasant. "Well, nobody's ever given Tim anything but praise for *Marianne*, so he needn't worry. He's just speaking theoretically. People do."

"Bah!" The older voice was sharp. "Why doesn't he write a sequel? Probably knows it wouldn't go over. I don't like the fellow. *Cave ab homine unius libri.*"

"Meaning?"

"God, it's a famous saying, Prestwick. You're a mathematician, and Plato said he had hardly ever known a mathematician capable of reasoning. I agree with him, but I thought, though you can't reason, you might have been subjected to a little Latin. It means 'Beware the man of one book.'"

An easy laugh. "Well, J.P., no one could say that of you. I've read all of your novels and enjoyed them. I don't see how you can head the English department, act as second to Father Farnum, teach, edit the school paper, and still have time and energy to write.

"And I *do* happen to remember some Latin, though not much. But, then, *errare humanum est.*"

An appreciative chuckle, but the other speaker, obviously Mr. Sullivan, was still irate. "To err may be human, but Cranston went a little too far the other day, in an English department meeting. He remarked, apropos of something flattering someone said about the quality of *The Hippo*, that 'those who can, write; those who can't, edit.'

"Insufferable impudence! And from a sentimental hack! God, I'd like to take him down a peg or two. Even if I had to frame him! And maybe I could make a good story of his not having writer's block but just putting *off* having it."

"Come on, J.P. That's not like you. Mellow out."

"Well, age certainly hasn't mellowed Cranston. Old Turbatt — he died about six years ago, just before you joined us — told me once he was the most charming boy. Taught him English, Turbatt did, and thought a lot of Cranston. Good manners, he said and even then a way with words. I guess fame — or royalties — have ruined him."

"I imagine money would ruin me. I'd get my clothes from Bond Street like Cranston, and live it up on imported brandy and champagne."

"Well, let's get some coffee, Harry. Whatever our hostess put in the punch is making me too loquacious. I'll be speaking French soon, though my accent is so bad the superior Tim Cranston would say, 'Those who can't speak French, shouldn't.' Humph!"

Another voice: "Here, Joan, I have a lighter. I wonder why Father Farnum still lets us smoke in Electra's *sanctum sanctorum.*

She's so against it."

"Oh, as you know, he's all things to men. As someone I won't name said of him the other day: 'Scratch his surface and you find — more surface!'

"I think we should suggest to someone that the Third Form get a break from its slavery. Electra evidently hasn't learned of the child labor laws. Hardly any of them have been able to say more than 'Yes, sir' or 'No, ma'am' before they rush back to the kitchen."

"Or the dining room. I've seen them sampling that bowl of punch Electra keeps refilling.

Although she was still a little lightheaded, Elizabeth Lamb's conscience began to operate. Peaceful as it was to sit and listen to faculty gossip, she decided to find a washroom, douse her face with cold water and then fare bravely forth to reduce any possible Third Form debauchery. "If any of them get drunk, it'll be just too bad for all of us," she thought as she gingerly rose to her feet.

She found Mrs. Farnum in a forbidding stance behind the punch. The Third Form, despite the child labor laws, was still performing its duties, although some of its members wavered slightly and many hiccups were heard. She was relieved to see that all of them, including Mary, B.B., and Josas, seemed, to a casual observer, to display no more than the natural fatigue caused by their duties. Many teachers, Elizabeth Lamb noted, had departed to their own cozy abodes or to hall duty.

Miss Curtain, though, was holding a sort of court and greatly impressing several students with her discussion of "stage presence." Her eyes never wandered far from B.B., at whom she frequently smiled, although as she saw Elizabeth Lamb, she smiled at her almost as warmly. Elizabeth Lamb noticed sadly that she was wearing, on her sleek platinum-blonde head, a pink hair bow that had long since lost its assurance.

She picked up a tray of small cups of coffee that appeared to be, at least, lukewarm. She paused beside Mr. Sullivan, now in the company of a nervous young man whose constant, obsequious repetitions of "Oh, yes, certainly, J.P.," indicated him to be a new member of the English department. "Look at that woman in pink, that actress," Mr. Sullivan was now saying indignantly. "As you know, they've put her in our department because she teaches something called 'creative writing.' Why the hell an over-the-hill actress should be considered qualified to teach any kind of writing — not that writing can be taught — is beyond me."

"Per . . . perhaps she's had experience writing scripts," the young man offered diffidently. "And . . . ah you think . . . you say that writing cannot be taught?"

"Of course not! How *not* to write can be taught, but that's as far as it can go. And what, in God's name, is 'creative writing,' anyway? What kind of writing is *not* creative?"

"Uh, perhaps writing that rates only a private printing?" the young man ventured, hesitantly and obviously innocently. He then laughed, to show he was attempting a joke. Elizabeth Lamb turned to Mr. Sullivan with interest.

His face had turned a dangerous shade of salmon pink, but he spoke casually: "'Writing that rates only a private printing'? You know, the last young person who said that to me came to rather an unhappy end; he recently drowned. Right here at St. Augustine's. I do hope the phrase does not carry bad luck with it.

"Now, if you'll excuse me, some of us are meeting at eight to sing plainsong on the chapel steps. I must pick up Salton and Prestwick." He extended a hand. "Good night, John, and the best of luck to you while you're with us. Yes, while you're with us."

He turned away, and then back, with a half-smile. "Oh, John, by the way, my novels and volumes of verse are privately published, financed by a benefactor who thinks they're pretty good. 'Creative,' she says."

Elizabeth Lamb dared to no more than glance at the hapless John, whose face was now a pinker color of salmon than Mr. Sullivan's had been, before carrying her tray over to the group by Mr. Cranston. This still consisted of four or five tall, sturdy, large-white-toothed young men with thick, curly hair and a hint of incipient jowls.

To Elizabeth Lamb, they resembled nothing so much as a clutch of Kennedys, except that to her (father-prejudiced) view, no member of that clan had ever been able to achieve such a convincing facial expression of honest sincerity. "Something about the eyes," she murmured to herself as she proffered her tray. A few cups were accepted, and she lingered to see if Mr. Cranston was as entertaining in private as he was when teaching French literature.

"Well, of course writers make mistakes," he was saying. "I believe Agatha Christie once said that she'd never written a book that didn't contain 'at least one first-class howler.' I've thought of writing a book with that title, to cover any mistakes I might make. A mystery, maybe. Now, don't any of you use that; it's my idea."

Appreciative laughter. "It would have to be about a dog, of course, a howling dog," one of the clutch offered.

"No," Mr. Cranston replied briefly, "no more dogs for me." He drank his cooling coffee.

"Oh, of course. Too many poignant memories," another of the clutch said hastily. And then, as a complete switch: "I was reading the other day that Flannery O'Connor said she was often asked if she thought the universities stifled writers, and she said her answer always was that they don't stifle enough of them."

More laughter, loudest from Mr. Cranston, who turned to deposit his unappetizing cup and found Elizabeth Lamb at his elbow. "Oh," he said kindly, "our young sleuth. Half the school's talking about you, young lady. You look intent. Picking up clues?"

"No, sir. I'm just sort of walking around intent on not — intent on staring at things. This is only my second day here, and everything's so different. I miss the *café au lait* I have always had every morning." She then blushed, thinking, "What a dumb thing to say."

"You must be destined to be a writer, if you stare at things. Miss O'Connor" — he nodded graciously to the man who had quoted her — "also has said that the writer should never be afraid of staring because there is nothing that does not require his attention.

"Well, gentlemen — and Miss Lamb — I think I've had a bit too much of our gracious hostess' hospitality. It's back home for some Fernet Branca for me. I learned in France that it is the only cure for — and a powerful preventive of, as well — hangovers."

"Did you just split an infinitive, sir?" one of the more daring of the clutch asked, in an obvious attempt to assert his sureness of himself.

"I don't think so," Mr. Cranston replied, smiling, "but," as he turned to go, "I must say I've never met an infinitive I didn't like — to split."

More laughter as he left, along with most of the remaining faculty. A few barked commands from Mrs. Farnum dismissed the Third Formers, most of whom looked ready to drop from exhaustion.

Miss Curtain secured Josas and Elizabeth Lamb and led them out with a firm hand on each girl's shoulder. It was now dusk and the tree-shaded grounds were almost dark except for a few lights along the paths. As they walked towards Madison Auditorium, they passed a group of people a little off the path, who stopped talking as they approached. As they passed, Elizabeth Lamb heard either a man, or a woman with a deep voice, say softly, "It would be best for her to stop the Nancy Drew act right now."

• CHAPTER 8 •

Art? Art's what dies at the boxoffice.

— Samuel Goldwyn (attributed)

M ISS CURTAIN tripped along, chattering happily. She had
evidently consumed just exactly enough alcohol (and no
more) to make her feel lighthearted. As they neared Madison, she
stopped and announced Elizabeth Lamb and Josas were to come to
her apartment for a moment, so that she could get two copies of
the script for *Earnest*, to give Elizabeth Lamb and Will "a bit of a
start." To Elizabeth Lamb's murmur that she and B.B. — "I mean
Will" — were quick learners, Miss Curtain replied only that "even
though *Penzance* is not yet polished, yet alone performed, I am
looking forward to my next production. I was always known on
The Coast for my eager anticipation," she ended gaily.

"I guess that's how it is with the pros in show biz," Elizabeth
Lamb answered solemnly. As they skirted the chapel on the far
side of the quad, the door to the bell tower opened and Mr. Salton
could be seen making an impressive entrance, the light from inside
casting a shimmering halo about him. A chorus of incantations
was heard before the door closed behind him.

161

"What's that?" Josas was startled. "Is it singing? I never heard anything like that before."

"It's Gregorian chant, I think," Miss Curtain answered absently. "A few of the masters sing medieval church music — plainsong — on the stairs to the chapel tower some Thursday evenings. Miss McMurtrie says women should be allowed in the group, but I doubt any music of the era was written for women's voices. And who with any sense wants to sit on cold stone steps for a couple of hours?"

"So Mr. Salton was right," Elizabeth Lamb thought as Miss Curtain led them to the porch of a white-painted house behind the chapel and unlocked a door on the right of the hall inside the entrance door. "They *do* sing plainsong. I bet all the other things Joylene said he lies about are just examples of student's digs at the faculty. Probably they say awful things about all the teachers."

Aloud she said, "I guess it's a male thing, like an old barbershop quartet. I can't see why any of the women teachers would want to do it. Or men, either."

"Oh, but," Miss Curtain said vaguely, "it gives the married men an excuse to get away from their wives on Thursdays if they want to do something daring like going to the bright lights of Bar Harbor or Ellsworth. If women were allowed in, they'd undoubtedly tip off the wives as to which of the men weren't there. Sisterhood, and all that."

By now, she had secured the scripts from a large portfolio, given them to Elizabeth Lamb and disappeared through a door across the room, which she left open. Elizabeth Lamb and Josie could see her reapplying substances to her already lavish makeup in front of a large mirror surrounded by theatrical-type dressing room lights.

"I insisted we have professional lighting like this in the dressing rooms at Madison Hall," she called to them. "Having good lighting is especially important for something like *Earnest*, for instance."

"Why, Miss Curtain?" asked Elizabeth Lamb, who was quickly reading the script to see if "Jack" and "Gwendolen" ever kissed.

"Oh, we'll have to make up whoever plays 'Algernon' to look enough like Will so he just might be his brother," she answered. "Unfortunately, the cousins in the Fifth Form who look almost exactly alike are hopeless on stage." And then, to herself: "That French actress was certainly right when she said 'the point where a woman passes from being desirable to not being can happen overnight.'"

Josas was slumped in a peony pink velvet chair, dreading the rehearsal although Elizabeth Lamb had told her it was the last time they had to fill in. Elizabeth Lamb observed the room. It was a combination of austere black, white and beige colors, glass and chromium furniture and lamps reminiscent of the Art Deco styling of the thirties. This severity was softened with many lush velvet and satin touches in Miss Curtain's favorite color. She moved to examine the numerous photographs on the walls and tables, all signed with impressive autographs and inscribed to "Darling Melinda."

"She has a sort of dual personality, I guess," Elizabeth Lamb thought, "and it comes out in her home. Both soft *and* hard." She then attempted to reassure Miss Curtain, who was looking downcast as she secured a pink mohair shawl preparatory to leaving. "Oh, I don't know," she said, "how important the face or the body are, in the general scheme of things. I was in the library today, trying to do an English assignment, and I was reading a lot of stuff. I read that somebody — I forget who — said that 'the human body is an instrument for the production of art in the life of the human soul.'

"So, I guess, Miss Curtain, that what the body does is more important than what it looks like."

Miss Curtain laughed, a little bitterly. "You know what Sam Goldwyn said about art, don't you?"

"No, ma'am."

"Well, it doesn't matter. But I am amazed at your memory; it bodes well for you in *Earnest*. Now, let's hurry. Joylene is holding the fort and must be tired by now."

Joylene was indeed very tired, and also the bearer of bad news: one of the girls whose sprained ankle was improving had tripped and broken the other one. Miss Curtain turned to Josas: "It's got to be you," she said, "for the duration.

"Let's start wherever you stopped, Joylene, and, please everybody show STAGE PRESENCE!"

Lara Jane's voice had remarkably improved, as Elizabeth Lamb told her after she, Dan and the other boy finished "Paradox." "It's due to Molly and Liz," Lara Jane muttered. "Somehow they got hold of two bottles of one-fifty-one-proof vodka and they insisted I have a nip. I'm half-zonked, or I wouldn't be telling you, but it certainly knocked out the laryngitis.

"Now, forget what I just said. I'm on the Student Council, and Molly, too, as you know. We've got to be above reproach. You promise?"

Elizabeth Lamb crossed her heart and hoped to die if she mentioned Lara Jane's descent into temptation to anybody at all. She was then seized by Joylene and forced into more tripping around the stage and more daisy-picking, during which ordeal she twice fell down. "We can't have a gap in the Daughters or it will throw everyone off," Joylene said with commiseration, "but it's your last night. Marcia can rehearse tomorrow, the doctor says.

"Hey, I hear you've suddenly become Miss Curtain's fair-haired girl. Congrats. For a Third Former here just two days, you're certainly making an impression. And an impression on your knees, too, I see; go get some alcohol for those scrapes. And, please, try not to fall again."

Elizabeth Lamb sat gloomily backstage, swabbing her knees. Two boys came to sit nearby, separated from her only by a newly formed pile of papier-mâché rocks. "You sure see something in Faith I never did, Dan," one said. "Or is it just a case of a bush in the hand being worth — " There was a loud thump and Dan stood up, rubbing his clenched fist with his other hand.

"Eat my shorts, Jim," he said calmly. "And shut your mouth about Faith." Jim, nose bleeding, staggered towards the washroom.

Elizabeth Lamb, in her turn, staggered toward Miss Curtain to beg release. She was standing at the side of the stage, listening to an earnest speech from Miss McMurtrie, with her eyes and ears nevertheless riveted on the patter of "I Am the Very Model of a Modern Major-General" being produced by a boy Elizabeth Lamb had never seen. "He's not fast enough," she was saying thoughtfully. "Maybe I should have made him the Sergeant of Police;

no, that requires Porter's bass."

Miss McMurtrie had been pattering along with the Major-General. "Harry's really been so worried," she was saying; "oh, I do hope everything turns out all right. You see, Melinda, he's talked to Lyman but now, well, of course — what *is* it you want, Elizabeth?"

"Just to go back to my room. Could I please, Miss Curtain? I fell again — well, you saw — and I just don't think I'm any help to the Daughters."

Miss Curtain sighed. "I know." But she affectionately patted the blonde head, almost the color her own had achieved by artistic applications, and said, "Go ahead. We can't risk any further damage to our 'Gwendolen.' Here, dear, take the scripts for *Earnest* and give one to Will when you see him." She turned to split her attention between Miss McMurtrie and the performance on stage.

While Elizabeth Lamb waited for a bus, Mr. Salton and the grim woman who had been with him at the reception were getting into a nearby car. Mr. Prestwick was walking away, shoulders slumped. Mr. Salton's voice rose in exhortation: "My dear, I was only singing on the chapel steps. You knew where I was going. And after that, I was cheering up poor Prestwick; he's a depressive, as you know, and something's really got him down. Ah, it's confidential; I can't discuss it.

"I'm sorry you had to wait for me and I regret your having an altercation with Mrs. Farnum, easy as that is to do. . . ."

"Lyman," the woman said harshly, "you've always got an excuse. Every Thursday. And if it isn't Thursday, it's Friday. If it isn't plainsong, then you get Harry or Tim to give you some alibi. He said you and he were absolutely nowhere near *anything* when that poor boy — "

The doors shut and the car started across the bridge.

"They must live over on the girls' campus," Elizabeth Lamb thought as she boarded the bus. "And Mr. Salton's telling the truth again. Although, with such an awful wife, it's a wonder he doesn't lie to her all the time. Maybe he does."

As she approached Room 13, she heard piercing voices. She tried the door, but it was locked. Someone inside began to shout and sob at the same time. Other voices were raised forcefully.

"Oh, no!" she thought. "Faith's in another fight. At least Josie's out of it this time. I'll just go around to the hall door, sneak in and get my books and finish my prep in the common room. This time I'm staying out of the whole mess."

As she crept along the hall, the door to Miss Greenwell's apartment opened and the housemistress, pale as usual and wearing another beautiful silk kimono, beckoned to her. "Could you open this bottle of aspirin, Elizabeth Lamb?" she asked. "I can never undo these child-proof caps and I've got a terrible, terrible headache." A scream from Room 13 was followed by the sound of a scuffle and more screams.

"Miss Greenwell," Elizabeth Lamb said diffidently, handing back the opened bottle, "there seems to be something awful going on. Shouldn't you — I mean, couldn't you — go in and — "

"No," Miss Greenwell said firmly. "With a headache like this, I must go lie flat. Molly, the dorm prefect, is there. I sent her in as soon as I saw Faith running across the quad dripping wet." She gently closed the door.

"Dripping wet?" Elizabeth Lamb repeated. "But why?" she asked more loudly, but received no answer. She walked to her own door and threw it open. Four heads turned to her and there was a sudden quiet, evidently more because the combatants were pausing to draw breath than in relation to her appearance.

"What's up?" she asked, foregoing her resolution to stay out of the fray. The sight of Faith standing in the middle of the room with only bare feet, wet blonde hair and a furious red face visible below and above the blanket thrown about her was too much for her innate curiosity.

"Faith got rivered. Somehow." Leigh's voice was as mild as ever. "We don't know who did it."

Faith opened her mouth and emitted a long and shattering scream. Immediately, there followed a faint knocking on their bathroom wall. Molly went over and closed the bathroom door.

"You did it," Faith shouted. "You and this creepy Liz and your scruffy friends. Don't think I didn't recognize you, even with that black stuff all over your faces. I'm telling, and you'll all get booted." She threw herself on her bed and pulled her knees up to her chin and the blanket over the whole of her.

"Why?" Elizabeth Lamb asked Molly, sitting down and preparing to be interested. She looked closely at Molly. "There's something different about you," she observed.

"You bet there is," said Molly, turning her head. Her blonde ponytail was gone and there were a few faint scratches across the shorn nape of her neck. "Faith was sitting behind me in the bus and she just grabbed my hair and cut it off. With a big knife. It hurt like hell. A lot of people saw her do it."

"So she got pushed into the river? Who by?"

"Who knows?" Liz asked with a small smile. "It just happened an hour or so ago. It was dark. We guess she was pissed at Molly because of what happened at the Council meeting. But you can't attack people. She'd get about a hundred years building walls if Molly reported her.

"Molly has a lot of friends, you know. But Molly herself has been here in the dorm, talking to Miss Greenwell, for over an hour. She has to report weekly to Greenwell."

"How come Faith was down by the river?" Elizabeth Lamb asked.

"Oh," said Liz, with another small smile, "a Fourth Former down the hall answered the dorm phone and someone who said he was Dan told her to tell Faith to meet him over there. Or maybe it really was Dan. *We* certainly don't know."

"Oh, the hell you don't," came a howl from under the blanket. "You know. And *I* know a lot of things I'm going to tell. I know Lara Jane's got keys that open every building in the school. I know — "

"Chill out!" Liz smacked the form under the blanket with a heavy hand. "Only Sixth Form girls know about the Key Ceremony and now you've ratted. I hate to think what's going to happen to you now that you've opened your big mouth in front of a Third Former. You're rasty, Faith; really rotten."

"I won't tell," Elizabeth Lamb said hastily. "But what *is* the Key Ceremony?" Leigh and Molly and Liz regarded her coldly. Faith uncovered her head and looked apprehensively at them. There was a long silence.

"I swear I won't tell," Elizabeth Lamb said firmly, hoping this was the last thing she'd have to swear not to tell, for a while, anyway. "I'll swear on anything you say. But once I know what it is, then I can be sure never to say a word about it, by mistake."

Liz and Molly both frowned. They looked at Leigh, who shrugged. "There's some logic in what she says. After all, she'll know in two years. Take her into the bathroom and make her take the oath. I'll watch the slasher."

When the three emerged from the bathroom, Elizabeth Lamb was decidedly paler than when she had gone in. She pulled up a desk chair and sat down. Liz and Molly moved to sit on her bed, facing her. Faith, still enshrouded in the blanket, sat up and watched, pushing her wet hair off her forehead.

"Back in the sixties," Molly said, "the first girl who was elected Sixth Form rep to the Student Council got hold of Mr. Sullivan's set of the school keys. She saw them fall out of his pocket as he was biking along. It was a Saturday, and she was going into Bar Harbor. She got the keys duplicated, thinking they might be useful. Then she returned them, saying she'd found them beside the path."

"A real credit to the school, she was," Faith observed sarcastically.

"Shut up. Anybody like you who's been on the rag for weeks has got no business commenting on anybody else's behavior," Molly told her. "And as for being a credit to the school, you—"

Leigh interrupted. "Anyway," she said in her soft voice, "ever since then the keys have been handed down, every May, right after the graduation of the Sixth Form, to the next year's Sixth Form rep. There's a ceremony, with candles and wine and everything."

"So Lara Jane has them this year. But what does she do with them?" Elizabeth Lamb asked.

"They've practically never been used, in all these years," Leigh answered. "If there seems to be some extraordinary need for a Sixth Form girl to have something opened—or if we think something should be got into for the good of the school—then six of the Sixth Form girls have to agree before the rep—Lara Jane, at present, like you said—is allowed to use them."

"It's just been sort of a tradition," Liz supplied. "I guess it makes us feel more important than the boys. But all hell would break loose if anyone told. So" — with a stern glance at Faith — "nobody ever has."

"Or ever will," Molly said grimly. "Or else."

"Well, of course I wouldn't, really." Faith had calmed down. "But," with more spirit, "it's no fun to be rivered.

"And there's things I *could* tell, like that you, *Miss* Urson, get somebody to sculpt half the things *you're* supposed to have done in SEXCA. Jay told me. He said he did some stuff for you because you're such a pathetic little nothing. Always coming on to him, he said. He was sorry for you and he was really talented and you're hopeless — "

"That sucked," Liz said succinctly. "You're just a — oh, my God! Leigh, get him!"

A large hairy spider had emerged from Leigh's jacket pocket, surveyed the scene with several of its eight eyes, and then jumped to the floor. It ambled over to the foot of Faith's bed and appeared to gaze thoughtfully up at her. She screamed more loudly than she had all evening, seized a jar of face cream lying on her bed and dropped it.

With a cry of anguish, Leigh leaped and, before she removed the jar from the tarantula's leg, slapped Faith hard on her face. She then picked up the creature and crooned over it. The other three girls watched with alarm, Faith rubbing her reddened cheek.

"Oh, Jerry, darling," Leigh cried. "Is your leg broken? No, sweet, it's only bent a bit. If it *had* been broken" — she looked at Faith — "*you* just might have got laked.

"And you know," she cast Faith a venomous glance as she put Jerry Garcia in her pocket and moved to the door, "how cold and deep the lake is. People drown in it. Remember?" She shut the door very quietly as she left.

"In your eye!" Faith said to the door. Then her pretty face crumpled and she began to cry, her mouth open and tears running down her face.

"That *was* a bit uncool," Molly agreed as she rose, beckoning to Liz. "Faith, calm down but just remember what's been said. You'll be watched. One more move against anyone — " She gathered her ally and left, murmuring to Elizabeth Lamb from the doorway, "And *you* remember the predicament you're in. You could make it bad for the whole Sixth Form if you narc, and if you did — well, think about it. Goodnight."

"Molly, wait," Elizabeth Lamb said as she crossed to her. "If the boathouse is new, just a few years old, how come a key from the sixties fits it?"

"They used the original doors, of course. They were so heavy and handsome they didn't want to junk them. Never mind the keys. Forget them."

Elizabeth Lamb watched Faith cry for a while, then wet a washcloth with cold water and offered it to her. "Wash your face," she said. "You'll feel better about all this. It'll be a while, but you will.

"And maybe it's not very cool to tell a Sixth Former this, but if *your* hair had been cut off, your friends would have done something. At least, Molly didn't report you to Dean LeStrange. And I think they mean what they say about the keys. We'll both be watched." She thought of adding, "Just because you talked too much," but decided Faith had had enough for one evening.

Faith nodded soberly and struggled out of her blanket and into a nightgown. "You're not so bad," she said. "But I'm still watching my money around that nigra. I'm going to bed. I'm dead.

"Hey, you shouldn't go out. It's almost nine-thirty. You'd better study here."

Elizabeth Lamb settled hopelessly at her desk with her biology and algebra. She gave up after a while. Josie came in, limping and full of tales of misery about the rehearsal. Elizabeth Lamb persuaded her into a hot bath.

Faith lay on her bed, looking woeful, with her hands behind her head, staring up at the ceiling. Elizabeth Lamb thought she might at least try to speak kindly to her. "Why were you so late in getting here to school, Faith?" she asked as she put on her pajamas.

"I was an intern all summer in Washington. Daddy got me a job in the office of one of our senators, a friend of his. Daddy says it's right pitiful that college kids have no interest in politics anymore, either on or off campus. He'd read that not since the fifties have they been so directed towards careers that just give financial security. And when they're not thinking, 'I'm for me,' they just do stuff like riding around in clothes dryers to blow off steam.

"He says I've got a good head when I want to use it and I don't need to make money. I'm the only child. So he thinks that after college, I should go into politics. He's got a lot of influence down home.

"Then after I got done in Washington, he thought I should have a rest in some nice cool place before I came back here, so he and Mummy took me to Switzerland for three weeks. He fixed it with Father Farnum. He donates a lot to the school."

As she brushed her hair, Elizabeth Lamb thought that Daddy, if he was wise, would engage some consultant in manners and charm before he threw the apple of his eye into the political arena.

Aloud she asked, "What did you do as an intern? Did you get paid?"

"Fifty dollars a week. We did clerical stuff and went to meetings. We interns all sort of hung out together. Caroline Kennedy was one. She's only sixteen, and I thought she was, well, sort of arrogant, but we got along. She was in her Uncle Ted's office. He's okay. We all called him 'Ted' though not always to his face."

Elizabeth Lamb thought of the things her father had called the gentleman, one summer a few years ago. She had only been eight, but she remembered.

"That's nice," she said vaguely. "Faith, you ought to try to sleep. I've got some aspirin. It must have been an awful shock, being thrown into that cold river."

"I took some when I got back here, but we're not supposed to have anything, even vitamins, unless the nurse gives them to us. Don't you know that?" she asked with a touch of her usual haughty contempt.

Then suddenly she began to cry again. "All I could think of when I went under the water was how Jay — Jay must have felt. And if I'd come back earlier, I could have at least seen him again," she wailed. "He was in France all summer, so I hadn't seen him since June.

"And if I'd been here, maybe he wouldn't have gone diving

every evening, and maybe he'd still be alive." She was now sobbing hysterically. Elizabeth Lamb was tempted to remind her that she would not have been allowed back at school as early as the "Augies of August," but decided to keep quiet.

Josie came out of the bathroom and immediately dived into her bed. Elizabeth Lamb went over and gently smoothed Faith's forehead. "I'm going to turn out the lights," she said. "You've got to go to sleep. Josie, too. And *I've* got two hours in the kitchen to work off before breakfast. Molly stung me."

Faith turned her head to the wall. "You're really okay, I guess," she said with some calm. "But getting stung your second day here's setting some kind of record. To add to your record of detection."

Elizabeth Lamb, with a sigh, got into bed. Faith was murmuring something. "What, Faith?" she asked. "Do you want something?"

Faith raised her voice. It was slow and groggy, but understandable. "I said, since you're such a detective, why don't you find out what happened to Jay?"

"Nothing happened to Jay, Faith, except he drowned." She set her alarm clock for five o'clock and went to sleep.

• CHAPTER 9 •

A hard beginning maketh a good ending.

— John Heywood

"W ITH LOVE to lead the way I've found more clouds of gray than any', ah, Curtain play 'could guarantee,'" croaked Elizabeth Lamb in a hoarse soprano, limping across the quad the following morning and regarding a lowering sky through which dawn might have been attempting to break. Through the mist ahead, the forms of Lara Jane, Molly, and Liz were faintly visible. They were gathered around Miss McMurtrie's little car, parked at the door to the girls' dining hall.

A nude male form approached, shouting in explanation, "It's a dare!" as he circled the quad.

"Watch it; there's a teacher coming out of the dining hall!" she warned him loudly. "Honestly," she murmured as she hastened her pace. "Joylene, or somebody, told me something called 'streaking' came in last summer, but Father Farnum said anyone doing it here would get bounced at once. That boy's an idiot, even though it is

173

practically the middle of the night."

Miss McMurtrie was ignoring the form as it ran towards the comparative safety of the boys' campus. She and Molly were handing bags of food to Liz and Lara Jane, now seated in the back of the car. Five more girls appeared. "You'll have to walk," Miss McMurtrie told them. "See you at the boathouse."

She regarded Elizabeth Lamb appraisingly. "You'd make a good cox," she decreed. "Want to try some early-morning crew practice? We have sort of a breakfast picnic before classes start.

"You haven't got a sport yet, have you? You need one, you know. Or a SEXCA. Or both."

"No, ma'am, but I'm going out for swimming. I'm no good at rowing. I fall out of boats. Swimming is every Saturday afternoon, isn't it, as well as Monday and Wednesday?"

"Yes," Miss McMurtrie answered grudgingly. "I'll see you at the pool tomorrow, then — no, it'll be my assistant, Miss Cooke. Be there. If you fall overboard, you'd better become a good swimmer."

Dora Dorr was handing three cartons of orange juice through the car window. "Humph!" she pronounced, looking caustically at Elizabeth Lamb as the car drove off. "'Born to hang'll never drown,' my mumma always said. So *you* shouldn't hev to worry, like that pore soul did.

"And why're you sayin' you fall out of boats? Up to somethin'? You never fell out of one that I ever see. And what're you doin' here so early if you ain't goin' to row, like them pore souls?"

Elizabeth Lamb ignored all but the last question. "I'm supposed to tell Mr. Pella that I've got two hours work duty. Is he here yet?"

"No, he ain't." Dora gave her a firm push towards the kitchen. "Sick he is, and only one other help showed up, 'sides me. Good thing you're here, and don't tell me what you done to git here; the less I know the less I can tell your grandma. She writes me, she does."

The next two hours passed frantically. Elizabeth Lamb was put to setting tables, switched to grilling bacon, to breaking several dozen eggs into a huge bowl, to emptying cartons of dry cereal into another, to pouring milk into pitchers and, finally, to slicing

174

the twelve loaves of bread with which she was provided, along with a long, sharp knife. Dora, seeing how pale she was, furnished a stool. "Git some weight offn yer feet," she advised.

"Mr. Pella baked that bread hisself," she stated, "last night just 'fore he come down with perfickly horrible pains in his stummick, pore soul. When he was takin' the last of 'em out of the ovens, he said somethin' that struck me, he did."

"What?" asked Elizabeth Lamb, wearily sawing away and wondering if Mr. Pella had eaten anything cooked and burned by Dora before he was struck with perfickly horrible pains.

"'If thou hast two loaves of bread, sell one and buy hyacinths, to feed thy soul,'" Dora solemnly informed her. "That's poetic, that is. I wonder how he come to think of it? They say he's a great one for readin', too."

"I guess he must be," Elizabeth Lamb agreed, barely able to speak because of the perfectly horrible pain that had suddenly appeared in the small of her back. She stood up, sawing more slowly.

"Yesterday," she thought, "was so terrible and so endless — so terrible except for B.B., anyway — that it was just like that book by Solzen-what's-his-name. Except it was so long it could have been *Two Days in One in the Life of Elizabeth Lamb Denisovich*. And I think today just might be worse."

Now that it was almost time for students, and whichever teachers were assigned or chose to appear, to descend upon them, Dora rushed about in a frenzy, exhorting her two helpers to greater speed in their struggles to scramble eggs, warm bacon and make toast. The whole time she maintained a tireless and unsettling monologue that nearly caused them to rebel.

Their nerves were frazzled by muttered observations about the nastiness of the kids who complain because a hard-working woman driven beyond her strength sometimes had occasion to make food "jest a mite brown" and the difficulties of managing when no one atall would help and the price of prime rib of beef that was downright scandalous at a dollar sixty-nine a pound and the ingratitude with which such a treat was received every other Friday and why hadn't Mr. Pella made sure to order it before he was took sick this being Friday and if that pore soul had had the sense to eat he would have had the strength he needed and it don't make no sense anyway to have beef on Fridays which all them Catholics used to call a fish day even though they been allowed to eat meat Fridays for seven years now it is I think but maybe it does make sense because they don't have to buy as much beef since there's some that still does want my good fish chowder on Fridays them priests and nuns for instance, and so on and on.

Finally, Elizabeth Lamb and her coworker were permitted to slump down at a small table in a corner of the kitchen and eat their meal. The young woman, with a wink at Elizabeth Lamb, secured large cups and filled them with coffee and warm milk. Elizabeth Lamb almost wept at the kindness. The coffee revived her and she whispered, "Thank you."

The woman whispered back that she was French-Canadian and she and her sisters and brothers had always had *café au lait* with their oatmeal before they walked three miles to school. "Carrying hot potatoes in our mittened hands to keep them from freezing," she ended.

Elizabeth Lamb, who had heard that one before, even from an old gentleman who had grown up in Georgia, smiled. Her new friend refilled their cups.

"Well," said Dora, stomping by them to fetch more coffee for a table occupied by Father Farnum and some other masters, "you two done good, by God, and you smiled all the time and you never let them see they wore us down. For pity Minerva's sake, don't you both look comfortable! Takes a young body to bounce back. Happy as a pig in shit, you are," she added, observing Elizabeth Lamb's cup. Then she hastily raised her eyes to the ceiling and muttered, "OhLordforgivemetakin'thynameinvain" — she stopped to snuffle — "andforbein'vulgarandinfrontofyoungwomentooAmen." Then she gave them more coffee and more toast.

Elizabeth Lamb was amazed at the transformation that working at St. Augustine's had caused in Dora. "Though maybe it's only when she's here," she thought, taking even more of the delicious toast. "This is awfully good," she added, aloud.

"Best thing to come along since sliced bread," Dora answered solemnly. The other woman laughed heartily. Elizabeth Lamb was mystified. Mr. Pella, entering and hearing, laughed, too. He looked pale as he pulled his kitchen whites on over his shirt and trousers, apologizing for being late. "I am much better, though," he added.

"Well we knew you was sick and not jest out gallivanting," Dora responded graciously. "We made out all right. These two was real good help." As he drank coffee, he peered through the hatch into the dining room, and then slammed his hand down on the counter.

"That woman," he sputtered, "is again filling a bag with bacon for her miserable dog. I swear I will go to Farnum about her. The money she costs the school!"

"Well," Dora said comfortably, "the pore soul needs somethin' to love. And those damned spoiled kids leave more wasted food on their plates than she takes for pore old Cerberus."

"Oh," the other woman smiled, "she does have something else to love, Dora. Although she may be wasting her time."

"That, too!" Mr. Pella struck the counter again. "She is hopeless. I have nothing against it for racial reasons, mind. I am part Creole and one of my grandmothers was a quadroon, but such an outright pursuit is demeaning to a teacher at this school."

"Maybe it isn't hopeless," ventured Elizabeth Lamb, who had caught on as to who was being discussed.

"But it is dangerous," Mr. Pella said solemnly. "She would do anything for the man, as she would for the dog. Obsessions are dangerous." He rose. "Well, to work. I must order the beef for tonight and — "

"And at a right scandalous dollar sixty-nine a pound," Dora burst out. "I don't know how pore people will be able to live, soon. Prices is goin' out of sight. Why, do you know that over to where I live, on the backside of the island — that's what they call it, hereabouts — there's a little island jest offshore that some Rocker-fellers bought for seven hundred fifty thousand. I ask you! Seven hundred fifty thousand! That's up a thousand percent, I hear tell, from what it sold for twenty years ago.

"And I'm right glad my daughter's finished college. I read some colleges are chargin' thirty-two hundred to five thousand jest for room and board and classes. I tell you — " Elizabeth Lamb and the

177

others escaped in various directions.

In Mr. Sullivan's class, Elizabeth Lamb again chose a seat between Caitlin and B.B., both of whom smiled heartily at her, B.B. with only a touch of embarrassment. The assigned work was handed in to Mr. Sullivan, who announced that the class was to read a chapter in the text while he assessed their homework. He was a rapid reader, and in ten minutes had glanced through the twelve students' work and gone back to read some pages more carefully. He then cleared his throat impressively.

"I am pleased beyond belief," he said. "You have all done your research correctly *and* your original poems and verses are astoundingly good. I am going to read Mr. Newton's to you."

He cleared his throat again. "James' poem is entitled 'Want Ad.' Here it is:

> I will pay for a place where a birch tree grows
> And mountain laurel dances white
> Against a sky serenely rose
> Before the soft approach of night.
> I want my place on a high, sharp hill
> From which I may snare a brilliant star,
> Or smile a dream as a young fool will
> Where mountain laurel and birches are.

"Now, *that* is poetry. I am forced to alter my long-held conviction that young people are not really able to appreciate beauty: that's why there are so few good young poets. But, at this moment, I have a young poet right here before me.

"Mr. Newton, tell us how you came to write your poem. If you care to?"

Mr. Newton, a thin black boy, clenched his hands together on the table. "Well, I grew up in the city and I never saw birches or mountain laurel till I came here. Just buildings and some trees in the park. But I always wanted a little, pretty place all my own."

He looked apprehensively at his teacher. "But — but, Mr. Sullivan, I didn't write that poem last night. I wrote it two years ago, in New York. I thought it was better than what I tried to do last night, though I write poetry all the time. Is — is that all right?"

Mr. Sullivan beamed. "Not only 'all right,' but A-plus. For

honesty as well as content. And the content is superb, although, like the ineffable Nero Wolfe, I might take issue with the title; I dislike the use of 'ad' when 'advertisement' is meant. But that's a small matter." Mr. Newton relaxed his hands and smiled shyly at his impressed fellow-students.

"Now," Mr. Sullivan went on, "Miss Worthington has done something clever inspired by the Parker verse, 'Resumé.' She calls it 'St. Augustine Resumé.' Here it is:

> Cliffs Notes too costly.
> Cuff notes too dark.
> Friends' whispers are off-key;
> Overhearing foes narc.
> Infirmary not gainful.
> Substitute risky.
> Neck-craning painful.
> Bribes call for whiskey.
> Concealed books need down vests.
> Dad's excuse prose too muddy.
> I guess, to pass all my tests,
> I might as well study.

Everyone in the class laughed, even Mark. "Very, very funny," B.B. said. "Miss Worthington," Mr. Sullivan asked, "I do hope this reference to Cliffs Notes does not mean you use them or have even seen the reprehensible things here? They may coach, but they don't teach, as I'm sure you realize."

"Oh, yes, sir; I know. But I've seen them. My cousin Gus went to St. Paul's and he's used them."

"Oh, St. Paul's." Mr. Sullivan dismissed that venerable institution of learning with a shrug. "I'm making no assignment for our next meeting, class, as I told you yesterday. But for Miss Worthington and Mr. Newton, I am making a special assignment now, which they may take several days to complete."

Both Elizabeth Lamb and the boy looked frightened. "As you know," Mr. Sullivan explained, "the school is doing *The Pirates of Penzance* for Parent's Weekend. And as you know, or should, the October issue of *The Hippo*, the school newspaper, comes out that weekend.

"What I want you two to do is research the two former performances of *Penzance*, those in '39 and '59, and preview a rehearsal of this year's production. Then collaborate on an article about the three productions, including a review of the current one. I am sure you, together, can uncover an angle, so to speak, for comparing the three.

"It will make interesting reading for the parents, who will see *Penzance* in just two weeks. Some of them may be alumni who appeared in the '59 show and, or, have a child in this one."

Mr. Newton swallowed and raised his hand. "How would we find out about the previous ones, sir?"

"Research, my boy. In the boys' library, on the mezzanine level, there is a room we call 'The Cage.' It is a screened alcove containing copies of *The Hippo* from its first issue, as well as the yearbooks of every graduating class. A student can get in only with a note from a teacher, which I will give you both.

"He, or she, is locked in The Cage by a librarian; there are full facilities for note-taking and a copying machine, since none of the original material may be removed. I am, ah, afraid you will be searched when you leave to be sure you have taken nothing but copied material."

"Suppose they forget and one or both of us gets locked in?" Elizabeth Lamb asked. "All night, maybe?"

"There's no danger of that, my dear young lady. The Cage is in full view of the librarians and any students using the library. There is also an intercom to the desk below, for use when you want to leave or if you have any questions for a librarian.

"It will be interesting and educational research and I'll expect an excellent article from it. Which, of course, I shall edit; the little editing I should imagine it will need," he added reassuringly. "I would hazard a guess you will both be writers someday, so you may as well get used to that dreaded practice, to writers, known as 'editing.'"

Elizabeth Lamb and Mr. Newton looked glumly at each other. "Will it take long?" the boy asked. "I have an awful lot of classes and I'm on the swim and the soccer teams."

"You are both excused from the next two sessions of this class.

You need only read ahead in your textbook. Well, to work."

He turned to his chalkboard and then back to consider his two star pupils. "Although why anyone would want to be a writer, I can't conceive. I just read that for any ten-dollar book published last year by Morrow, four-sixty went to the seller, two-seventy to overhead and profits, one forty-five for manufacturing costs — and a big one twenty-five to the author."

He sighed. "As the quotation goes: 'Be careful of what you make your heart's desire, for you may attain it.' All I wanted to be was a writer, when I was your age; and in a way, but only in a way, I am. Ah, well. Now, class — "

Mr. Newton raised his hand. "Excuse me, sir, but what you said a while ago about young people not being able to appreciate beauty — do you mean you have to be old to have a sense of aesthetics?" He pronounced the word to rhyme with "hay-ess-thetics."

Mr. Sullivan sighed again. "No, not exactly. I feel that one must be old and have realized beauty for some years, and seen how fleeting it is, to write true poetry. I'll go into that another time. But, young man, in 'aesthetics,' the letter *a* is silent." Mr. Newton was confused, as were some of his fellows.

Mr. Sullivan went on. "You must know what a 'silent letter' means. Didn't you ever hear the old story about how the actress Claudette Colbert answered the actress Jean Harlow when Miss Harlow addressed her as 'Miss Colbert' with that last syllable rhyming with 'hurt'?"

The whole class was now confused. "She said," Mr. Sullivan recited, 'Miss Harlow, the letter *t* in my last name is silent, as is the *t* in Harlow.'" It took a minute, but then the class burst into hilarity, Mr. Newton laughing loudest of all.

In Elizabeth Lamb's next class, her Latin translations went well and Miss Greenwell smiled approvingly. She left with a full and no doubt valuable knowledge of how a *villa rustica* differed from a *villa urbana*. In biology class, Miss McMurtrie was extremely excited by the previous day's announcement of the 1974 Nobel Prize for Science: three researchers had won for their work on cells. She continued with her class' study of cells with as much fervor as if she expected to receive a call from Sweden at any minute.

Elizabeth Lamb was completely lost, a fact not unnoticed by the ardent Miss McMurtrie, who requested her to be at her house at 6:45 that evening, for some coaching. "But I have to be at Mr. Prestwick's at six-thirty," she was told.

Miss McMurtrie suddenly looked depressed. "Then come to me a little earlier; Mr. Prestwick has an engagement at six-fifteen and may be late getting home," she said, frowning. "My house is just next to his, behind Falls Dorm. We'll see how much we can cover before he arrives."

Algebra went no better, and Mr. Prestwick reminded her to see him that evening. Lunch was a relief, until Caitlin, B.B., and Josas began to delight in how, the next day being Saturday, everyone would be free after his first three classes. "A bus takes us to Bar Harbor, if we want," B.B. said. "We might get some 'za and see the sights."

After this was explained, Elizabeth Lamb, who was feeling dispirited, told them she hated pizza, had seen everything there was to see in Bar Harbor, and asked, if their later classes were cancelled on Saturdays, how they made them up. This resulted in a complicated explanation of how every student, each week, figured out his rescheduling, which she could not begin to understand. "Never mind," Josas assured her, "I'll tell you every morning what classes you're supposed to go to till you catch on to the system."

As they left the dining hall, Caitlin whispered, "Look, there's some stranger eating at Farback Farnum's table. Do you suppose someone's been fired and he's a new master?"

Elizabeth Lamb glanced at the table. Sitting beside the Headmaster, eating slowly and listening to the talk of the other men while speaking little himself, was a familiar face and form. Her mouth opened in surprise. "He's cute," Josie said. "I think men with short brown hair and long, tanned faces are the handsomest! And those horn-rimmed glasses set off his eyes just dickty."

"Nice tweed jacket," B.B. observed. "Looks intelligent, too. Wonder what he teaches. You're staring, Elizabeth Lamb. Do you know him?"

"I've met him," she answered, moving along with the others. As she did, the man looked across the room and their eyes met. He was surprised for only a moment, and then silently mouthed, "Wait." At her surprised expression, he jerked his head towards the door and then continued listening.

Josas, B.B., and Caitlin had not observed this. "Anybody want to go to the pool?" B.B. asked. "I've got some time before my next class. Come on; a swim would do you girls some good, the way you three pigged out. And, you know, President Ford told one of his aides that 'fifteen minutes in a swimming pool is as good as two martinis.'"

"Josie and I have a class, and you know it," Caitlin answered. "And why are you talking about martinis, which have no effect at all, bad or good, on *you*? Remember when you drank four at Aunt Vicky's wedding last summer before they caught you? But maybe Elizabeth Lamb would like to swim.

"Or is that what you were aiming at?" she asked knowingly. "A twosome?"

B.B. was unabashed. "Sure it was," he said. "With you along, I won't get the tee martooni effect, Elizabeth Lamb. You have — ah — a different effect on me. Stabilizing; well, sort of."

"The 'tee' WHAT?" she asked. "What are you talking about?"

"Oh, it's a scuba slang term for going down too deep and staying too long. You get too much nitrogen in your system, or something, and it's as if you were drunk. You know, as with two, or too many, martinis. Sometimes you get so disoriented you release your mouthpiece and so you get no air from your tank. You just drown."

She stared at him. "No," she said slowly. "Thanks for asking, but I don't think I'll go swimming right now. I'd better go to the library and get into that awful Cage and start looking up the stuff for Mr. Sullivan.

"Another time and I'll have my swimsuit in my knapsack. See you."

As the others left, she walked over to a bench by the door on the portico of the dining hall and sat, thinking. "Why is Buzzie Higgins here, and eating with Father Farnum? What's going on? And why's he making faces at me? I wonder if he's still a lieutenant? Or if he got promoted? Maybe he did and does public relations, or something, now."

Very soon, Father Farnum and Buzzie emerged and shook hands firmly. "Then I'll see you Monday, Lieutenant," the Headmaster said, thereby answering one of her questions. "And I'll arrange for the others to see you again. I realize you're required to do this, but — " He shrugged and strode away.

Buzzie turned to her. "Lieutenant Alfred Higgins, at your service, ma'am," he said pleasantly. "And may I ask what in tarnation you're doing here?"

"I told you last summer I was going away to boarding school," she answered. "This happens to be the school. What are *you* doing here? You said you hoped there wouldn't be any murders at any school I went to; don't tell me there's been one!"

Several students and teachers coming out of the dining hall looked curiously at them. "Let's walk across the grounds, here, private-like," Lieutenant Higgins suggested. "No, there's been no murder I know of but there was a boy drowned here about a month ago, a feller named Jay Colket, and his parents can't believe it was an accident.

"The family's got a lot of political pull, to put it mildly, and we got orders to investigate further. Now, just don't tell me you were here when it happened. I didn't see you when we came before."

"No, I only got here a couple of days ago. My plane from Pakistan was late. But didn't you already investigate all this? From what you're saying, you did. I thought the boy just ran out of air and drowned."

"That's what the Medical Examiner said. And, of course, the feller in charge here, in charge of the scuba stuff — nice feller named Prestwick — had to fill out a complete Underwater Accident Report. It was very detailed, four pages: everything from what the weather was like, and the wind, and the water, from what you ate last — which in this case was nothing much — down to swimming experience, scuba diving experience, height, weight, who you were diving with, hours of sleep in the last twenty-four hours —

184

which was like eighteen or more — if you'd had a drink in the last twenty-four hours — oh, Lord, it covered just about everything except color of eyes and hair! And everything about the equipment; everything you could think of especially how much air was left in the tank — which was none. It went over the whole works.

"And by gorry, it was just plain simple: the kid ran out of air too deep in the lake and drowned. We interviewed a bunch of teachers, the ones who were around then, and the kid he went diving with, and anybody else we could think of. It was plain cut-and-dried."

"Then why are you here?"

"Told you. Orders. Now, being as how you've helped me out more than once, I just thought I'd see you a minute and put it to you: have you seen or heard any of the kids say anything that might indicate they thought the drowning suspicious?"

"Well, I guess — no. He wasn't liked and I've gathered he was something of a blackmailer. When I say he wasn't liked, I don't know about the kids, but I've heard teachers saying things, when I wasn't supposed to."

"You're good at that. So what's your feeling?"

"Well, I don't feel that anybody thinks there was anything funny about it. Except his girlfriend. She's my roommate and she keeps saying he was too good and experienced a diver just to drown.

"And if he was so good and experienced, how come he didn't have enough air in his tank?"

"Good point. We asked his buddy, Dan Garde, and he swears the Colket kid's tank was full. They planned to dive only about forty-five feet, to explore some queer rock formations on a ledge they'd noticed before, and there was plenty of air.

"This Garde is qualified to teach scuba and it's automatic with him to check his equipment and everybody's he dives with. He said sometimes the Colket boy was a little careless and didn't refill his tank, cleaning it first, all the rest of it before diving, but they'd cleaned their stuff the night before, after that night's dive, and filled the tanks from the compressor the school has in the boathouse and everything was absolutely okay.

"And they went down together, of course, and stayed close at first, but then something on the rocks caught Garde's attention. A minute or two later, when he looked, Colket was nowhere. Garde swam around for a time, then surfaced, but Colket hadn't come up. And no bubbles were visible anywhere. So he went down again, and again and after the third dive, he saw Colket, just easing up to the surface, sort of, with his mouthpiece floating free.

"So he got him up to the air, and started mouth-to-mouth resuscitation right there on the surface of the lake. He saw he was getting nowhere, so he dragged him to shore and did artificial respiration for at least fifteen minutes. Then he ran like hell for help, and right off found Mr. Prestwick. And *he* tried everything he could. It was just no go. So they called for an ambulance, but the kid was dead, obviously, even before he got to the hospital. And the M.E. certified it as death by drowning."

"And nothing was wrong with the air gauge on the tank, or whatever you call it?"

"No, we checked the gauge and the tank and all the rest of his equipment, very thoroughly. Its condition has to be described in the Underwater Accident Report. It was a couple of hours later, what with all the commotion, trying to bring the boy around and then taking him to the hospital. That's from where the doctor called us in, because it was an unexpected death, but later that night Mr. Prestwick and one of our men who dives went all over everything. It was the boy's own special equipment, very expensive, his initials in gold all over it, for pity's sake, and it checked out A-OK. Everything worked right. They refilled the tank and there was no leakage."

He looked thoughtfully at the chapel tower. "Only thing was, we finally got out of this Garde that he and Colket had shared one marijuana joint before they went over to the lake. But he said they always did. Sweating bullets, he was, when he admitted it, because they're pretty strict about it here, he said. But he gave us to understand that some of the other kids and even some of the teachers knew they did it. All sort of implied."

"Buzzie, did you tell Father Farnum this?"

"Well, no; for one thing, he wasn't here. We kept it to ourselves because the Garde boy was so scared. It's in my report, of course, and it was, at first, my boss' idea that the pot just may have affected the Colket kid's judgement — maybe he went down too deep, or something.

"But our doctors say it's highly unlikely, since he habitually did it. And the tank *was* empty. He drowned. I suppose it's possible he hit his head on something and lost his regulator — his mouth-piece — but there were no marks on his body and, anyway, he was experienced enough, not only to know what to do but to signal Garde."

"But maybe the pot made him think he had more air than he did, so he just wandered around till he ran out!"

"The doctors say no, not the small quantity the Garde boy swears they both smoked. And the Garde boy was perfectly all right; Mr. Prestwick insisted the hospital go over him thoroughly. This was before he knew about the pot, of course. When he found out — the Garde boy was so upset at the memorial service they had here at the school the day Colket was buried down in New York, that he came out with it to Prestwick — all hell broke loose. I gathered, from what a feller I know who works here says, that Mr. Prestwick put the whole crew through hours and hours of extra practice, had them run cross-country every day till they about dropped, and made them all sign statements that they would in-stantly report any crew member who used pot, or anything else. Or, he said, they were off crew for the duration. Prestwick's some former big athlete, I guess, and he's dead set against drugs."

"He didn't tell Father Farnum, when he found out what Dan and Jay Colket had done?"

"It was over by then, and I guess he figured he took care of any possible reoccurrence. He's mighty proud of the crew here, my friend said, and I suppose he thought they might all get expelled, or something."

"Hmmm. I guess he was right. I mean, Jay was dead and it seems to have just been an accident. But maybe he smoked more pot than Dan said. Did they do an autopsy? Would it show in the body?"

"As I said, they didn't do an autopsy. There seemed no reason to. I've got a feeling, though, that if we don't dig up anything more here, the family will go for disinterment and an autopsy. He wasn't cremated.

"It's been about a month now and I don't know what it would show. Wouldn't show alcohol, but the Garde boy swears they didn't drink anything. Probably might show poison; *might* show how much marijuana — as I say, it's been a month and it's touch-and-go whether anything would be discernable.

"Naturally, there's no blood in the body so pot won't show in it, but *if* he'd consumed a large amount, it just might show in the tissues. Not too likely, though, from what Garde said. See, Elizabeth Lamb, they were roommates and that whole day, just about, they were together. Garde feels responsible for his death; don't you realize that if there were any out at all for him — anything that would show Colket brought it on himself, Garde would spill it?

"I just wish the Colket family had requested an autopsy at the time. But they were in shock; the mother was all to pieces. They'd been flown up in their own private plane and she kept screaming that all she wanted was to take her boy home. And now that they've most likely made up their minds, it'll no doubt be too late."

He looked at his watch. "I've got to be in Ellsworth in twenty minutes. Look, just keep your eyes and ears open. There's probably nothing to this, but I, and maybe a couple of others, have to come back Monday. I'll try to see you then. You know my home phone number so call if you even have a faint idea of a line we might follow. You're pretty experienced, you know, and you're right on the spot."

"And I've got to go do some work in the library. I'm late. Buzzie, exactly who else, besides Dan Garde, did you talk to last month? All the teachers who were here then?"

He took a small notebook from his inside breast pocket. "Let's see: a Ms. Melinda Curtain — she insisted we not call her 'Miss'; Mr. Prestwick, of course; the Headmaster's wife, Mrs. Farnum — Father Farnum was away on some fund-raising trip; a Mr. Alsop; a Mr. Cranston; a Miss McMurtrie; a Mr. Salton; a Miss Greenwell; a Mr. Sullivan, and every one of the boys on the crew team. They all, of course, knew the Colket boy and we thought one of the kids might know something besides what Garde told us.

"And all of them, by the way, said Colket and Garde only ever smoked one joint between them. Mr. Prestwick wasn't in on this at the time — he had enough on his hands, but, as I told you, when he found out that his boys were using pot, even a little, he hit the ceiling.

"Any of these people, you think, would want Jay Colket dead? Or even just approve of murder, on principle?" His manner was not entirely facetious.

Elizabeth Lamb swallowed. "Well, not really, I guess," she answered. "Didn't you tell me once that, in a murder, one always asks: 'Who benefits?'"

"That's right. First time I ran into you, five years ago. Four cases ago, as we might put it.

"Anybody the victim had hurt, or was going to hurt, or whose friend he had hurt, or anybody who owed him a lot of money, or whom he had something on. Or anybody who had something he wanted. You know."

"Yes, I know. Well, I'll hope to see you Monday, but I don't think I'll have anything startling to tell you."

As she arrived at The Cage, she found Mr. Newton also requesting admission. A librarian signed them in, showed them how to use the copying machine and the intercom and told them to call when they wished to leave. They sat across from each other in the middle of a long table, got out their notebooks and pens and then each stared blankly at the other's face.

"If we're going to be locked in here together, Miss Worthington, for God knows how many hours," the boy finally said with a smile, "I guess we'd better use our first names. Mine's Jim."

"Mine's Elizabeth Lamb. But you don't have to say all that."

"I like it. My little sister's name is Catherine Aurora and she makes us call her the whole thing. She's only eight but she's got a very strong personality. My mother thinks she ought to become a nun; she'd be Mother Superior in no time, she says.

"Well, where shall we begin?"

Elizabeth Lamb sighed. "For starters, why don't you take the '59 *Penzance* and I'll take the '39?"

It took them very little time to find the necessary editions of *The Hippo*. The 1939 production of *The Pirates of Penzance* had received a rave review. All of the performers' acting and singing were highly praised, special notice being given to the "delightful, controlled soprano" of a Lisa Cassidy, borrowed, as were most of the other female characters, from the Bar Harbor High School, who had played "Mabel," and the "profound and dramatic bass" of Tim Cranston who had played the Sergeant of Police. There were several photographs of the cast and Elizabeth Lamb was not surprised to see in the youthful features of the Sergeant of Police, somewhat blurred as they were, a distinct resemblance to her present-day teacher. She found no other faces she knew, and had soon copied the essence of the review.

Since Jim was heavily engaged with the more fulsome article on the '59 production, and since she still had some time before she was due at a class on the girls' campus, she wandered around the room. There was a notebook listing everyone from the beginning of time who had ever used the resources of The Cage. Not many had, and she saw no familiar names except two: Joylene Treble and Jay Colket, both with the permission of Mr. Prestwick, had signed in, Jay in late August, Joylene a week ago. No one except Jim and Elizabeth Lamb had used the facility this term, since Joylene.

She closed the notebook and went over to the yearbooks. On the top of the case was a plastic folder that held a list of all the graduates of St. Augustine's who later taught at the school. She sat down to see which of the teachers she knew besides Mr. Cranston, were alumni. "Or *alumnae*, after, when, maybe 1961 or '62?" she thought. Idly, she listed the familiar names in her notebook: J.P. Sullivan, Theodore Alsop, Timothy Cranston, Father William Farnum, Father Paul Rogers and Harry Prestwick.

Paging through the list, she had noticed the name of Anne Jane Lamb, 1963, and since her own mother's name had been Jane Lamb, she went to the case and got the yearbook for '63 as well as for the years in which her teachers had been graduated.

In the '63 yearbook, the young face of Anne Jane Lamb was startlingly familiar. "It's been, let's see, eleven years, but I *know* it's that Ursuline nun who wouldn't drink Father Farnum's cheap wine," she said aloud. "Sister Mary Anne, he called her." Jim looked up in surprise and then went back to his research.

She deduced that Miss Lamb had evidently been something of

a swinger in her school days at St. Augustine's. The carefully-phrased but illuminating paragraph under her picture contained hints that she had broken a number of rules but gotten away with it, and was exceedingly popular with the male student body. She had participated in just about all the athletics offered to girls, appeared in a number of plays and concerts and been elected Sixth Form girls' rep to the Student Council. She had also been co-president of the social club, the Bon Vivant Society. The yearbook editors predicted that she would become a rock singer.

"And now she's a nun," Elizabeth Lamb thought. "Gee, it just shows, as Grandmother is always saying, that life holds a lot of surprises for you." Now more curious, she took the other yearbooks in sequence and read the descriptions of her teachers.

J.P. Sullivan, 1927 — full name Jermyn Percy Sullivan; no wonder he went by his initials in later life — presented a round, boyish visage topped by a head of heavy curls that, except for his wire-rimmed spectacles, did not at all resemble his present face. He had been Senior Prefect of Boys, president of the Literary Club and the History Club, assistant editor of *The Hippo*, and it was predicted that he would be a Pulitzer-Prize-winning writer.

"Oh, my!" Elizabeth Lamb thought and went to the 1934 yearbook. Theodore Haynes Alsop looked much as he did now, allowing for the passage of forty years, except that he had a full head of hair and no moustache above his tightly-clamped mouth. He had been on the varsity swim team and president of the Classics Club and, for some reason, it was thought he might enter the Church. "Ha," thought Elizabeth Lamb, who had by now learned what the Sixth Commandment was, as well as the Second her grandmother had quizzed her on.

The 1939 yearbook showed Timothy Morrow Cranston with a stern young face, his smooth, square jaw firmly set and his wide eyes regarding the camera with a severe but open expression. He had been on the varsity crew, appeared in several plays, been president of the French Club and the Orthographic Society and sung in the choir. The editors thought he would end up in the diplomatic service. "Well, he is fast-talking and witty," Elizabeth Lamb thought. "Maybe he could have been a diplomat."

William Alcott Farnum, in the 1947 yearbook, looked somewhat like his present-day self except that his forehead was covered with abundant blond curls and his smile was more sincere. Even in the black-and-white photograph, his eyes seemed to be twinkling. "Looks happy," Elizabeth Lamb thought. "Well, this was long before he married deranged old Electra, I guess." He had been stroke on the crew team, Senior Prefect of Boys, a member of the choir, and evidently something of a jokester, from veiled references to pranks. It was predicted he would enter politics. Elizabeth Lamb laughed. "Well, he sort of did," she thought, remembering how Miss McMurtrie, in the girls' dining hall, had described Father Farnum as going about "working the house."

In the 1952 yearbook, Paul Orville Rogers was almost as handsome as he was in 1974, although he wore no Roman collar below his classic features. He had gone out for most sports, been president of the Classics Club, the Orthographic Society, the Photographic Society, acted in various plays and, surprisingly, been co-president of the Bon Vivant Society as well as active in the Catholic Youth Ministry. It was thought he would become either a priest or an actor. "They were half-right," Elizabeth Lamb thought. "Maybe whole-right."

The 1954 yearbook depicted Harry — ("not Henry, please") — Prestwick with a very jovial expression, quite unlike the serious-looking Prestwick of the last few days. He had been Senior Prefect of Boys, president of the French Club and, obviously, from the florid praise, the biggest star on the crew team in the school's history. It was predicted that he would someday be an Olympic winner and end his days as a teacher. "Well, hurray!" Elizabeth Lamb thought. "At last some editors with brains, if not ESP."

She replaced the yearbooks and glanced at her watch. "Jim, have you got a sixth period class?" she asked. Jim, still engrossed, nodded. "Well, it's almost two now," she said. "I've got one too. If you'll put the rest of the stuff back where it goes, I'll make a stab at calling the librarian."

When one appeared, he thoroughly searched their knapsacks and looked though their notebooks before ushering them out. They raced off in different directions. Elizabeth Lamb, just missing a bus, ran all the way to the girls' campus. She appeared, breathless, in Mr. Cranston's classroom. He raised one mobile eyebrow at her and pursed his mouth so tightly that the cleft in his chin deepened.

"Why is it, Miss Worthington," he asked, "that you are late two days in a row? Do you have a pressing romantic rendezvous just before this class?"

"Talking to the handsome detective," informed a low voice that ended in a subdued chuckle. Mr. Cranston turned to Dan Garde. "I didn't ask you to narc on Miss Worthington, Mr. Garde," he said coldly. "Well, mademoiselle?"

"I was only talking to the detective a minute or two, after lunch, sir," she stammered. "He's an old friend of mine and I was surprised to see him here. Then I went to the library because Mr. Sullivan had assigned a boy and me to look up previous productions of *Penzance* and"—her voice broke effectively—"we got locked in The Cage."

Mr. Cranston smiled, with some humor. "Well, of course you did, but didn't they tell you how to use the intercom?"

"Yes, but neither of us are mechanical and we just couldn't do it right," she improvised. "Not the first few times." She thought, "And that's not *far* from the truth."

"Hmmm," said Mr. Cranston. "I think I used that excuse myself once or twice. Well, take your place. Now, class—"

The students were, uniformly, in an unusually dense state of mind. Mispronunciations of French words abounded, and, after a half-hour or so, Mr. Cranston was rubbing his forehead in despair. Elizabeth Lamb noticed his eyes were bloodshot and thought possibly he had been speaking the truth at the Headmaster's party when he said he'd had too much of Mrs. Farnum's punch. This caused her to remember something. She raised her hand but Porter Cornwall's was recognized before hers.

"I read, Mr. Cranston," he said, "that alcohol loosens the tongue and makes it easier to pronounce foreign words correctly. Some researchers at the University of Michigan were quoted as saying that. Maybe if you gave us some *vin ordinaire* before class, we—"

Mr. Cranston waved him to silence. "Yes, Miss Worthington?"

"That's exactly what I was going to suggest! But it comes from something my Aunt Isabella said once. And she speaks five languages fluently and she also drinks a lot."

Mr. Cranston was obliged to laugh. "I think we've all had enough class for today," he said lightly. "Your assignment for Monday is on the board. By then my headache will be gone and your tongues will be looser, though it had better not be because of alcohol. *Bon jour!*"

As the students happily scrambled for freedom, Dan Garde clapped Porter on the shoulder and said, "Well done, big fella!" He smiled at Elizabeth Lamb. "You, too. If you're going to your room, I'll go along with you. I want to find Faith. Miss Curtain said we ought to practice *Penzance* all we can.

"Outside the room, of course," he added hastily.

As they walked across the quad, Elizabeth Lamb ventured: "Dan, I've known that detective I was talking to since I was eight. He — ah — he lives near my grandmother's summer place on the west side of MDI.

"He was just mentioning, sort of, that you said you and your friend Jay had shared only one marijuana cigarette on the night he drowned. Is that really so, because — "

Dan stopped dead. "Shut up!" he said forcefully. He looked around nervously. "Please lower your voice, I mean. *Why's* he telling people that? I could get booted!"

"He only told me because he knows I won't talk. And he and the other police won't tell Father Farnum, unless he asks, which he's unlikely to do after all this time, because they don't think it affected Jay. But *something* must have, don't you think? He was too good a diver to be affected by half a joint. But *is* that really all he had?

"He was your friend, and Lieutenant Higgins told me he's been sent here to look into the thing again and, please, you keep *that* quiet. They're really trying to find out why he drowned, because his family's agitating everybody. And don't *you* want to know?"

They walked on more slowly. "Of course I want to know!" Dan said fiercely. "But he only had half a joint! And we *always* shared a joint before diving. And we hadn't had even a beer, either. I'll swear to that on anything the fuzz want.

"And I dived and dived looking for him. It took around half an hour to use up my air at the level I was, maybe less, because ascending and then descending uses more air. When I got him, my tank was just about empty, and, as they found, there was no air left in his."

"Well, forget it. I didn't mean to upset you. I just thought you should know you'll be questioned again, on Monday. But if the whole crew team and some of the teachers, as Lieutenant Higgins says, knew what you and Jay used to do, it can't be such a big secret. Maybe somebody's told Father Farnum by now and he's just going to ignore it."

"Well, I don't think he knows. I don't think anybody knows except Prestwick, and he's straightened us out, all right. And they won't, if your old buddy keeps his mouth shut. You promise me, here and now, you won't spill to anyone?"

Elizabeth Lamb crossed her heart and hoped to die if she did. Dan relaxed. Faith emerged from Room 13 and joined him, with a civil smile at Elizabeth Lamb. She came back to the room in a moment and asked politely, "Would you mind reaching up to the shelf in my closet and handing me my light blue pullover? My shoulder got hurt in that mean — ah — incident, and I can't raise my arm very well."

Elizabeth Lamb rummaged around in a disorganized pile of sweaters and found the one requested. Faith thanked her, even more politely, and left. "If she can't reach up, she'll never find anything in that mess," Elizabeth Lamb thought. "Why don't I be decent and straighten it up for her?"

The shelf was high and the closet deep. She climbed upon a light desk chair and folded the jumbled mass of sweaters. In the very back corner of the shelf, her hand encountered something hard, an object a little larger than both her fists if held together.

Curious, she reached for it and as she did, she overbalanced on the chair, which tilted and deposited her on the floor with a crash. There was a smaller crash from the object she had dropped as she fell, which was now in two large fragments of dried clay. She got to her feet and picked the fragments up and with them the folded piece of paper that had fallen out of the object. Fitting the pieces together, she sat on her bed staring at an unmistakable likeness of Faith O'Malley.

The head had been sculpted about one-third life size, and appeared to have been crafted hastily, but the resemblance was exact. "Oh, no!" she said aloud. "It's probably a study for a head her doting daddy commissioned of her and she probably values it. She'll kill me!" And then she noticed that, scratched under the hairline, on the back of the neck, was the inscription: "JAY C."

She sat and thought, holding the head together. "But if she cares for it, since Jay did it, why isn't it out where she can brag about it? Why was it hidden? Maybe I can get to a SEXCA class in sculpture and learn how to fasten the pieces together before she ever notices it's gone."

She got a heavier chair and poked the split head back into its corner. The piece of paper it had held which she unfolded was a neatly-clipped Xeroxed photograph with text under it.

"Why in the world!" she thought. "Maybe Jay revered this as representing an idol of his, the way people put treasures and memorable things in cornerstones of new buildings. But I can't put it back till I fix the head." She had hidden the clipping under the underwear in her dresser drawer just as Josie came in.

"Let's go over and practice some basketball shots," she invited. "I had a free period so I did all my assignments, not only for tomorrow but for the classes I'll have on Monday."

"I can't. I've got stuff to do. I'm going to the girls' library to work but I'll see you at dinner."

To reach the library, she had to pass the large arts room. The door was open and a tall man stood considering an almost-life-size clay model of a Labrador retriever. She knocked on the door jamb. The man turned, a smile lightening his heavy, tanned face.

"I can't see how Peter, talented as he is, ever got Cerberus to stand still long enough to do that," he said, speaking confidingly although she, to her knowledge, had never seen him before. "But Miss McMurtrie will love it. He's going to give it to her. I wonder how he's doing in biology," he added, to himself.

"Well, what can I do for you? I'm Mr. Dipietro. I don't think I've met you — no, I'm wrong; you were at the Headmaster's reception

196

for the Third Form last night. I noticed you because you were observing people; with an artist's eye, I hope?"

"I'm Elizabeth Lamb Worthington and I just got here a couple of days ago. I'm certainly no artist; at least, I don't think so, but I wonder how would I get into a sculpture class for my SEXCA?"

"Quite simply. You sign this form and appear on Tuesday and Saturday afternoons. At three, if you can make it; at four, if you can't. I'll report you to your dean as having chosen sculpture for your SEXCA. Have you ever done any?"

"No, not ever. Except maybe with Playdoh. But I'd like to do portrait heads, or try to, anyway. Could I just look around a minute?"

Mr. Dipietro nodded and returned to contemplating the clay Cerberus. Once he said, as if to himself, "Just remember that in sculpture, there are no concaves." She received this without understanding it, and was about to dispute it, but instead remained discreetly silent, wandering about the room observing completed oils, watercolors and half-finished sketches. There was a shelf with several clay heads of boys, the faces of some of which looked familiar.

"Who did these, Mr. Dipietro?" she called.

He turned. "Oh — a — a former student. He was very good at getting a quick likeness of his friends. I really should pack those up because his family might want them. He is, ah, unfortunately no longer with us."

"Were they — were they done by Jay Colket?"

"Why, yes. Did you know him? He arrived early each year with the rest of the crew, for August practice, and I always let him come in here and work when he had an hour or two. He was extremely talented. I wasn't here this year when he came, but the arts room is usually unlocked."

"No," she answered slowly, wondering if she should ask his advice about fixing the broken head, but he had taken off his smock and was back to her, splashing noisily as he washed his hands at a nearby sink.

"Well, thank you, Mr. Dipietro," she said. "I'll be here tomorrow afternoon." She put her name on the list he had indicated and left

197

for the library, to begin writing up the notes she had taken on the production of *Penzance*. And to think.

She arrived at the dining hall just in time for dinner and did justice to the overpriced prime beef. Mr. Pella had prepared Yorkshire pudding and steamed Brussels sprouts to go with it. She and Josas went back twice to the serving table.

She looked at her watch as they ate their applesauce and ginger cookies. "I'll see you at the room, Josie, after I go to my tutoring in biology and algebra," she said, sighing as she left. Josas sighed, too. "I won't be there. I have to go be one of those stupid fatten Arab chorus girls," she replied gloomily. "I'm beginning to hate even the thought of daisies and parasols and rocks."

Miss McMurtrie, a soft blue sweater slung about her shoulders against the coming evening chill, was sitting reading in her picket-fenced-in yard as Elizabeth Lamb opened the gate. The black dog lying beside her stood up and growled.

"It's fine, Cerby," Miss McMurtrie assured the dog, who stopped growling and advanced, wagging his tail. Elizabeth Lamb presented her fists, clenched together, for him to smell, dropping her books as she did. Cerberus licked her hands approvingly, presented her with a sort of Lab smile, and, before Elizabeth Lamb could pick up her books and close the gate, the dog rolled heavily about in a bed of flowers and then, one eye on his mistress, dashed out of the yard.

"Oh, no!" Miss McMurtrie wailed. "He's been trying to get out all afternoon; I can't imagine why. He always runs all the way down to the river, for a swim. Labs just love the water. Oh, well; he knows his way home.

"Oh, no!" she wailed again, as she inspected her crushed flower bed. "He's rolled in the poppies and delphinium, and they're very, very poisonous, you know. If another dog licks his fur, it could get, at the least, very sick. Well, let's hope he heads straight for his swim. And before he takes it into his foolish head to lick *himself*.

"Now, come over here and we'll start. Good, you have your notebook as well as your text." She lit a cigarette to brace herself for the coming ordeal.

They struggled for what seemed a very long time to Elizabeth

Lamb, but Miss McMurtrie's attitude indicated it was not as much of an ordeal as she had expected. "Although, you will need about two more tutoring sessions, to catch up. And, since you have a quick mind, I'm going to try to get you to lighten up a bit by assigning you *The Lives of a Cell*, by Lewis Thomas, to read by next Wednesday.

"It came out just last May and it's awfully good. It's in the library. It'll make you see biology can be fun. Now, why don't you go inside and get us the pitcher of lemonade you'll find in the refrigerator. There are glasses on an open shelf above the counter."

The little house was cheerful and pretty. Even Cerberus' water bowl, on the shining white kitchen floor, was of hand-wrought pottery with a design of running Labs. "I like your house, Miss McMurtrie," she said, returning with the lemonade.

"'Beware of on what you set your heart, for you may attain it,' as J.P is always saying," Miss McMurtrie answered heavily. "What I always wanted was a nice little house all to myself, because I grew up in a large, poor family and we were all crammed into a tiny apartment. And it's lonely," she finished.

"But there's lots of nice teachers around to be friends with," Elizabeth Lamb said consolingly.

"That's true. Living completely alone makes one small-minded. Living in a community like St. Augustine's, even though it is often an ingrained, self-centered community, gives one a sense of family, of association. One is not only in a world, even though it's a small world, but an educated community like this gives you a window on a larger world."

Elizabeth Lamb thought this over, smiling agreeably.

"And not only is the house rent-free," Miss McMurtrie said, "but the school pays all utilities, even heat. So I can save for what may be an even lonelier old age."

Elizabeth Lamb smiled encouragingly, hoping she would receive more information. Miss McMurtrie smiled only slightly in return, sipping her lemonade. Her face brightened as they heard a car driven into the yard next door.

Mr. Prestwick's widely smiling countenance soon appeared at the fence. "It's okay, Theo — Miss McMurtrie," he said. "It's all covered. He was extremely understanding."

Miss McMurtrie jumped to her feet, dropping her glass. "Oh, I'm so relieved — oh — ah, Mr. Prestwick, this is Elizabeth Lamb Worthington who was tutoring with me and is now due to see you, I believe."

Mr. Prestwick leaped lightly over the low fence. "I know Elizabeth Lamb, Theo — she's one of my students, as you said, or else she wouldn't be here! You're excited, and no wonder.

"Why don't you, young lady, go over to my house and get your things ready. The door's unlocked. I want just a word with Miss McMurtrie. And some of that lemonade," he added, laughing.

Elizabeth Lamb, in his living room, staring without comprehension at her algebra assignment, heard low murmurs and happy laughter from Miss McMurtrie's yard. She heard something else: the spurt of what sounded like a wooden kitchen match being ignited. Mr. Prestwick exclaimed loudly in annoyance.

Elizabeth Lamb moved to the open door and listened hard. "Theo, I wish you wouldn't," Mr. Prestwick was saying. "If you get caught, Farnum will be far from agreeable. And you know I hate the stuff."

"Just one, Harry, to celebrate," Miss McMurtrie answered. "I promise it'll be my last ever. I'll throw the rest away. I do promise, darling."

The aroma of burning marijuana came to Elizabeth Lamb's nose. She raised her brows and got back into her chair, just in time. Mr. Prestwick was striding up his front walk, looking very happy.

"Did Cerberus come back?" she asked.

"No. When he gets out, he's apt to stay a while. Out of revenge for having to wait hours for Miss McMurtrie to come home, I guess. Dogs," he ended thoughtfully, reaching for a textbook, "do a lot of waiting."

"They do, don't they? I never realized that. If only they could read! But Miss McMurtrie could leave the radio on for him. My Aunt Sarah does that for her kennel dogs. She raises Dalmatians."

"I have a feeling you're trying to get me off algebra and on to dogs." He smiled. "Now, let's begin here — "

Thirty minutes later she understood more algebra than she

would have thought possible. During her tutoring, she was aware of sounds in the kitchen. "Probably Miss McMurtrie, chaperoning," she thought, remembering what a teacher had said at the party about not tutoring students of the opposite sex alone.

Mr. Prestwick stood up and stretched. "It's after eight," he said. "Don't Third Formers have an early curfew? You're coming on, I might add, but I'd like to see you tomorrow evening — no, that's Saturday. Monday, then. Same time."

She was trying to put off her departure in case Miss McMurtrie called some interesting endearment from the kitchen. "Why are grades called 'forms' in private schools?" she asked.

"I've wondered that myself. No one seems to know. I've thought that maybe, way back in the Middle Ages when the first schools were started, probably in churches, the students — all boys, of course — sat on those wooden benches that can be called 'forms.' The first form, up in front under the monk's eye, would be where the smallest boys sat. And so on, going back, with the largest boys on the sixth form. It's just an idea of mine."

"It could be true! But there's something else nobody's ever told me: why is the school magazine called *The Hippo*?"

"Because Saint Augustine was Bishop of Hippo, obviously. Now, my dear child, I've been teaching long enough to know when I'm being conned. You cut off to your dorm, and right this minute!" His smile softened his words.

She stood outside his front hedge, loosening her taut shoulders and breathing deeply of the surprisingly warm, clear night air. Although it was by now fairly dark, she detected a black form off to her left, past Miss McMurtrie's house, down the forbidden road. It was crouched beside a taller hedge that separated Mr. Cranston's house from the road.

"Cerberus," she thought, walking stealthily toward the form. "I'll grab him and get Brownie points from Miss McMurtrie and maybe they'll be saying something interesting when I drag him back. I wonder what they're so relieved about and I wonder if Cerberus remembers me. I certainly hope so."

Cerberus did. Although he was sitting staring into the hedge, he wagged his tail and grinned before he turned his attention back to the bushes. Elizabeth Lamb knelt down and peered in.

A small black cat was lying on a pile of leaves in a little open but sheltered area in the hedge, and it was most certainly giving birth to a number of kittens. Elizabeth Lamb gasped. Cerberus merely wagged his tail again and continued to watch the proceedings. She grasped his collar and tried to pull him away, but though amiable, he was immovable.

"He might hurt the kittens," Elizabeth Lamb thought. "Eat them, maybe!" She turned to go back for Miss McMurtrie but she heard a series of coughs from Mr. Cranston's garden. She ran to the tall gate and opened it slightly and, as she did, she again smelled marijuana. "This whole road's what Dora would call an opium den," she thought. "No wonder they don't want students wandering along it!"

A lanky male form was visible lounging in a lawn chair under a tree. Beside the chair was a small table that held a bright battery-powered reading lamp. There was a book open on his lap and, as she looked, the end of his cigarette glowed brightly as it was deeply drawn upon.

"Mr. Cranston?" she called hesitatingly. There was a low but distinct exclamation of *merde!* as the glowing object was tossed into a portable barbecue faintly visible near the chair.

"Who's there? What the devil do you want?" Mr. Cranston's voice called irritably as he came quickly to the gate. "Students are not allowed on this road!

"Oh, it's you, Miss Lamb. Well?"

"Mr. Cranston, I was just coming out of Mr. Prestwick's. He was coaching me in algebra and I *was* going to go back to my dorm the way we're supposed to but I looked down here and saw Miss McMurtrie's dog sitting staring into your hedge. So I sneaked down to see why and there's a cat having kittens. I thought Cerberus might hurt them." She stopped, breathless and a little frightened at Mr. Cranston's glare.

But he spoke gently. "So that's where Midnight is! She was due any day and I had a perfect birthing box all ready in the kitchen closet. But, cats being as independent as they are, she's ignoring it. I was sitting out here hoping she'd wander home. But let's see the happy event."

Cerberus again wagged his tail. Mr. Cranston seized his collar firmly and hustled him up to Miss McMurtrie's gate, through which he ungently thrust him. All the kittens were now born and the mother was washing them. Mr. Cranston knelt and caressed his cat. "You go in and find the box. It's in the open closet right beside the back door. I'll keep an eye on them."

As she ran through the garden, the odor of marijuana from the barbecue was very strong. "He must have been waiting for hours," she thought. "Oh, well, I guess he was worried. But he doesn't seem to be affected by all he must've smoked. But then, Grandmother was reading once a Yale University report that said pot has little effect at all on a very well-balanced individual."

The mother and kittens were carefully deposited in the box and carried into the kitchen. Mr. Cranston drew in a deep breath of relief. "I've been extremely nervous and I've got you to thank for Midnight's safety, so let's go out and sit calmly and have a drink. I think that crisis-averted demands it.

"Ginger ale for you; port for me. I think we both deserve it. If you hadn't come along, it's just possible Cerby might have tried to play with the kittens or dragged them home to his doting *maman* with Midnight following. Then there'd have been hell to pay. Miss McMurtrie's terrified of cats."

He pulled up a garden chair for her after he had quickly moved the barbecue far back against the house, emptying the ashtray from the table into it. He produced a package of Marlboros from his shirt pocket and lit one, carefully putting the match in the ashtray, now back on the table and smelling only faintly of what it had held. "I'm afraid I smoke too much," he said, closely watching her face. "It's a habit I picked up in France during the — during tense times. It's a habit I hope you don't adopt. One gets a bad cough from it."

She nodded agreement, looking as innocent as she could as she sipped her ginger ale. He relaxed his scrutiny of her and leaned back in his chair, rolling his wine glass between his hands. "This is another habit I picked up; the French drink port as a cocktail and now I prefer it to whiskey or gin. Or Mrs. Farnum's punch," he added with a smile and an exaggerated shudder. "But then you've never tasted that, have you?" he asked, with a mischievous half-grin.

"Oh, no, sir," she said, looking innocent again. He laughed aloud. "You're good at deception, Miss Lamb," he announced. "I heard the whole Third Form, almost, got buzzed on it."

She laughed, too. "Well, I did have a little. But none of us will admit it, officially." She thought it was time to change the subject. "Have you had Midnight long?" she asked, trying to prolong her stay and thinking of B.B.'s face when she told him tomorrow that she had "been having drinks with Mr. Cranston in his garden."

"No, just since I arrived back this fall. She'd been smuggled in by an 'Augie'—a crew member—and Mr. Prestwick discovered her. It would have been the Humane Society, or maybe the lake, so I adopted her, although I had told myself 'no more pets'"—he stopped, laughed heartily.

"What is it?" she asked.

"I just remembered her original owner's name is Milton— Milton Rosenberg, Rosenbaum—I forget. And don't you know the poet Milton's lines: 'of Cerberus and blackest Midnight born, in Stygian cave forlorn'—no, I guess you don't.

"Anyway, considering that my hedge might qualify as a 'Stygian cave,' I suppose one of the kittens will have to be named 'Melancholy.' Look up your Milton and you'll see why."

She thought she would avoid any more research than it was Mr. Sullivan's constant practice to assign, but avoided saying so. "Well, the kittens *could* have been born in a nice kitchen. I think yours is the best one I've ever seen. It's like a French restaurant, all stainless steel and black iron and handsome wood. It made me think of France, where I lived for a while, as I told you in class the first day."

He was pleased. "I like to cook. I grew up on French food and then France, the home of good cooking, was my 'calf country,' as they say. And where one spends those early days, even under difficult conditions, as I did, influences one's whole life."

"I would have thought here at St. Augustine's was your 'calf country.' Mr. Sullivan has me doing research on early productions of *Penzance* and you were in the '39 one, I read."

Mr. Cranston made a grimace of distaste at the mention of his fellow teacher. "Just what he *would* think of putting in that dismal school newspaper.

"No, the cooking here, then and now, would hardly influence a young person towards an appreciation of food — at least, not favorably.

"So you read about the '39 *Penzance*. Did it mention how miserably I flatted during my rendition of 'A Policeman's Lot Is Not a Happy One'? My cousin, who came down to see it, laughed about it for years, even when we in the *Maquis* had little to laugh about."

"No, it was very tactful; a rave, really. But didn't you read the review at the time? Or you could now, in The Cage."

"I was in a number of plays here, and I never read one review. When a thing is over and done with — well, it's over and done with. I've never been one for postmortems."

She was lingering over her drink, hoping to delay the time when she must return to Room 13 and just possibly fall into a recital of another of Faith's misfortunes, or be asked how her clay head got broken.

"Well," she said, "I never can live just in the present. It always bothers me when I say or do dumb things and it takes me a long time to get over them. Like last night, for instance! At the reception I said a dumb thing to you: I said I'd never before been in a place where I couldn't have *café au lait* for breakfast. That had nothing to do with anything. I felt so stupid."

His laugh was very pleasant. "Even though I was suffering the effects of the punch, as I recall the conversation, it was reasonable that your mind was on coffee because you were at the time serving some horrible version of it. So don't feel too bad. It's just *l'esprit l'escalier*. It's happened to me.

"But, as I said, I don't dwell on things. Although when I was young, in my forties" — he laughed again — "I many times felt it."

She was puzzled. "Felt what? That translates as 'spirit of the stairs' but I don't know what it could mean."

"And you grew up in Paris! Well, I suppose you were too young to go to parties, receptions and so on. It's a phrase that refers to how you, as you're leaving a gathering — going down the stairs — always think of what you either should or shouldn't have said while you were there."

Now she laughed. He was very amusing, she thought. "Did you live in Paris, ever?"

"I was a student at the Sorbonne. That was after the war. I lived in Switzerland for some years and taught English in Paris for a time. Then I came back here — urgent invitation from the Headmaster. One of those offers you can't refuse, as they say. That was five years ago, though it seems longer."

"Because you don't like it?" she dared to ask.

"Not at all. I've never lived in such a charming community, one all to itself with its own civilities, customs, loyalties, personal gossip, academic intrigue — never known anything like it. I'm glad I came back."

"Wasn't it like this when you were here before? Miss McMurtrie said something like what you just said, but she wasn't a student here."

"My dear Miss Worthington, a girl as astute as you surely knows that students, although the school is supposed to revolve around them, really count for very little. They are transient; the community remains."

He rose. "And *you* have remained here far too long. I have a feeling your housemistress may be looking for you. Well, tell her that I'll verify you assisted at a birth. That should shake her." He glanced at the face of his Rolex watch, putting his wrist under the lamp to see it. "Better run. Where's your dorm?"

"Right across the road. It's Falls. My roommate has a boyfriend who fixed the door at this end so she and he can get in and out. I'll just sneak in."

He shook his head playfully as he closed the gate behind her. "You shouldn't reveal things like that to a member of the Establishment. Except that I'm not a very loyal member of it. Too many years of defying authority, I fear. Take care."

Neither Faith nor Josas were in. Elizabeth Lamb took a leisurely bath, again hearing through the bathroom wall Miss Greenwell's and Mr. Alsop's reaction to "the martini effect," and went to bed relaxed and happy. "I guess the only thing I really don't like about being here is that I miss adult conversation," she said aloud. "Grandmother and *Nonno* always talk about interesting things. I'm glad I found Midnight and could hear Mr. Cranston talk, and Mr. Prestwick and Miss McMurtrie, too. This day ended a lot better than it began."

She turned on her side and went instantly to sleep.

· CHAPTER 10 ·

Ars est celare artem.

— Latin proverb

WHEN ELIZABETH LAMB woke, she glanced first at Faith's bed, which was empty, and then apprehensively over to her closet. Faith was there, reaching up stiffly for a sweater. She tossed the blue one Elizabeth Lamb had got for her on top of the pile and closed the door. She left the room with a small but polite smile.

"At least she hasn't noticed the broken head yet," Elizabeth Lamb thought. "If only I can find out this afternoon in SEXCA how to stick it together!" She frowned in bewilderment at the thought of what had been concealed in it, but shrugged it off. "I don't understand her and I certainly don't understand her former boyfriend," she thought. "Maybe it meant something special to them." This, upon reflection, made little sense, but she gave up and raced for the bathroom to beat the stirring Josas to it.

At breakfast Josas told her to attend her first three classes, as usual. "Then on Monday, I'll tell you the ones to go to." Elizabeth Lamb spent her Foundation In Learning class time in The Cage, imprisoned again with Jim Newton. They consulted their note-books and decided on the title for their *Hippo* article: "Thirty-Five Years of Piracy." "It's not very inspired," Jim decided, "but maybe a better title will come to us. Let's get started on it, separately, and then we'll combine our masterpieces."

She disagreed. "No, I think we should catch tonight's rehearsal before we begin. It's in Madison at seven; Miss Curtain is going all out because tomorrow is the last rehearsal before she takes off for California, a girl in my dorm said. There'll probably be a run-through when she gets back, before it opens at Parents' Weekend, but tonight and tomorrow are *it*. I guess tonight's may go on forever, since tomorrow's Sunday, but if we can't hack the whole thing, we can pick the rest up tomorrow night."

Jim received this news glumly and Elizabeth Lamb went as glumly to her Latin and biology classes. Only she and a few other girls were in their dining room for lunch, the majority of the stu-dents having taken advantage of their half-holiday and gone off to the cosmopolitan atmosphere of Bar Harbor. The meal was heated-up beef left over from the night before, which Mr. Pella had defiantly enhanced with a spicy herb gravy and served with hashed-brown potatoes. Elizabeth Lamb went back for two extra helpings.

Dora was in an agreeable mood and chatted pleasantly with her about life at The Bungalow in past summers. She expressed ap-proval at the large meal Elizabeth Lamb was demolishing. "Some-thin' good in your stummick's what you need to get through all this studyin'," she intoned, "and this here beef's the best. Lots of protein. I read up about all that before I come to work here."

Elizabeth Lamb was reminded of something. "Dora," she asked, "you said something yesterday morning about if some poor soul had had the sense to eat his beef he would've had the strength he needed. Who'd you mean?"

"That pore soul what drowned, that's who. I specially noticed because there wasn't many here for dinner, only the crew members and a few teachers. They eat over here, the men, too, before term starts 'stid of over to the boys', because this hall's smaller. A little protein in his stummick might've helped."

"What teachers were eating here?" Elizabeth Lamb asked idly.

"I got more to do than count faces! I know who wasn't here, though: Miss McMurtrie and Mr. Prestwick. Somebody said they went to Ellsworth for dinner. Mr. Pella was put out because you heard what he thinks of *that* situation. But at least she wasn't here to grab beef for her Cerberus; that made Mr. Pella a mite happier."

Elizabeth Lamb ate her stewed apricots thoughtfully, trying to remember something that didn't jibe with what she had just learned. She glanced over at the door, which a departing girl had left open. As if he had heard his name mentioned a few minutes before, Cerberus pushed the door further open with his black nose and entered, wriggling happily. He made his way over to Dora's feet, wagging his tail, then coughed horribly and promptly vomited what looked and smelled like very old fish onto the spot-less polished floor.

Dora shrieked. Mr. Pella came running and took Cerberus out. With the help of a third worker, the mess was cleaned up. "It still stinks terrible," Dora decided. "And I scrubbed and scrubbed."

"Get some ammonia diluted with water, and go over it," Mr. Pella advised. "Ammonia takes away just about any odor." Dora departed for the supply closet in the kitchen mumbling about "damned nasty animals spoiled beyond belief and if people took proper care of 'em—" She was soon back, announcing that there was no ammonia to be found.

"Of course there is," Mr. Pella frowned. "I ordered a full case of it, six gallons, as soon as I got here, along with other cleaning supplies for the term. We haven't used any of it, that I know of."

After a search, he was forced to admit that Dora was correct. Elizabeth Lamb left them arguing as to whether applying Clorox would remove the finish from the floor, and went to her room for her swimsuit.

Miss Cooke gave her a few elementary tests and then announced she was permitted to swim in the pool, only with a buddy, of course, and then decided that she should practice to try out for the girls' swim team. She provided another bathing suit to put over the first. "It increases your drag, and slows you down, so you're able to swim faster in competition, when you wear only one."

Elizabeth Lamb took this information and the extra suit with composure and dutifully plowed up and down the swim lanes for an hour, along with other promising girls, all of whom were wishing they had eaten less lunch. Miss Cooke was pleased with her and announced she would recommend to Miss McMurtrie that Elizabeth Lamb was a definite possibility for the team. "She'll want to see you here Wednesday afternoon."

Elizabeth Lamb took this news with less composure, morosely got on a bus and appeared at the art room. Students were doing oils at easels and several sat at tables, painting in watercolor. One girl was constructing an armature for a clay figure, the sketch of which was beside her.

Mr. Dipietro introduced Elizabeth Lamb to the others and sat her down at a table with an apple, a banana, a large piece of reddish clay and an ordinary butter spreader. "Do these life-size," he said, and went off to look at the work of the others. He was back shortly, expressed amazement at what she had done so fast and so accurately, and produced an armature for a head. He began to tell her the rudiments of portrait sculpture, giving her front and side photographs of a woman's head to attempt to copy in clay. She progressed rapidly and was sorry when the class was over.

"Mr. Dipietro," she asked hesitantly as she sprayed with water and then covered her unfinished work, as he instructed, "is it possible to put a clay head together so it doesn't look mended? I dropped one my roommate has and it split into two pieces, right down the center of the sides. I'd like to fix it so she won't know."

He frowned. "The clay is dried, of course? Well, bring it to the next class. Perhaps I can do something with it. And it will not, naturally, be the same, if I must wet it and apply some touches to cover the mend. Well, there is a Latin proverb that goes: 'Art lies in concealing art.' Maybe it applies here."

"The features are not harmed, you say?" She reassured him. "Of course," he said, "the head will not be 'sincere.' Do you know where that word comes from?"

"No, but I always like to know things like that. My grandmother says I have more information on things that nobody would ever want to learn than anyone she's ever known."

"It comes from the Latin meaning 'without wax.' Ancient statues, you see, which were broken or cracked often had wax inserted into them, to fool the buyer. Now you have more useless information."

She went smiling back to Room 13. Her smile vanished at the sight of Faith sitting at her desk and staring at the broken head, the two pieces of which she was holding together. She looked up, her forehead wrinkled in bewilderment.

"Can you imagine?" she asked. "I was looking for a sweater that's absolutely *not* here—no doubt pilfered by your friend and hers, that Josas—and this was way back on my closet shelf. It's of me, and Jay did it! See, here's his initials. But how did it get in my closet and why did he make it in halves?"

"Maybe he broke it putting it in there, as a surprise for you," Elizabeth Lamb suggested weakly. "He knew you'd have this room again, didn't he? I've just come from the art room and there're other heads Mr. Dipietro said Jay did of some of his friends, in August when he—when he was here early. That must be it; he did it as a surprise for you!"

She swallowed hard, and thought: "That's just one big lie—except, maybe it is true he did mean it as a surprise for her. And it'll save a lot of hassle if she believes it."

Faith wiped her eyes and nose. "It's all I have to remember him by and it's ruined."

Elizabeth Lamb continued, somewhat, with her untruths. "A girl told Mr. Dipietro in class that she had dropped a clay head and he said bring it in and he'd try to fix it, as long as the features weren't hurt. It isn't really ruined; I can clearly see it's you. If you could wrap it up carefully and put it in a box, I'll take it along the next time I go to my SEXCA."

"Oh, would you? I just want to cover it and not see it till it's fixed. It makes me feel so terrible while it's all broken, just like—just like Jay's life." She began to sob. Josie came in, eager to describe her afternoon amongst the bright lights of Bar Harbor, but quickly backed out.

After much rummaging about, they found a box in the bottom of Faith's closet. They carefully wrapped the pieces of the head in two small towels, closed and sealed the box, and Elizabeth Lamb put it under her bed. "So you won't have to think of it till it's mended. But remember, Faith, he may not be able to make it perfect."

Faith said she didn't care if it showed some flaws since she — (with the only sign of humor Elizabeth Lamb had seen in her) — had a few herself. She expressed her gratitude very nicely and left. Elizabeth Lamb looked out the window and saw Dan Garde waiting outside.

She sank on her bed, sighing in relief. She settled down and half-dozed, until aroused by a gentle knocking on the door to the quad. Buzzie Higgins stood on the steps. "Something happened?" she cried.

"Now, just calm down. Nothing happened except I ran into your Aunt Isabella in Bar Harbor and she asked me to drop this off for you — I told her I'd seen you — so I thought I'd deliver it now on my way home and not wait until Monday.

"Nice-looking feller with her," he added, smiling.

Elizabeth Lamb, as she took the envelope, felt Buzzie was being very gracious, since he and her aunt had only a year ago spent two weeks in Paris together. "But maybe it was so traumatic he's managed to forget about it," she thought, as she motioned him to sit beside her on the step. "Whatever happened in the hotel — and I don't even want to imagine that — I bet she dragged him to every bistro in Paris."

Inside the envelope was a twenty-dollar bill and a brief note in Isabella's indecipherable scrawl. "Can you read that?" she asked Buzzie. "You're a detective."

"No, I can't, because I was brought up on the Palmer Method of handwriting. Feller in my department says you can read the writing of the public school people who learned Palmer, but the rich ones, men and women both, who went to private schools write what he calls 'snob hieroglyphics.'"

"Well, I think it says she's sorry I didn't get much to eat on the way when she drove me up here — *much*; I didn't get anything! So she's sending this for snakes, or snacks or smocks or swatters or something.

"I'm sorry I can't ask you in, but it's a rule. I could walk over to your car with you or, now that I'm rich, buy you a Coke at the Snack Bar. Or, as it's Saturday, I could go for a short drive as long as I'm back for dinner. I just have to put a note under my house-mistress' door as to where I'm going and who with."

Buzzie politely refrained from saying he had issued no invitation to spend some time with him, so, the note in place, they drove sedately down the school driveway and headed for one of the roads in Acadia National Park. "You know, Buzzie, I've been thinking about the teachers you said were here when Jay Colket drowned and I've been wondering about 'who benefits?' or, as I *think*, from what Latin I've learned, *cui bono*?

"I can tell you I heard he blackmailed Miss — or Ms. — Curtain to give him any part he wanted in any school play, but that had been going on for a couple of years and everybody says he was a good actor, so why would she suddenly now benefit from his death?

"And Mr. Alsop and Miss Greenwell evidently have been carrying on a love affair, even though he's married, for some time, and Jay's girlfriend, Faith O'Malley, has had a room next to Miss Greenwell's apartment for three years now. I'm in that room with Faith and you can hear Greenwell and Alsop talking, and doing other things, from our bathroom. And Jay evidently was often in Faith's room, so he could have heard.

"So maybe he tried to blackmail one or both of them. But what for? Better grades? I don't know if he had classes with either of them. And I heard he was rich, so why blackmail for money? But there's — darn it, I forgot what I was just going to say. I think all this studying is destroying my brain cells."

"Never mind. I'll check as to when and if either of them taught, or was going to teach him. But, you know, there's a saying that you can never be too thin or too rich. Maybe he wanted more money.

"Anybody else?"

"Well, Mrs. Farnum, the Headmaster's wife, was here. She drinks a lot, but everybody knows that, so she couldn't be threatened about drinking. Unless he was going to complain to the Board of Trustees; I didn't think of that. There's one funny thing:

I went to one of her classes and she distinctly stated her view that murder was sometimes justified. If someone was going to hurt you, she said. If Colket had something on Father Farnum, she might have killed Jay. But how?

"Mr. Cranston. Well, he knew Jay, and maybe he didn't like him. He helped Mr. Prestwick with the crew team. Jay might have seen Mr. Cranston smoking pot in his garden as I did last night. His garden gate's almost directly opposite a hall door in our dorm that's now fixed so Faith or her new friend Dan can sneak in or out. Maybe it had been like that before, when Jay was here, and that's how Jay would have known. By smelling.

"But Mr. Cranston's a big asset to the school, the author of a world-famous book, and I don't believe Father Farnum would fire him, even if Jay had told. He'd probably just warn him to smoke pot inside the house, not outside. But something — "

A bicyclist approaching them suddenly swerved sharply towards the car. Buzzie had to pull over into the bushes on the right side of the road, cursing under his breath. When they were mobile again, he asked, "What 'something'?"

"I forget. I was just nearly scared to death. Gosh, that was close!"

She went on. "Now, there's Miss McMurtrie. She's just crazy about Mr. Prestwick and people have said she'd do anything for him. I heard her talking to another teacher and she was saying Jay was sort of making insinuations about Mr. Prestwick, as if he had something on him. The school cook's said, practically, that she would be violent to protect Mr. Prestwick. Or her dog. She's devoted to him, too. And she grows poisonous plants in her garden. And I think she might — "

Buzzie interrupted with a laugh. "Did this Colket have anything on the dog?"

She laughed, too. "I don't know. And you said Mr. Sullivan was here. He didn't like Jay; from something he said at a party, Jay had sort of insulted him. But I don't believe that, just that, would make him kill, and I don't see how he could. Mr. Sullivan's old, and not athletic, but, you know, he has keys to — "

Buzzie cursed loudly and braked quickly as a woman coming

towards them with a small child on a carrier behind her bike seat hit a bump on her side of the road that caused her bike to overturn. The child's head rested just inches from the car's wheels. Buzzie and Elizabeth Lamb got out and righted the bike. The mother comforted the screaming child, who luckily had been wearing a helmet. Buzzie reprimanded her firmly, controlling himself as to what he would really like to say, and advised her to walk the bike home and ride alone until her cycling improved.

He got back in the car, wiping his forehead. "My God, these flatlanders!" he said. "It's October and I'd hoped they'd all be gone by now. If they don't kill themselves, they'll kill off the rest of us, for sure. Good thing I was practically crawling along.

"Now, what were you saying?"

"Oh, nothing important. Let's see, what other masters were here? I think my mind's going; I can't remember anything for five minutes."

"That'll be the day! Oh, one thing: there were 'masters,' as you say, who were back at the school a few days before Colket's death, but they'd taken off again for the weekend. Three there were, I think, and I can't remember the names except the head of the music department. I remember his because it's Emerson and can you imagine what they christened him?"

"Not 'Ralph Waldo'?"

"You got it. Poor guy. But, you know, on Monday I think I'd better talk to Mr. Emerson and the two others. They might've noticed something."

"If one of the teachers killed Jay — and you still believe it was probably an accident — there're getting to be too many suspects. Now, you said Mr. Salton was here. I can't think he'd have anything against Jay Colket. There's one of those rumors that always go around schools that he lies a lot, but I found that a couple of things the kids said were lies were absolutely true. I think, since he's the Admissions Officer, that he may just stretch the truth a bit to make the school more appealing to prospects, but that wouldn't endanger his position. Or would it, if Jay found he'd told some really awful lie?"

Buzzie made no comment. She went on. "Then Mr. Prestwick's

the last, of the ones who were here when Jay drowned. If Jay *did* have something on him, then I guess Mr. Prestwick could have done something to Jay's scuba gear. But you said nothing was wrong with it? And you couldn't have checked the wrong equipment, by mistake?"

"No way. His initials were all over it, and Garde had just pulled it off him when he ran for help. And there was nothing at all unusual about it. Our man went over it, with a fine-toothed comb, to coin a phrase. Went over and over everything, even though he was coming down with the worst cold I ever saw. And Prestwick was with the body from the moment Garde found him and got him to the boathouse, and so was Garde, by the way, right beside Prestwick.

"Prestwick went with him to the hospital and then came back with the others and me. Right then, we started checking Colket's gear. Prestwick didn't have a chance to hide anything he might've done to it.

"Anyway, he and Miss McMurtrie alibi each other. Right from when he finished with crew practice, they were together. First they went to dinner in Ellsworth and were going to go to that *Deep Throat* that's playing at the drive-in. I gathered she was the one who wanted to see it — 'just a *little* of it,' she said, 'to see what all the fuss is about.' But he talked her out of it. Said he not only didn't want to go, but he had a funny feeling they should come straight back to the school."

"Don't you think that's queer?"

"Not 'specially. And Miss Greenwell and Mr. Alsop say they were together all evening. And afternoon, before that. Doing some research on a book they're writing, they said. They had dinner at her apartment."

"Well, naturally they'd say that."

"Ms. Curtain says she was reading scripts at her place after having a drink and a sandwich for dinner. Mr. Sullivan said he was alone in his house, reading. His wife's dead and a daughter lives with him but she's a nurse on the three to eleven P.M. shift at the hospital, and she was on duty. Mr. Cranston says the same. Says Mr. Salton asked him to go over to Manset for a lobster dinner with him, because Mrs. Salton hates lobster, but he just felt like staying home and reading, after heating himself some soup."

"Mr. Salton. Did he go out to dinner by himself, then?"

"Says he did. Wife says he went alone, since no one would go with him. He says he got back fairly early, and sort of walked around to settle the lobster, though I've got an idea it was just to stay away from the wife for a while. Ever meet her?"

"I've seen her. I think you're right."

"Anyway, Salton says that, when he was wandering around, he distinctly saw Ms. Curtain reading in her living room, Mr. Sullivan in his, and Mr. Cranston in his. Says he saw Greenwell and Alsop writing at the desk in her apartment — evidently nobody at your school ever pulls the curtains."

"Hmmm. Did he talk to any of them?"

"Says he didn't want to disturb them. But he swears he rounded both campuses several times and saw them all each time.

"Look, I'd better be getting you back. Now listen, Elizabeth Lamb, and listen good: if you get any ideas, do *nothing*. You understand? *Nothing*. You call me. Repeat: *me*."

"Buzzie, you said you're sure the drowning was an accident. How could I get any ideas?" They were now back at the school grounds, and she spoke quickly.

"You might. First time I ever met you, you got an idea and told nobody but the murderer and it nearly got you killed. Just remember what I said. Even if it *was* an accident, you might get some ideas about something somebody doesn't want you to know. As maybe Colket did.

"Here's as far as I can drive you. See you Monday. I promise."

As she crossed the quad to her room, she encountered Jim Newton, strolling along hand in hand with a tall, pretty black girl. "Jim, I was thinking," she said. "Maybe we should see the rehearsals of *Penzance* separately, so as to get independent viewpoints. Which do you want?"

He looked affectionately at the girl with him. "Well, Alma, here, would like me to sneak her in to see a rehearsal, but she can't go tomorrow night because she's in the girls' singing group, The Augustas, and they rehearse on Sunday nights. So we'll go tonight, and you go tomorrow, if that's all right with you."

Alma smiled at Elizabeth Lamb. "I voted for you for our Third Form rep. I thought you were terrific. As a dean-handler, I mean; I didn't know you could write, as well.

"And if Jim falls asleep tonight, I'll wake him up. It wouldn't be fair to you if he saw only half of the rehearsal."

Elizabeth Lamb expressed her thanks, and went on her way, after agreeing to preview the Sunday rehearsal, having no idea that what she had promised them, and what Buzzie had promised her, would never occur.

• CHAPTER 11 •

Things are seldom what they seem.
Skim milk masquerades as cream.

— W.S. Gilbert

E VERYONE IN ROOM 13, as well as the rest of the school, slept late the next morning, since the first meal on Sundays was, in both dining halls, a combined breakfast/lunch served at 12:15, after the Episcopal service on the boys' campus was over. At ten, Josas gently shook Elizabeth Lamb awake. "Want to go to the Catholic chapel with me?" she whispered. "You have to go at ten-thirty or else over to the boys' chapel at eleven. But *we* get juice and graham crackers after Mass, to hold us till brunch."

The thought of both seeing the handsome Father Rogers in action and of something in her stomach before 12:15 was more appealing to Elizabeth Lamb than another half-hour in bed. They dressed quietly in their good dresses, put on white socks and patent-leather slippers and walked slowly across the quad.

"Lots of the girls wear nylons and shoes with half-high heels with their best things, but my mama says she wants to keep me a little girl as long as she can," Josie confided. "Anyway, I'm only fourteen and nylons are expensive and they rip all the time."

"That's what my grandmother says, too," Elizabeth Lamb replied despondently. "I've got a feeling I'll be in socks and Mary Janes until I'm in college."

They both, despite the appeal of Father Rogers, half-dozed through the opening hymn and introductory rites, although they managed to mumble the General Confession along with the others. Faith and Dan were on opposite sides of the chapel, looking at each other occasionally, but like strangers. Elizabeth Lamb observed that the small chapel was crowded, about two-thirds of the congregation being girls, before she yawned and closed her eyes while the lector read from the Old Testament.

She paid attention to the responsorial psalm because it was not sung by all, but was a solo by a boy with a beautiful alto voice. "I just love to hear him," Josie whispered. "But his voice'll get deeper soon and it's a shame. Isn't it funny how boys' voices get deeper when they get older and girls' don't? Not so much, anyway."

They were both more awake when the New Testament reading was announced. "This time, thank goodness, it's not a letter from St. Paul to the Corinthians," Josie whispered. "It seems to me he wrote to them all the time. I wonder if they ever wrote back?" Elizabeth Lamb laughed silently and settled down to half-listen to the reading, which was from the fourth chapter of James. She was jolted to attention by a distinctly pronounced sentence: "You desire what you cannot obtain and so you resort to murder." She stared up at the lector in amazement and heard the rest of the Mass through a haze, wondering about Dan Garde. "Did he really want Faith so much he drowned his friend?" she thought over and over. "But how did he manage it?"

A warm farewell handshake from the idolized Father Rogers diverted her only slightly, as did the promised juice and crackers. She left Josas with the hurried excuse of being so tired that she had to lie down until brunch, found a tree with a bench underneath it and sat, staring absently ahead of her and seeing no one who passed. There was a paperback book, somewhat damp, lying on the bench. She had noticed that many of the students left books and notebooks almost anywhere in any weather. The book was *What You Ought to Know About Drugs.* She read a chapter with interest.

A little before 12:15 she went to the girls' dining hall and joined Josas, B.B., and Caitlin. Mr. Cranston and Mr. Salton honored them with their presence, Mr. Cranston muttering that he thought "being assigned to dining hall duty for Sunday brunch is a bit unnecessary."

"Oh," Mr. Salton answered him, smiling happily and shinily, "I like it. Even though you've got the duty here today and can certainly handle the riotous crowd, I told Martha you asked for my assistance. Her cooking, you know. . . ." He became aware that the students were listening eagerly and blushed to a stop. "When his face is red," Elizabeth Lamb noticed, "it shimmers even more. I wonder if he's got an overabundance of minerals in his system, or something." Then she went back to thinking of Dan.

Her friends were eager to tell her of their half-holiday in Bar Harbor. They had found, so B.B. said, a "super" Chinese restaurant and he just wished she had been able to enjoy it with them. Elizabeth Lamb replied that to her all Chinese food tasted like something that could well be termed "dim sum moo gloo" on the menu. B.B. was somewhat cast down.

They were cheered by the lavish meal provided. Not only were there scrambled eggs, sausages, slices of cold smoked ham, sautéed mushrooms, three kinds of fruit juice, corn muffins, Danish pastry and hot chocolate, with *café au lait* for the teachers, but Mr. Pella stood agreeably at one end of the steam table, poaching eggs to order, which he served on toasted slices of his bread. Even Mr. Cranston stopped looking disgruntled and ate with gusto.

Their enjoyment was interrupted by the sudden appearance of Miss McMurtrie and Mr. Prestwick. The two threw themselves, beaming, into empty chairs and, both at the same time, asked, "Just guess what?"

Elizabeth Lamb's mouth, of course, opened to ask, "What?" but she quickly closed it, in deference to Mr. Salton and Mr. Cranston. They were staring at the newcomers, who were now openly holding hands. Mr. Cranston took a deliberate swallow of his coffee before he asked, "Well, my dear friends, *what?* If it is suitable to be

222

heard by the young persons present, that is?"

"We're engaged!" Miss McMurtrie exclaimed. "We're going to be married as soon as possible!" Mr. Prestwick said at the same time. "Father Farnum is going to perform the ceremony," they added in unison.

There was a loud chorus of congratulations from the table, Mr. Cranston's pleasant tenor rising above the others. The other students stopped eating and stared. Standing up, Mr. Prestwick announced: "Miss McMurtrie and I are going to be married," upon which shouts of congratulations resounded. During them, Elizabeth Lamb wondered if the old law about a wife not having to testify against her husband, or vice versa, still applied.

When the tumult had subsided, the happy couple, Miss McMurtrie blushing and Mr. Prestwick not, went to get their food. Mr. Pella's expression was impassive as he regarded them and said, "My best congratulations."

"Thank you, Sancho," Mr. Prestwick responded.

"I was looking at the lady," Mr. Pella answered blithely. "But I got it wrong and I apologize: I look at *you* when I say, 'Congratulation,' and at *her* when I say 'Felicitation.' But since I made a mistake — and I make many such — I say only to you both that I wish you all the happiness you deserve."

This was graciously received and only Elizabeth Lamb, who had approached for a second poached egg, saw the slight smirk on Mr. Pella's face. "I suppose he just had to get a dig in at her," she thought. "But they're so involved with themselves that they didn't get it. And that's good, I guess."

Replete and happy, the students departed to their various Sunday afternoon diversions. B.B. said he was going for a swim and Caitlin agreed to join him. Josas had engaged to do some typing for one of her teachers. "I hate to type," she said, but then, more happily, "but the money I'll make will be chilly. Good, I mean." Elizabeth Lamb went back to Room 13 and changed into a shirt, jeans and sneakers.

She lay on her bed, a number of unconnected things running through her mind. Suddenly she sat bolt upright. "Of course"; she said aloud, "the look! And the clipping in the head — that Jay must have Xeroxed from stuff in The Cage — and all those other things. 'Who' and 'why' have been right in front of my nose all the time!"

She retrieved the clipping from her drawer and considered it carefully, nodding once or twice in satisfaction and once frowning in puzzlement. She tore a page from a notebook and wrote some names and questions on it, then put it and the clipping into her pocket.

"First the library," she thought. "It's open on Sunday afternoons. Oh, why doesn't Faith own a dictionary! She has just about everything else."

As she walked down the corridor in the Girls' Schoolhouse to the library at its far end, she had to pass the door to the arts room. It was closed, but through its glass panel she saw that Mr. Dipietro was working at a drawing table. She knocked lightly and went in.

"I'm sorry to bother you," she said, "but there's something some friends and I were arguing about and I think you'd know the answer."

He put down his pen and nodded agreeably. She asked him a question. "I've never heard of it," he answered. "The reverse can happen, though." She thanked him and he nodded again and resumed his work.

In the library, she sighed in satisfaction. "It's not real proof," she thought, "but it sure doesn't agree with what was said in my instructions. And then after what Mr. Dipietro said — . Now for Mr. Emerson."

She went to the boys' campus and found the head of the Music Department on his front porch. There was a pitcher of iced tea and glasses on the table beside his chair. He held a piece of sheet music, at which he was staring despondently.

"Yes?" he asked. "You want something? Not to join The Augustas, I hope."

She reassured him and told him her name. She introduced her question with the same words she had used with Mr. Dipietro.

"Oh, almost definitely not," he answered. "I'd say it was quite impossible. The opposite, too." He pondered. "You know, I think someone else asked me that, and quite recently. I can't remember who it was.

"Would you like some iced tea?"

She accepted, grateful for a respite from things she knew she had to find out. "I noticed you at a couple of rehearsals of *Penzance*, but I think you haven't been at the last few," Mr. Emerson told her.

"I got out of it because I was so awful. The most terrible performance this school has ever seen was what I would have given."

Mr. Emerson poured more tea, shaking his head. "No, Miss Lamb, the most terrible performance this school has seen to date will occur on Parents' Weekend. I'm glad you don't want to be involved in it."

"What do you mean, Mr. Emerson?" she asked.

He considered. "I shouldn't be saying this to a student, but my wife and son refuse to listen to me any more and maybe if I get it off my chest I can face the inevitable."

She nodded, having heard that musicians were extremely temperamental, and required more understanding than most artistic people. "Even writers, poor things," she thought, while she smiled encouragingly at Ralph Waldo Emerson.

"It's this new girls' singing group, The Augustas. *I* have to coach it, of course"—he sounded bitter—"and they insist on singing 'Rum and Coca-Cola' at the Parents' Weekend concert. I can't talk them out of it, and when they all agree on a number, I've been told to go along with it.

"Now, I ask you, can you just imagine a bunch of gangling young female Wasps trying to emote with the sultry sophistication the song requires? Have you ever heard it? Yes—well, then, you must see what I mean. They're just pathetic."

"I can see they might be. But are they all white and awkward?"

"Actually, no. There's a girl from Jamaica who's great and an Indian who's not too bad. And one blonde who knows what she's doing. But that's all."

"Well, why don't you put them in front of the piano—I guess there's a piano? And put the others behind it."

He laughed and emptied his glass. "Now, that's an idea. Except that one of the terribles is so short she'd be hidden and she's the one whose father is a trustee—why d'you think I have to—never mind. And the piano isn't big enough to conceal all the frozen performers who'd be behind it. But you've cheered me up. Glad I could answer your question."

She walked slowly away. "I guess I really do know 'who' and 'why' but I can't imagine 'how,'" she thought. She found she was directly in front of the boys' library. She went in and asked a librarian what there was on scuba diving.

He produced two books. "But this one's better. It's the third and newest edition, the '74, of *The New Science of Skin and Scuba Diving*."

It took her about an hour to get an idea of the fundamentals of scuba. She leaned back in her chair and took in a deep breath, thinking. "So," she said to herself, "it would certainly have been possible. But how was it done?"

She sat for a while, alternately staring out a window and then shifting her view to a framed motto above a tall section of bookshelves that read: "Before the Gates of Excellence the high gods have placed sweat."

She went to the librarian again, thinking, "I don't know about excellence, but I'm certainly sweating this thing out," and asked where the drama section was. When she had found what she wanted and had read it carefully, she again sat, staring at nothing. Before she could return the books, the voice she least wanted to hear, of all those in the school, spoke behind her. "Why're you working on a great afternoon like this? Going to be a grind?"

"Oh," she answered, rising and picking up the texts and hoping their titles hadn't been observed, "I'm quitting now. It's all this research I have to do, you know."

As she escaped from the library, she thought, "Now, Joylene. I have to have a little more before I call Buzzie." On the other campus, she got directions to Joylene's room. The door was opened to her knock by a tall, beautiful Middle-Eastern girl. "Is Joylene here?" she asked the girl and then, since the large room obviously held no one else, "Are you her roommate?"

The girl motioned her to come inside. "Joylene's the Senior Prefect of Girls, you know, so she has her own room. I live next door and she's letting me use her typewriter while she's at the cookout. I'm Sophia Hassram, by the way."

"Elizabeth Lamb Worthington. What cookout?"

"Oh, at brunch the smoked ham got a boy from one of your southern states all nostalgic. He started talking about the different ways his family barbecues meat — meat, ugh! I'm a vegetarian. Well, Joylene and some of the other Student Council people who were at his table — he's on the Council too — got the idea of a sort of barbecue at the old smokehouse, put on by and for the Council.

"It's about a hundred-fifty years old and decrepit, but it's been made into a sort of picnic area. We can use it with permission. So Joylene asked Father Farnum and he said okay, as long as the Council members restricted themselves to one guest each *and* invited at least six of the faculty."

"He's smart. I guess he figured somebody'd get beer in somehow. The faculty invitation stopped that. Maybe."

"But, Sophia, you can't smoke meats in a couple of hours. I know that much."

"Of course not. The smokehouse hasn't operated since the school bought the property. As I said, it's just a place for picnics and the ham gave the boy the idea and it just went from there."

"Where is it? I'm on the Council so I guess I can go, though nobody asked me. And would you like to come as my guest? They probably have something besides meat."

"Thanks, but no. Even the smell of it almost makes me sick. At home, sometimes, when my father is hosting a big dinner, I have to eat a bit of lamb, to please him, but I can barely force it down."

Diverted from her quest by her innate curiosity, Elizabeth Lamb asked, "Did you ever have to eat a sheep's eye? I read — "

Sophia interrupted her quickly and with a violent shudder. "I guess Joylene couldn't find you, to tell you about the picnic. She and some others went all over both campuses looking for Council members. You can't miss it; the place is a little behind the girls' soccer field and there'll be a repulsive smell to lead you to it."

As Sophia had said, the site was easy to locate. She went to the soccer field and followed her nose. The party was in full swing. Someone was playing a guitar and a group was singing folk songs, more or less to its accompaniment. Another group was tending a cluster of backyard barbecue grills.

In spite of the large brunch a few hours before, students and a few teachers were heartily consuming hot dogs and hamburgers and spareribs, washed down with quantities of soft drinks. "I guess Father Farnum must really like cookouts, to agree to the school's providing all this food," Elizabeth Lamb thought. "I bet his wife doesn't know."

Father Farnum was gnawing on a large piece of barbecued pork, with evidence of great enjoyment. The other faculty present were Miss McMurtrie and her fiancé, Mr. Alsop, Mr. Cranston, Ms. Curtain and a few other unknown, to her, teachers. Ms. Curtain was protesting that she could eat very little because, "I'm always nervous before a performance and tonight's is the last full rehearsal of *Penzance*."

Elizabeth Lamb found Joylene, and reluctantly accepted a grilled frankfurter encased in a roll. With the help of a little mustard, she was able to eat a bite of it. Then, before Joylene could rejoin her group, she asked her a question.

"Gee, I really don't know," she was answered. "And I can't imagine why you want to. My uncle's right over there at that table. He'd know because he was there."

"No," Elizabeth Lamb replied quickly, "I don't want to bother him when he's just engaged and having such a good time." Then she saw Porter Cornwall emerging from a clump of trees. "Senior Prefect of Boys or not," she thought, "I bet he's got some beer in there. And that there're others in on it, too." She intercepted him and asked him the same question she had asked Joylene.

"How would I know?" Porter answered defensively.

"Haven't you ever heard of it? Come on; it's only for some research I have to do. I thought you knew almost everything. The kids say so."

Porter was as susceptible to flattery as most people. "Well, I didn't really *know* the guy who told me something about it." He indicated, between his cupped hands, a space about eight by twelve inches. "I didn't even know his name," he added nervously, looking over her shoulder and then loudly telling her, "Okay, I'll see you there."

Elizabeth Lamb turned casually. Dan Garde was very near them, also coming out of the woods but from a slightly different direction. "See you where?" he asked jovially, putting his arm about Elizabeth Lamb. "Trying to steal my second-best girl, fella?" He had very obviously been drinking.

She laughed politely. "We're just talking about something I have to do for the Council and Porter's going to help me. Listen, Dan, if I were you I'd keep away from the teachers for a while."

As she walked away, she thought, "Of course it was Dan who told him. Oh, well." Skirting the happy picnickers, she heard Mr. Salton saying in an undertone to a young teacher, "But you really should go; I mean, to realize what our culture is now." His face glistened with earnestness as well as ketchup. "Bet he's talking about *Deep Throat* and bet he had to sneak away from that awful Martha to see it," she thought.

As she passed the table nearest her escape route, she heard the new English teacher who had affronted Mr. Sullivan asking what he could expect to happen at Parents' Weekend.

"Oh," Miss McMurtrie answered him, "you have to talk to the ones who want to know how their darlings are doing, of course. They'll make appointments with you. And it would be wise to show up at all the entertainments. Look healthy and trustworthy the whole time."

Elizabeth Lamb lingered to hear Mr. Prestwick agree: "And I'm afraid the newer teachers have to see every parent who asks. I get out of most interviews by being with my boys. We have two shells on the river for races several times each day.

"Melinda Curtain, having seniority like me, gets convenient migraines when parents want to see her to inquire about their kids' chances of winning an Oscar. And, being a former" — he looked around — "*being* a celebrity as well, and a temperamental *artiste*, besides, she gets away with it. Ralph Emerson, also, trades heavily on the latter image."

"And Tim Cranston, too," Miss McMurtrie added. "As a star like Melinda, he's always tied up with a phone call from a publisher in Iran, or something."

"Don't think he's had more than one or two interviews since he's been here," Mr. Prestwick added. "And as for J.P., he absolutely refuses even one. And then there's — " Elizabeth Lamb eased away from the festivities.

In her room, she sat at her desk and began to list, as they came to her, points to discuss with Buzzie. "What Miss Curtain said," she wrote, thinking she had better not be more specific on something that might be lost or stolen, "and Mr. Cranston, and Mr. Pella and what Buzzie said regarding *that*.

"And Dora, and whoever it was who lied about that; except I only know about it from hearsay. Still, it's a point, if the time. . . . And remember the kitchen helper. And that Jay's room was all torn apart and that Faith had the same room for three years. And what Mr. Salton said, way back.

"And what Joylene told me; then Porter today. And what I found out in the library — make that both libraries — and from Mr. Emerson and Mr. Dipietro. And that look today. But most of all, what Miss McMurtrie said, way back. And, sort of, what I heard today. And then, as for Parents' Weekend — "

She stopped writing. "But Buzzie's going to ask how in the world it could have happened. And I only half-know." She got up and walked around the room. Then, "Oh, my God!" she screamed aloud. She clamped her hand over her mouth and thought, "And *that* was *certainly* right in front of my nose, as well as 'who' and 'why.'"

She read over her list and arranged her facts, or summaries, in the order in which she would present them to Buzzie. She used initials, substituting the letter that followed in the alphabet, as a precaution. Then she drew in a deep breath and walked down to the telephone booth at the end of the hall.

Buzzie's phone was answered by a young female who seemed on the verge of hysteria. Elizabeth Lamb was told that Lieutenant Higgins would not be back until seven-thirty; that the speaker was his "puppy-sitter"; that the damned animal had bitten her twice and, while she was applying iodine to her wounds, had eaten most of a sofa pillow and one of her employer's best shoes.

"Who's this?" the girl asked hopefully. "Could you come over? I just don't think I can last another two hours. I might kill myself!"

Elizabeth Lamb avoided giving her name, in case Buzzie had

noted it on his desk along with one of the school's telephone listings. "She's so out of it she might call here and try to make them send me over," she thought. "And I don't want anyone to know I'm calling Buzzie."

Aloud, she told the puppy-sitter that she would call back. "You could tell him that someone who has an idea called," she added. She went back to her room and sat staring at a copy of *Watership Down* Josie had taken out of the library.

Faith and Josie returned almost at the same time. Josie rushed to the bathroom to soak her typing-tired fingers in warm water. Faith went to her closet and took out an expensive-looking dress, putting it on after she had removed her church dress and thrown it on the bed. "It's Yves St. Laurent's new 'loose look,'" she announced. "Mummy and I went to him on our way back from Switzerland."

Josie came to the bathroom door and timidly said that Faith looked just dickty. Faith looked up at the ceiling and wondered aloud what had happened to her new red sweater. Josie sighed and returned to the washbasin.

Elizabeth Lamb said quickly that the dress was beautiful. "You look *haute* to trot," she murmured. When Faith grasped this, she almost smiled. "Well," she said, with a graciousness unusual in her manner, "after dinner I've got to be at the *Penzance* rehearsal, of course. But I just might stop off first at a party over — "

She suddenly realized that Elizabeth Lamb was looking searchingly at her and that there had been a cessation of splashing from the bathroom. Coldly, she said, "You two'd better get to dinner on time. It's early on Sunday nights, you know." She then removed M. Laurent's 'loose look' from the contamination of those remaining in Room 13.

Elizabeth Lamb was unable to eat much dinner. Josie also ate little and then, muttering to herself various uncomplimentary things about the whole cast of *Penzance*, especially "Mabel," went for a solitary walk before rehearsal. At seven-thirty, Elizabeth Lamb was again at the Falls Dormitory telephone booth. Someone occupied it, apparently giving her mother an endless list of clothes she expected to be brought to her by her parents the next weekend. Finally, she opened the door, saying a perfunctory, "Thank you and see you soon, Mummy," as she did.

Another girl ran down the steps behind the booth and intercepted Elizabeth Lamb, begging to be allowed to go first. "It is just simply vital," she said dramatically. "My whole life might depend on it!"

Elizabeth Lamb went back to her bathroom to wash her hands and face in cold water. Faith came into Room 13, Dan with her. "Look," Faith was saying as she rummaged in a drawer, ignoring the half-shut bathroom door, "why can't you get it for me? Even though fifteen dollars an ounce is highway robbery. Last year he charged twelve dollars for the best stuff."

"We all promised the coach," Dan said firmly. "Come on. We'll be late. And — "

Elizabeth Lamb had turned on the water faucets full force. When she came out of the bathroom, Faith and Dan had gone. She went back to the telephone and made impatient gestures at the girl using it, no matter what her life was depending on. By the time the phone was finally free, Elizabeth Lamb's face and hair were again damp with sweat. She took her reminder list from the security of her back jeans pocket and held it unsteadily as she dialed. Buzzie took a long time to answer, and he sounded harassed and impatient. She drew a deep breath and said, "It's me, Elizabeth Lamb, and I'm sure it was murder and I'm sure I know who did it. And why."

"What?" Buzzie shouted. "Say that again!"

And then the line went dead.

• CHAPTER 12 •

Vindication is a bucket with a hole in it.

— Italian saying

ELIZABETH LAMB hung up, set her jaw, and dialed again. "Damn dog!" Buzzie answered. "He knocked the phone over. Look, I want to know everything that makes you think so. Every bit!"

Consulting her list, she explained in detail. It took a long time. Once she was interrupted by an angry shout from the telephone. "What did I say?" she asked.

"Never mind. The blasted animal just got out the back door. Go on."

She continued. "You could be right, I guess," he responded slowly. "You haven't been obvious?" She told him of the library incident. He drew in a deep breath and loudly exhaled it.

"Look," he said, "I'd better come over tonight. I think it's best the presence be removed. Or call it 'X.' You understand me and we're not saying the name again on this line. Under the circumstances, I don't need a warrant for 'X.'

"Where are you calling from?"

"The phone in my dorm hall," she answered. "It's in a booth," she added quickly. "Buzzie, who was the last person you interviewed, before?" He told her. She sighed in satisfaction.

"Give me the number where you are and stay by it," Buzzie directed. "If I'm to avoid a suit for false arrest, I want to be a mite more sure. Just let me make two calls. I'll get right back to you, whether I get answers or not."

When the phone finally rang, she grabbed it. "I checked with our newspaper files in Augusta and then I called the Colkets," Buzzie told her. "From what they say, the boy well could have — listen, now, and listen good: you're to go to a friend's room and stay there until it's all over and I send you word. You are to be *with* someone the minute you leave that booth. You are *not* to get any helpful ideas and act on them.

"As soon as I find that mutt, I'll start. I should be there in half an hour. Now go do what I said."

Just a little frightened by Buzzie's serious tone, she went to the room next to hers, the one occupied by Lara Jane, Molly, Liz, and Leigh. Her knock was not answered. She passed Room 13 and tried at Miss Greenwell's door. Again, no response.

She returned to her room and glanced out the window. Very few lights showed in the buildings around the quad. From outside, a survey of the exterior of Falls Dormitory revealed every window dark.

"They're probably at the rehearsal," she thought. "Well, this is great; I'm practically alone on the campus! And I can't just show up at the few rooms with lights, where the girls probably never even heard of me. They'll think I'm crazy."

As she returned to the room through the door to the quad, she locked it behind her. "What'll I do?" she said aloud. "How long before Buzzie gets here?

"And," she thought, "he has to find his dog first. Suppose it takes longer than he thinks and suppose being seen with the scuba book in the library, and the other one, too, made 'X' — I don't even want to think of the name — realize I was on to something. Maybe

Buzzie would need the tangible evidence, if it exists, but 'X' might get to it first. Or already have got it. But if it's still there, it might help Buzzie to avoid a suit for false arrest. It just might."

She got an empty white canvas laundry bag from her closet. "The book said it didn't weigh all that much," she thought, "and I could drag it out and hide it till Buzzie gets here. Somewhere in the bushes, maybe." She pulled on a sweater over her shirt.

Recollection of the firmness with which Buzzie had spoken made her stand still. She turned to return the bag to the closet, then thought: "But I can't stay here alone. I'll go over to the boys' campus where there'll be people and if I think I should try when I get there — " She searched among Faith's possessions for the flashlight she would undoubtedly possess, forbidden or not, and found it.

Leaving the door to the quad locked, she left by the other door, cautiously crossed the hall and slipped out the fire door to the forbidden road. No lights were visible in any of the houses. She ran to the end of the dorm building and peered around it. By the building's farther corner, nearest the quad, she could most distinctly discern a bicycle lying on the ground.

"A sign, maybe," she breathed, and, slipping the flashlight into her back jeans pocket and stuffing the laundry bag down the front of her sweater, she mounted the bike. She pedalled fast to the other campus, glancing frequently over her shoulder at the dark road behind her.

The boys' campus was more brightly lit than the one she had left and a number of people were walking about. Most of them were headed in the direction of Madison Auditorium. "Probably the rehearsal's just starting," she thought.

She put the bike in a rack and began to walk slowly towards Madison. Then she stopped. "I'm sure there's no danger," she said aloud, and thought, "Even if I *am* being just like one of those dumb heroines in whodunits, who goes right where she shouldn't. Buzzie just might need it."

She turned and ran along the path to the river. There were no lights in the boathouse. "Dumb, dumb, dumb; that's me," she thought. "Of course it's locked. I'd better try to get Lara Jane out of the rehearsal and convince her it's important enough for her to give me her keys. Or maybe come over herself, if there's time when she's not on stage."

Feeling suddenly weak, she leaned against the heavy door, to catch her breath. Her weight made it swing slowly inward. Not only was it unlocked, it had not even been tightly shut.

"My God," she whispered. Afraid to use the flashlight, she slipped into the building. Her sneakered foot encountered something lying on the floor just inside the door. It was a key on a plain metal ring. "What in the world?" she thought.

On an impulse, she inserted the key into the lock. It fit. She listened for what seemed an eternity and heard nothing. She shut the door, in her nervousness making a slight sound as she did, locked it from the inside and left the key in the lock. She again stood listening and again heard no evidence of anyone's being in the boathouse. Using the flashlight, she quickly and quietly found her way amongst the racks of rowing shells to the place along one wall near the back where the scuba gear was stored, next to the air compressor used for filling the divers' tanks.

"The book said it was rare to have your own compressor," she thought, "but they teach scuba almost every day and I guess some rich parent donated one." Jay Colket's well-monogrammed equipment was easy to locate, just behind the rest. With difficulty, she inserted it, or most of it, into the laundry bag and began to drag it towards the entry door. "I'll hide it in some bushes and run as fast as I can to Madison," she thought. "I hope the parts that wouldn't fit in the bag aren't getting scraped so that they won't show anything they possibly could."

Halfway to her destination she stopped, dodging behind one of the racks. One of the small windows had suddenly darkened. As she hid, the window swung inward and a form, with some difficulty, pushed through the narrow aperture.

She was almost paralyzed with terror. Then she let go of the bag and ran for the door. The form moved to block her way. Gritting her teeth, she attempted to turn the light on it but before she could press the switch, the flashlight dropped from her sweaty hand. She bent down and unsuccessfully fumbled for it.

"No need for a light, Miss Lamb," said Mr. Cranston's pleasant voice. "I can see in the dark. It's a talent of mine that has proved useful more than once."

Her own voice was no more than a croak. "How did you come through that little window? They're made that small so nobody can. And they're supposed to be locked."

"I discovered in the *Maquis* that it's really true that where a man's head can go, his body can follow. And I've had this window unlocked for some time. Prestwick never checks them.

"But why are *you* here? And you seem to be making off with Colket's scuba gear. Strange."

Her voice was a little more controlled. "I was — I'm getting it for his girlfriend. She's my roommate and she wanted it to remember him by. Mr. Prestwick wouldn't let her have it, so I — "

"So you, somehow, got Mr. Prestwick's key and came in here to retrieve it. Hard to believe, Miss Lamb.

"But you did get a key. I tried the door first. You must have locked it from inside. I knew you'd be here, you see. I followed you at a distance as soon as you slipped out the dorm door opposite my garden. And I calculated you were on to something, after seeing today in the boys' library what you were reading.

"I had heard of your talent for detection, in casual conversation with some other teachers, after the Senior Council meeting. All great minds run alike, they say, and it appears yours is as great as mine." He actually sounded, not pompous, but absolutely serious.

"I don't know what you mean, Mr. Cranston. I was just getting this for Faith — "

His laugh was as pleasant as his voice. "And today you were surely reading in *The Merry Wives of Windsor*. One of its lines is: 'Faith, thou hast some crochets in thy head now.' How did you know Colket quoted that? He was drunk, of course, and as egotistical and foolish as usual.

"Everyone knew of his gift of modeling likenesses in clay heads and I surmised he'd hidden something in a head of his girl. But it certainly wasn't in his room; I took that apart. I suppose you found it somewhere?"

"You admit it?" Now she was extremely frightened. This man

was so sure of himself, so certain of always getting his way. "Talk about egos; his is that of a maniac," she thought. How would Buzzie ever find her here?

"I'll never admit it to anyone but you. And it will go no further." His laugh was now not so pleasant.

"Mr. Cranston, I told Lieutenant Higgins how I knew Jay Colket was killed and how I knew you did it." She wished she could see his face. "I told him just a little while ago. He's on his way here. If you kill me, too, that'll be the end of you. Lieutenant Higgins knows everything I figured out."

He laughed again, with real amusement, it seemed. "My dear child, you've read too many mystery novels. The victim-to-be always says the police are on the way. Sometimes it's true, but in this case — no. You're certainly lying. As I would, were I you. We're very much alike."

"Why do you think I'm lying? I'm not." She was beginning to tremble. "If only I can keep him talking," she thought. "When Buzzie can't find him and can't find me, he just might come here. Why didn't I have the sense to leave a note? But he probably went through my room first, to see. He's smart."

"I know, not think, you're lying," he answered, "because you're as much of an egotist as I am. You'd want to present all your evidence at once, including Colket's gear."

"I don't think there's any evidence in it," she said, with some calm. "The ammonia you got from the kitchen and cleaned the tank out with while they were all at the hospital destroyed almost all of the smell of marijuana. And the detective checking it had a cold.

"Except that a little was left. A boy who used the gear a few days ago felt some reaction. I heard him talking once, at lunch. But it's probably all gone, by now. Still — "

He made a slight movement towards her. Loudly she said, "You thought of everything. A lot of people including you knew that Jay smoked pot before he dived, and even half a joint would keep him from realizing that the air in his tank was full of marijuana."

He paused. She wondered why. Then his lighter flickered and she saw the glowing end of a cigarette. "How long does it take to smoke a cigarette?" she thought, desperately. "But maybe he won't finish all of it and — "

He spoke in his usual tone, as if he were stating something to his class. "You *are* clever. I have to admire you. And I'm as curious as you are. We have — I have — a little time."

"So tell me why I did it?"

"If you'll tell me your real name. You're the Canadian cousin, of course, but I don't know your name, although they'll find out.

"The real Timothy Cranston wrote *Marianne* and when he died, it had already spread all around France. Buzzie checked in old papers as to the date he was reported killed. I don't know why you took his identity; I don't think you had yet realized how famous and profitable the book was going to be.

"Well, you're smart. Maybe you did. Maybe you're even the one who betrayed your *Maquis* unit, as Mr. Salton told me it was betrayed, so you could switch. Or maybe you'd had police trouble in Canada before you went to France with your cousin and so that's why you impersonated him. Cousins can look very much alike — as Miss Curtain once said, and the other *Maquis* — if any were left who knew you — would have more on their minds than you. And after the many years you took before you dared come back, I guess you felt it was as safe here as in Europe.

"But you refuse to see many parents, and maybe it's because some of them are, or could be, men who were boys here when the real Tim Cranston was. And they might wonder."

From the back of the boathouse, there was a stirring neither of them heard. He drew on his cigarette again. "Why did *you* wonder?"

"Good," she thought, "he's getting interested. Oh, God, when will Buzzie come?"

Aloud, she said, as slowly as she could, "There were a lot of contradictions about you that I sort of registered in the back of my mind, but I didn't really exactly *wonder*. It was just today in the dining hall when Mr. Pella was congratulating Miss McMurtrie. Mr. Prestwick, standing beside her, thought he was the one being spoken to.

"Then I suddenly realized that the insults and hints Jay Colket was coming out with, that day in August I heard about, that day

Mr. Prestwick had the crew at his house for champagne and pizza, weren't being said to him though everybody thought they were. You were standing beside him and Jay was looking at *you*. You realized he knew from what he said — 'like a fair house built upon another man's ground' and 'I cannot tell what the dickens his name is' — and the other things, that you really weren't Timothy Cranston.

"He probably talked to some old *Maquis* when he was in France this summer. His family think so. And heard something that made him suspicious. Then he got here and looked up the real Cranston's yearbook, and other stuff, in The Cage and figured out the contradictions I did. He Xeroxed the yearbook page and put it in the head of Faith — "

"And where is it now?"

"Where Buzzie will find it. I tell you he knows all about you."

He very deliberately threw down his cigarette and stepped on it. "And I tell you I don't believe you. And you know as well as I do that there are a lot of teenage suicides. It'll be considered just another one when they find you in the river."

She gasped and tried to step farther back into the rack of shells. He calmly went on: "You thought you'd vindicate Colket's death. Colket was worth nothing and, sadly, you are worth much. The Italians say, 'Vindication is a bucket with a hole in it' and, for you, the hole will be that you're silenced."

"No!" she screamed, her voice covering the slight sounds of movement coming towards them from the rear of the building.

His voice was gentle and even regretful. "It will be quick. You deserve that. And you'll feel nothing. As nothing will show on — "

A small bright light appeared at the very edge of her limited field of vision and at the same time whatever hurtled past her knocked her down. She heard only a soft sound from Cranston and then the collapse of his body to the floor. She found the light she had dropped and turned it on.

Cranston was lying on his side, below a rack of shells. Liz Fyordberg knelt beside him, vomiting horribly. The light Elizabeth Lamb had seen before Liz rushed by her came wavering up to them. It was a flashlight held by Leigh Urson, in whose other hand, raised as a weapon, was an empty vodka bottle.

Leigh sank to the floor. "Liz got him?" she whispered. "We heard — awfully drunk — took a long time to catch on and move." She gasped, turned her head and emulated Liz.

"Liz," Elizabeth Lamb said quietly, "what did you do?"

Liz shook her head, still gagging. Finally she sat back on her heels, wiping her mouth with her hand. "Dizzy," she managed to say. "When we realized, just went straight for him. Got him by the shoulders and pushed him back from you. Leigh was going to hit him with our bottle."

"He's out cold," Leigh offered, gulping. Liz crawled to the recumbent form and shook it. She put her head to the chest. "Not breathing," she said. She turned Cranston over onto his stomach. In the top of the back of his neck, there was a small, deep gash that was bleeding, but not heavily.

They stared at it, puzzled as well as frightened. "It's from that piece of metal that holds the clamp on the end of a shell's rigging," Elizabeth Lamb decided. "You pushed him right into it. Hard."

"Oh-my-God," Leigh said slowly. "It pierced what they call the brain stem, or something." She paused to cough. "That's the part of the brain that controls breathing." Her voice was now barely audible. "I heard my father and another doctor talking once —" She started to vomit again.

With difficulty, Liz turned Cranston onto his back. "I'll try to start him breathing while one of you runs like hell to get somebody." She pounded several times on his chest. "There's something new," she said vaguely, "but I don't know it — I hate to touch the snake but I'll try mouth-to-mouth."

Elizabeth Lamb felt too weak to stand. She slumped to the floor beside Liz, who had cupped the back of Cranston's neck with one hand so that his head fell backwards while with the other she pinched his nose. She shuddered as she placed her mouth on his.

Leigh moved unsteadily to the door. There was a cry of "Damn!" as the light she held went out with a crash. "Key was in the door," she said, "but I dropped it and my light too. Broken." She began to cough again, choking as she did.

Elizabeth Lamb took in a deep breath through her mouth, and

then another. She got slowly to her feet and found her way to the door with her light. Although she felt all over the floor and shook the choking Leigh's clothes, she could not find the key. "It's nowhere, the key," she called to Liz.

Liz removed her mouth briefly from Cranston's. "Well," she panted, "he's still not breathing. He'll die and I'll be up for manslaughter, or something. Didn't this damned dink come through the window?" She bent down and continued her efforts.

The window would not open, no matter how many ways Elizabeth Lamb tried to manipulate the catch. She reached for an oar and swung it against the glass. It cracked, and she swung the oar again, and then again to clear the fragments of glass that still hung on the frame.

As she eased gingerly through the opening, she felt a sharp pain in her upper left arm and heard her sweater catch and rip as small pieces of remaining glass held her back. "Hurry!" yelled Liz. With one more push she was through. As she fell to the ground she landed partly on her left hand and an agonizing pain shot up her arm. She could feel that her entire left sleeve was wet and sticky. "It's blood," she thought, "and lots of it. Oh, God, I forget the pressure point for the arm!"

Clamping her right hand around her bleeding left arm, she staggered a few feet in the direction of the quad. Its lights suddenly blurred and she swayed. "I'll never make it," she thought. The pain in her hand had settled into a dull throb. She managed to move a few more yards and then, almost directly behind the boathouse, between it and the Headmaster's residence, saw a small house on the river path she had never before noticed.

Gritting her teeth, she headed slowly for the lighted porch. She could no longer think very coherently as she muttered, " 'Bucket with a hole in it,' he said. Well, the hole's in his neck now — "

She crawled up the steps and, through the blackness that was slowly making its way across her eyes, she saw the front door open. "What the devil!" a man's voice exclaimed.

"It's Mr. Sullivan," she thought, as the blackness completely closed in. She felt him catch her as she fell and very dimly, from far, far away, heard him call, "Mary, come here! Mary — "

242

• CHAPTER 13 •

Head of the Charles

THERE WERE alternating periods of white and black, sound and silence. Finally there was a small room in which the bright light above revealed anxious faces bent over her, green walls visible behind them. Her arm hurt from wrist to shoulder. She was lying on something hard. A voice said, "She's coming to, again," and then there was a sharp, quick pain in her other arm and then nothing.

She woke in a bed beside a window through which she saw the boys' campus of St. Augustine's in the golden glow of early evening. Her left wrist was in a cast and there was a bottle somehow suspended above her from which a colorless fluid emerged and trickled down a plastic tube into a needle inserted in her right arm. A young woman in white stood at the foot of the bed, holding an enormous sheaf of gladioli.

"I'm dead, right?" asked Elizabeth Lamb. "There're always gladiolas at funerals. And I happen to hate them."

"Then we'll give them to someone else," the nurse agreed cheerfully. "But they're from the Student Council and it's said they took up a collection so we'd better keep them for a couple of hours.

"My, you've slept almost right 'round the clock!"

The flowers were put in a large vase of water and placed on the sill of the other window where they were obvious to anyone entering by the door in the opposite wall but not to the patient. "There!" the nurse said. "And you're not dead; you're in the school infirmary. Lucky to be here, too. I'm Mrs. Roberts, by the way."

"Why?" Elizabeth Lamb asked. "I mean, why am I lucky to be *here*?"

"With the blood you lost, you're lucky to be anywhere! It was touch-and-go by the time they got you in the ambulance and rushed you to the hospital for a transfusion. And they set your wrist there. You must've broken it when you fell through that window.

"Then they called your grandmother — she was in California but she'll be here tomorrow — and she said couldn't you be moved back to the school? She said you were terrible in hospitals and would have a fit when you woke up."

"I sure would have. Hospitals make me throw up. I'm serious. I try not to but I do, all the time, whenever I'm in one. Which hasn't been often."

"So the doctor said you'd be okay and they brought you back. Your grandmother wants you watched constantly. She told them to hire three nurses at her expense and I'm one of them. The third. The other two've already done their shifts for today."

"Well, well," said Elizabeth Lamb. "I see. Though why Grandmother thinks it's necessary to have somebody staring at me all the time, I can't imagine. It doesn't look as if I could try any more dumb tricks.

"I'm hungry, Mrs. Roberts. And how is it you know about the window? Did I talk while I was out of it?"

The nurse looked at her watch. "The IV can come out now. That's good, or else I'd have to spoon-feed you. And if you vomit easily — Just a minute; I'll go call for a tray."

When she returned, she answered the question. "How do I know? Just about everybody on the island knows. The story even made the Bangor paper, somehow, though the school tried to keep it quiet. Someone in the hospital talked, no doubt; I've heard it said it's impossible to breathe anywhere on Mount Desert Island without getting your rate of respiration counted. And having it told.

"The A.P. picked up on the thing. You're quite a celebrity. Nobody knows the whole story, though, and Father Farnum isn't talking. And won't let anybody else talk, so the fuss will soon die down. The reporters, after a day or two, will have something new to get on.

"His book, though, I hear, is selling out 'at bookstores everywhere,' as the ads always say."

"His book? Oh, Mr. Cranston's." She hesitated. "What happened to him?"

"Dead as a doornail. Would have been brain-dead in four to six minutes anyway, without oxygen, so it's just as well. Save the State of Maine the money for a trial, or hospital for life. Those girls did what they could, but it wasn't enough and it was too late.

"They broke down after it was all over, when a teacher with a key got to the place. They told the whole story, afterwards, all they knew, when they could. How he was going to kill you and what they did. But that's all most of us know, because, as I said, Father Farnum has shut everybody up now.

"He wants to see you as soon as the doctor checks you over. I called him after I sent for your supper, and told him you were awake."

The doctor arrived just before the tray of thin soup, salted crackers, rice pudding, and weak tea appeared. He satisfied himself as to her condition, gave the nurse some instructions and began to leave with a gay wave and a "Good work! A brave young lady."

"What's the button you're wearing?" Elizabeth Lamb asked him. "That button that says WIN?"

"It's for President Ford's new 'Whip Inflation Now' policy."

"My grandmother says that doctors' incomes have gone way, way up, far above the inflation on other things."

"Er — indeed. Just relax and don't think too hard. And do get better soon," he added hopefully, making a hasty exit.

Elizabeth Lamb quickly disposed of the food and called wistfully to Mrs. Roberts, who was reading in a lamp-lit chair across the room: "Oliver Twist?"

"Who?" Then she laughed. "Oh. I'm not sure. You've been out for hours and I'd better ask the doctor. He's checking those other two girls. They're in here, too. I'll go find him as soon as Father Farnum comes."

Father Farnum strode in, managing to look both solemn and joyous at the same time. He sat beside the bed, patted her good hand, and cleared his throat. "Going to make a speech," Elizabeth Lamb thought. "Like a politician."

But he didn't. He merely said, "For once, I am at a loss for words. The cleverness you showed, and the courage! I've been talking to Mr. Vincentia, who will come tomorrow with your grandmother, and he told me of things in — ah — your past. I had no idea.

"And I heard more from Lieutenant Higgins, too. He asked me to tell you he had to go to Augusta today. He'll come tomorrow morning. But he showed me his notes on all you had told him. He got to the school, you know, while you were in the boathouse with — while you were in the boathouse, and organized a search. Just as you reached Mr. Sullivan, Mr. Prestwick and I and some of the others got to the scene."

"Father Farnum, what's going to happen to Liz and Leigh?"

He now managed to look both solemn and reassuring. "Well, of course the school must show *some* reaction to their drinking. Probably required attendance at AA meetings in Bar Harbor for the rest of the term. And they'll be on social probation." He sighed. "They had a flashlight, too. But then, so did you, but your roommate admitted it was hers, so we'll just forget about those flashlights.

"*And* they had a key to the boathouse they got from somebody who shouldn't have had one." He sighed again. "But between us, Mr. Vincentia has announced his intention of presenting Elizabeth Fyordberg with something like a diamond as big as the Ritz." As he smiled, his face lost years and he looked again like the happy boy in the yearbook picture. "And one perhaps the size of the boathouse to Leigh Urson.

"Mr. and Mrs. Colket are coming to the school on Wednesday. They'll want to see you, if the doctor permits. I think I can say they'll be most generous in expressing to you in a tangible way their gratitude for discovering the truth about their son's death."

"I don't want anything. I was just curious. My grandmother says it's a trial I'm made that way; that I hear and see things and put them together."

"We-l-l, *my* grandmother used to tell me: 'Always take anything you're offered and say thank you.' But it's up to you." He regarded the ceiling and told it: "A full scholarship in their son's name given in perpetuity at four-year intervals to a deserving applicant would be a wonderful gesture."

Elizabeth Lamb regarded the cast on her wrist and told it: "I'm very worried about that key. I guess Liz and Leigh had to explain where they got it. I think if I wasn't so worried about Lara Jane Oliver and the rest of the Sixth Form girls I could remember everything I might want to say to the Colkets."

Father Farnum actually laughed, and loudly. He continued to laugh until the nurse rushed in. He dismissed her with a reassuring gesture. She frowned and left.

"You'll be able to remember. The keys held by the Sixth Form girls' rep have been confiscated, of course. The entire body of Sixth Form girls came to me and told me the history of the Key Ceremony. And Liz and Leigh say they took the boathouse key from Miss Oliver's key ring after she left for rehearsal and they had decided the boathouse would be a good place to finish their vodka.

"They say they'd had some of it before they went to the boat-house and so when they dropped the key just inside the door they were — to quote them — 'feeling no pain.' They merely left it and neglected to lock the door behind them. As I told them, their flouting many of the school rules led to your being able to get into the boathouse and so nearly caused your — ah, early demise."

"So nobody gets thrown out? Or punished?"

"Only what I told you for Miss Fyordberg and Miss Urson. Nothing for Lara Jane Oliver and the rest of the form." He looked at his watch. "Mr. Sullivan came over with me. He wants to see you. The doctor said we could have fifteen minutes and I've used up my share."

He touched her hand gently and rose. "Don't worry about anything or anyone. And when you're better, I'd like to hear in detail how you figured this whole thing out. I can only say again that I'm both amazed at what you did, and proud of you. I'm very glad you chose St. Augustine's."

Mr. Sullivan had obviously been lurking in the hall. He bounced in almost before Father Farnum had finished speaking and left with a regal nod to the nurse. As she entered, Mr. Sullivan was close behind her.

Mr. Sullivan ignored the nurse's crisp "I must very soon get this child ready for the night, you know."

"Well," he exclaimed, "I can't wait to hear! You look frighteningly well, Miss Worthington!

"Now, in the time I'm allowed, please tell me how you came to suspect that creature of murdering the Colket boy? And how he did it? Say you're not too tired!"

"I'm okay," she answered, and to the nurse, "Please could I have more to eat?"

"Coming up," said the nurse. She went out with a look at Mr. Sullivan that indicated her thought that he might be a possible child-molester. Mr. Sullivan grinned at her.

As soon as she had gone, he, with a wink, produced a large shiny red apple from his pocket. Elizabeth Lamb took it gratefully.

"Well, I'll try," she said between bites, "but I am getting sort of tired, Mr. Sullivan. Were you told what Liz and Leigh remembered about what they heard Mr. Cranston and me saying in the boathouse?

"And what *is* his real name, do you know?"

Mr. Sullivan sat back, prepared to enjoy himself. "He was the Canadian cousin, as you surmised, and his name was Theodore Candage. Evidently he'd visited here while Cranston was a student, and knew something of the school. Cranston had the money and took him to France in '39. Candage was, as you thought, in some trouble in Canada: a fifteen-year-old girl. Maybe, when Candage assumed Cranston's identity, the identical initials helped with passports, identity cards — I don't know.

"And, yes, Miss Fyordberg and Miss Urson seem to have

remembered everything they heard. They told Father Farnum later. I was present; that's how I know what I do about you and Candage. Or let's call him Cranston.

"It's quite strange," he added, "or so my daughter Mary, a nurse, thinks, that those two girls could have drunk a bottle of one-hundred-fifty-one-proof vodka and still be not only walking around, but in full possession of their faculties after Prestwick and the others got into the boathouse."

"They'd thrown up most of it. From fright, I guess."

"Yes. Mr. Prestwick was in a rage about the boathouse floor. Threatened to have them building stone walls all winter, as soon as they were released from the infirmary here."

"Father Farnum didn't say that. Only AA meetings and social probation for them."

"Right. Several boys, among them our friend Jim Newton, and Will Dickinson, and Porter Cornwall and Dan Garde, too, said they'd clean up the boathouse if Prestwick would let the girls off. Said they'd do it in honor of you. Evidently you have admirers."

"Gosh!" She finished the apple reluctantly. The capacious pocket of Mr. Sullivan's sagging tweed jacket provided another.

She leaned back on her pillows and chewed more slowly. "So you know a lot of it. But there were things that made me see Mr. Cranston wasn't really Mr. Cranston. And I think Jay Colket discovered them, too.

"But you're sure Liz and Leigh told everything they heard, Mr. Sullivan? Else there'll be holes for you in what I say."

"*Ab*solutely sure. No one's admitted here who isn't extremely intelligent, and it's been noticed of those two since Third Form that they have incredible memories."

"Well, then, you know it was that look in the dining hall Sunday — was that only yesterday! — from Mr. Pella to Miss McMurtrie that put the whole thing in focus for me. And you've heard of the look from Colket that was thought by everybody to be for Mr. Prestwick but was really at Mr. Cranston, beside him.

"You know, Mr. Sullivan, *you're* responsible for my getting on to some things about Mr. Cranston — Candage — whatever. You sent me to The Cage to look up the previous productions of *Penzance* and while I was waiting for Jim, I looked in old yearbooks, too.

"Now, Miss Curtain had said, at a rehearsal, that Mr. Cranston had 'the best tenor voice' she'd ever heard. Something like that. But the *Penzance* review said he'd sung the part of the Sergeant of Police in 'a profound and dramatic bass.' And I'd heard her say that part requires a bass voice.

"So yesterday I asked Mr. Emerson if men's voices could change with age, from bass to tenor. My roommate, too, had said in chapel something about boys' voices getting deeper as they get older. And Mr. Emerson said it was just about impossible for them to get higher.

"And Timothy Cranston's yearbook photo showed his chin as absolutely smooth — no dent or dimple in it. Mr. Cranston — Candage, I mean — had a deep dimple in his chin I noticed the first time I saw him. It was almost a cleft. Yesterday I asked Mr. Dipietro, who knows faces, if he'd ever known of a dimple to appear as someone got older. And he said no, though they could disappear with age.

"And the yearbook said Mr. Cranston was the president of the Orthographic Society. That didn't register on me at first, but I looked up the word yesterday in the girls' library. 'Orthography' means correct spelling, to make it simple. So I guess you'd have to be a demon speller to belong to the society. Is that right?"

Mr. Sullivan nodded assent. She went on: "Well, Mr. Cranston, in giving me an assignment, said he'd never been a good speller. So that, with all the other things, made me wonder.

"And he told me he'd 'grown up on French cooking.' His mother, or her cook, could have done French cooking but I thought of what a kitchen helper had said. The kids call them 'wombats' but I think that's disgusting. She said that as a child in Canada she'd had *café au lait* every morning. So maybe Mr. Cranston had grown up in Canada."

"Candage," said Mr. Sullivan. "Yes, of course he had."

"Well, all this later stuff was just supposing. But he kind of implied, one night in his garden when I was talking to him, that living at St. Augustine's was sort of a new experience. I just got that feeling.

"And I heard a teacher saying that someone — she couldn't remember if it was Mr. Prestwick, Mr. Salton, or Mr. Cranston — had said he'd seen Jay eating heavily the night he drowned. Well, Mr. Prestwick wouldn't have said that because he was out to dinner. And he'd know that, if Jay drowned, the Underwater Accident Report would have to say what he'd eaten. If there'd been an autopsy, it would have shown. And a cook told me he'd eaten almost nothing.

"And Mr. Salton wasn't at dinner. And, you know, I asked about this while I was talking to Lieutenant Higgins last night: Mr. Salton was the last one interviewed by the police. So he'd probably have been told by the teachers before him what they said. I think he'd gone off to see *Deep Throat* and — why're you laughing, Mr. Sullivan?"

Mr. Sullivan controlled his mirth and, just as the nurse appeared with a second supper tray duplicating the first, whisked the apple cores into his pocket. "Why do you think, Miss Worthington? And you're right, you know."

"Well, he knew you and Mr. Cranston had said you were reading, and what the others said. So *he* said he'd been walking around the school grounds for a long time and saw you all doing what you'd told him you told the police you were doing."

"Figures. Thereby concealing from Martha — from anyone, I mean — where he'd really been. Just like Salton. Ingenious. Has to be, I suppose."

"So Mr. Cranston must've been the one who said Jay ate a lot. Just as a sort of reason for his having drowned. But *he* wasn't at dinner, either. I guess he didn't know about the Underwater Accident Reports, as Mr. Prestwick would."

"I see. But *how* did he do it? The girls didn't overhear anything about that."

She was eating very slowly. "I'm getting really tired. He drove to the boathouse with his portable barbecue grill while everyone was at dinner and burnt marijuana in it beside the air compressor. Then he filled Jay Colket's scuba tank from the compressor. Then he let the contaminated air out of the compressor. He had been here five years and Mr. Prestwick's niece told me it was only a couple of years ago that some kids did that here, to get extra high by breathing pot from a tank filled from a compressor they'd burned pot beside. And I read a book on drugs I found on a bench and I gathered that just one pot cigarette, or part of one, would have left a taste in Jay's mouth so he didn't realize he was breathing in more pot from his tank.

"And I read some books on scuba. For every fifteen feet you dive, the pressure at which you breathe the air in your tank increases. If Jay'd been breathing in pot from his tank on land, where the air pressure is 14.7 pounds a square inch, he would just've gotten high. Dan and Jay went down about forty-five feet, Dan says. There's a complicated explanation of the effect of pressure on your organs and tissues — nitrogen gets into them, or something, if you go too deep or stay down too long. The books call this 'the martini effect' or 'nitrogen narcosis' and I read that Dr. Cousteau called it 'rapture of the depths,' or 'the deep,' or something like that.

"Maybe you see mermaids or underwater cities. Maybe you even think you're above the water. I don't know. And Jay was breathing in marijuana in very concentrated form, even though he was only down forty-five feet. He would soon have got dizzy and disoriented. He must have got so stoned that he let go of the mouthpiece. He just drowned."

"But," Mr. Sullivan objected, "Garde told Prestwick it was only a few minutes before he went looking for Colket. And Colket's tank was empty. How could all his air have been used up in that short a period?"

"Well," she said, "that bothered me, too. But I read that when the mouthpiece is dropped, if it sinks facing upwards then the air can be released from the tank, if the tank's been properly adjusted. But if it's facing downwards, the air stays in. Anyway, the mouthpiece obviously was facing the right way to let all the air out.

"Mr. Cranston was lucky, because if there'd been air left, Mr. Prestwick and the police would have realized it was laced with pot."

Mr. Sullivan sighed. "Cranston, you'd think, would've known it might be chancy, since he helped Prestwick with crew and maybe was around the scuba classes. Or maybe he wasn't. Or maybe the point just never came up. It would've been sort of an obscure thing for Prestwick to mention. But the luck of the devil is what Cranston had. Till you came along," he added with his usual grin.

She wearily pushed the tray away. "As to how he almost got away with it, see, he smoked marijuana in his garden and dumped the — the roaches? — in the grill, as probably the other teachers on his road knew and could say, if anyone wanted to know why the grill smelled. I suddenly realized how he'd done the murder at the barbecue on Sunday, when I looked at the grills. I had asked Por — I asked a boy there how much pot you'd have to burn beside a compressor to get high. And I realized the amount would've fitted into a grill.

"When the emptied compressor was refilled with clean air, there'd be almost no taint of pot in it. But there would be in Jay's tank. The THC or something leaves a sticky coating. So, while everyone was at the hospital, he got all the ammonia from the girls' kitchen and cleaned out the tank. There was just a little pot residue left, and it slightly affected a boy who used it later. But the detective who checked the tank after it was cleaned had a cold, and Mr. Prestwick probably wasn't functioning too clearly. But I think if you asked him he'd remember smelling a hint of ammonia."

"I will ask, and I bet you're right. Well, I'm going. You need rest and the nurse will throw me out in a minute, anyway." He stood up, rubbing his hands together in satisfaction.

"There's one wonderful thing that's come out of this," he said. "The book is selling furiously."

"So the nurse told me. But I gathered you thought it was the work of a 'sentimental hack.' I heard you call him that. I have to say I loved the book, you know, whoever wrote it.

"So why're you pleased about it?"

"You're young. You'll develop a better judgement of writing. I'm pleased because 'Cranston' told Father Farnum a few years ago that since his wife had died in Switzerland — wonder if he had a hand in that? — and he had no heirs, his will left everything to St. Augustine's.

"My dear, why d'you think the road on which Cranston lived was shut off to students? Father Farnum is no fool, you know. He was aware of Cranston's habits but he — well, he's a politician. *And* he, very honestly and realistically, wants the school to prosper. He wants the best for it."

"I guess," Elizabeth Lamb said slowly, "I realize both those things."

"So," Mr. Sullivan went on, "young talents like Jim Newton's will now have even more chance to prosper here. And — "

But she was sound asleep. With one last grin, he left.

When she awoke, the window beside the bed showed only blackness in which the glow of a small lamp across the room was reflected. Another nurse sat in a chair beside it, knitting. There was a most delicious aroma from somewhere nearby. She sat up, and saw a large gardenia tree in almost full bloom on a long table at the foot of the bed. She stared at it.

"Feeling better, I'll bet," the nurse decided, coming over to her. "They said to let you sleep all you want. It's the best thing for a body. 'Long's you wake up." She laughed heartily. Elizabeth Lamb glanced briefly at her and went back to staring at the tree.

"That came just a little before midnight," the nurse told her. "Special order, or something. Here's the card that was with it."

Elizabeth Lamb took the card from its envelope. "Fate often sends you what you thought unseemly and undesirable and you end up liking it. With thanks and with love," she read in an undertone. "I don't believe this!" she said more loudly. "But it's written in what Buzzie calls 'snob hieroglyphics' and I remember saying it to her. But how could *she* remember it? And to send me a gardenia tree — not Faith!"

"Faith?" the nurse questioned, as she presented a bedpan that was scornfully waved away. "Is that what you said last? Did you want her? She's here with another girl, you know. They were acting up something awful over at the other campus, I heard."

"Who was?" asked Elizabeth Lamb, somewhat muffled by the warm, wet washcloth that was being passed across her face. "What do you mean?" She winced as her left hand was lightly gone over, and then her right arm, more strongly.

The nurse merely pointed to the floor in a far corner of the room. Dimly visible were two occupied sleeping bags. In one a curly blonde head could be seen, and a curly black head in the other.

"What-the-hell?" asked Elizabeth Lamb. The nurse was offended. "That's no way to talk!" she said sharply.

There was movement in the bags. "Hey there," came in Faith's unmistakable Georgia drawl. "Hi," came in a soft Bermudian tone. Elizabeth Lamb leaned back and closed her eyes. "I'm dreaming," she told the nurse quietly.

When she opened her eyes, Josie and Faith were standing beside the bed. "We were so worried," Josie said. "Nobody would say much and I went to the chapel to pray and Faith was there and we started to cry and holler. Father Rogers came in and called Miss Greenwell and we told her we had to see you before we could sleep. Even if it *was* midnight."

"We pulled one hell of a fit," Faith said cheerfully. "We had to know you were okay. Greenwell called Farback Farnum and he said it would be best for us not to excite the dorm. So he had Greenwell drive us down and here we are.

"I — ah — found that red sweater I was creatin' about," she added. "It was in Dan's — Dan had it. And this kid here's not so bad, I guess. She yells just fine."

Josie was beaming. "Will gave me a letter for you, 'case I could get to see you. I guess he's your bye — boy, I mean. We're just so glad you're all right. There was a rumor going around that your mind might have been — "

The nurse interrupted, loudly. "Now, look," she said. "I was told you two could sleep here but not that you could excite the patient. And her mind's as good as yours, miss."

"Yes, ma'am," Josie said obediently. She lightly touched Elizabeth Lamb's cheek, and assured the nurse. "I'll just go to the bathroom and then straight back to bed."

Elizabeth Lamb indicated to the nurse that she would like to follow Josie. When she returned to the room, Faith smiled at her and then retreated towards the corner where Josie was yawning herself to sleep.

"Wait a minute, please, Faith," Elizabeth Lamb said quietly. "How could you remember what I said to you the first day I walked into Room 13 with all that uproar going on?"

Faith laughed. "Nobody who can't remember things gets into this school," she answered. "I want to say something else," she told the nurse firmly.

"Elizabeth Lamb," she whispered, "I can't rightly say all I feel. I just can't believe what you did and I don't even know all of it. But Liz and Leigh told Lara Jane some things and she thought I should know, since Jay was — "

She wiped her hand across her eyes and drew in a deep breath. "Jay never made it to the Head of the Charles this year," she said. "And he never will again. But you — what you did — well, maybe wherever he is he thinks what you did is like his own Head of the Charles. Because you sort of got even for him. And thanks."

Elizabeth Lamb nodded solemnly. "Well, thank *you*, Faith. See you tomorrow," she said. And to herself: "Though I'll bet the way you're acting now only lasts till you lose another sweater, or something." Then she felt ashamed and said a brief prayer before she turned on her pillow and settled into sleep, Will's note clenched in her right hand.

The nurse turned off the bed light and the room was again in semi-darkness. The quiet there was as deep as the lake, and as peaceful.